PLUCHE, OR THE LOVE OF ART

Jean Dutourd

PLUCHE

or the Love of Art

Translated from the French by Robin Chancellor

Garden City, New York

Doubleday & Company, Inc.,

1970

All of the characters in this book
are fictitious, and any resemblance
to actual persons, living or dead,
is purely coincidental.

PLUCHE OU L'AMOUR DE L'ART by Jean Dutourd © 1967,
Flammarion et Cie

DESIGNED BY RAYMOND DAVIDSON

Library of Congress Catalog Card Number 71–89114
Copyright © 1970 by Doubleday & Company, Inc.
All Rights Reserved
Printed in the United States of America

To Jean-Claude Roussel, my lifelong friend,
who has helped me, stood by me, blindly defended me,
and loved me better than a brother since boyhood,
I dedicate this novel.

J.D.

PLUCHE, OR THE LOVE OF ART

CHAPTER I

First Day of Sterility

> I should stop myself from
> dying if a good joke or a
> good idea occurred to me.
>
> **VOLTAIRE**

The urge to embark on a work of creation after a period of
sterility is like the desire to make love, very violent, but it
can be appeased by failure. This is what happened to me
today. I flopped over a painting. And yet I had risen early
and in the best of spirits. The smells of linseed oil and turpentine were stirring my blood, like those of moist earth or
horse dung. I had lighted my pipe. I still needed some aroma.
I made coffee. In short, all the conditions proper for a good
day's work. Result: I never applied one stroke of color. My
drawing wasn't worth two pins. I had believed myself to be
filled with inspiration, but inspiration, as it came out of me,
went up in smoke.

A lousy day! It's now five in the evening. I have been bored
since six this morning. Nobody could say I haven't persevered.
Dusk is beginning to fall; my studio is all blue. Even this
blue, which turns everything such a bewitching color, bores me.
So I have chucked it all—the brushes thick with paint, the

smeared palette, the spoiled canvas. Tomorrow the paint will have begun to dry on the palette and brushes: it'll be the devil of a job to clean them, but what the hell! I haven't the courage to do it this evening. When I have worked well these little chores cost me nothing; actually they amuse me. I happily scrape away at my palette with the knife, I put the brushes to soak, I wash them in soapy water. I cannot tear myself away from my creation, I could go on prowling around it for hours, busying myself with a thousand little odd jobs; I am seized with a commendable thirst for order. But when I have achieved nothing I have only one desire: to flee from the scene of my defeat, leave everything flat like a routed soldier taking to his heels, heedless of whether or not the dead will be buried. This isn't panic but disgust. I no longer have the heart to rise above it, I have to look the other way. That's how I am right now.

At the start of this I wrote: "First Day of Sterility." A lie. I'm at my fiftieth or sixtieth day of sterility. For three months now I've had no taste for anything, I can't get anything going, I bore myself to death, I have the blues, my head is filled with cement. The smallest stroke of the brush costs me an immense effort. Now, with me creativity conditions my health and my temper. When I'm not painting I feel unwell and morose. Everything *gets me down.* Any little vexation which at normal times I would put up with quite philosophically plunges me into despair. I am ten times more sensitive than usual; I even have gusts of bitterness, like those bourgeois who rebel against the world when they lose on the stock exchange and start envying their friends. I know this *ordeal by sterility.* I've been through it before. I have triumphantly come out of it before. But past experiences do not lessen present difficulties: this time it may perhaps be final. Perhaps I am cooked, finished, done for, empty. Perhaps the reserve is exhausted.

For a creative man the inability to create is the supreme humiliation. Personally, it makes me humble on every level, fearful, timid, cowed. Ugh! "His misfortunes had not humbled his pride." A phrase to meditate on, to repeat to myself every hour of the day.

I believe that I have a thorough knowledge of painting. When I paint a picture there is nothing I cannot convey, and even with facility. Without wishing to boast, I am almost as good at it as the old masters. With my talent for painting I feel a complicity of the same nature as the champion sprinter has with his knees or the muscles of his thighs. The sprinter, on his mark and getting set for the hundred yards, knows nothing distinct about his body but he has an experience of this body: he knows how he must nurse a tricky muscle, how to control his breathing, and so on. These complicities give him confidence; he takes in his stride, so to speak, and with supreme ease, the distance to be run. Once past the post he perceives that he couldn't possibly not have won the race. This intimate union of heart and body, this secret understanding between self and self, I feel absolutely when I paint. I hold my talent gathered up in the palm of my hand and I use it to the utmost. But the essence of this talent I do not know. I do not know where this talent dwells, the reasons for which it reveals itself or stays hidden. Sometimes it sweeps me up to stupendous heights; I bestride the roc of fable; better still, the roc obeys my slightest whim. With its giant wings it performs aerobatics of a delicacy worthy of a swallow. Snug and warm in its feathers, I have made some intoxicating journeys. The flight over, the winged creature gently sets me down, scrams, and for quite a while that's an end of these aerial excursions. Here I am again, heavy, opaque, aching, flung back into the miseries of the human condition. Above all myopic, unable to see six feet ahead of me when but a moment before my gaze was piercing the clouds. I am a larva, a slug dragging myself pitifully over the ground. I was recently contemplating the austere splendors of paradise; now I am chained down in hell amid the circle of the frivolous damned, where everything is mere diversion, where one only hears rank stupidities, where one only says stupidities oneself, where one is bored to death without ever dying.

And so my life has two faces and I spend my time being now very happy, now unhappy. In these latter periods I naturally seek the means to become happy again, that is to say to rediscover the mysterious paths of creation. It is then that I realize the deep folly into which I have been plunged. For the thirty years and more that I have been putting color on canvas, I haven't yet learned the way to bring on the creative urge when it doesn't exist within me. For thirty years with a mulish obstinacy I have indulged in the same pretenses, although I know them to be futile, hoping nonetheless that one day they will set in motion the mechanism of inspiration. At these times I am wholly an animal, an obtuse beast mindlessly going through the same motions which have no bearing on the situation but which men or nature have taught it. I am like a bitch whose puppies have been taken away to be drowned, tirelessly seeking for them where they cannot possibly be. For instance, one of my cherished fancies is that it is impossible for a painter to be sterile. It is enough for him, think I, to arrange a bowl, a bottle, and a loaf of bread on a table, set himself down before them, and reproduce them on canvas. It's almost a mechanical function; the mind hardly plays any part in it; only the hand amuses itself, and that makes one picture more. A completely idiotic reasoning; its falseness has been demonstrated to me two hundred times over and yet I simply cannot root it out of my mind but willy-nilly pursue it again every time I feel myself, as now, a hundred miles from inspiration. Only yesterday I said to myself: "In spite of everything let's just try one little still life. You never know . . ." As I mentally spoke these words, I knew already that such a venture was absurd, that I had lost before I even began, that the little still life would turn my stomach after three strokes of the brush. Notwithstanding, I went to fetch from the kitchen those appalling objects, namely a saucepan, a sugar bowl, an old newspaper, two apples, a dishcloth. I shudder to look back on it. The most astonishing thing is that I know perfectly well that even if I painted all the still lifes I wanted, took endless pains, drove myself to the brink, pursued this superhuman labor to the end with my last gasp, these paintings would still be failures. The heart isn't in it, the mind isn't in it, and in such cases the hand counts for nothing, even the hand of Rembrandt. In short, I am going through one of those glacial periods when I have no curiosity about what I am capable of doing, no curiosity about the being that is myself and in quest of whom I follow the road of painting, no love for my calling, for the world, or for the self I discover at the end of my calling.

I am writing this with the thought that maybe the practice of an art unfamiliar to me—literature—will once again set in motion my factory for producing forms and lines. This notion came to me just now as I was reading the newspaper. I was slumped in my armchair, my spirits at rock bottom; I was holding the rag in a limp hand, idly running my eye over the advertisements, lacking even enough power of concentration to read an article. All at once I lighted on that old line of fast sales talk that has been trailing through the press for a hundred years: "If you can write, you can draw." Very well, said I to myself. Since I can draw, I must equally be able to write. I note this to demonstrate how much absurdity enters into serious decisions. As a rule I hardly write at all, for the very simple reason that I express myself fully by means of lines and forms and have nothing left to say by any other method. But after all, the arts resemble each other; I maintain that everything I know as a painter can very well be conveyed by other means; it's enough to apply oneself and I like hard work. There are in words, in the stringing together of words, the composition of a book, all the equivalents of what I put into my pictures. I am told that a musician, let's say a piano virtuoso who knows nothing about the clarinet, is capable of playing that instrument within a few days. The relation between painting and writing is no doubt of the same order.

Will my foolish remedy for sterility, which never works, now succeed? Instead of setting apples and a jug before me, I propose to set a fragment of my life, the one that began today, and try to reproduce it. Shall I be able to? Or will sterility, that toothless goddess with pendulous dugs, debar me from writing as well? We shall see. Anything is preferable to this inertia, this lethargy, this drifting state I'm in. Enough for tonight. I must go and brush myself up since I have a date with Lucienne, who is silly as a goose.

CHAPTER II

One Thousand Five Hundred Francs a Month

> In this I am like Diderot, who believed himself ordained to dwell in a hovel and saw death approaching when he was installed in a fine apartment.
>
> **DELACROIX**

My life is extremely well organized, being based on selfishness. I use this word for two reasons, firstly because it is the right word, secondly because it shocks me. I am addicted to calling things by their correct names; I take the same pleasure in this as in drawing a good likeness or finding the exact color, and this sort of pleasure always shocks to begin with. All truth commences with a sting or a wound. In this respect I flatter myself that I am covered with scars.

The selfishness of an artist is not of the same nature as that of an ordinary man. I am selfish with honorable intentions—those of producing my own paintings, which, whether many or few, will have added something to the world. My selfishness is like a steam engine's stock of coal. It is essential so that the engine may run, so that it may cover the greatest possible distance. In consequence I couldn't possibly set aside the smallest lump of coal for anyone else's benefit.

For a number of years my paintings sold pretty well, which surprised me somewhat. Thank God, it never turned my head; I knew this success didn't add up to much and that my pictures were being praised for the worst possible reasons. From time to time I used to build up illusions: I told myself I was finally out of the woods, that by dint of liking me for the wrong reasons the public would end up liking me for the right ones, so the outlook was promising; but this didn't last long, given that I'm a pessimist by nature. In short, with the money I made from daubs I almost blush for today I earned enough to produce good paintings in peace, meaning paintings after my own taste and not after that of contemporary fashion, which to my mind stinks. Perhaps one day I shall be rediscovered. In all sincerity I'd be delighted if I were, since I don't find this demiobscurity into which I have lapsed so very amusing. But I've got to be true to myself and I don't want to be famous any old how.

My balance sheet is as follows. I am the owner of my own studio in Paris and the adjacent apartment. This is situated in a rather dingy house in the Rue Boissonnade. I am very fond of this quarter, though its looks are against it. In 1953 it was still charming. As the house stands halfway down the street, I don't hear the din of the Boulevard Montparnasse and the Boulevard Raspail. At certain times of the day it is even so quiet that one can distinguish the footsteps of people in the street. This sound of footsteps rings happily in my ears; all at once the world is a hundred years younger. Alas! The Rue Boissonnade is beginning to go downhill. I mean that, little by little, its population of artists and working-class people is dwindling, giving way to people of taste, that is to say the bourgeoisie. What a calamity, people of taste! In the old days the middle classes had no taste; they remained parked in their hideous buildings in the *smart parts of town*. It must have been idyllic. Today they are spreading all over the place like germs, they admire beautiful things, they respond to the charm of picturesque old corners, they comb through the antique shops, they read art magazines, they are even stupider than their forebears. So much taste will lead to the galleys, as my dear Degas used to say. How true! Never have people had so much taste as in the past twenty years, and never has the true creative spirit been so impoverished. It is in periods without taste, periods of vigor and simplicity, that art flourishes best. The aristocrats of the eighteenth century in France, who used to put their Louis XIII armchairs and chests carved by Jean Goujon in the attic or on the fire, had no taste compared with the middle classes of today. Even so, I would have got on a damn sight better with them than with the Brigantins, Dupuy-Fritons, Gérard Kahns, and Lambinets who buy unspeakable Napoleon III coffee tables in mother-of-pearl-encrusted ebony at fabulous prices. In a few years' time my poor Rue Boissonnade will be as antipathetic as the Avenue Henri Martin or the Boulevard de Courcelles; I shall feel in exile here; I shall have to move, flee from the barbarian hordes. I've a good mind to take my gun and shoot at the invaders.

With the money from my bad paintings I treated myself in 1955 to something I had always dreamed of: a house at Le Cannet. It was a slightly crazy idea but one dear to my heart, I don't know why. The proximity of Cannes, a rather raffish town, pleased me, as did the view of the sea and the fine weather one enjoys there all year round. Truth to tell, I like towns. Menton is sinister, Nice is full of old folk, Toulon is a bore, Marseilles is too big. There remained Cannes, which for three or four months of each year is a reflection of the Avenue des Champs-Elysées, with the same hazards as the Champs-Elysées.

Lastly, I have some money put by. A hundred thousand francs[1] slumbering in the bank since I know nothing about

[1] $20,000.

playing with stocks and shares, an activity that bores me and
that I distrust like the plague. With this I can get along
for several years provided, of course, I don't do anything
foolish but live like a church mouse. All the more since,
however out of favor I may be, I still manage to sell a
painting here and there. I have preserved a faithful few who
believe in me, not to mention the abominable Ravuski's monthly
check. Such a life suits me perfectly. I spend barely more than
fifteen hundred francs a month, girl friends included. I pass for
a stingy man in the eyes of the world, but one has to choose.
I've chosen to pursue a certain kind of painting; this means
tightening my belt for everything else.

A word about Lucienne. I never think without pleasure of this
beautiful woman. People talk of "marriages of convenience."
With her I have a "liaison of convenience"; she suits me and
I suit her. On certain days of extreme affection I tell myself
that this is perhaps the most pleasant side of love. Apart from
this, not a single idea in common, not a single taste. Why the
hell are we lovers, and remain so? It is a mystery, but a charming mystery.

CHAPTER III

The Picture by Mesnard

> Idleness is the finest thing
> in the world provided one
> doesn't suffer from it.
>
> DEGAS

Again spent a good part of the day doing precisely nothing,
with the firm intention from early morning of doing precisely
nothing. With me, laziness is all-consuming. I could turn these
long, empty days to advantage by answering twenty letters
lying in a heap on my table, going to pester Ravuski, visiting
some exhibition, polishing off a dozen lithographs I've left half
done in the studio, and a mass of other things. But no. I do
nothing, I don't feel like doing anything. I am wallowing in
my idleness. I have no will power left. I feel that within me
there is, at this moment, no new form, no unfamiliar curve. My
mind exudes nothing but old, hackneyed ideas, tedious repeti-
tions. It is an attic full of dust, which repels me before I have
even opened the door. Besides, everything goes together; when
I am enjoying a good period of creativity nothing is too much
for me; even after painting ten hours a day I still have
enough energy left to deal with matters outstanding. There
will be time enough to answer those letters when I am wholly

immersed in painting. Just now I am not alive. I am dead. A dead man doesn't answer letters.

Nothing is so shameful as impotence. The most beautiful thing requiring expression seems to me futile, useless, absurd, unworthy at any rate of occupying thirty seconds of my time. I have no mind, no spirit left. My life has taken refuge entirely in my body; it no longer projects itself into the infinite through my work. I have once again become like ordinary people who live each moment in succession, who slip through time without anything to hold them back. Above all, I am deprived of that most precious of gifts which goes with the work of creation and enables one to see the inner, profound meaning of things. Sterility confines me to outward appearances. Previously I was at the very heart of the world, at its most central point. I have been expelled to the periphery, to keep company with all men who spill their incoherent actions over the surface of the universe. I am no longer the sounding board of the world but merely one of the countless hammers that strike it.

I only thrive when in a state of metamorphosis; between one bout of painting and the next, my aim is for my style to renew or extend itself, for my creative faculty to become as diverse as the world it reproduces. It is through boredom that I am sterile, because all repetition is boring. However hard I try, I cannot manage to repeat myself. I have sometimes envied those prolific artists who will tirelessly embark on endless series of pictures; occasionally I have forced myself to follow their example but it has never lasted very long. My mind goes too fast for my inspiration. Where it takes another painter two hundred canvases to exhaust a certain manner, all I myself need is seven or eight. When I have come to the end of something, it's done with and ceases to interest me. Cézanne, whose work is an endless metamorphosis, must have been the same.

In short, I'm in the mood to go jump in the lake, a mood due largely to a long daydream in front of the picture by Mesnard that hangs in my studio. It's the only picture of his

I have. He painted it when he was twenty and this, despite the opinion I have since formed of the artist, still fills me with admiration. One of these days I shall try to describe this picture. It will no doubt be a good literary exercise, since I am dabbling at being a man of letters.

It's now about twelve years since I lost my respect for Mesnard as an artist, which doesn't mean I don't feel friendship for him as a man. But wait, here's a remark written too hastily and already it needs to be qualified. As a man, Mesnard is very likable, rather blithe, generous, stylish, etc. I mean that outwardly and in the eyes of those who know him well, he's a fellow full of charm and courtesy. But it's impossible for a gifted artist who has at the outset all the means to produce first-class work yet abdicates in his thirties and begins to paint deliberately bad pictures, to remain basically decent. When one prostitutes one's gifts for a worthless goal, in this case wealth, one at the same time debases one's soul. When I say that I still feel friendship for Mesnard, this is at once true and false, or rather, the nature of the friendship I feel for him has changed. I no longer like him at forty-five the way I liked him at twenty-five. And as I am incapable of putting on an act, we see much less of each other nowadays than we used to. When I spend an evening with him I am bored, I don't know what to talk about. I can't bring myself to take an interest in his work. To my eyes it is shameful rubbish. He's aware of this, since for quite a while now he has ceased to show me what he is doing. So what's left? We are like two ordinary men brought face to face. Out of tact I don't discuss my own researches, my flights of fancy, my masked balls of the imagination. He for his part refrains from asking after them. It's a bit much when two artists as intimate as we have been—and brothers-in-law to boot, since Mesnard married my sister Marie—never exchange one word about their main preoccupation! There is as it were a tacit agreement between us: the subject of painting is taboo. Grotesque! Most grotesque of all is the fact that Mesnard must rather despise me for not being as rich and famous as he is. Unless he envies me, which would be quite possible in view of the remarks he drops from time to time about how happily I accept obscurity, how lucky I am to be able to paint what I like, my sunny nature thanks to which I don't give one monumental damn for public opinion. Poor Mesnard! If he knew the extent to which I pity him he would hate me! And not even a cynic! For a long time I hoped that he didn't at least take himself in, but I've never managed to extract a single word from him on that score. To all my allusions, a face of wood. Mesnard, you're nothing but a scoundrel, for if you aren't a cynic with me then you aren't with anyone, and certainly not with your innermost self either. I believe by now you are so blinded that you are the dupe of your bad pictures. The more so since they aren't as bad as all that; they have a certain elegance, a fashionable air, a slickness, wit, and even a sort of applied craziness which can be impressive. Nevertheless, had you at twenty been able to see such work you would have rocked with laughter.

CHAPTER IV

Five Hours at the Bottom of the Sea

> *An artist's touches are some-*
> *times no more articulate than*
> *the barking of a dog who*
> *would call attention to some-*
> *thing without exactly know-*
> *ing what.*

SAMUEL BUTLER

I have to admit it: few landscapes have set me dreaming more than this courtyard in the Faubourg Saint-Antoine. To the left are cabinetmakers' workshops and to the right a little house. The latter's façade is quite flat, broken only by a gutter running along the first-floor level. There is a door on the ground floor, painted chestnut brown and surmounted by a glass canopy There is some greenery and a bay window behind which one glimpses the head of a craftsman at work. On the first floor, three half-open windows. The wooden rail of the balconies is peeling. The balconies are made of that rather crude gray cast-iron tracery one finds only in France. Come to that, where outside France would one find a house like this? Down to its color, which is peculiar to Paris and like the pallid com- plexion of poor young Parisians. The air of Paris colors or bleaches faces and stones alike. It is this close resemblance that, according to me, makes the modest houses built from the days of the Second Empire down to the beginning of this century so moving. They are chlorotic, tuberculous, but not lacking in a certain gaiety beneath their sickly melancholy. The house I am talking of puts one in mind of a little laundress or dairy girl of 1890; poor but clean and even clad with a sort of modest elegance. This façade is as eloquent as a pair of eyes or a piece of clothing; it tells of things at once secret, poetic, and insignificant; it evokes average virtues, happiness without ambition, the peaceful and humdrum life of the people, who speak French and do an honest day's work. In the center window is hung a cage with a canary. Since there's no breeze, the muslin curtains hang motionless. Yes, I like everything about this house, even the drainpipe falling straight down from the gutter into the concrete yard.

The building which extends beyond this house is equally flat but two stories higher; it is all windows and wooden frames. Curtains with broad red and white stripes hang half drawn behind the casements. Outside one of them someone has suspended a bow saw. The scene in the yard is charming. In an open shed on the left are piles of planks; outside the workshops, wood put out to season alongside a rudimentary carpenter's bench; in front of the house, finally, someone has deposited— doubtless to make more room inside—a cane chair lacquered black and the carcass of a Louis XV sofa. The silence of cities in no way resembles that of the countryside. Here a wholly Parisian silence reigns. The noises of the city are very distant and muffled. One can only (or should only) discern the sounds of human activity: an occasional word, a snatch of song, the chirp of the canary, a clock striking, the tuneful blows of a hammer on a nailhead. Down below on the left one can decipher the name MESNARD, signed in rather a limp hand and with a small M, after the fashion of Manet and Marquet.

Phew! I've certainly performed a literary exercise. I've described the picture by Mesnard that hangs in my studio and that I like for a number of reasons. First, because it expresses a

certain poetry of Paris so perfectly that as I look at it my eyes
fill with tears. Certain works of art have the gift of moving
me in this way, which I don't find at all ridiculous since it is
clearly not the sadness of the subject matter that stirs my feelings but the beauty of the painting. Besides, there is nothing
sad about Mesnard's picture, painted on the contrary very
blithely, with such a delight in lines, brushwork, and composition
that it never fails to enchant me each morning. Secondly, it is a
remarkable painting, worthy to my mind of those seventeenth-
century Dutchmen Ter Borch, Van Ostade, and Pieter de
Hooch, although entirely modern as to composition and technique. But beautiful works of art have this peculiarity, that
they share a family likeness. The soul which presided over their
birth, even with a gap of several centuries between them, is the
same. A Velázquez is more akin to a Van Gogh than to a
Meissonier. Thirdly, my Mesnard is a wonderful illustration
of the doctrine of landscape, namely that the beauty of it lies
not in the subject but in the artist who reproduces it. The
most beautiful landscape can become a picture postcard; the
poorest, most arid can make an enchanting picture. And so
Mesnard, in painting this, attained one of the hardest goals
in art—conveying a likeness—and at the same time experienced
the greatest possible joy for an artist.

I should like to know why I am thinking so much about
Mesnard at this moment. He's not a man very dear to my
heart as a rule, even though, being my brother-in-law, I see
him from time to time. This way my mind persists in harping
on him bothers me. I know this kind of warning. Sometimes,
for instance, I think of some friend I haven't seen for ten
years: three or four days later the friend shows up; either
he writes to me or I run into him in the street. Everyone
has had this experience. It's just as if we had evoked the
absent one by means of our private magic; without knowing it,
we summon him through thought. The summons, so it would
seem, never fails to be heard. I have observed how it's the
same with great writers and artists who are dead. Only last

week I said to myself for no reason at all: "Why, it's a long time since I looked at any painting by Bonington!" Why Bonington? Why not Veronese or Patinir? A mystery. The next day I received in the post an art magazine containing a whole article on this painter, with color illustrations of his pictures. These illustrations moved me like old photographs taken long ago, having a bearing on my life and rediscovered while rummaging in a drawer. I was carried back to the time when I was eighteen, the time when I discovered Bonington and his charming romantic ideas, almost more literary than pictorial, and when I was dazzled by his way of imbuing parody with poetry. In short, Bonington turned up dead on time.

What's going on in the same way with Mesnard? He is thinking of me, since I am thinking of him. But how is he thinking of me? Certainly not the way I'd like. The private magic isn't only benevolent; it can equally be malevolent. In truth, I fear everything coming from a character like Mesnard. A man who is capable of doing good painting but has chosen to do bad painting inspires me with total mistrust.

Mesnard was twenty-five when he married my sister Marie, who was then nineteen. It's odd how, while I was devoted to Mesnard at that time and admired him with all my heart, something inside me disapproved of this marriage. I swear it wasn't due to extreme brotherly passion or any murky jealousy. Such things are at the opposite pole from my character. I felt friendship for my sister but was in no way in love with her, if only because she's six years younger than me. For a twenty-year-old boy to want to make love to his nineteen-year-old sister is conceivable if the circumstances lend themselves, that is if, for example, the family lives a withdrawn life in a secluded district where there's no pretty girl for fifteen miles around, if the sister is pretty herself, if the two children have the feeling that they are the only ones of their species, and so forth. But when I was twenty Marie was fourteen, we lived in Paris, I used to see naked women every day at the Academy of the Grande Chaumière, and I wasn't a virgin. Although I have nothing

against incest, which strikes me as a fairly natural act, it would
never have entered my head to lust after a little girl whom
I'd known since her birth, who had had chicken pox and
scarlet fever under my nose and who happily strutted about
before me in her panties. Finally, I have a strongly developed
taste for friendship. Marie was the first person to bring out
this feeling in me.

In the history of art and literature one can count several
famous sisters: Lucile de Chateaubriand, Eugénie de Guérin,
Pauline Beyle, Caroline Flaubert. It was this last-named with
whom, in the old days, I used most readily to compare Marie.
Besides, even in its background (though ours wasn't as smart
as that of Dr. Flaubert in Rouen) our childhood was fairly
similar to that of the Flauberts: the love of art, the family
jargon, the contempt for the bourgeoisie, the wild laughter, the
complicity, the boy's marked predilection for his younger sister,
his desire to instruct her—we knew it all too. Marie filled an
essential role in my youth: she was my first mirror. It is when
he is young that an artist has the greatest need of disciples.
Later on he has his paintings in which to study himself.
But at twenty he has hardly begun to paint. Whence the need
to fashion a being who reflects his own image, whereby he
perceives that he can, by force of ideas, modify the world
and make it like unto himself. Marie gave me that, little girl
though she was.

There are some people one has loved so deeply at a certain
period in one's life that one recoils later on from sincerely
questioning oneself about them. In me friendship leaves the
same mark as love does in others. I have always derided
those nitwits who cannot recall without emotion some floozy
who cheated and ditched them long ago, but in my way I am
like them. And so, when I think of Marie, it is not so much
the woman of today I evoke as the young girl who had my turn
of mind, my way of reacting or not reacting, of setting on
actions or feelings values people don't normally ascribe to them;
who talked like me, with turns of phrase shared by the two

of us alone and almost constituting a private language; who
was high-spirited, with a way of refusing to be concerned about
trivialities; and who, moreover, was naïve, a trait that particularly suits intelligent people.

Marie has certainly preserved many of these qualities, but
some have become heightened, others have faded, and the
lighting has entirely changed. In twenty years time has left
its mark on her; she has gone in directions I would not have
taken; in place of the imprint I had set on her, life has sub-
stituted other imprints. Why the hell do I so stubbornly refuse
to accept this fact, which is quite natural? It's really absurd
and even unpardonable for a man like me, who prides himself
on his clear-sightedness. The idea that Marie no longer shares
my philosophy, that she has compromised on certain counts,
that her preoccupations have shifted, that she wants different
things from those I want, vexes me as if somebody had repainted
one of my pictures behind my back. Several times I have told
myself bitterly that I'd given this canvas to a different painter,
who had retouched it and wrecked it. Whence, of course, an
increase in my antipathy toward Mesnard: the fellow hasn't
contented himself with ruining his own work, he has also had
to go and spoil something I had made a success of. In which I
am unjust. Marie is not an object but a human being, blessed
with free will. If she has taken one path rather than another, it's
because she chose to.

When Mesnard married Marie, I had a strange feeling; it
was as if he had asked *me* for my hand in marriage. The
weird notion of my own life bound by sacrament to Mesnard's
gave me a momentary glimpse of what a difference in kind
there was between someone like him and someone like me—or
like my sister. Such revelations unfortunately do not last. Reason, sensible arguments rise up at once to dispel them. They
certainly did so on this occasion.

I can easily understand the fascination Marie exerted over
Mesnard when he first met her. I was his best friend; in her
he saw a feminine version of myself, having my ideas, my mind,

and a girl's body. For Marie a similar phenomenon occurred, of which I obviously had no inkling any more than she did, but which today seems to me undeniable: in Mesnard she saw me. In actual fact, each was seeking me in the other and both believed they had found me. Both desired something I alone was able to give; both were obscurely aware that I was their natural complement. They felt in me a hardness, perhaps a certain form of simplicity of mind they lacked and which it was vital to procure for themselves if their lives were to succeed. None of the three of us realized at the time that there was a vulnerable side to Marie's character which was susceptible of being contaminated by Mesnard, and vice versa; that they were weak in the same places; that this marriage was in fact a misunderstanding.

What an odd business writing is! My pen is leading me into the most unexpected places. Little did I imagine, when I began just now, that I would be expatiating like this about Marie and my youth! I feel as if I had made a dive of two hundred fathoms and spent four or five hours on the sea bed, pawing over objects submerged for twenty years. And suddenly it's over. Here I am in a flash returned to the surface, sitting in my chair, looking at the habitual world around me. Mesnard's picture gleams on my studio wall. It's a reflection of his soul at twenty. Studying this picture with my new eyes of a deep-sea explorer, I can understand better why I wanted my sister and Mesnard to marry all those years ago. Time has flown this afternoon.

CHAPTER V

Art and Money

> *I think I could have lived*
> *very happily in prison, pro-*
> *vided I had the wherewithal*
> *to smoke and write.*
>
> LEAUTAUD

I am not a free man. I have a slave driver. His name is Ravuski and he is a picture dealer. He pays me a thousand francs a month in return for two paintings. By the end of the year this brings him in twenty-four paintings, which is a profitable undertaking for him and possibly a less profitable one for me. Two pictures are both nothing and a great deal. Some months, I give him only rough sketches done with ten strokes of the brush. Then the brute protests. There is a hideous argument. What a pest this Ravuski can be!

From time to time I try to squeeze a bit more out of him, improve on the ridiculous contract I signed with him three years ago. Nothing doing. Ravuski is hard as rock. What is signed is signed. Which doesn't prevent him from dishing out sweet talk on the beauties of poverty, the delights of sacrificing oneself to one's art, and other twaddle. This infuriates me. "We

shall never understand each other," I retort. "You are a poet,
I am in trade." One might as well try one's irony on a dog.

This contract with Ravuski is just the sort of sensible folly I
periodically commit. Three years ago the outlook for me wasn't
very brilliant. My work had completely stopped selling. I still
had something owing on the house at Le Cannet. I got into a
panic. Whereupon the jackal Ravuski, lured by the scent, appeared on the scene full of honeyed words. He had brought
with him his "little contract." I confess my head spun. I was
Faust, he was Mephisto. With his thousand francs a month he
was giving me two things finer than youth: time and peace of
mind. He was putting within my reach one of those absurd
and sleazy dreams I have had all my life: the one of having a
steady income, like a civil servant. I was so thrilled by this
windfall that at the time I never questioned it. Ravuski seemed
to me as beautiful as the day itself, kindly, and eager to be my
friend. In the desert I was crossing he suddenly appeared like
an angel. So I wasn't wholly forgotten then, not wholly dis-
credited. A famous dealer had come to see me, honored me
with his confidence, staked his money on my genius. My emotions that day got the better of intelligence, which often happens with me. Had I bargained with him I could have had
two thousand francs. I realize that very well today. With two
thousand francs at this present moment I would be a pasha.
But I was idiotically touched, so bursting with gratitude that
I simply couldn't see straight. I could only grasp one thing—
that Ravuski was prepared to risk his money on me. I was
then going through a period of sterility like the one I am
going through right now. I was in the depths of depression
and dark thoughts, and humble to the point of imbecility. The
unexpected faith of Ravuski, a true connoisseur, a scoundrel
but knowledgeable, set me up in a flash. Even so, I mustn't
make myself out stupider than I am: I certainly realized that
if Ravuski had come to me, this was because he thought it in
his interest to do so and that sooner or later my painting would
be appreciated. But we live in the present and a thousand

francs a month seemed to me far more useful than remote and uncertain riches.

For a long time I pestered Ravuski to arrange an exhibition of my pictures, or at least to show some of them. After months of empty promises and delaying tactics I finally divined his purpose, which was to pile up my canvases in his cellar and then, one day, God knows when, to exhibit some of them, launch a publicity campaign, jack up their price, and make as much money as possible. The contract is for five years. When it expires he will possess a hundred and twenty canvases which will have cost him in all sixty thousand francs and on which he will make ten or twenty times as much. Let's be quite frank: this transaction annoys me when I think about it, but not unduly. Besides, the pictures are good; I've by and large had a lot of pleasure in painting them. I sell them for a pittance, but perhaps without Ravuski I wouldn't have sold them at all. Besides, I have one superstition, namely that *one must choose what matters most*. I have time, creative ability, I live more or less as I like. That's already a lot. It's even more than most men have. To want *everything* is the height of imprudence and in any case must sour one's character. A little constraint is excellent for the health.

My contract with Ravuski and these questions of finance have put me in a certain train of thought. I have never seen the relations between art and money treated in depth. And yet it is a splendid and absolutely vital subject on which it is indispensable for an artist to have a healthy outlook. Let's be sensible: there can't be any question of despising money. On the contrary, one's painting has to bring it in. But one mustn't paint the kind of pictures that bring it in. These two propositions, so it seems to me, accurately sum up the problem. I loathe those hypocrites who act as if they despised the good things of this world. I don't want to be poor; but I don't want to be rich at any price. I don't want to exchange for money something more precious than money—my time, in other words my talent, in other words my soul. These considerations somehow impel me to evoke Mesnard. The difference between him and me is that for him time is money, whereas for me money is time. Mesnard knows that in an hour he can earn ten thousand francs. I know that with ten thousand francs I can paint for six months. For him, painting has become a way to get rich. For me, it has always been an end in itself. From this I have never swerved.

Those things that are really precious don't cost very much. Now what is the most precious thing for an artist? Time, in which he does his work. I, while I am less rich than Mesnard, have more time than he. Only what is bad, tedious, or noxious is costly. I have experienced this twenty times over. Happiness or pleasure has always been given to me. On the other hand, every time I've wanted to buy boredom or worry, I've had to pay its weight in gold. Nothing better illustrates my proposition than evenings in nightclubs, where one is bored to tears while spending a fortune.

What a shabby ambition it is to have fine furniture, beautiful carpets, cars, masses of clothes! Does anyone need all that? It's neglecting the essentials for side issues. I offer myself better things by painting, by building up my *oeuvre*. I offer myself palaces, treasures, marvels. From one second to the next I am a millionaire, I am a king, and served with more alacrity than Louis XIV. We artists are not made to collect beauty since we create it. An object of the humblest kind, but full of memories, tells us more about beauty than the most magnificent Boulle cabinet. And this is precisely what we need: eloquent objects. Signed pieces of furniture are dumb.

It's a long time since I charted the fatal course of Mesnard's life: debts that must be paid, mounting taxes, a hellish race. The wretched man is condemned to earn more and more money, in other words to paint more and more pictures and, of necessity, worse and worse ones. Unlike me, he hasn't the means to wallow in idleness.

With his panoply of a great lord, his *needs*, his extravagances, his luxuries, his collections, he provides a terrifying picture of the way destiny takes shape. I have watched him commit himself ever more deeply to spending money. After ten to fifteen years of this it's no longer possible to alter one's way of life, to cut it out, become poor again, even if one sees that here lies the only way to salvation. Luxury is an implacable habit: to repudiate it would induce an intolerable sense of downfall (a ridiculous and typically bourgeois notion, incidentally). To sacrifice one's wealth lightheartedly, on an impulse, to take such a startling decision would demand tremendous moral courage, a sort of saintliness. A bachelor might achieve it, possibly, but a married man and a father? There's always the wife, mercilessly preventing him from doing anything foolish; what's more, her arguments are most reasonable. By contrast with this hellish existence, I take a delight in brooding over my savings, keeping my little cashbook, being stingy in every respect. I balance my accounts every week like a grocer. I waste not one scrap of what the world provides for my subsistence. People who aren't smitten with this kind of miserliness don't know what joys they deprive themselves of. Every hundred-franc note I have saved brings me an almost metaphysical happiness, since it represents one hundred francs of freedom. My only master—and only very spasmodically—is Ravuski. For the rest, I am indeed as free as air.

You may say I have the soul of a shopkeeper. Yes. But thanks to my shopkeeper's soul I have the soul of Rembrandt or Rubens when I paint. I fancy that Cézanne, who pulled a long face when any of his guests at table said something improper in front of the maid, must have been a fellow of the same type as myself. I guess as much from his famous self-portrait in a bowler hat. There's the face of an old skinflint for you, that's for sure. A great painter and miser: these things go together more often than people think. The root of the matter is that material preoccupations bore me and the only way to rid oneself of them when, like me, one is not well off is to organize one's life once and for all on a very modest and very simple basis. In order to avoid having to think anxiously about money all the time, one has to think about it carefully every evening. I might add that living on these lines has its charms.

I have always been struck by the fact that there are two kinds of food for men: simple, rustic, sustaining food like beef stew, sardines in oil, Camembert cheese, and Beaujolais; and sophisticated food like caviar, *foie gras*, lobster thermidor, champagne. Similarly there are two kinds of women: the honest ones we love, who are not very beautiful or elegant but have tenderness of heart; and the adventuresses, who are pretty creatures, well dressed, well coiffured, well perfumed, movie starlets, cover girls, fashionable beauties. The latter, just like the caviar and *foie gras*, strike me as unreal and I know why: it's because one can have them for nothing. I know certain types—publicity men or theatrical agents—who live free. They drink champagne which is paid for by some firm, that is to say by nobody, and they sleep briefly with birds who either regard them as steps on the ladder or are quite simply kind-hearted. To pay fabulous sums in order to buy what these parasites get for nothing seems to me the height of folly and futility. Yet that is what the prodigal do, and what in a different way M. Mesnard, my brother-in-law, does. I would say meta-phorically that he nourishes himself on caviar and champagne. Not only does this bring him no benefit but it also undermines his health. While I, who live on stew and beans, have the delicious feeling that I am eating real things, wholesome and cheap, that I am enjoying the honest-to-God things of life which don't deceive one, since one knows what they cost and has paid for them exactly what they're worth. To carry on my metaphors I would say that, thanks to my system, life clothes me like a good loose-fitting suit in which I feel comfortable, whereas M. Mesnard is laced tightly into a superb doublet which restricts his breathing and is splitting at every seam.

One last idea comes to me before I put down my pen for the day; this is that above a certain level of wealth money ceases to have any value. I have had this feeling in the past, when I was earning as much as I wanted and with the greatest of ease. I was like those women in Spanish chocolate factories who are allowed to eat as much chocolate as they like. After a couple of days they are so sick of it that they never touch it again.

A final note which cropped up while rereading today's jottings. I have laid down two propositions seemingly contradictory in appearance; that happiness is not expensive, and that caviar is of no interest because it costs nothing. The way I see it, these two conceptions go very well together but I'm damned if I'm able to prove it. Anyway, it's of no importance. Thirty years' practice as a painter has taught me that truth and logic rarely go hand in hand.

CHAPTER VI

A Brother

*Nelson at Trafalgar, instead
of prating to his men of glory
and posterity, issued a simple
proclamation saying: "Eng-
land expects every man to do
his duty."*

DELACROIX

During my creative periods I am in an enchanted mood. Everything amuses me. Even the dreariest people interest me. During
bouts of sterility, on the other hand, nothing can relieve my
boredom. Were Descartes himself to come and talk to me, I
should yawn. My mind is far away. Where? I wonder. In
limbo, a place that has always intrigued me and which I picture
as a vast nursery whose walls, once white, have yellowed down
the years; it is furnished with little iron bedsteads and rust-
colored balding rocking horses. Over everything there reigns
the sour smell of babies and a musty odor of memories. In
1957 I made a trip to Moscow and visited Tolstoy's house,
where they show you just such a room as I have described,
preserved intact. This place, where toddlers had lived and
played who would be a hundred years old today, was for me

a momentous experience. It made me quite dizzy. I was in a supernatural spot.

This picture returns to my mind whenever I subside into idleness and impotence, as if there were taking place in me then a sort of retreat toward childhood, the age above all of tedium, of waiting, of pure and disjointed impressions.

It is when I have no wish to see anybody but only to pickle slowly in my own boredom, drown myself in it, that the bores unfailingly appear. My brother Georges turned up in my studio this afternoon. I could gladly have done without this treat. I have a horror of people who take everything in life as a tragedy, especially the bourgeoisie. Now here's a bourgeois from top to toe, to the extent that I begin to wonder—whenever I chance to think of it, which isn't too often, thank God—what odd combination of genes has made us blood relations. This man has not one single idea, not one feeling, not one scrap of philosophy in common with me. The two of us are as different as a Chinese and a Zulu. We barely speak the same language. I have always kept as far away from him as I could. Someone so alien to me by temperament and so intimately related by blood is bound to land me in difficulties. With the artless and boorish ways of his kind, he started off by explaining how he had come to me because he was in trouble. This type of person loves the word "trouble." It is as if merely pronouncing it makes them aware of their existence. The trouble gives them substance. Naturally, I didn't listen to a word of all this. My thoughts were in the Tolstoy family nursery in Moscow. They were shy little girls got up in frills and furbelows and button boots, listening to their milk teeth dropping out. Even so, I must have caught in passing various lamentations concerning my sister-in-law Véronique's growth, which isn't malignant but will have to be operated on one of these days, Alain's failure to pass his college exam in mathematics (six months old, this item), Marie-Christine's cold, etc. Everything is tragic to such a man. A cold is tragic. The bourgeoisie exude tragedy like sweat. This inability to rise above things, this lack of philosophy in a word, fills me with horror. Truly I was beset by childhood today. The sight of my brother voluptuously creasing his brows as he evoked his various woes plunged me back into my early youth: I could see my father, hear him over the distance of forty years. He used to bewail events in the same way, used to build up the same tragedies out of nonsense. In reaction to these small-time Orestes, I go out of my way to be flippant, I laugh at everything and quite likely shall be making wisecracks on my deathbed.

Before embarking on the chapter of more serious accidents, Georges changed his tune: "And what masterpieces have you been hatching out lately?" he inquired in that peculiar tone of his, a blend of polite curiosity, contempt, and superiority. Note the words "masterpiece" and "hatching out." That's how you talk to artists, in imitation of their language. The friendly derision in the word "masterpiece," as applied by my brother to me, could easily drive me to violence. There followed the obligatory ballet, with me setting up my canvases on the easel and putting them back against the wall; and him examining them with a critical eye, drawing back a step or two, enthusing over the only bad one of the lot. Here is another exasperating characteristic of bourgeois behavior: the ritual aspect of life. What a ludicrous rite, after all, forcing me to display my canvases! Georges doesn't give a damn for what I paint; I don't give a damn for what he thinks of it; he doesn't understand the first thing about it; I derive no pleasure whatsoever from his esteem. Even so, I have never had the courage to tell him all this, as a real cynic or a Quaker would do. Cursing inwardly, I join in his absurd game. I see quite clearly that we are both wasting our time over such antics. But these things apparently have to be gone through. Society is based on buffooneries concealing an absence of any genuine feeling. Napoleon, said Stendhal, had "imprisoned his life in a serious comedy." This is the very definition of the bourgeoisie, and Napoleon is the biggest bourgeois of them all. But he, at least, liked good painting.

My brother, although as bourgeois as may be, isn't even on the level of the contemporary bourgeoisie I was describing the other day. He hasn't discovered antiques; he has no taste, he is quite unsullied in his bourgeoisness. But whereas this same unsullied state ought, relatively speaking, to please me, I still cannot stomach him. I am six years older than Marie. He is five years older than I. Even when we were young he was already a stranger. He came into the category of grownups who say tiresome and untrue things and whose every remark can be predicted before it is made. When I was twelve, he was seventeen. He was good at his studies, he had girl friends and possibly mistresses. A wall divided him from us. Although I am now thirty-three years older, the wall is still there; nothing has been able to demolish it. I am still a gifted child, secretive, complex, wayward, whereas he is a normal adult, that is to say a machine run on prejudices and clichés. What children most rebel against, or so I believe, is the constant realization that adults always miss the point. They never see the world clearly; it is masked for them by a screen of ready-made expressions, acquired emotions. This explains the intolerable boredom of their remarks, always inadequate and always so futile. Writing this I understand why, on the rare occasions when I meet Georges, such a violent taste of childhood wells up in me from the depths. It is because he is the perfect example of a grownup, identical in every way to those who surrounded us when Marie and I were small and who almost wholly disappeared from my life twenty years ago, not that I have become a grownup myself, in that sense of the word at least, but because my friends are artists, connoisseurs of art, men of the world whose frivolity or upbringing prevents them from talking too much nonsense.

Who will hymn the irresponsibility, the folly, the unscrupulousness of the bourgeoisie? Hardly anyone, if my reading is anything to go by. In works of fiction, even by the greatest writers, it is always the same convention: the good bourgeois bleeds himself white to pay off the debts or extravagances of the poet. Rubempré ruins Séchard. The reality is very different and history offers us numerous examples of honest artists reduced to penury by the rash doings of their relations. Flaubert and Degas, to mention only two whose life stories I happen to know. A misfortune of the same nature is about to descend on me and I was quite right to be not unduly pleased when I saw the mournful figure of my brother framed in my studio doorway. Listen to me, young artists: never open your doors to a bourgeois (unless, of course, he comes to buy), for it's tragedy that enters with him. We artists carry no tragedy within us, even if we are in despair and do away with ourselves like poor Gérard de Nerval, for our minds stand back to watch us suffering and thereby mitigate the pain as it were, push our troubles into the background, transform them into a spectacle over which we can joke or philosophize. For an artist the one really irreparable disaster is sterility. I don't mean the sterility besetting me at this moment, which is only temporary and almost pleasant, but the final and irreparable inability to create. Whereas for the bourgeoisie it's a different kettle of fish altogether. To exist being their only preoccupation, everything is serious, everything bears down hard on them. No standing back, no detachment, no philosophy, no refuge.

After having inspected my canvases with his mind on other things, even rather put out, so it seemed, that there should be so many of them, my brother went to seat himself on a chair and assumed the important air of one who, having offered his sacrifice to the indispensable futilities of social convention, is at last about to approach the root of the matter. Here again a gust of childhood blew over me, namely panic. "What catastrophe is this fool about to announce?" I wondered. My apprehension must have registered on my face, or else Georges guessed at it (which wouldn't surprise me; I've always been struck by his perceptiveness; it is remarkable in so limited a man and must be a sort of animal instinct), for something now happened which, while I was prepared for almost anything, nevertheless left me aghast: Georges buried his head in his hands

and burst into tears. How strange the way life repeats itself!
Thirty-two years ago I took part in a similar scene. I was thirteen and it was my father who was sitting before me, his head
in his hands, ruined, weeping, calling me "my dear boy"
through his sobs. And now, thirty-two years later, I was filled
with the same disgust and the same anger, not at seeing a man
faced with disaster but a man hitherto so arrogant, so sure of
himself, so domineering, facing up to this disaster so badly, going
to pieces before my eyes, revealing without shame his weak and
terrified soul. At the same time it was for me as if the years
had telescoped together; for a moment, so oddly identical were
the two scenes, I no longer knew whether I was thirteen or
forty-five and whether it was my father or my brother who
was weeping. At such times one perceives how closely life resembles a work of art. It has the same unity, the same hue, it
is based on four or five great themes which give it its balance
and particular stamp. My mind has undergone a profound
change since my childhood, and so has my heart; one thing,
however, has remained exactly the same—that is the essence
of my being, in other words my soul—since the same scene
re-enacted after an interval of thirty-two years provoked in me
the same reactions, I would almost say the same passions. I
felt no more pity toward my brother than toward my father,
and no remorse at being unable to feel any. On this occasion as
on the other I had only the feeling, at once pleasant and bitter,
induced by the discomfiture of someone whose sham superiority
one has known for a long time. Boredom too, since I could
have recited in advance what Georges was about to say. The
most violent shocks never manage to inspire such people with
anything but banalities.

"I'm in a hideous jam," said Georges in a sepulchral voice.
(I was waiting for that "hideous.") "So I've come to you. After
all, family feeling . . . You're my last hope. You can't imagine
what's happened. And I don't mean the disgrace: one doesn't
dishonor oneself any longer nowadays (cliché of more recent
origin). I've already paid out a hundred and ten thousand

francs. If I don't manage to find another hundred thousand within the next two months I'm a ruined man. I'll have no choice but to blow my brains out (blackmail, bunk). I'll be prosecuted. Dear Pluche, can you lend me these hundred thousand? You needn't worry, I'll pay you back. I'll start again from scratch. I'm not afraid of hard work. And with my contacts . . ."

I am quoting Georges's words very precisely. It is barely credible that a man could infuse his genuine anxiety into these ready-made phrases, said and repeated a thousand times over. Yet there it is, and it was a man of my own blood expressing himself in this lamentable fashion. I don't feel enough courage to carry on in the same style. No doubt I have hardly any experience at writing, but at least I express myself in my own way. After stammering on for five minutes, Georges wound up by explaining how he had landed himself in this situation. I'm sorry I have forgotten the details, since it's so fine, so moral, so magnificently bourgeois that future generations might well turn it to advantage.

The hallmark of the bourgeois, as I've been saying over and over for the past twenty years, is irresponsibility. Accordingly nothing attracts him more surely than a scoundrel. One might say that this represents a sort of anti-instinct, all-powerful and infallible. The crook appears to the bourgeois in the guise of a perfect gentleman, big-hearted, an unrecognized genius, an undreamed-of friend. I have pondered long over the origins of this marked predilection, of which I've seen a hundred examples each more comic and deplorable than the other. I have finally concluded that this must be laid to the account of the original sin concomitant with the quality of being bourgeois. There is in fact no reason why the bourgeoisie should have any knowledge of men, since they have built their lives entirely on lies, errors, prejudices and fleeting fashions bearing no relation to anything truly beautiful; since they detest art insofar as it is an accurate transcription of life and like it only when it debases itself and indulges in cant. A crook is to an honest man what a bad painting is to a good one. The bad painting pleases the bourgeois to the extent to which it lies, that is to say presents a false and hence simple and reassuring view of the world. Conversely, the good painting displeases because it offers a true and hence complex and disturbing view of the world. The crook, whose essential characteristic is falsehood, is by definition a very simple, immediately comprehensible individual; immediately likable too, for he has the deceptive veneer of cheap gold plating, the tinsel glitter that dazzles small minds, which in turn regard it as the height of luxury.

As one might have expected, my brother has run across one of these fine-feathered birds, and at the age of fifty, what's more. All he needed was to get himself well and truly swindled. The poor devil's now complete. From the way he described this lad, who is called Emile Marchepied (what a name!), I myself, the hermit, the dreamer, the so-called unworldly poet, would have sniffed scum a mile off and taken to my heels. But the bourgeoisie are of an unimaginable blindness and credulity. This Marchepied came one day to my idiot brother with a dazzling proposition. It had to do with buying a plot of land somewhere or other in Paris—Vaugirard, I think—building a block of apartments on it, and selling these off individually, etc. Marchepied had all the plans drawn up: there would be thirty-two apartments costing a hundred and fifty thousand francs each and fetching double that amount. Profit: one hundred and fifty thousand multiplied by thirty-two, say four million, eight hundred thousand francs to be divided between the six morons financing the enterprise. My brother was the sixth of them, naturally. A decision had to be reached within twenty-four hours, since another goon was champing at the bit and frantic to be the sixth man. I can picture now my brother seated behind his desk, declaring self-importantly to Marchepied: "I can't take any decision until I've studied the matter thoroughly." I can see him reading through the documents, frowning; I can see Marchepied being very affable, rather patronizing, fully conscious of the windfall he's providing but

very firm and brooking no delay. And then I can imagine
Georges that evening, confiding in Véronique of the non-
malignant growth, checking the details of the speculation over
and over again, totting up his "liquid assets" and investments,
calculating his profit—almost a million, imagine!—rapturously
describing to his bourgeois wife the sublime Marchepied, whose
sole mission in life was quite plainly to bring fabulous wealth
to people he didn't know. Such a staggering scene would
have made me laugh when I was younger, but I have seen
too much of this type of thing to find it amusing any more.
Why is my father no longer here, who so often set Georges
up as an example to me, Georges the well-behaved, the reliable, the model pupil, the son with a big future! I get
rather a kick when I realize that all the boys who were held
up to me as good examples have either gone to the bad or
else failed to rise above poverty, as if the mere fact of being
admired by grownups were a curse from which no child re-
covers. Georges had so far been missing from the list of my
father's hapless paragons. This surprised me, I must confess, and
I was vaguely expecting some catastrophe.

Indeed, Master Marchepied, after having collected the money
from his suckers, purchased the land, and signed agreements
with the contractors, began to dip into the till in no uncertain
fashion. "Butter wouldn't have melted in his mouth," said
Georges in his special jargon; he was bald, plump, in his sixties,
with the stealthy ways of a cat and the requirements of a
prince. When the scandal broke (for a scandal there was, apparently, though it was news to me. "True," Georges here
remarked, "you never read the papers, my poor Pluche.") When
the scandal broke, I say, it transpired that Marchepied the
miracle man had embezzled nearly two million francs. The
contractors, unpaid for the past two settlement dates, had
stopped all work. Those who had paid deposits on the apartments, numbering around twenty, began to squeal, and so on.
This tale bores me so much that I haven't the heart to go on
with it. All the more since it is, so to speak, a classic. There

have been at least ten similar cases since the end of the war.
To cut it short, they had to raise more capital and ask for
extensions from the purchasers, who squealed all the louder
and started legal proceedings. In the meantime the sexagenarian
Marchepied absconded to Brazil with a tart. There remained
the six financiers, on whom a hail of writs and summonses
descended in a horrendous downpour. Naturally all six of them
were severally and jointly held responsible since Marchepied—
no fool, he—had consistently arranged things so that it was
they who signed all the relevant documents. Conclusion:
Georges is trussed up like a chicken. He has to raise a hundred
thousand francs, failing which, as he put it in his own inimitable
way: "I'll land in jail." And it's me who has to provide these hundred thousand francs. "There now, you know everything," he declared in the tone people usually adopt when proffering this
type of remark. "I'm only a poor man," he added. "Véronique's
on the verge of a breakdown. That's all I need!"

Now here's a curious trait of my character. Directly Georges
began to tell me his pitiful tale I knew it would inevitably
lead to his asking me for money, and I also knew that I would
lend (or give) this money. The tale at its moment of telling
bored me more than I know how to express. During the time
it lasted my mind took flight. I thought of other things. I could
almost have said to Georges: "Spare me the details. Come to
the point! How much do you want?" Why are the disasters
that befall our kith and kin always so annihilating? Because
they are so dismal in the telling and always end up by involving
the listener in some bloody mess.

It's really infuriating. Here am I, having to lend Georges the
money he needs. I can hardly do otherwise. A question of
honor, duty, brother standing by brother, etc. I can't leave this
idiot to get hauled into court. He's in a lamentable condition,
quite unable to think straight. Luckily I have a cool brain. I
explained to him how he must play for time, not pay over
everything at once. What I found most painful of all was the
avid and passionate way in which he kept gazing at me. As I

talked on, I had the impression that common sense and courage were gradually returning to him. He promised me he would dispute the matter. He even talked of stalling for two months before coughing up. Two months would provide a breathing space. If I could avoid the financial hemorrhage I'd be mighty glad, but there is little likelihood of it. Before he left, I was again treated to a nauseating scene. He effusively clasped my hands in his and insisted on embracing me, which gave me no pleasure. Lucienne's embraces are much more amusing and cost me far less. When is he going to say: "You're saving my life!"? I wondered. This came out on the landing. I shut the door before it entered his head to evoke our childhood days together.

God, what a sickening business, and how ludicrous! The ant coming to weep to the grasshopper: what could be more absurd? It will engulf all my savings. Possibly I shall even have to mortgage my poor shack at Le Cannet. Just when I was counting on ten years of peace, that's to say a happy and enormous output of paintings, carried out at leisure! All in all there is something utterly senseless about it, and the injustice of it revolts me. I have a series of pictures to produce, works which I know will be unique, disturbing, profound, and add to the world a little something that didn't exist before me; I had made everything ready for it; I have reached the most vigorous and productive period of my life and now, through the fault of a nitwitted slob, the whole thing is put in jeopardy. I am going to strip the useful artist bare for the sake of the dumb and useless bourgeois, who will pass over the earth like a puff of smoke. And why? So as to fulfill an absurd demand of my heart, a sort of private code of honor that hardly makes sense nowadays. What an appalling thing duty is!

I'm perfectly sure I'll never see my hundred thousand again. How will the poor fool ever be able to pay them back? And when? I must talk it over with Marie tomorrow. Perhaps the affluent Mesnard will agree to join in with helping his inept brother-in-law, if only out of consideration for the boundless admiration in which Georges holds him. If each of us would give fifty thousand, that would suit me fine.

Could anyone conceive of a more arid and sinister venture than sacrificing oneself for somebody one dislikes and for whom one has no respect whatsoever? Such is my lot. I who profess that self-sacrifice is a positive and uplifting affair can see nothing positive in all this. I can only regard it as a complete and unmitigated pest. I can't even feel a twinge of pain, great or small, to stir some impulse in my heart.

Be it noted that it's not eighty or a hundred and fifty thousand that Georges is asking me for, but a round hundred. Exactly the amount I possess. Not a penny more, not a penny less. This is just the kind of practical joke Destiny keeps playing on me: it always arranges to present me with accounts *which I'm able to settle,* which leave me without a cent but do not positively put me in difficulties. Everything occurs as if there were a tacit agreement between Providence and myself; it ensures me the necessities of life but takes away anything that might strictly speaking be looked on as superfluous. I am a sort of Polycrates, happy and ruined. To have peace of mind one must, I suppose, cast a ring into the sea every day. If one day one should forget, the fish leaps out of the waves to claim it.

CHAPTER VII

The Squirrel

Felix was a beggar who had nothing; Olivier was another beggar who had nothing: say as much of the charcoal-burner, his wife and the other characters in this story, and conclude that as a rule complete and staunch friendships can hardly exist except between men who have nothing.

DIDEROT

Night is the comforter and nurturer of artists. At night all difficulties resolve themselves, inspiration recharges its batteries, the mind draws fresh strength from mysterious depths. There have been times when I have wrestled five hours on end over a picture, failing to get anything right and going to bed in despair. The next morning I completed the picture in twenty minutes, singing as I worked, and it turned out a success. These are the happy mysteries of being an artist. It seems to me that when I am asleep or dozing a door opens within me and I find myself confronted with a landscape full of strangenesses. Feelings there are as palpable as trees. There is a huge, murky lake, an expanse of sluggish water in which the whole of my subconscious seethes. In my good creative periods the gateway of the subconscious opens while I work. But it opens silently; I do not know that it is open; it remains open without my being aware of it. I am myself open too, as untrammeled as when I am asleep. I have known myself to place certain colors on my canvas with the infallibility one has in a dream, yet wholly with the reasoning of a waking man. Nothing is impossible at such times, everything is easy and the painting blazes like an unquenchable fire. That, basically, is what inspiration is: this door of the subconscious opening while one is awake. I am sterile just now because the door is closed. And herein also lies the fundamental difference between artists and the rest of mankind: the latter never know the indescribable joy of contemplating their secrets with open eyes.

Why should I have begun these pages with this "Hymn to the Night"? Because, I guess, I woke this morning viewing the world through rose-tinted spectacles after having slept like a log. Even the memory of yesterday and of Georges, although it immediately rose up before me, failed to plunge me back into gloom. I shall have to pay. I can't avoid it. So I put it out of my mind. I had been to make my coffee and put some bread to toast; a delicious smell was pervading the apartment. It was six in the morning. I watched the sun rising over the Rue Boissonnade, which is a perfect sight with grays, pinks, reds, and ochers, the whole covered by a film of blue. One nice trait in my character is lightheartedness. I thought of Georges lightheartedly. I told myself how I was going to have to cough up a hundred thousand francs and at bottom this was of no importance.

All at once I felt a consuming desire to see Boulard, whom I hadn't seen for ten days. I felt a need to contemplate his cheerful mug, to have a good three hours' talk with him, to pick everything to pieces—our art, our souls, life in general, sex —in short, to talk of things sublime. Dear old Boulard! My eyes almost brimmed with tears! I called him up. I heard his gruff voice say: "Hello, you old sod!" and the world became even more delectable than it already was.

"We've got to lunch together," said I. "It's my party."

"Not possible," cried Boulard.

"As I have the honor to inform Your Excellency. There will be ortolans, venison pasties, haunches of wild oxen roasted over charcoal, twelve dozen oysters, a salmi of mandarin duck, a whole young wild boar stewed in caramel, and to wind up, a floating island as big as the Grande Jatte. Wines: Sancerre, Chambertin, Krug."

"Cheesecake?"

"But naturally. We don't do things by halves. There will be amazing houris nurtured exclusively on Turkish delight from the age of four and a quarter, with flesh as white as chicken's breasts and tender as the inner tubes of a child's bicycle; they will be clad in pantaloons of gold-dusted muslin and veils hung with silver drops. There will be Circassians with eyes ringed with kohl, blue tresses, and powdered tits; Negresses from Nubia, thin as rakes with breasts like pears; Swedish typists who always work in the nude; English girls armed with whips; and even two scrawny teen-agers picked up at Aubervilliers. Will that do?"

"Splendidly. What address?"

"Mother Cruchon's, Rue Froidevaux."

"Well, you're laying yourself out, I must say. It'll set you back fifteen francs a head at least. Mother Cruchon's, for God's sake! Oh thrice blessed day."

"To hell with the expense. I'm ruined. That calls for a celebration."

Our snack at Mother Cruchon's was a delight. We consumed alarming quantities of sausage, tripe, pasties, fried potatoes, Roquefort cheese, and apple tart; we drained three bottles of Beaujolais (the boss's special), not to mention after-coffee liqueurs followed by a chaser. In short, a real get-together in the finest sense of the word. Since when have I known Boulard? My reason assures me that I met him for the first time at the

Ecole des Beaux-Arts in '39. That would be twenty-six years
ago. In spite of this, the illusion persists that he has been my
lifelong companion; I find it hard to imagine that I went
through childhood and youth without him. He stands in the
foreground in my image of the world. His face is for me the
very face of friendship and friendship is, of all sentiments, the
one I love best. I even incline to prefer friendship to love.
Love absorbs too much time, too much emotion; the joys and
sorrows it brings are too overwhelming; nine times out of ten
it's a fearful nuisance and when it isn't a nuisance it's worse.
One drops everything to run to it. One is at its beck and call.
Two passions are too much for one heart. I already have one
for painting, which is enough to keep me busy. When I love
a woman, I am torn the whole time between her and my work.
What I give the one seems to be stolen from the other, I feel
remorseful, I don't do anything wholeheartedly, and in the
end it's painting that wins the day. Ah, to think of all the
charming passions I've laid waste! Whereas friendship is never
demanding. If love is a taskmaster, friendship is the most discreet and exquisite of chambermaids. Now there's nothing better, for an artist, than ancillary pleasures. When you get down
to it, I have really loved only a very small number of women.
Three, to be precise. Even at the height of my passion for
Monique seven years ago, there were times when this beauty
bored me and I can remember occasions when I left her alone
to go and chew the fat for a couple of hours with Boulard
about serious, diverting, superfluous, and subtle things—matters
for men, in a word.

I've done ten portraits of Boulard and he has done ten of
me. He's a good painter, full of ideas and imagination, but he
lacks that touch of madness which makes a picture sing. Since
he is lazy and consequently doesn't paint much, he falls into
the error of putting too many things into his pictures; he tries
to say everything at once. This leads to an impression of over-
crowding, of verbosity, of semi-impotence, although with remarkable bits in them, for he's as skillful as Van Eyck and as

intelligent as Delacroix. Impossible, of course, to cure him of this since economy, the control of talent, can be learned only at the price of years of slaving. He's a head shorter than I am; he has a round face, a thickset body. He follows the contemporary style with hair down his neck and sideburns. This dandified manner he loves to assume gives him the look of a chestnut vendor, which is apparently the height of chic. I had nearly forgotten his mustache; this is of the handlebar variety and he wipes it with the back of his hand, like the workingmen in a Zola novel, after a good swig of Beaujolais. I've painted this mustache in every color of my palette, from Veronese green to burnt sienna via yellow ocher; I've had a lot of fun with it.

He is garrulous, by nature didactic, and has his own opinions on every possible subject. In short, his conversation is a pure delight; the more so since we know each other inside out and when it comes to art—the only perennially captivating topic in the world—each of us knows as much about it as the other. He knows all my mannerisms; he has an eagle eye for spotting my faults; he criticizes my paintings as I would criticize them myself, had I not painted them. I do as much for him in return. Nothing draws people so close together as this passionate, uncompromising concern each brings to the other's work. With Boulard I don't grow old; I am still twenty, with all the brashness, brutality, affected language, and excesses belonging to that age, and I confess I do nothing to rid myself of them. On the contrary, these seem to me the essential concomitants, the indispensable accessories of friendship, above all of friendship between artists. I've forgotten where I once read that friendship is a virile emotion; the more rough and pitiless it seems, the more tender and high-minded and attentive it is at heart; it is the spirit of a young mother in the body of a rhinoceros. An excellent definition, to my way of thinking; at any rate, this is the way we are together, Boulard and I.

It is difficult to tell Boulard anything; he keeps interrupting the whole time in order to crack some joke, draw some moral lesson, express some view, develop one of his pet theories. One would think he was paying no attention to what one was saying, absorbed as he is by what he's thinking or about to say himself; but this is a false impression and I am always surprised to discover that in spite of his bursts of laughter he listens most carefully and proffers excellent advice. Moreover, after yesterday's session I needed to be back among my real family. Boulard is one of those soothing people who put the world into perspective and reduce events to their true proportions. As far as tragedy goes, he is completely the opposite of my brother: tragedy is something he knows nothing whatever about, to which he offers no hold. In this respect he is exemplary. He is even more lighthearted and mocking than I am. It was vaguely in my mind to treat him to a fine and detailed account of my brother's misfortunes in order to bring myself some measure of relief, and then, damn it, the talk got swept away on topics so much more absorbing that I whizzed through it in two minutes flat, just to bring him up to date and let him know that in two months' time I am going to blow the bottom out of my bank account. A man of commoner clay would have yelled the roof off, protesting that there was no reason for me to sacrifice myself to a Philistine idiot and so forth. But not he. With his artist's eye which immediately penetrates to the heart of any matter, aiming straight for its deeper significance, he approved while advising me strongly to touch Mesnard for as much as I can, though this didn't prevent him from adding a moment later that Mesnard won't contribute a cent.

"Money earned by bad painting never goes to help a bankrupt," he said. "Bankruptcies are paid for with honest money like yours. Money that hurts. It's the law of nature. You won't get out of it. It's a pity, all the same, that you've managed to save so much! If you had spent your dough as you made it, like any normal man, you'd be ruined in the same way, but ruined on your own account, and so your ruin would be more gratifying and would no doubt have left you a few happy memories. Whereas the way things are the thought of your ruin will always be linked with that calamitous character, your shit of a brother. You wait and see: you'll never look back on it with any pleasure, I promise you that, I who've been on the verge of bankruptcy at the end of every month since I was eighteen."

"What you say may well be true in absolute terms but it isn't true for me," I replied. "It's part of my nature to save money and it's because I live like a church mouse that my painting is good. If I had spent my earnings as I made them, the way you recommend, my painting would have been quite different, certainly worse, since for the past twenty years each time I painted a picture I've had the feeling of stretching my powers to the utmost and being incapable of doing better. I'll tell you something more: I would go on putting money aside even if I were certain I'd never touch it. D'you understand?"

He had understood so well that we talked of other things. In particular the horses of Van Dyck, which are superb, painted with love, their fat, gleaming rumps, elegant heads, and flowing manes looking like charming young girls. This is one of the pleasures of talking with Boulard. I am aware all the time how, without any collusion, we share the same weird ideas. I too have always more or less unconsciously compared Van Dyck's horses to women. Besides, everything in Van Dyck's pictures is feminine, down to the stout, bearded, and swarthy gentlemen, which would doubtless tend to prove that he himself was excessively virile. Boulard and I agreed with one accord that the famous equestrian portrait of Charles I led by his groom is more lascivious than Ingres's "Turkish Bath." Such considerations, when one records them in writing, don't appear to add up to much yet to my mind they provide evidence of a profound mutual understanding and depict friendship and the strange joys of friendship more surely than any long and sentimental colloquy. I could almost define friendship as a taste for the same oddities and this implies, obviously, a shared sensibility.

I hadn't much inclination to leave my old friend Boulard and get back to my studio, surrounded by my dried-up paints and my canvases doing penance with their faces to the wall. As it was quite a fine day, I suggested a stroll. We went on foot from the Rue Froidevaux as far as the Jardin des Plantes, passing along the quays, gabbling fit to burst our lungs and gesticulating like Italians. At the Jardin des Plantes Boulard made a few sketches of the lions which he botched completely, so we gave them to the camel, who chewed them up and swallowed them down with gusto. Every once in a while I love to go for a long walk like this with a close friend. At such times I am tireless. I could easily cover forty miles non-stop. I think mankind has lost a great deal through the invention of the motorcar, on account of which no one walks any more and so never meets anyone. To my mind, though I don't know why, a man who crosses the world on foot is completely happy; if he has the luck to have a good companion at his side he could ask destiny for nothing better. To place one's foot on the ground, advance at three miles an hour, talk, look around, stop, start off again, meet all kinds of people, tell them one's life story, listen to their adventures, pay one's whack by drawing the farmer's or innkeeper's portrait, have all one's time ahead of one, no worries, thick hobnailed shoes, a bundle, a stick—who the hell could offer me anything nicer? In *Monsieur Nicolas*, Restif de la Bretonne's masterpiece and my bedside book for over twenty years, what possibly moves me most is the good Nicolas's great walk from Auxerre to Paris and his arrival before Villejuif. I, who as a rule hardly feel much desire to live in another age than my own, am overcome with nostalgia for the eighteenth century, when such delights were still possible. Another work moves me in the same way, gives me the same image of happiness, and this is the famous picture known as "Bonjour, Monsieur Courbet!", in which the great Courbet painted himself arriving on foot at the house of some friends. One can feel he has had a good journey, that he is sweating profusely, and that his immense hike has done him the same amount of good that people nowadays expect from vitamin pills. It is a curious thing to observe that, in the arts, these are

just the subjects to which I am most responsive: I like travels,
I like characters who keep moving, who traverse the world the
way a very thin sharp knife slices through cheese. For me the
finest novels are those in which the hero is a man on the move,
who covers a lot of ground: Don Quixote, Gil Blas, Jacques le
Fataliste; and the most beautiful music is the kind that gives
me the feeling of being taken on some everlasting ramble shot
through with unexpected visions. I have a particular weakness
for the symphonies of Brahms and Mahler; they carry my
mind off on endless perambulations, and at my own pace,
which is not too fast. An odd product of our overcivilized state:
walking is no longer enjoyable in France save in one place
only, the most civilized, the least natural of all, namely Paris,
where the opportunities have remained as numerous as ever,
whereas they have more or less completely vanished from the
countryside. Walking in Paris one can have the same encounters,
strike up the same conversations, find the same surprises, the
same joys as two hundred years ago. Men change less than the
landscape.

When I left Boulard around four o'clock my inclination for
a stroll was far from being appeased. My legs still had a
lot of strength left in them and my mind was still in an in-
quiring mood. My conscience, too, was easy since I am incapable of doing any painting just now. There was a gray
tint to the air induced by a light ceiling of clouds, and this
caused me the keenest pleasure. I must remember this special
shade of gray and put it in a picture one of these days. Not
necessarily a landscape. I turned down the Rue Buffon and
headed loiteringly toward the Parc Montsouris, where Mesnard lives. I had no particular thought in mind, save that
I might drop in on Marie, who is often at home at the close
of the afternoon. My lunch with Boulard and the animal smells
of the Jardin des Plantes had put me in the highest spirits.
Although thoughts of the idiotic Georges and his follies, so
ruinous for me, kept flitting from time to time through my
mind, even these couldn't manage to cast a cloud. Here is

another of the beneficial effects of a good walk: the profound
sense of felicity that never fails to sweep over one and which is
due to nothing precise: just that the blood is circulating
freely, the body feels light, the ground speeds by beneath
one's feet. Deep inside me I even felt that delicious crack
(I can find no other word for it) that opens up in one when
the creative spirit moves into action again. Yesterday I was humble and impotent; and suddenly I am once again full of ambitions, shapes, curves, colors. There returned to me as I walked
an appetite for painting such as I hadn't had for weeks. This
doesn't mean very much; at any rate it didn't mean that the
true, all-powerful creative spirit had resumed possession of me;
but it was good to hold onto at the time and rather encouraging.

From the Jardin des Plantes to the Parc Montsouris is
quite a stretch, with various temptations on the way. I stopped
only once, at a junk shop in the Avenue Reille, seduced by its
air of dust, dirt, and general mess. I don't really care for
antique dealers, who are for the most part tradesmen specu-
lating on current fashion and knowing the price of everything.
With antique dealers nowadays all the thrill of discovery is
gone. They have drawn up a huge catalogue of the furniture
and objects of the past, from which nothing is omitted. They
know down to the nearest penny the value of what they stock.
Buying a regence commode for six thousand francs from a man
who expatiates into the bargain on its beauty strikes me as no
fun at all. I want to find it for myself, in the shop of some old
devil who doesn't give a fig for it and will let me have it
for three hundred francs "to make room." For an antique to
be a real source of pleasure it must also be "a bargain." Poor
Cousin Pons would be very unhappy among the antique
dealers and people of taste of 1965.

I think there are possibly still a few bits and pieces to
be found around the junk shops, although up to now I've
hardly spotted any treasures in their dens. At least when
poking about among their rubbish I still have some hopes,

THE SQUIRREL

whereas with the dealers I have none at all. My hands get
covered with grime, I sniff up the chill and spicy smell exuded
by objects from the past, I gossip with the proprietor, who
is nearly always a simple soul with no more regard for his
wares than a dealer in secondhand tires. My junkman in the
Avenue Reille was cut out to please me in every way. He's
a man who has clearly spent fifty years of his life ferreting
in dustbins and who stinks as vilely as his emporium, which
appears in the guise of a shop with a wooden façade painted
a hideous chestnut brown. The window is almost opaque from
dirt. Through this fog one can discern piles of old magazines,
wicker chairs, an occasional table which first saw the light
of day during the rule of President MacMahon, several candle-
sticks, two or three paraffin lamps. What impelled me to enter
was a stuffed squirrel holding a nut in its mouth, which I
coveted at once. The junkman sat reading his paper in a
Voltaire armchair. He raised toward me a big, surly moonface.
Not a smile. Not one word of welcome. Here was a man
after my own heart. I sought his permission to browse around.

"Anything special you're looking for?" he asked in a rather
gentle voice.

"Certainly not," I replied. "I'm a genuine seeker, I am. Not
one of those smart lads who rave about anything and everything
and then buy nothing. If I find something good, I shan't tell
you and I'll offer you as little as possible for it."

The man smiled and the conversational ice was broken. "You
now, you're an artist," he declared. "I could see that right
away."

"How?"

"I don't know. Your manner. Besides, I guess you might be
a bit stingy maybe. Well, not exactly stingy, but counting your
pennies."

"Well I must say, you know a lot about artists. It's true, I'm
pretty closefisted. I earn my living by the sweat of my brow.
You've a quick eye. I congratulate you!"

After five minutes of such dialogue the junkman was completely tamed. He even took such a fancy to me that he went and rummaged in the back of his shop for a bottle of wine and we proceeded to clink glasses. The wine was rough but decent enough, added to which it had the savor of friendship. The fellow confided his name to me: Raimondet. Forty years of scrounging old junk, a widower, etc. He wanted also to let me into a bargain, which wasn't so jolly. This was the MacMahonesque table, all in mahogany. I could have had it for fifty francs. In short, I spent a good three quarters of an hour with old Raimondet, who followed me around like a dog as I explored his lair. A fruitful exploration, since behind a set of shelves I found an admirable book—Ingres's *Thoughts*— and solidly bound, what's more. Whereupon I steered toward the squirrel, which was a bit moth-eaten but had a graceful pose. The lot cost me twelve francs. I've had a wildly extravagant day! Papa Raimondet wrapped up my treasures in an old newspaper, we swigged a last glassful, and I promised to go back next week. "I can see the sort of things you like," he told me as we parted. "I'll keep my eyes open."

M. Mesnard, my brother-in-law, lives in one of those narrow streets bordering the Parc Montsouris, in a house about which I could say a great deal and which I dislike for all kinds of reasons, the first being that Marie likes it, or at least has made it her home.

The Parc Montsouris is charming. I would gladly live there myself if I could afford it and it is certainly not the surroundings I disapprove of, nor even the street where the house stands. It is the house itself and nothing else that repels me; I find its features boring, respectable, and middle-class anyway, but worse still, they are in that excessively impoverished and depressing middle-class style of 1930. It has a flat façade in which something is eternally wanting. What? The talent of the architect who designed it, of course! The ugliness of architecture nowadays is characterized by an impression of being left unfinished. The buildings have the air of being sketches of buildings, clumsily designed by people without imagination, incapable of working other than with a ruler. This particular one, which I often mockingly call "Mesnard Hall," the "Palazzo Mesnardi," or the "Castel de la Mesnardière," exudes the same sort of lugubriousness as the Napoleon III pavilions flanking the Bois de Vincennes, wherein generations of bourgeois thirsting for money have spoken millions of empty words. An even worse lugubriousness since one can, if pressed, respond to fancy pastry work and cast-iron ornamentation, which in the present instance are cruelly lacking. In 1860 the middle classes loved frills and furbelows; in 1930 they were taught to love austerity, in other words ugliness laid bare, without remedy. Given the equal absence of talent among the architects, I prefer overdressing to nakedness. I prefer shoddiness disguised, bowed down under absurd adornments, to shoddiness laid bare. Long live the Opéra, down with the Palais de Chaillot! Or rather, down with both of them, but let's blow up the Palais de Chaillot first.

It's a good ten years now since Mesnard bought his house by the Parc Montsouris; I still wonder how such a subtle chap—so full of aestheticism, so sensitive and even rather too refined for my taste—was ever able to put up with this soulless, styleless barn. One would almost conclude that he had needed a house at the earliest possible moment, that he bought the first one offered to him directly he had the means, so as to have something to show for his affluence, a material translation of that spiritual element that is talent, in order to dazzle himself as he thought: "This tangible, solid, three-story stone building has sprung from my brain and my fingers." When we were young it was one of his goals, I remember, to own a house near this self-same Parc Montsouris, which he regarded as a sort of artists' Faubourg Saint-Germain. I suppose there weren't very many for sale in these latitudes and so he pounced on this one. All of which strikes me as exceedingly comic. What does it matter whether one lives here or there? For myself, I think I would die of gloom and despair in the Palazzo Mesnardi. I would feel in exile. Besides, it is unquestionably fatal to acquire in one's maturity what one has longed for in one's youth, especially when it is something as banal as a house with garden and garage near the Parc Montsouris. In fact, whatever one passionately, deeply desires one always gets, but at the expense of what one doesn't really want. I know this well from having experienced it a hundred times. Like everyone else, I have had any number of wishes, fancies, absurd ambitions. For instance, I too would very much have liked to have a house of my own in the Rue Notre-Dame des Champs, or at the end of one of those alleys in the neighborhood of Denfert-Rochereau. This wish has never been granted me because at heart I wasn't all that keen and only one thing really mattered to me: to paint well. And I do paint well: at least, so I believe. I have this, and almost nothing else. My shack at Le Cannet couldn't be more humble and its furniture barely merits the name. My apartment in the Rue Boissonnade is of a poverty I would define as heroic. Every time I contemplate the Palazzo Mesnardi I feel a surge of pride and at the same time a vague regret that my sister should be content with it.

For a long time, too, the interior of Mesnard's house has gotten on my nerves, and since I've taken it into my head to write I don't see why I shouldn't unburden myself of this irritation. I am tempted to regard as a complete jerk any man who takes so much care over what the art magazines call the "environment." And here Mesnard seems to me the chief culprit: his habitation is a perfect reflection of his soul. Marie doesn't count for much in all this, even though I hold her almost equally guilty for never having said anything, for having let him go ahead and even fallen into line with him. When I visit Mesnard's place everything, down to the smallest object, describes for me the sort of person he is. To begin with, I'm not overenchanted by the flunky who opens the door, in a striped waistcoat in the mornings and a white jacket in the evenings. Certainly it's no sin to have a manservant; all the same, I don't know why, this doesn't seem to me to fit in with the status of an artist. To me it's just showing off, wanting to be like the affluent bourgeoisie or bankers, and this distresses me. An artist, like a priest, has a maid or an old housekeeper who sees to everything, grumbles all the time, and is utterly devoted. The artist is a private citizen whose life should not be dazzling; that, at least, is my idea. The true splendors one carries in one's head. The gilding, the carved paneling, the four-poster beds, the marquetry tables are for people with no imagination. I'm not too happy either about the gorgeous cars softly gleaming in the darkness of the garage: a Mercedes for Monsieur, an Austin for Madame. These are publicans' vehicles, as Diderot would say. I can't believe that these objects don't in the end do an artist harm and I would far prefer it, I admit, if Mesnard, like Harpagon, were to convert his riches into bars of gold.

What perhaps repels me most about the Palazzo is what Mesnard himself has added to it: he has painted *trompe l'oeil* murals—still lifes, anecdotal scenes—all over the place. There are far too many of them and behind this welter of clever designs one senses a passion for self-indulgence which is hateful. Mesnard has done for himself, free of charge, what painters in the past did for princes in return for payment. To put oneself to so much trouble for what is not a work of art but a mere job, and not to get one penny out of it, seems to me the height of perversion. Better, to my mind, to remain sitting on one's hands, better to be pickled in sterility and eat one's heart out while contemplating one's impotence. In impotence and sterility there is something terrible and tragic acting as a leaven for the great works of the future; whereas there is nothing in such ludicrous five-finger exercises as painting *trompe l'oeil* decorations in a dining room. Were I fair-minded I would certainly admire the skill with which Mesnard's murals are done; I would relish his pictorial erudition, his charming pastiches of Lancret over the doorways, of Oudry for the panels in the dining room, of Benozzo Gozzoli on the walls of the drawing room, of Giulio Romano on his bedroom ceiling, etc., but I'm not fair-minded. Moreover, from the strictly professional point of view these ironic pastiches are far less well painted than the originals. They have a quality of being perfunctory, only approximate, and this turns them into something more like parodies than imitations. Even when merely amusing himself in this way, Mesnard didn't have the small amount of application it called for. I shan't describe the splendors accumulated in the house. That would take up too much time. It's a mass of Louis XIV clocks, Renaissance sideboards inlaid with ivory or ebony, Louis XV commodes in the Chinese style, Aubusson carpets, ornate opaline chandeliers. Even down to the studio on the third floor, which is clean, neat, and tidy as a boudoir. Another of Mesnard's manias: stuffed birds. I can count at least fifteen, from the heron to the owl. On the stairs a blue-black eagle with outspread wings, seven feet in span, seems about to swoop down on the hapless visitor. Every time I see it I regret coming without my gun.

I cannot describe how much all this bric-a-brac fills me with horror. I cannot conceive that Mesnard isn't occasionally bored by all this perfection, that he doesn't ask himself what accumulation of ideas, whims, purchases, visits to antique dealers and curio shops has led him to concoct such a house for himself. The suspicion must cross his mind at times that this is not the setting of a true artist, that he has gone to inordinate trouble over something that called for far less. Does he sense that these objects, each of them beautiful or interesting on its own, produce a nauseating effect when crowded together? In fact, there is in this a strange fatality very similar to the one that has accompanied Mesnard throughout his life; his house is a pretty accurate portrait of his character, in which the sum of many virtues hasn't produced a forceful whole. Some corrosive element is at work in the depths of Mesnard's soul and its effects emerge precisely in the inability he has always suffered from of giving full rein to his good qualities so that his personality may fully expand. Whenever he chances to glance back over his past life I am certain that he finds in it a color he hadn't intended, and this shocks and surprises him. The appearance of his life doesn't correspond to the actions that have gone to make it, or at least to the intentions he believed he had. An experience like this ends by becoming a philosophy. At forty-five Mesnard's philosophy, so far as I can judge it from the brief conversations we have together (brief and hypocritical, since he has reached a stage of totally mistrusting my heart—which has remained the same while his altered course—and of lying to me as to an art critic), his philosophy, I say, is that effects hardly ever correspond with the causes and that after having chosen a certain path one ends up at the opposite place from the one aimed at. A philosophy completely the reverse of mine, since I see nothing of the kind in my own life and experiences, where, on the contrary, effects always correspond exactly to their causes. True, I knew very early on what I was, what I wanted, and have never changed my direction, whereas Mesnard is a man who lives in darkness or, if not darkness, in a half-light—as most men do, incidentally—and is quite unaware of this save during rare moments of soul searching, which are unpleasant and therefore brief.

I see I have forgotten one vital shortcoming in my description of Mesnard Hall, namely that the rooms are all small in size and consequently ill suited to the sumptuous furniture that fills them. Whence its overcrowded look, its air of being at once opulent and meager. One can hardly picture Cesare Borgia or the Prince de Condé living in a studio-kitchenette-shower bath. Such is the impression created by Mesnard's treasures in his tiny rooms.

I hadn't seen Marie for three weeks. I found her rather off color, with a worried look about her; this, however, didn't prevent her from welcoming me with a wide smile and manifest delight, as if my mere presence were a gala occasion. So she used to welcome me in the old days in our parents' house when I came home in the evening, my day's work done. She would fling her arms around my neck and plant great smacking kisses on my cheeks, artlessly demonstrating that I

was the only person in our circle whom she really and truly
loved. She has always been this way with me; she has still
kept for me, at thirty-nine, the same feelings she had when she
was sixteen. The faith she had in me when I was twenty-five,
her certainty that I was a man of genius singled out for a
prodigious future and destined to astound the world have remained intact, although I am now forty-five and not exactly
a figure of renown. A sisterly love so great that it takes no
account of the shabby reality but sees beyond the circumstances
and has had for twenty-five years the same unswerving regard
for my soul, which has not changed, is something truly remarkable. To be frank, I am almost embarrassed by it at times,
since I myself criticize Marie, disapprove of the life she leads,
and occasionally quarrel with her about it. I brutally remind
her of our principles in bygone days over which she has long
since reached a compromise. In short, I am not *easy* on her.
But she never bears me any grudge. I must confess I like being
loved in this way. Perhaps, without this unfailing love, I might
during these last ten years have drifted apart from Marie,
after more or less lumping her together with Mesnard. I would
have become cooler toward her out of a blend of jealousy,
resentment, disappointment, and philosophy.

Physically, Marie was fairly ordinary as a little girl and none
too pretty as a teen-ager. At ten she was thin as a rangy cat;
at seventeen she hadn't yet fined down, as they say. But even
when a skinny kid and lumpish adolescent she had superb
eyes: the long eyes of a Scheherazade, black, oriental, astonishing in such a roguish little Parisian face, with lashes half an
inch long. Rarest of all, these lovely eyes don't give her the
mysterious look of a doe but sparkle with considerable mischief.
More than she really has, actually. From what Levantine or
Spanish forebear can they stem? Georges too has handsome
dark eyes, rather feminine, but without the faintest spark in
them. My own are small and blue: with them one has no merit
in appearing intelligent. I've done twenty portraits of Marie—
as a child, teen-ager, young wife, and so on—in twenty differ-

ent ways. I even once painted her as Salome (her eyes all ringed with kohl) holding up Georges's head augmented with a beard. I couldn't know this face any better. But I've never painted it since she became pretty. For in fact, as she was approaching thirty she went through a final metamorphosis: everything changed, in her figure and even in her face. Subtly changed. Suddenly she was no longer quite the same nor yet quite somebody else. What had been clumsy in her body became graceful; what in her face had been merely pleasant became attractive; the features ceased to be banal, to become something harmonious, and this in turn made them arresting; her skin, thanks to the beauty parlor, gained in delicacy what it had lost in freshness. Lastly her hair, thanks to the best coiffeurs, is now of a silkiness, a glossiness and abundance I would never have thought possible. To put it in a nutshell, Marie is now a beautiful woman. She is extremely chic. This new state delights her, from what I have observed, and doesn't help to remind her of the views she held when she was twenty—which were mine.

When I arrived at the Palazzo Mesnardi it was about six in the evening. Two minutes before I went in the figure of Georges crossed my mind and I told myself: "Above all don't forget to talk to Marie about that fool's bankruptcy; don't forget to ask if Mesnard can help in the refloating operation." I should have known better. Whenever I exhort myself in this way to remember some important piece of business I can be sure it will immediately slip my memory. Directly I saw Marie and we began to talk I gave no further thought to Georges, and since neither of us mentioned his name, nothing brought him back to my mind. Only now, tonight, as I write this, do I remember about him. My built-in ready reckoner functions in a strange way; trivialities can obsess me for weeks; I move heaven and earth over nothing at all; on the other hand, when some vital step or decision is involved I am negligence incarnate. Even so, it's a weighty matter for an impecunious fellow like me to know whether all I possess is to be taken from me or only half of it; my peace of mind, my very life almost, is at stake and deep in my heart I am less concerned about it than about some petty obligation such as taking Ravuski his two pounds of flesh on the thirty-first of the month at twelve sharp. I am rather glad to have this detail down in writing as it is very revealing. Since I signed my contract with that usurer I've never missed a single delivery date. He has always had my two paintings on the last day of the month at twelve sharp. He's even surprised at this himself and I'd swear this absurd punctuality lowers me in his eyes. Like all tradesmen or bourgeois he imagines that regularity, a respect for one's word, the planning of one's work don't go with the artistic temperament; that genius is by definition temperamental and that a man who delivers his wares on a fixed date, as agreed, is little more than a manufacturer. This fact dawned on me a long time ago. I know very well that if I treated Ravuski casually, if I kept him waiting, if I pocketed his money regardless of the terms of our contract, he would be far more accommodating, far more humble and obsequious, whereas now, on the contrary, he is niggling and cantankerous in direct proportion to my punctiliousness. But it's something stronger than I am, I'd rather be hacked to bits than change my ways.

I suppose this attitude forms part of my general and implicit design for living, in which the little things are regulated once and for all, like so many pieces of self-winding clockwork, in order that no material considerations need ever hamper my thoughts. I am a type after the manner of Kant, who every day at three-thirty apparently walked eight times up and down the Lindenallee at Königsberg with such unfailing regularity that passers-by used to set their watches when he appeared, and who always placed his handkerchief on the same spot on his desk so as not to waste time looking for it if his nose began to drip while he was writing. Nonetheless a life like mine (or Kant's), so organized that the body encroaches as little as possible on the mind, has its inconveniences. Both Kant and I are flea trainers. We have tamed all our fleas. But by dint of looking at nothing but fleas we end up by seeing nothing else. Now it sometimes happens that a lion appears on the scene. Not, of course, that we wouldn't know how to tame lions too if we took enough trouble, but we don't pay any heed to it. This huge beast—so incongruous, so out of the ordinary—fails to catch our attention. Instead of organizing a safari and shooting the animal on the spot we look the other way, we think of other things, in return for which we get eaten. I shall be eaten up by Georges as surely as two and two make four. Eaten whole and not just by half. But what the hell! It's not very painful being eaten. One doesn't die from it. Even if the lions eat me, at least no flea has bitten me for the past twenty years. That's one great compensation. People who kill their lions never stop scratching the rest of the time. I prefer my fate to theirs and here as everywhere else one has to choose.

But to return to Marie. Because she looked so unwell and preoccupied I made a great effort to be cheerful. I unpacked my purchases from old Raimondet; I described my lunch with Boulard, the camel, the Jardin des Plantes, and so on. This distracted her and after ten minutes of banter I saw a little spark light up again in her eyes. In this I acted with a trace of selfishness, I must confess. I was in a good mood; I wanted to remain so. I had no desire to learn about someone else's troubles today, not even my beloved sister's. A moral dilemma; which is better, to share one's own good mood like a cake with someone who is visibly under the weather, or relieve that someone of part of his depression by taking it upon oneself, in other words swallowing a dose of vinegar? I opted for the cake, and now that it's too late I am sorry I didn't choose the vinegar. A rejected dose of vinegar burns the stomach worse than if one had drunk it. I realize as much this evening from the acidity I feel inside me. Marie, I'm quite certain, is worried about something pretty serious. I already felt sure of it this afternoon. My intuition where she is concerned is never wrong. Doubtless my jokes, my good health, my stories helped to cheer her up, but maybe she would have felt even more comforted had I let her confide

her worries to me. I am sure she would have liked to tell me
about them and afterward listen to my comments as to an oracle.
I use the word "oracle" advisedly. In fact, I believe I am
Marie's oracle to the extent that she religiously accepts everything I say but thereafter almost wholly disregards it because it
doesn't fit in with her normal train of life, her habits, her
comforts, etc. I continue nonetheless to lavish my advice and
comments on her every time the occasion arises; this amuses
both of us.

She asked me at length for news of Boulard, a character who
appeals to and irritates her at the same time, because she is as
jealous of my friends as a wife. To certain subjects, including
Boulard, she still reacts with all the pungency of our youth.

"You obviously only go for failures," she said.

"Forgive me, but you're wrong," I replied. "Boulard's a very
good painter, a bit lazy but full of excellent qualities."

"Get along with you," she exclaimed with a laugh, "you can't
kid me. If poor Boulard had a shadow of talent you wouldn't be
able to stand him. I've seen you with talented people: you go all
wooden, you don't know what to say, you look as if you were at a
funeral. With Braque, with Segonzac or Bellmer, with Chagall,
who's enchanting, you're simply not yourself. And they are just
as starchy as you. It's like two politicians meeting, who watch
every word they say and glare suspiciously at each other, each
bogged down in his pride, each studying the other with the eye
of a cobra to see if he hasn't got something on him or else
something that could usefully be pinched from him. Don't you
dare pretend it's not so! By contrast, when you're concerned
with a washout like your dear Boulard you're an angel. Basically
all you want are foils or admirers. Don't imagine I didn't realize
long ago that the only living painters you are fond of are those
who will never do anything good. For them you have an infallible instinct. Mind you, I'm not saying you don't recognize
superior talents: I'm only saying that you don't find them
attractive. And I suppose it's natural. No doubt you don't need
any masters since you're a master yourself. So you cut the

masters out if ever, by chance, you're anywhere near the point of getting friendly with them. Take your relations with Braque, for instance. He liked you a lot, he liked your painting, he did everything to make you like him, which with him, God knows, was pretty unusual. But you, you never followed it up, you always found excuses for avoiding him, crying off dates and so on."

"I've never been mad about Braque. For me he's a minor master. Like Mérimée, he played only eight notes on his piano. What he was looking for doesn't interest me."

"And insincere into the bargain! Obviously, between Braque and the brilliant Boulard there's an abyss!"

At this moment there entered the prettiest creature in the world, aged twelve, namely Mlle. Lise Mesnard, who has the face of Verrocchio's "David" in the Bargello Museum, that is to say features at once childish and perfect, if these two adjectives may be combined, since a childish face has something open about it, something unfinished, overgenerous, malleable, the opposite of perfection, which is always complete and final. And yet there exists a certain perfection of childhood, belonging to childhood alone and lifting it into a class of its own. With Lise I think this comes from her almost horizontal eyebrows, the slight heaviness of the lower part of her face, and her grave and attentive mouth. This child is devoted to me and I return her devotion. She will be my sole heir, if I have anything to leave apart from my pictures. Even her hair—wavy, chestnut, dressed in pageboy style—is like the bronze hair of "David." Lise has a charming way of addressing me, which is neither "Uncle" nor my family name of Pluche; when she speaks to me she calls me "Maestro," a nice invention, well in keeping with the jargon her mother and I use between us.

In some little girls it is as if two beings existed side by side; a child who marvels at everything, asks naïve questions, has quaint desires and whims, suddenly becomes absorbed in futilities; and an extremely wise, judicious adult with whom one can discuss matters of the gravest moment. My niece is one of these. It is in no way a question of any molting operation, of a little girl casting her little girl's skin and beginning to change into a woman; there are really and truly two distinct persons contained in the same individual, who have always been there however far back one goes. Even when quite tiny she was already like this and I can remember long conversations I had with her when she was five and when she astonished me by her levelheadedness, her ease in expressing herself, her gravity. It was just like talking to an adult. My sister when she was small never had this dual personality; she was purely childlike, with an almost blind strength and passion. From mother to daughter one can see an undeniable evolution of the species, due to the rise in the social scale, environment, and upbringing. Marie had a vigor that Lise hasn't got but the latter, in return, has a subtler nature, perhaps a more civilized one. You might say that one is an extension of the other, that these two generations of women form but one single destiny.

Phew! It's two in the morning. I've been writing for six hours without a break. These are fine days of sterility indeed! I feel as battered as if I had been painting a fresco forty-five feet long. Maybe I could take Marie to lunch at Mother Cruchon's to-morrow? That's not a bad idea. I'll call her up first thing in the morning and suggest it. She's got to have her mind taken off things. And now for bed! Somehow I can't put my pen down. I shall read a few of Papa Ingres's thoughts before going to sleep. I'm really delighted with the squirrel. I'll do a painting of it tomorrow. I've an idea how to tackle it.

CHAPTER VIII

Twenty Years of Marriage

> Clavigo: *No, sir, your sister, Dona Maria, is a lady overflowing with wit, amiability and goodness.*
>
> Beaumarchais: *Has she ever during your acquaintance given you any occasion to complain of her, or to esteem her less?*
>
> Clavigo: *Never! Never!*
>
> **GOETHE**

I painted the squirrel during my sleep. By this I mean that, having concentrated on it for a few seconds with my eyes closed before going to sleep, I woke this morning with a longing to commit my last night's vision to canvas. Such experiments never fail. In half an hour, without one false stroke, I dashed off a squirrel which is a huge success. I made of it one single patch of russet brown, sinuous, shifting in tone, exactly the faded russet verging on grayish yellow of my model. The texture is all creamy like the Fragonards in the Louvre depicting "L'Etude" and "Inspiration," or Brouwer's "Smoker," or again Monticelli's plates of fish. I've had a lot of fun with this squirrel and I'm damned if I regret my twelve francs.

From close to my sketch looks like an old glove or a pear. Viewed from a short distance it is my squirrel down to the smallest detail. You can even see how the little creature's fur is moth-eaten in places, and the nut stands out as if it were real. "One would think it was about to speak," as Boulard would put it. It's a long time since any painting has given me such pleasure. Why? Because I have reproduced one object while painting something else. I have achieved an almost literal likeness by the means proper to poetry, in other words what I would call a "roundabout way." What's more, I have seen my squirrel with the eyes people will have in thirty years' time, after they have learned to see according to my method—if they ever do learn. One of Pluche's thoughts for the aesthetes of the twenty-first century: "Bad painters never achieve a likeness because they reproduce exactly what they have before their eyes. Good painters achieve a likeness because they work like poets and, when they contemplate the ocean, begin by seeing horses." There are also the humbugs who never look at anything at all, a species rather widespread at the moment.

The attribute of the great painters is to modify the eyes of the world and hence the world itself. Since Turner, the sea is no longer the same as it was before him. Since Monet, Rouen Cathedral has ceased to be a religious edifice of stone adorned with sculptures and become a sort of prism, spectrum, kaleidoscope. At least I can never conceive of it in any other way, this cathedral, this work of art treated like a flower, like some manifestation of nature, out of which Monet made another work of art superimposing itself on the first. Sometimes when I have been painting at some length and with some success I think that the world after Pluche may well be slightly different from the world before Pluche. I will have brought to it a few curves that are real but which nobody had perceived before me, and a few colors, real as well, but which nobody had sought precisely where they may be found. All this in connection with a squirrel painted at top speed on a Number 5 canvas! Bah! A painting isn't good simply because it is vast and has caused one a lot of sweat. My squirrel, such as it is, is excellent and I wouldn't exchange it for the ceiling of the Odéon. My day has not been wasted.

A small (or large) work of creation promotes a great deal of energy. Four days ago I was incapable of any undertaking, everything bored me or discouraged me in advance; I barely had the strength to get dressed; even yesterday there was nothing that didn't seem difficult, overwhelming, insurmountable. This morning, just because I'd found pleasure in painting for half an hour, I felt ready for anything, as if I had grown enormously and the world had enormously shrunk. My misgivings about Marie now seemed absurd; I interpreted them as being mainly the result of the weak state of mind I was in. As it was too early to call her up, I wrote half a dozen letters. There's still quite a pile that I haven't answered yet, but if my new-found energy lasts I hope I shall get to the end of this chore in a few days.

Whenever I telephone Marie, I never hear her bright voice saying: "Hello, is that you, Pluche?" without a faint thrill. At such moments my whole life, my whole youth rises up before me. Marie's voice is the same as when she was twenty, the same as when she was a little girl. Perhaps I am at fault in seeing art everywhere, but this voice, these words, always the same amid our changing lives, amid things growing old, amid the world becoming denser, bring me the same joy as a phrase of music written by some composer of genius, Beethoven or Schumann, which will accompany mankind to the end of time. They unfailingly revive those happy and unhappy days of my childhood, an age when everything was at once pure and symbolic. One of the reasons why I have a special affection for my niece is because she has Marie's voice, above all on the telephone, to the point that I have on occasion confused the two of them, particularly when the child, in imitation of her mother, cries: "Hello, is that you, Pluche?" in the same way. This morning Marie's voice was fresh and gay just as it usually is. Hearing this voice, which has echoed for so long in my innermost self and forms such an integral part of my feelings and my memory, I once again had the charming and fleeting illusion that life hadn't moved on, that the world was still the same, that the years between had never happened. Even so, Marie was feeling tired. We would go to Mother Cruchon's another time; today she didn't feel like going out, not up to driving. But why didn't I go and have a *tête-à-tête* lunch with her instead? Yes, she happened to be alone.

In the cold light of day I found her looking even less well. And sadder too. All at once I felt a pang of remorse; confronted by her drawn face and unhappy eyes, I thought that by and large I can't possess much tenderness of heart or charity. Seeing my sister as she was, pale and looking older, I was suddenly and forcibly reminded of all our friendship, our memories, our past faith in each other, of that feeling that still binds her to me. For a moment I was so moved by this that I found myself blushing. The frailty of human beings appears to me now and then in this way, and every time it arouses in me a kind of shame. Shame at being so unconcerned, so personal, so exacting with them, at bottom so hard. Is it because I am an artist that I give so little of myself to others? And are they aware of it? Marie, at any rate, is certainly aware of it. I had proof of this today. Who am I then, in God's name, to be ceaselessly casting judgment the way I do, and to subordinate to these judgments the impulses of my heart? One must care for people as they are and not as one would wish them to be; that is true charity, and I have a hell of a long way to go along that path. There is in Marie's heart a love for me that has never swerved, that is wholly pure and has nothing to do with what she has made of her life. Isn't this enough to inspire an equal amount of love in return? Apparently not. She must in addition have adhered to all my principles. Oh Pluche, Pluche the stiff-necked, pride has not done with making you suffer!

Whereas Marie yesterday was anxious to unburden herself while I resisted all attempts at confidences, so today when I was full of remorse she was in a reticent mood. That's how it always goes. I had to badger her for quite a while. I could see I was annoying her, but the impulse was too strong for me. When one thinks of something too late, one has a moral rebound resulting in an excessive display of zeal in order to make up for what one failed to do the day before. In the end I had my way. Marie heaved a deep sigh and said:

"It's true, Pluche, I am unhappy. I didn't want to tell you about it because I noticed yesterday you were going through one of your periods of hibernation and not exactly inclined to share in the woes of suffering humanity. But since you insist. . . . You'd better know that everything in my life may possibly change. So I'm feeling rather scared. And I also need to have you around. Shall we go to the root of it all as we used to in the old days? During the past ten years I've often had the feeling you were drifting away from me. I don't mean that you were becoming a stranger, no, but we no longer talked about the same things, or we'd talk about them in a different way, as if you had shut a door in my face. An inner door, very deep inside you, which had always been open to me before. I've known you too long and too well not to have sought in myself as much as in you for the reasons that caused you to drop me. It has more than once made me very sad. But you must have noticed that I've never shown any sign of it, that I've remained always the same in my relations with you. This wasn't difficult for me, since I have never wavered in my attitude toward you. What I felt as a child I still feel now. For me you have never ceased to be the great Pluche, the boss. A boss one disobeyed, of course, because the boss doesn't exist who isn't disobeyed, even while one admits he's in the right at the very moment of doing the opposite of what he wants. I have often done the opposite of what you'd have wanted. I'm deeply aware of it, you know. And I've a pretty strong suspicion it's because of that that you've drawn away from me. To put it as briefly as possible, I've let you down. Yes, I've let you down, and each time I've done so, that's to say each time I've acted in a way you disapproved of, I've known it. I would reproach myself for it, fret about it for several days, telling myself it was I who was digging the ditch between us, but I was unable to do otherwise. There was always a sort of fatality impelling me to adopt certain points of view; to take certain decisions that were in contradiction to what you had taught me or given me to understand in the old days. It seems to me you first became aware of this about ten years ago. But it had begun long before. In fact, it began when I married Albert, when we parted company, you and I, when we no longer saw each other every day, when I stopped looking at the world through your eyes. Something happened then which I grasped only much later on. So long as we were young you took the place of everything for me. You weighed so heavily on me, you wrapped me round so closely that I wasn't even conscious of it. I had the same thoughts as you and I said the same things. I was convinced we were as alike as twins. Because of this a whole part of myself eluded me. I never saw it. I didn't even know it existed. Directly I became a woman, directly I began to live a life of my own with a man I loved but who hadn't got your weight, this other part of me which you had so long relegated to the shadows came out into the open.

"Please don't mind, Pluche, if I reproach you for something. I've told you I disappointed you. It's true. I have been disappointing. But one's always wrong to be disappointed: it only proves one hasn't been seeing straight. That you shouldn't have seen me straight when you were twenty-five is only natural. What on the other hand was not fair is that you should have gone on looking at me with the same eyes and never noticed as time went on in what ways I was different from you or, to put it more modestly, was not your equal. And yet the thing stares you in the face: I am a woman, Pluche. A woman is not a man. Forgive me for harping on something so silly but you still aren't really aware of it. Our whole misunderstanding lies in that. It never occurred to you that we were not of the same sex, you and I. Besides, it's quite understandable. When I was a child, it wasn't a little girl who listened to you but a sexless companion in whom all you were conscious of was the heart or the intelligence. As a girl, I still had the sturdy spirit of the young. Finally I became a woman, a wife, a mother, and everything shifted. A child, a young girl, is hard like a boy. A woman is soft, malleable, she has need of a hand to mold and remold her the whole time. As it happens, these feminine characteristics came out in me when I left you, and it was to Albert that the task fell of fashioning this new being.

"When we were young my relations toward you were the same as those of a novice toward his superior, that is to say there was a hierarchy between you and me. Besides, if I may put it this way, we lived on an abstract plane. We had no material preoccupations in common. With Albert things were immediately different. To begin with we were equal. Following this, we had to live. You don't know what it's like, Pluche, to be a hard-up young couple. You've never had to worry about anyone but yourself. When there are two of you it's quite a job to survive. And this is where, if one isn't careful, the feminine influence starts to grow, asserts itself, proliferates, and even becomes abnormal. For years Albert and I could barely afford to live. During this period I believe I was a great help to him. I talked to him as you would have talked to him. I never complained. I even found a sort of pleasure in the wretched meals we ate, and in sharing them with you when you came every week. I told myself that the luck of living with two men like Albert and you was well worth a sacrifice. I never minded having to wear the same sleazy dress for four years on end, the same beret, the same down-at-heel shoes. Anyway, I was sleazy too. Without taking into account that at home I'd been taught to be thrifty. One thing you always forget is that I had a lower middle-class upbringing. Papa and Mama stuffed my head with a mass of petty notions, petty maxims about prudence, petty reservations, petty precautions which you would

sweep aside whenever you paid some attention to me but which
never really disappeared. After I started seeing less of you,
when I had a house of my own to run, all this more or less
rose to the surface again. You had given me the mind of an
artist, I was married to an artist, I lived among artists, but I
still had my middle-class atavism. This absorbed all the more
of me in that I wasn't an artist myself, that is to say I didn't
have any creative gift. Your chief grudge against me, as I see
it, is that I haven't known how to hold Albert to a certain
path, that I let him give free rein to his facility, that I never
sounded a warning note. You would have liked for me to say
to Albert ten years ago: 'Look out, you're beginning to produce
bad paintings in order to earn money. Stop it. Let's remain
poor and sublime.' Am I wrong? But things were never so
simple. To begin with, I admit it freely, I didn't realize Albert's
painting was no longer what it had been. He was working
like a slave, painting night and day; I thought that from such
a formidable output—uneven, of course, but when one is turning
out a mass of stuff one can't help being uneven—there would
gradually emerge an original body of work. After which, as
you know, he had his first successes and these first successes
dazzled me. For the first time we began to be better off, I
no longer had to perform miracles in order to buy new sheets.
Maybe too I sinned out of modesty. I felt intimidated by
what they were saying about Albert in the papers, the rising
prices of his pictures. I assumed that the world was right and
I was wrong. This money which came more and more easily,
our standard of life which was improving every month, blinded
me. I'm going to say something that will horrify you, Pluche,
from what I know of you: I had a longing to be happy. A
longing for that foolish happiness you despise so much and
which takes the form of dresses, pretty underwear, a comfortable house, servants, cars. I had a longing to put something
other than Pond's on my face. And on top of this I longed to
have a child. Now that we could afford to bring one up, I
wanted this child more than I can say. I had to have one. I

was twenty-eight. Up to that age I had deprived myself of a child. After all, I can't help it, I'm a woman. Albert's painting has brought me happiness. You mustn't ask too much of a woman. How could you expect a woman, a member of the female sex, cautious, grasping, haunted like all her kind by a fear of going in want, to condemn paintings thanks to which she is happy, and the man who makes these paintings? No, Pluche, she can only love such paintings, want them to spread all over the world, display their rewarding colors on every wall of every house. I know that you reject lock, stock, and barrel everything Albert has done for the past ten years but I can't bring myself to do so. For me, in what he paints, even when it's slapdash, there is some quality which is his alone, which has never ceased to give me pleasure, which still speaks to me, in a faint and distant way, of our past twenty years of life together that are now coming to an end."

I have transcribed all this without a break, since that is more or less how it was said. I didn't have the heart to interrupt her, although much that she said was questionable. I was too disturbed, too filled with pity to quibble over details. By and large Marie was right. I realized that she had been as clear-sighted as I, if not more so on certain points. I am hard, no doubt, but it takes very little to open up my heart. At bottom, I believe it's enough just to talk to me intelligently and sincerely. This instantly crumbles my defenses. Listening to Marie, I felt amazed and grateful. I was rediscovering a being I had really and truly forgotten, I was again seeing in her virtues I had believed extinct. For the rest, lucidity never fails to have a beneficial effect, for Marie, who had been decidedly mournful and dejected when she began this examination of conscience, became more animated as she went on. I could sense in her that special kind of exaltation, conveyed so clearly by the tone of voice, felt by people in pursuit of their truth.

This exaltation, however, didn't last. With her final words Marie subsided again into gloom.

"Tell me what's upsetting you so," I said. "It's true, all these last years I have been rather remote. Forgive me. It's been my fault, and yours, and the fault of Mesnard's painting. You've seen all this quite clearly. What you have just been telling me has touched me more than you realize. I should like you to be quite sure of one thing, darling, and that is that I love you, that you are the dearest person in the world to me."

"Pluche," she said, lowering her eyes, "Albert wants a divorce. He told me so a few days ago. It's silly but I wasn't expecting it. And yet I had reasons to expect it. One can only presume that my bourgeois life as an artist's wife has made me timid and blind—which, incidentally, would amply justify your judgment of me. This business of a divorce has come at a bad time. Last year I could have stood it better. But right now I feel quite crushed by it. I never told you I was ill. The thought that, on top of this, I am going to separate from the man I've lived with for twenty years, whom I love for all sorts of reasons, who no longer loves me for the same reasons no doubt, that I am going to have to busy myself with the details of a divorce, find an apartment, consult a lawyer, explain it all to Lise, no, it's not possible!"

"You're ill?" I cried. "But why didn't you say so? What's wrong?"

"Oh, women's troubles. It's for that very reason I haven't mentioned it. Not even to Albert. Someday soon they're going to have to open me up and God knows what they won't have to remove. It's not so much the prospect of the operation that gets me down as what it implies. I'm thirty-nine. After they've put me through the hoop, I'll be a sterile old woman and this is the moment when Albert decides to divorce me. Just when I'm going to need so much to have him around! When he brought up this divorce I had a fit of despair. Everything was deserting me simultaneously! I'm not like you, my poor Pluche, I haven't the comfort in my unhappiness of telling myself: 'It's good for inspiration' or 'There's still *me* left, and that's enough!' I just felt totally abandoned. Abandoned without recourse, with-

out anyone to turn to. I am not a strong woman. And I didn't
dare ask you for help. That's funny, isn't it? From time to time
you scare me. I've felt scared of you these last few days. Just
imagine, I have a growth like Véronique! We've had pretty
good laughs, you and I, about that growth of Véronique's, which
she and Georges have made into a family institution! I guess
we were even pretty savage about it. Well, now I'm being
punished. Now I've got a growth in my turn and the idea hor-
rifies me. Swear to me above all that you'll never say anything
about it to Véronique. She'd be calling me up every morning
to discuss our growths. I can't tell you how it revolts me, the
knowledge that this thing has grown inside me, that it is there,
that I'm carrying it in my belly like a crab. I've also got the
windup. I'd never admit that to anyone but you. This filthy
thing may be malignant. They don't yet know; they're still
making laboratory tests. I've been examining my feelings very
seriously: it's not the thought of death that frightens me, but
the thought of dying of cancer after being carved up three or
four times. If they confirm the worst, no operation, no deep
X ray. Nothing. Promise me, Pluche, you won't let them touch
me. I want to die intact. I don't want to leave behind the
memory of someone become monstrous and deformed by surgical
mutilation. I was so depressed when Albert told me he didn't
want me any more—and he couldn't have been more gentle
and considerate, as you can imagine—that I thought: 'Maybe
I'll be dead before the divorce goes through. That would be
a good way to settle the whole business! Why hasn't he had
a bit more patience?' Of course, I try to be reasonable. I tell
myself it's ludicrous to torture oneself about one's carcass, that
if my time has come it's just too bad, there's nothing to be
done about it except bow out as decently as possible. But I'm
afraid it's not quite so easy. Fatigue gives rise to a physical
depression on account of which one can't help seeing the black
side of things. This morning I had another hemorrhage. And
then the world of doctors and hospitals is so frightful. Gynecologists here, analyses there, I've had about as much of them

as I can stand when the business has only just begun. Later
on there will be the clinic, the operation, all the nursing. Nowadays being ill is such a complicated affair. Not to mention how
hateful it is spending all one's time looking after one's body. I
could almost chuck the whole thing!"

I was appalled by these revelations. I could feel inside me
that sort of hollow void, that total confusion which comes over
me when by chance I witness any real grief or pain. It's not
that I'm insensitive but my mind is never prepared for such
occasions and I don't know what to do or say; I'd be no more
embarrassed if I had to cope with delivering a baby. In reaction against myself, instead of joining my lamentations to
those of the afflicted I become aggressive, which isn't such a
bad method after all. Indeed, to feel sorry for people means
one tacitly acquiesces in their misfortune, whereas with a little
hectoring one shows that one doesn't regard them as passive
victims of destiny but as beings endowed with free will and
capable, given a little energy, of overcoming their misfortune.
Apart from this, I suppose that brusqueness is more in my
character than sniveling.

"You mustn't get into a panic just because you have a growth!"
I burst out. "All women have their growths. You're by no means
a rare specimen. Whoever would have thought that one day
I'd be holding up Véronique as an example to you! She makes
everyone's life hell with her growth, I grant you, but at least
she doesn't make a tragedy of it. You don't look well, it's true,
but you don't look in the least like someone on her deathbed.
If you had cancer I'd know it; I'd have sensed it. As for being
an old woman, don't try to kid me. Just look at yourself: you're
a darn sight better-looking than you were at twenty and you
know it perfectly well."

"You're right," replied Marie with a smile. "But admit that
people are obsessed nowadays by stories of cancer. I am like
everyone else. I don't mind dying a bit, but not any old how.
Véronique has an advantage over me in that she's told the whole
world about her growth. Over the past five or six years she and

Georges have exorcised it. But I haven't yet mentioned mine to
anyone except you. I'm all alone shut away with my growth. It
doesn't make very lively company. I shan't know the result of
what they call the biopsy for another eight days. It's a long time."

In situations in which my responsibilities are involved I am
gripped by a dual emotion: a feeling of boundless discouragement and simultaneously the certainty that I shall do everything
that may be necessary, out of a sense of duty. I note this in
passing, since it is one of the odder things about me, function-
ing quite independently of the love I bear for people. I'm
going to have to look after Marie, protect her; I know I shall do
it, and even throw myself into it, but it will cost me just as much
as if I were doing it for someone toward whom I'm quite indifferent. I went on talking nonsense for a few minutes and then
thought of a good way to calm Marie down, which was to
nudge her into describing the circumstances that have led
Mesnard to break up a marriage of twenty years' standing.
Indeed, there's something about it all that doesn't fit in with
his character, which is more disposed to sin through an excess
of self-denial. A man who seeks a divorce is a man who shows
the world that he thinks above all of himself, aspiring selfishly
to a certain form of happiness. Now Mesnard has prided himself
all his life on an altruism of the most pronounced kind; he has
displayed an ostentatious consideration for others, striving the
whole time to prove he's never been concerned with himself. I
shall have something to say one of these days about this wholly
fabricated attitude, which has contributed a great deal to the
shipwreck of his talent. The fact remains that this divorce is a
flat contradiction of his behavior ever since I've known him. I
thought that if I could succeed in luring Marie into the maze
of a psychological analysis, I could distract her from this obsession about her health which made her so humiliated and depressed. I wasn't mistaken and thanks to this my sister recovered
the strength of spirit she had displayed at the beginning of my
visit.

I had arrived at the Castel de la Mesnardière around half

past twelve; I didn't quit Marie until nearly five. We had talked
for over four hours. As I loitered on my way home to the Rue
Boissonnade I wondered just what hour of the night my
writing would keep me up to, and more especially whether I
should be able to thread my way through this mass of emotions
and words. Not to mention the frame of mind I'm in. Now
would be a fine moment to start feeling sorry for myself! I who
have a horror of complications have netted two king-sized ones
in two days! I thought I had enough to do, coping with
Georges's bankruptcy. Now on top of it I'm landed with a poor
sick woman who has nobody left but me to care for her.

I am always startled to realize how people's lives, even the
seemingly most futile and incoherent, all have a predestined
and so to speak harmonious curve to them. Every event in
them is prepared way in advance. In its way, Mesnard's life is
a work of art and, as I try to sort out this afternoon's conversation, I can see how it could have no other outcome than what
is now going to happen, namely his divorce and possible re-
marriage to a certain Mademoiselle Juliette Duchateau. Yes,
everything was leading to this little upheaval, which is, like the
majority of upheavals, more of a putting things in order.

That Mesnard should have a mistress in the person of this
Duchateau girl is of no importance and I don't think she can
be the first one since he married twenty years ago. When he
and I were young he was an indefatigable womanizer, a real
old goat—at least he was always happy to play this part—and he
would chalk up conquest after conquest, making me gape in
admiration since I was far less sharp than he was. Such habits
don't cease merely because one has taken the marriage vows, the
more so in that Mesnard had a philosophy regarding these
which he expounded to me a hundred times, as they formed
part of his general system of life, and the falsity of which I finally
rumbled. Here's something else I shall come back to one of
these days if I take it into my head to explore his character in
this journal, since it's instructive and permits one to grasp how

a man, through a continual effort of will, can end up by never being himself.

I suppose, I repeat, that in twenty years of marriage Mesnard must have had a certain number of mistresses, but no one has ever known. He has always been exrtemely discreet, extremely correct, since his whole life is based on being correct. Now, what better opportunity is there for being correct than in adultery? Toward Marie he has always shown himself endlessly attentive, tactful, and considerate; all these attitudes were probably more deliberate than spontaneous and more the fruit of his head than his heart, but nonetheless they have made him very delightful company, there's no denying. I'm not surprised that Marie should be devoted to him. The more so since from what I know of him—and from the way most male individuals behave—he must have redoubled his charm every time he has deceived her. However shrewd one may be it's easy to let oneself be taken in by these antics. Judging by the rough picture Marie gave me of La Duchateau, it seems the affair is beyond remedy. Indeed, what drove Mesnard into her arms was neither lust nor lack of occupation, nor any of the usual emotions that provoke adulteries. It was something deeper. This girl is exactly the type toward whom Mesnard was bound to be led by ten years of second-rate painting. To employ a stock phrase, she is "the woman of his life" in the sense that she resembles far more closely than Marie the life he has built up for himself. She is the crown of this life, she completes it, heightens the colors he has put into it just as a discreet touch of vermilion makes the greens in a picture sing.

Mlle. Duchateau is twenty-two years old; she is pretty the way girls are nowadays, that is to say she has the stereotyped charm and elegance of fashion models whose pictures one sees in black and white and color in women's magazines. For me, this type of girl is the exact equivalent of luxury motorcars or those planned interiors subtly blending modernity with Louis XVI which smart decorators devise for rich grocers and the art magazines love to reproduce in order to tempt other rich grocers. Nothing in common with my dear Lucienne, who is, no doubt, far better informed on questions of chic but who is a timeless woman, a kind of dryad, with the forms feminine beauty has had since time began, until our good-for-nothing century discovered beauties sick and wan. I have never seen Mlle. Duchateau and it is most unlikely that I ever shall, but I can picture her with her perfect tailor-mades, her Chanel gowns, her matte complexion, her pensive eyes, her mocking mouth of a well-brought-up young girl, her black hair, clean and bouffant. To my way of thinking, there's not much difference between dolls like this and the handsome objects all in chromium, plastic, and "studied" lines that industry turns out these days. In the same way I can imagine what sort of mentality the girl must have, as daughter of a modern bourgeois family without principles or traditions but not without money. It is a mind as trim and fashionable as her body, furnished with the most elegant scraps of contemporary "culture": a little psychoanalysis, a few dull but distinguished novels, abstract painting, what makes a happy marriage, the gulf between the generations, progressive political ideas. It appears, moreover, that Mlle. Duchateau *does* art history at the Ecole du Louvre. This completes her picture. Incidentally, I can never manage to understand how people who know about painting, however little, can possibly enjoy abstract art; anyone would think they understood nothing about the masters in whom they claim to be interested. Manessier is incompatible with Titian or even Bonnard. In short, Mlle. Duchateau seems to me a perfect example of her type; she was the ideal choice for poor Mesnard, who had had more than enough of Marie's complicity and Pluche's silent disapproval. Basically something very odd and very original has happened to Mesnard: he's had enough of being understood, enough of being known too well, of being too transparent, too much helped. Enough of that twofold Cousine Bette that Marie and I have been—she by fondly encouraging him in his sinister virtuosity, I by now and then tendering my advice willy-nilly on his lucrative daubs. I find this point quite fascinating. Mesnard has followed the opposite (and probably far truer) course to what one normally expects from an artist (to wit, misunderstood at home, he goes in search of understanding elsewhere). He himself has been so well understood, so bolstered, poor man, that he sighed after a little incomprehension. Incomprehension meant comfort, relaxation, freedom! What a dream, to have to deal with people who are indifferent, who are totally ignorant, and who can be made to swallow any bit of hogwash on the grounds that it's avant-garde! This dream Mesnard has fulfilled with his little mistress, who knows nothing about painting, nor the exacting demands this makes on one, nor the fact of hard work, and who is flattered to have a famous man in his forties chasing after her. Besides, he may possibly be in love, if only out of vanity at having aroused the interest of such a pretty girl. With her his heart and mind relax from their usual tension; not only can he sit back and enjoy the pleasure of being admired, but also he has a delightful sense of superiority. No more need to watch his step; he can say whatever he likes in the certain knowledge that it will be respectfully listened to. Finally there is the novelty, I mean the joy of appearing new in someone's eyes. Indeed, it isn't the novelty of Mlle. Duchateau that has captivated Mesnard, I imagine—he'll have soon got over that—but the fact of being for her a highly complex being, someone very difficult to understand and whom it will take her years to fathom. Perhaps I have just discovered here one of the most frequent causes of adultery: the longing a transparent man feels to become opaque. He suddenly finds himself wrapped in mystery, as if he had bought a new suit. This mystery is most becoming; it conceals the fact that the left shoulder is lower than the right, it nips in the waist, it makes the leg more slender. Oh, it's a marvelous tailor! This unexpected new suit makes you look fifteen years younger.

When a man of forty-five divorces in order to marry a chick, the world at large will have it that he was hankering after fresh young flesh, that he was overcome by a fit of middle-aged lust, and other nonsense. For my part, I believe this to be the least important aspect of the affair. To begin with, one should

look around at the sort of men who divorce. They're not the
seedy sort: those lack the means to maintain two wives. The
poor man is monogamous out of necessity. Since time began
polygamy, whether legal or not, has been the privilege of rich
men. Take, for instance, the Hebrew patriarchs, the Negro kings,
and the Mormons. Divorce is a form of polygamy adapted to our
society. So it is the rich who divorce at forty-five, and even then
not just any of them: those who are entirely self-made, who
have really had to work, who have earned their money the hard
way. They perceive all at once that, twenty years late in the
day, they can artificially re-create the gilded youth they never
knew, they can have the smart wedding with all the presents,
tail coats, and honeymoon in Venice that was denied them
when they were young. Not to mention the intoxicating feeling
of bringing a fortune, an opulent and easy way of life to the
girl of their choice. If there is any desire to recapture lost youth
it is in this that it can be found, in this puerile illusion of a past
life that can be blue-penciled like a bad draft and begun again
by virtue of a marriage contract.

Alongside such novelties the former wife doesn't count for
very much. She has everything against her, poor thing, but
above all the fact that she was the witness of the hard times.
She knows too much about the gentleman. She has too often
seen him struggling to make ends meet at the end of each
month; she has helped him too much. A woman married in
one's youth is in a way one's mother. She has all the earnestness,
the outdated if not common ways, the superiority, and, most
tedious of all, the trustfulness of a mother. The attitude of a
man of forty-five who divorces seems to me hardly any different from that of a self-made man toward his parents, of whom
he feels ashamed.

In spite of the anxiety Marie's state has thrown me into and
that I can feel reflected in various parts of my body such as
my diaphragm, which is constricted, or the hollows of my elbows, where that sort of impatience has lodged that is felt by
people dominated by the sympathetic nerve, I can't help finding

pleasure in writing. It seems to me that my style reflects this. In spite of the gloom spread all through me, I find in it a sort of gaiety quite out of tune with my heart. It only goes to prove that in the practice of this less familiar art I have the same spirit as in painting. The gaiety of a work comes from I don't know where, perhaps from that flinty kernel that lies at the bottom of every artist's heart. I can no more restrain my pen than my brush. It runs along, it dances as if the mere fact of writing made it joyful.

Writing here of Mesnard reveals to me a trait in myself to which I hadn't paid any heed up to now: this predilection I have for justifying people, for seeking explanations of their actions. I ought to be in a cold rage against this fool who is exchanging a pearl for a piece of tinsel and who in any case has done nothing else but that throughout his life; I ought to be seething with hatred for this irresponsible man who not only fails to notice his wife's poor state of health but even adds to her misery by telling her he means to leave her. But no, I can't manage it. His motives, his arguments, his passions interest me more than his responsibility. I cannot bring myself to mount the platform of morality in order to judge him and declare: "This is good, that is bad." Even the fact that Marie is involved doesn't make any difference. Were I Mesnard's victim myself, it would still be the same. Memories come back to me, as I write this, of various occasions when some fellow has done me in and yet I couldn't bring myself to bear him any grudge, because his motives interested me to such an extent that all I could see was the cause and not the effect, which was harmful to me.

I asked Marie how she was so well informed on the love life of Mesnard and Mlle. Duchateau, considering that it isn't generally in her character to be curious about such matters. It seems that this came about of its own accord. Mesnard met the girl seven or eight months ago at one of those smart dinners he loves to attend. A classic dinner with two or three ambassadors, one or two writers, two countesses, an industrialist, and

so on. Duchateau was there as a stopgap, because she was dec-
orative, not too stupid, and also the hostess's niece. At the dinner
table she was seated next to Mesnard, with whom she prattled
at great length. Mesnard was charmed by this beautiful child
who had been to some of his exhibitions, who told him how
much she admired his genius, not to mention the course she
was taking at the Ecole du Louvre and what makes a happy
marriage. She rolled her beautiful black girlish eyes at him, she
smiled her beautiful velvety girlish smile; Mesnard, as he
munched his cold salmon mayonnaise, had a bird's-eye albeit
oblique view of beautiful downy girlish arms, beautiful firm and
rounded girlish breasts, beautiful soft and awkward girlish hands.
I fancy the scene must have been particularly well lit and that,
along with the saddle of lamb, he relished a faint shadow on
the round cheek of Mlle. Duchateau, which shadow surely
gave him as much pleasure as the 1943 vintage claret and
may even have inspired some tender thoughts. I know how the
minds of painters work! After dinner Mesnard and Duchateau
went to sit on a sofa at the back of the drawing room; they
continued to talk with much animation and gaiety. It made
Marie feel rather foolish. Happily some ambassador from Greece
or Turkey took up with her, making a thousand and one vacuous
remarks in that flowery and syntactically impeccable French
spoken fifty years ago in chancelleries. Now and then she would
glance over at her husband busy making his conquest. On the
way back to the Parc Montsouris in the Master's Mercedes
Marie, out of pique and with that gentle perversity of honest
women, said to him: "She was a charming creature, that girl you
were talking to!" Mesnard, the utter nitwit, replied offhandedly:
"Oh, d'you think so? I found her pretty ordinary. She's one of
my admirers." To herself Marie thought: "He'll be in bed with
her next week." In short, banality itself. All the same, it's distressing that Mesnard, whom I've known so blithe and cynical, having all the girls he wanted, should have made such a life for himself that he's reduced at forty-five to the most conventional,
middle-class adultery, at least in its beginnings. I can picture him

at his smart dinner: the spitting image of the young captain of industry, head of a dynamic concern, not looking his age, keeping up with the times. The ideal of every well-bred girl. Not surprising that Mlle. Duchateau should have swooned away before such a matinee idol. A famous artist who looks like a publicity agent is irresistible, the hero of every heartthrob magazine. God, how absurd it all is! I don't really like running down mature men by comparing them with the young men they once were since generally speaking the fifty-year-olds are worth far more than the twenty-year-olds, but I'm forced in Mesnard's case to admit that at twenty-five he was quite a different person from what he is today. His shortcomings hadn't yet borne their fruit, if I may put it that way; they hadn't yet attacked his talent and his soul.

As she thought "He'll be in bed with her next week," Marie was surprised to feel nothing but a dull shock. She concluded from this that something in her life had come to an end, namely a certain form of demanding, jealous love she bore for Mesnard. She told herself despondently that she was joining the ranks of resigned old women for whom their husband's peccadilloes hardly matter any longer because there are "other things." Her husband's conventional attitude was far more painful to her than the thought that he would soon be unfaithful. This attitude bored her, by which I mean it gave her that sense of discouragement one gets when someone behaves in a conventional way or, in a given situation, says just what one was expecting him to say. I can understand this reaction better than anyone, being ultrasensitive on this point and only caring for what is surprising, unexpected, original. One has to admit there are very few people capable of providing it. And I also know why I have such a horror of scenes of violence or affliction: it's not that I'm afraid they may upset me but because I know in advance what people are going to say and how they will say it. Marie, hearing Mesnard lie the way every husband lies, instead of being offended or annoyed simply thought that, since a man so close to her, who knew her so well, was adopting such vulgar behavior, it must mean that he despised her or had become indifferent and consequently no longer loved her. In the end she told herself that Mesnard's love for her must already have died some time before, although he possibly hadn't been aware of it. Indeed, love does die discreetly, above all between married people who have many other interests and habits in common. Often those who believe they love each other, or at least never question themselves about it, have ceased to do so for several years. Married love can be like a cracked cup, which may remain whole for a long time but breaks if one dips it in boiling water. This comparison comes from Marie. The chance meeting with an insignificant girl was enough to destroy Mesnard's cracked love for her completely.

After this pretty beginning, Mesnard's amour developed along standard lines. He began to go out in the afternoons, which was something new, given that at this time he normally gets through a lot of work and even, on some days, knocks off two canvases. Then he took to going out in the evenings. Then he spent two or three weekends in the country. Explanation: "I need to be alone, I have to think things out by myself, etc." The poor lad has decidedly gone bourgeois, even down to the lies, even down to the vocabulary. And what a pathetic excuse to think up, what lack of discernment! Did he believe a woman like Marie would be taken in by his clichés or didn't he care, as she presumes? She wasn't for a second deceived as to the true meaning of his need for solitude even though on these expeditions he would take his sketchbook and a paintbox for appearances' sake or out of politeness. What surprises me is that Marie didn't tell me sooner about these goings-on. I reproached her for all this secrecy she's been practicing for eight months now.

"Oh come on!" she retorted, "I wasn't going to bore you with all of this. You already don't much care for Albert; it wasn't worth throwing fuel on the flames. I was sure his little adventure wouldn't lead him very far. Besides, I've reached the age when husbands sleep out, haven't I? That's nothing to make a drama about. Let me quote you a Pluchesque maxim: 'It's bad enough to have worries without talking about them!' Basically this whole business stinks of boredom. Whichever way you look at it, it's deadly. My husband, his mistress, myself, it's enough to drive anyone round the bend. There are a few situations in life like this one which are really appalling, because they leave no opening for saying or doing something original. And Albert doesn't make things any easier: he's the image of the perfect gentleman divorcing in a haze of honor and dignity, he looks on me as his best friend and so on; in short, he's the hero of a distinguished novel on adultery among the upper crust of society. As we married under the community property system, I shall have to take with me the half of his worldly goods; he's determined on this point and has told me as much. In this connection we've had a battle as to who can be the most noble. My first impulse, stupid like every first impulse, was to refuse. I said to him grandly: 'Albert, if you get rid of me I shall go as I came, without a penny. I'd rather die than take one cent of what you've earned with your painting. That's yours, not mine!' At the same time I thought: 'What I'm saying is too silly. What he has earned with his painting he owes partly to me. I've given him the regular and orderly life that has enabled him to produce so much; I've defended him, encouraged him, supported him, idolized him; I've even landed better terms for him with his various dealers.' But you know how it is: one thoughtlessly adopts a noble attitude, gets bogged down in it, and it becomes impossible to turn back. The funniest part of it is that by my refusing any kind of compensation or alimony I've unintentionally provided the only argument likely to make Albert have second thoughts about the divorce. He finds the idea that I might be more generous than he quite intolerable."

"It seems to me," I said, "that there's another argument to prevent this generous man from divorcing. Your operation. You don't quit your wife just at the moment she's going to have her insides opened up. It simply isn't done. I think you've been a little too tactful not to put him wise to it."

"After he'd made his announcement it wasn't possible. It

would have looked like blackmail. Blackmailing people through illness is horrible, Pluche. You would never do it. Besides, I've made up my mind: when I've had the results of the analyses, when the doctor has fixed the day when I go into the clinic, I shall pack my little bag and tiptoe off in secret, without telling a soul. You'll be the only one to know the name of the clinic. One evening when he comes home Albert will find me gone. There are two possibilities: either he'll heave a sigh of relief or else he'll fly into a panic. If he panics, it will mean he still loves me. He'll be touched by my discretion and maybe we shan't divorce. I should so much like that to happen."

I told Marie I found her scheme somewhat melodramatic but ingenious. She remonstrated hotly: ingenuity didn't come into it; it was more of a wish to run away, the desire one has to hide when one feels no longer loved. I let that pass. People seldom go through with this kind of crazy project; no surgeon would be a party to it; besides, Lise would be even more panic-stricken than Mesnard. To take her little bag and creep away is the wild fancy of someone who has been churning over a problem all alone for days without anyone to advise her.

I am extremely alarmed by the word "biopsy" that Marie used this afternoon. The idea that she may have a cancer, that we won't definitely know for another week, gives me the cold shivers. I feel the heavy, sick apprehension that descends on one when imagining the secret workings of disease in the bodies of those one loves, of one's impotence in the face of these ravages one only learns of when it is too late to fight them. Pray God Marie hasn't developed something really grave! Just to think about it makes me quite distraught and almost paralyzed. I don't know how to stand up to events. Thirty years of egotism and rigorous preservation of my freedom of mind have endowed me, where this sort of thing is concerned, with a complete supineness that has become as it were a component of my nature. Lost causes and beings arouse in me a sense of fatalism and although I greatly reproach myself for this feeling I cannot dispel it. It is like an instinct. I can see quite clearly what

intellectual discipline has led me to this point: it is my inability
to persist over a picture that has gone wrong. When a painting
has started off badly, when every brush stroke takes the wrong
direction, when instead of blossoming out, instead of opening up
wider and wider vistas as it grows, the picture only leads me
to a dead end, I don't persevere with it; I smear the whole
thing over or burn it and begin another, completely different
one. I have a similar way of behaving in life, even with regard
to the people I love. I've had occasion to observe this three or
four times, always to my sorrow, certainly, but without any true
remorse since I can't help it. It's beyond my powers to hang onto
something that is disappearing. I have always been struck by
the attitude of David in the Bible, in the Book of Kings, when
the son Bathsheba has given him dies. Directly the child is
dead he snaps his fingers, turns his mind to other things, and
gets to work with the queen over producing a new heir. I have
this same quality to the highest degree. Is it ridiculous to think
that my selfishness sometimes weighs me down, and that I curse
the lack of concern it imbues me with on almost every occasion?
Indeed, I've always done well to deny the tragic side of things,
since due to this nothing tragic has ever happened to me. But
such an attitude is perhaps only compatible with youth and I
have reached an age when, in spite of all the philosophy we
are armed with, all the habits, the strength of character we
believe we possess, destiny and its cruelties creep up on us. At
forty-five I am no longer young; these last years I have had a
suspicion that tragic events were drawing in on me like a ring of
wolves circling the fire lit by a traveler lost in the wilds. Is the
fire I have lit less bright than it was five or ten years ago?
Are the wolves growing bolder? Ah no! Not that! Better to
become a Stoic philosopher. And do everything, first and foremost, to escape the wolves. But enough, there are no real
grounds for all this. I suppose it is impossible to love someone
without thinking of his death.

My God, how late it is! It seems to me I've forgotten nothing
in today's record. What sort of mood am I in at this precise

moment? None too good, in spite of the satisfaction I've had from such a long dose of writing. These days I wake up happy and go to bed sad. I miss my painting badly. When will inspiration come back, the lousy swine? Without it I feel naked and defenseless. Even my body has turned against me. I've got pains in my stomach, pains in my head, a feeling of general discomfort. All things absolutely unknown to me when my painting gets going. And Georges's hundred thousand—I'm going to have to pay the whole lot! I had forgotten this charming detail. But there can't be any question of touching Mesnard now. Life's a bitch! If only I could lay hands on Lucienne tonight! I simply must see her tomorrow, the angel. I need to treat myself to a little pleasure. Looking at things coldly, Lucienne, dumb though she may be, is the only person just now who offers me something positive, something happy. She is always gay, always glad to see me. A presence light as a feather. Not one word of reproach when I show no sign of life for a week. In short, a treasure. Sweet Lulu. I shall lull myself to sleep trying to think of you. Tomorrow I'll stump up a pot of geraniums.

CHAPTER IX

A Perfect Mistress

> *What breasts! My God,*
> *what a breast! Apple-round,*
> *full, overflowing, set well*
> *apart from its pair and weigh-*
> *ing heavy in the hand. There*
> *are fecundities there, and*
> *sweets of love to die for.*
>
> **FLAUBERT**

Through a benevolent disposition of fate, calamities usually descend on me during periods when I'm not working, so that I have all my time free to grapple with them and try to restrict the damage. Georges and his hundred thousand francs' worth of debts, Marie and her divorce constitute major events in my orderly existence. What a catastrophe if they had occurred during a spell of intense creativity! They would have absorbed all my thoughts and got in my way. But one can look at it from a different angle. Indeed, I've often noticed how work, when one is completely immersed in it, forms an effective shield against the world, a cushion, a rampart of sandbags between the artist and external worries. It creates a vacuum around you, sucks you in, and there is no time left for living, in other words for being put upon. Friends melt away, enemies fall silent, the bores go to ground. It's paradise. Occasionally one feels a twinge of regret at not having a spare moment to go and visit Charles or Caroline. But there's nothing to be done about it. One's work sweeps one along like a train. It's their loss—the poor stay-at-homes who are left behind on the platform waving their handkerchiefs. This morning as I woke up I thought nostalgically of those glorious times when I am immersed in my work, of those dives into it for several weeks or months on end granted by heaven at times when I least expect them. It's as if every clock had stopped. I settle down before my canvases. A moment later I get up to find that six months have sped by. As I write this I could almost weep with emotion. Are there some men for whom the whole of life passes like this, mighty spirits whose powers of invention flow on without a break? Lucky devils! Titian, Michelangelo, Tintoretto, Goya, Delacroix, Rubens—were they men of this stamp? Well, I can think of no more enviable fate, and I'd gladly give all the riches and honors in the world for a permanent stream of inspiration. Take the case of Mozart, who died at thirty-five after having had a hellish life in every conceivable way: I've never been able to feel sorry for such a man, who surely never had one single empty hour throughout his brief existence. If I add up all the time in forty-five years I've devoted to work, I reach a ridiculous total: seven or eight years maybe, give or take a little. It's no use telling myself that the rest wasn't wasted, that one needs time to recharge one's batteries, I am nonetheless very small beer. Boulard tells me I'm "a force of nature"; where the hell does he get such an idea from? More like a weakness of nature, a frail nightingale who rapidly gets rusty.

It's odd to note how, in private journals of this kind, one has a tendency to whimper, moan, and exaggerate the black side of things. What can this imply? That directly one starts thinking about oneself one feels self-pity and subsides into melancholy? No, since there are often times when I think about myself and it doesn't depress me in the least. The truth is that depression drives one to write, and since one hasn't much to write about one reproduces one's depression. Obviously it was some such feeling that prompted me, without my realizing it at the time, to embark on this narrative, begun nine days ago now. I was very down in the mouth then, and I have to acknowledge that I am less so now in spite of Georges and Marie, in spite of my inability to paint (I don't count the squirrel; one squirrel doesn't make a spring).

I have one very useful faculty which simplifies life a great deal: I possess a mind fitted with drawers. When some activity or problem has preoccupied me for what I consider to be long enough, I shut the drawer and instantly stop thinking about it: my mind becomes as free again as if nothing had previously been preying on it. I think my most pronounced characteristic, which is unconcern, comes essentially from this gift of being able to detach myself at any moment I choose. This doesn't only hold good for worries but also for work, love, friendship, and ambition (whenever I chance to have a fit of it). All at once something goes click in my head and heart: the matter instantly ceases to interest me. Sometimes it is I who turn off the switch. Today I had no wish to think about Marie or Georges, nor about Boulard, nor even old Raimondet, despite my liking for him, as for me he is linked with the idea of Marie since I only made his acquaintance the day before yesterday on my way to see her. So for twenty-four hours I decided to shut the drawer holding all that. I know I shall open it again tomorrow, that nothing in it will have shifted, that my feelings will be the same, and so on. Consequently, no compunction. On the other hand I can never concentrate my thoughts for very long on any one object. I have to move on to something else, my problems have to drop down into my subconscious, which then proceeds to knead them, grind them down, work at them, and possibly solve them. Meanwhile the only person I felt like seeing today was Lucienne.

And so I saw her. She came and spent four hours with me here in the Rue Boissonnade. There's no denying, love is really fun only in the afternoon. Probably because normally one works in the afternoon, so that one is sacrificing a useful activity to a pleasant one. On top of this, when one makes love in the afternoon it always involves a ceremony, it assumes the aspect of a solemn rite. At all events, Lucienne is lovable in every possible respect, even down to her conversation, which never bores me although it is made up of trivia, tiny preoccupations, insignificant projects. Since when have I known her? About three months. Like all the women who have attracted me, I found her in a setting unfamiliar to me. Love (or desire) is the most beguiling path down which to explore society. In forty-five years I have known a certain number of women; each of them captivated me to the extent that she brought me a way of life different from my own, a special language and odd ways peculiar to her environment. We talk much about how change is a sexual stimulus. To this I would add being taken out of one's normal environment. A salesgirl in the Galeries Lafayette offers me as much that is picturesque, as much folklore, as a geisha girl or a houri, and half the attraction she has for me stems from this.

This makes me appear a Casanova, which I can hardly claim to be! I can on occasion spend months on end in a state of absolute continence, especially when I am working. I make up for this during my bouts of artistic sterility. I came across Lucienne in front of Ravuski's window in the Avenue Matignon. She was pretty enough to eat, and so elegant that I felt quite bashful. If I hadn't thought I detected a twinkle in her eye, I would never have had the courage to approach such an awe-inspiring creature. But that morning I had just finished a picture with which I was pleased, I was feeling lighthearted, and my mind was tuned in to the outside world. I had just come through a vast bout of creativity and was feeling that for some time to come I wouldn't have much further urge to work. All of which, added to the vague smile of this passer-by, set my heart pounding. I smiled back and said the first thing to enter my head, which was just what was needed. I pushed open Ravuski's door. At the back of the gallery was hung a picture of mine, nicely framed. I led Lucienne up to this masterpiece. She pronounced it superb, blindly and because its author was holding her arm. In the half-light of the gallery this charming girl, like Manon Lescaut, had an air at once so gentle, so tender, so bewitching that love instantly started galloping through my head. Such memories are delicious and fraught with poetry. Lucienne is what she is; for all that, at a certain moment of my life she dazzled me, she etched her smile forever in my memory, where it will remain one of the sweetest things I have known.

Some people are blessed with the gift of simplification. For them everything is easy, everything runs on the smoothest possible wheels. Never any dramas or misunderstandings. This is either the fruit of great wisdom or else of a complete lack of imagination. Lucienne has so little imagination, she is at once so practical and so placid that I wonder if I will ever leave her. I see her as seldom as I choose, my absence doesn't oppress her and my presence seems to please her. There's no question of any "love-passion." And what "love-taste" we share is so light, so undemanding that I don't see how I could ever grow tired of her. But wait! I mustn't get carried away and talk nonsense. I've already tired of Lucienne several times, since I'm the same as all men: anything too calm, too clear, too easy bores me. There are times when I wish Lucienne would get mad with me and scratch my eyes out. But it's no use expecting anything along those lines, it's just not in her nature. So I have to amend what I've just written: in two or three months' time I can see myself saying goodbye forever to this adorable mistress and faintly regretting her for the rest of my life. Only faintly. Just enough to give my memories of her a twinge.

I, who am the prince of misers as we know, then did for her something prodigious, something I still can't get over whenever I think of it. The day after our encounter, following which she had made me "the happiest of mortals," I was so delighted with her and myself, so full of gratitude and tender feelings that after leaving her I went straight to a florist's and sent her a sumptuous bouquet with my card bearing the words: "In homage to one of nature's masterpieces!" A miracle even more noteworthy: not only did I never regret this bouquet and the fortune it cost me but it even added further to my contentment. Not to mention the pleasure we all derive from playing a part that is out of character—on this occasion that of the lavish lover, which, God knows, is far from my normal way! Among her other virtues Lucienne has one to which I fairly often succumb, to my eternal surprise: she attracts gifts. I can never manage to explain how she does it; it is an entirely new experience for me (and, I hope, one without a future). She never asks for anything; she is a model of tact and discretion, of unfailing sweetness, constant little attentions, with an air of always being perfectly content, and nevertheless one feels a strange obligation to give her yet another bauble or flower as if to thank her for being so nice. One gets the impression that she expects it, that it wouldn't matter in the least if one didn't give her anything but that it would be *fitting* to take her some present. The miracle of the bouquet is repeated every time I make Lucienne some offering: it delights me to do so. Sometimes it's a paperweight unearthed in some junk shop, sometimes a lithograph by Daumier, sometimes one of my own watercolors. She has an inimitable way of accepting these. She thanks you and gives you a spanking kiss. The most trivial object enchants her, sends her wild with joy, is in her eyes an object of wonder. Following this the matter is dropped and the object vanishes into God knows what chest or cupboard, to join all the other treasure she has amassed in twenty-eight years of existence, which must be as vast as it is heterogeneous.

I wrote a few days ago that Lucienne is "silly as a goose." A libel. I should have written "silly as a cat." A cat doesn't read Plato or respond to the painting of Michelangelo, but it has a sort of intelligence about life and this is precisely what my mistress has. Besides, when she talks to me—and on occasion she can prattle away nineteen to the dozen—she never bores me. Her thoughts don't cover a very wide field but they are full of good sense, gaiety, a certain predilection for jokes and even a measure of humor. And everything is always so simple! Of a simplicity which at times comes close to shocking me, I swear!

Thus, in response to a very casual question put more out of politeness on my part, given that I'm the least inquisitive of men, being too taken up with myself and my work, she embarked on her whole life story without a qualm. In fifteen minutes I learned the number and names of all the lovers she's had since she was eighteen, the dates of her two miscarriages, and the unpleasant aftermaths of these lamentable events; I similarly found out how, at the age of twenty-four, she met Monsieur Valhubert (Léon-Charles) the textile king, an admirable and generous fellow who is about my age, who has furnished the apartment she lives in in the Rue de Prony and pays the rent for it, who forks out a handsome allowance every month, to whom she is deeply attached, and to whom she hasn't been unfaithful for four years with anyone but myself. In short, as far as discovering a new world goes, I was amply provided for. In the fair Lucienne I had stumbled on an anachronism, one of those exquisite kept women of whom the novels of 1900 provide us with such alluring portraits, a modern version of *Mon Amie Nane,* and here was I relegated to the rank of gigolo! Such a notion enchanted me. Pluche—a forty-five-year-old, poverty-stricken artist, stingy, sober, and a strenuous worker—the lover of Emilienne d'Alençon, how supremely comic! This eminently respectable and traditional status of my fair Dulcinea provided me with an explanation for her furniture, which equally belongs to another age. Lucienne lives in the apartment of a cocotte from a Feydeau farce: Louis XV poufs, brocade curtains, embroidered doilies, pink lampshades covered with lace, marquetry commodes, finicky little tables, suggestive eighteenth-century engravings depicting "The Stolen Kiss" or "The Bride's Awakening." The bedroom is worthy to be in a museum of amorous dalliance with its vast imitation Louis XV bed upholstered in pink satin, its cheval mirror, dressing table, and picture in the manner of Chabas: "Lascivious Nymphs Crowning a Sleeping Faun with Vine Shoots." Such is the taste of M. Valhubert, who strikes me as a splendid fellow. To have created such a setting for one's number one mistress isn't the doing of any ordinary

man. It indicates a sensibility I would venture to define as
literary. Lucienne has promised to introduce me one day to her
Maecenas, who would, it appears, be "very glad to know me."
This is typical of the artlessness of my pretty bedfellow, who I
am convinced sees nothing perverse in bringing together her
steady and her sidekick, merely regarding it as a praiseworthy
and desirable action, the sole aim of which is to establish ties of
friendship between two men equally dear to her.

Although Lucienne must be at least seventeen years younger
than I am, she always makes me feel as if I belonged to a
younger generation, she is so calm and self-assured and so
obviously never questions herself about the meaning of the
world, fate, life, death, and other superfluities. She welcomes
me into her arms as much like a mother as a lover. Such
sensations are not unpleasant for an artist—far from it. Here
again is someone who has no sense of tragedy, although with her
this is not the outcome of a philosophy but quite simply the
result of a vegetative nature. Better still, she destroys tragedy,
either by reducing it to practical terms or else by ignoring it. In
truth I would be very hard to please were I to turn up my nose
at such a paragon! There won't be many women in my life who
suit me so well and I can honestly say that I haven't been so
happy during the past nine days as I was this afternoon: damn it
all, one should never be afraid to show enthusiasm! Lucienne
came round about three o'clock this afternoon, dressed like the
princesses in the women's weeklies, in a leopard-skin coat that
must be worth at least fifteen thousand francs with a toque to
match. The general effect was dazzling. She was late, so that
I'd had into the bargain the pleasure of waiting for her, which
is the best part of love. Directly she came in her beneficial
influence made itself felt. Confronted by her smooth face, her
artless smile, her familiar and affectionate ways, a feeling of
security and gaiety instantly swept over me. Whereas I find it
painful and even humiliating to rediscover a taste of childhood
when dealing with idiots like my brother Georges, with Lucienne

I find it has great charm. Georges is a grownup; Lucienne is more of a tutelary goddess. When she rings my doorbell it's not so much my mistress who is there as some kindly aunt, some elderly cousin, come to see little Pluche, who is bored and feels a need to be loved, coddled, distracted, caressed, protected. It amuses me to record this fact, as it is so out of tune with the rest of my character.

As always, Lucienne catechized me about my health and the events in my life. I was in such a confiding state that I told her all my troubles, that is all three of them. My present sterility, Marie's operation, and the bankruptcy of the fool of the family. She listened with every mark of the keenest interest, solemnly declared that I had "enormous talent," that I shouldn't get worked up about it, that it was quite normal to take a rest every now and then, and that very soon I would recover my creative powers. Funnily enough, these platitudes comforted me. Besides, they were said with great conviction and tenderness. As for Marie, I had to write down the names of three gynecologists, including one who is a professor at the Faculty of Medicine. But I have kept the best bit for last. I had fetched the notebook in which I am writing this and read to her the passage describing Georges's visit; this made her laugh several times, which in turn flattered my literary vanity. She then assumed a pensive air that I know well and which warns me that she is cooking up some scheme at once beneficial, obvious, and nutty.

"Listen, darling," she said, "I've been thinking. I am going to talk about this to Léon-Charles. As a matter of fact, he's taking me out tonight. He's very rich, you know. For him a hundred thousand is nothing. For instance, why shouldn't I ask him to commission two or three pictures from you? This place is stacked with them. You'd only have to pick out the biggest ones. Let's say four pictures. That would make twenty thousand each. It's not asking a lot. Léon-Charles can lose a hundred thousand in one evening in the casino at Monte if he feels like it. I don't see why he shouldn't treat himself to four of your paintings, do you?

In a few years they'll be worth five times as much. And why shouldn't you paint his portrait? Don't worry, my pet, I'll think it all out and settle it somehow or other, I promise."

Isn't it marvelous that Lucienne should call Monte Carlo "Monte," the way they used to in 1900? There is no way around it, this girl is purest perfection. I must confess that while her proposal made me burst out laughing (which surprised and annoyed her), I found it for a moment deeply tempting and it took me something approaching courage to turn it down! Poor M. Valhubert! It is bad enough for me to go poaching on his territory without on top of this selling him for an exorbitant sum goods which, according to Ravuski's price schedule, are worth infinitely less! No, really, this venal episode doesn't in the least fit in with the general aspect of my life. It isn't so much a question of morals as, I would say, of harmony. It falls into the same category as my hatred of buying bonds and gambling on the stock exchange. I tried to explain as much to Lucienne but I'm not at all sure I managed to convince her. I even feel she was rather put out by it.

"I just don't understand you," she said. "Thanks to this idea of mine everything would have been settled and everyone would have benefited from it. God, how complicated you can be! Artists are past understanding."

I should add, to complete the picture, that Lucienne is in no way amoral. She has just as much morality as anyone else, but as with most people whom we define as amoral, her morality is not in the places where we normally find it in the common run of mortals. Anyway, I insisted so strongly that she make no approach to her dear Valhubert that I hope she keeps her mouth shut, although I can't be sure she will. We parted around seven amid hugs and kisses. I was as hungry as a wolf, so I went and treated myself to a gargantuan dinner at Mother Cruchon's, where the main dish was everything I could have wished for: pickled pork with lentils, of which I ate fit to burst; not to mention the *pâté maison* to begin with and the *crème caramel* to round it off. The whole washed down with a bottle of Châteauneuf-du-Pape. I feel as blithe as a lark and lighthearted as a conscript. My worries can wait till tomorrow. Lucienne has made me feel twenty years younger. Dear Lucienne!

CHAPTER X

"Au Chic d'Alésia"

> *A definite soul, or entity,*
> *or spirit-thing glimmered be-*
> *hind his dog's eyes, already*
> *fond with affection for this*
> *hair-grizzled god who talked*
> *with him he knew not what,*
> *but whose very talking car-*
> *ried delicious and unguess-*
> *able messages to his heart.*
>
> JACK LONDON

And supposing I went away? Supposing I chucked everything, supposing I sheered off to the south, supposing I went and barricaded myself in my villa at Le Cannet? It's only a shack, but when one opens the window the whole Mediterranean pervades it. We have reached the middle of March; it must be glorious weather down there. Fresh enough in the morning, hot in the afternoon, and really cold in the evening. I could slop about all day in sandals, corduroy slacks, and a checked shirt. At approaching twilight I should have the pleasure of pulling on a thick sweater; I should go and dine in the seedy cafés round Cannes harbor, where you can get a meal for eight francs including tips. It would be marvelous. I often have sudden

desires like this to run away. There is absolutely nothing to stop
me catching the train tonight. I would put the key under the
door. I would take wing. I would melt into the atmosphere. No
more Pluche. He's vanished. Let suffering humanity get along
without him! Apart from anything else it would be an excellent
thing for me to go and spend three or four months in the south
just now. The light there is completely different from that of
Paris and it might very well set my painting factory going
again. I know, for instance, that when the sun is in a certain
position and of a certain strength the iron balustrade of my
balcony casts on my bedroom floor a shadow of a pronounced
blue—akin to Prussian blue—which often makes my mouth water.
Similarly, at this time of year the sky has a pale blue tint
verging on yellow. Moreover, I should be very happy to paint a
palm tree or two. People talk about the "raw light" of the south.
That is another bit of sheer nonsense. The light of the south
isn't raw at all; on the contrary, it is baked and baked again
like a piece of pottery, it has endless shades that you find nowhere else and particularly not in Paris, where everything is
insipid, watered down, faded. A pox on "the grays of Paris"!
I've seen enough of them. Even in Hubert Robert they get me
down, though I'm mad about his painting and find in it an incomparable poetry. All the more so, then, in Quizet, Marquet,
Utrillo, and the other painters of cities. The one reproach I have
against my revered master Degas, who died alas before I was
born, is a certain dignified coldness in his palette, due beyond
doubt to the baneful influence of the light of Paris. I feel sure one
of the reasons for my present sterility is the fact that my eye is
bored. It is bored from having nothing to look at but these hues,
familiar to the point of nausea and already exhaustively recorded by thirty painters during the past hundred years. There's
nothing left to be discovered in Paris which wasn't discovered
in 1880, 1910, or 1930. Paris is finished for painters, just as Delft,
Amsterdam, and The Hague were finished in 1680, just as
Venice was finished after Canaletto and Guardi. A city is like a
human being. Two or three great artists paint its portrait, express

its spirit, and there is nothing left to be gotten out of it. Whereas the countryside, that is to say nature, is inexhaustible. Even so, there are a few cities left whose portrait no one has yet painted—London for instance, in spite of Turner and a fleeting attempt by Claude Monet. But I have no desire to settle down in London and squeeze that sooty lemon, even if it has retained all its juice. I shall leave that to someone else. What I need are fields of flowers and fields of corn, absurd little huts, bushy and bright green trees, a stretch of water which is not the everlasting Canal Saint-Martin, people rigged out in loud and badly cut clothes. When I go down to buy my bread in the Rue Boissonnade, what wouldn't I give to meet one of those fat females from Marseilles, half fishmonger, half whore, weighing two hundred pounds in her Sunday best with her raven-black hair, her face made up fit to kill, swaying on her stiletto heels!

I don't know what has filled my head with this violent nostalgia. Maybe it's the happy day I spent yesterday. This morning as I woke up I felt one of those waves of discouragement that sometimes sweep over me when life gets too grim. At such times I come very close to abandoning everything. It's odd, really, this horror of lost causes. From time to time my life seems to me like a lost cause and I have only one desire: to quit, by which I don't mean commit suicide but run somewhere miles away, change my skin in a manner of speaking. Alongside these impulses toward desertion and flight must be set another impulse I sometimes yield to, sometimes resist: the desire to go to ground when things are going badly, to stay in my hole doing nothing, as if I were smitten with paralysis or complete loss of will power. The world could well collapse around me and I wouldn't even stick my nose out of the window. For all that I know my inertia is fatal, that life outside is mounting engines of war against me, that I should assert myself, get moving, lay down defenses or prepare a counterattack, there is nothing to be done. Impossible to lift even a finger. I wait stupidly for events to grow worse, until the situation becomes so intolerable that it finally forces me out of my lair and drives me to desperate

combat. This tendency isn't confined to daily life. I also encounter it in the artistic sphere. In fact, the periods of sterility I
go through from time to time could very easily be cut short.
When they are drawing near their end it would need only a
slight effort of will on my part to start working again, but I
haven't the amount of will necessary, as if impotence made me
numb. I know the creative instinct has returned, I feel it seething
inside me, I know that were I to make just the slightest effort,
in the shape of setting up a canvas on my easel and squeezing
some colors onto the tin tray that serves me as a palette, the
machinery would be set going and everything would proceed
smoothly. But I am quite incapable of that effort. I wait another
week, a fortnight, a month, until finally I can't bear it any
longer and the painting comes out of me like a voice, like words.
Then I get down to it double-quick, I paint for twelve hours on
end like a lunatic, in three days I turn out Ravuski's two monthly
pictures, which I deliver to him before they are even dry, I am
seized with a wholly ridiculous creative panic calling for ten
times more exertion, intellectual effort, and physical endurance
than if I had sensibly taken my time at the cost of only the
slightest self-constraint.

It's funny how vividly my childhood has remained with me.
For there is something childish about these inner doldrums. I
was already prone to them when I was seven or eight. I had
periodic lapses of energy during which I would let everything
drift: horrified, I would watch situations get out of hand while
helpless to do anything about them. Later on, at school, I once
let things slide for a whole term, for no reason, just because I
didn't feel in the mood. I forged my parents' signatures on the
reports, I didn't learn a single lesson, I did no homework, I
larked about, knowing full well that I was heading for disaster.
And of course one day the whole thing blew up, I was called
on the mat, forbidden to attend school for a week, and there
was an appalling scene with my parents, who threatened to send
me to a reformatory, confined me to my room, confiscated my
paintbox, and so on. Whereupon, reinvigorated by this ordeal, I

worked like an angel the following term, came out top in French and even—superhuman exploit—climbed up to twelfth place with a pass mark, believe it or not, in mathematics.

I believe I understand the deep-rooted cause of these "lapses of will" which must form an integral part of an artist's character. In the first place, however strange it may seem, they stem from an unshakable self-confidence. Even at the murkiest stage of my bouts of despondency and inertia I can always hear deep down inside me a sort of small voice telling me that in spite of appearances all is not lost, that I may well indulge in a few months of flabbiness without any dire consequences, that I have huge reserves thanks to which, when the moment comes, I can more than make up for the time I have wasted. Second cause: my wholehearted loathing for action due to the ease, the omnipotence to which the practice of painting has accustomed me. To be an artist, to create a work of art, is something exquisite, since in the act of creation the will knows no bounds save those of one's talent or one's skill in execution (and in that respect I'm all right). When I paint a picture I offer myself anything I want, I offer myself the impossible. No external will intrudes to hamper me. Whereas when taking action one has to be content with what is *possible*, that is to say with what little all the other wills in the world permit you to seize on. These hostile wills pitting themselves against mine bore me and reduce me to despair before I have so much as begun. I can foresee, before even applying myself to it, that the outcome will be so distorted, so imperfect that I am immobilized and haven't even the minimum amount of courage necessary to set some action, or merely some reaction, in motion. A man accustomed to the tremendous freedom of artistic creation can never bring himself to put up with the strict subordination of action. And that is why I am so deliquescent today, and in the mood of a hibernating animal. A revealing detail: ordinarily it is at night, before I go to bed, that I scribble down my thoughts and tribulations of the day in this journal. Today, however, I began to write the moment I woke up in order, of course, to escape from life just as, before resigning myself to painting, I rush round in search of various harmless little jobs—fixing a nail, stretching a canvas, calling up some slob I know—in order to postpone for as long as possible the moment of finding myself face to face with the devil. It is 11 A.M. I have been writing since seven this morning. I have a superstitious notion that whatever happens I mustn't set aside this journal, that it protects me, that directly I put down my pen life will dash at me like a ravenous crocodile. I had thought my high jinks yesterday would change my outlook, as they say. They have changed it only too effectively! By distracting me from my worries they have taken away from me what courage I might have had to face them afresh; they have made them recede far into the distance; it will take me a good day to catch up with them. After all, why the hell shouldn't I treat myself to a day off? I am an artist, by God! Nobody seems to be aware of this fact because generally speaking I am a decent sort of fellow, unaffected and easygoing. But an artist is a "delicate organism" who needs handling with infinite care. Well, that settles it. I shall grant myself these twenty-four hours the world denies me. What are twenty-four hours more or less?

Nine o'clock at night.

Called up Marie. Nothing new. Her voice sounded young and gay. Apparently my visit the day before yesterday cheered her up considerably. Hearing her "Hello, is that you, Pluche?" for the thousandth time, I couldn't prevent myself from having a sinister thought: I told myself that perhaps one day this well-loved voice would fall silent, that I should telephone in vain, that never again would I hear those five joyful words and familiar tone of voice, that this love my sister has for me would cease to exist. What on earth puts such ideas in my head? No doubt the tense emotional state induced by my present inability to paint. For all that, it's painful at the time. Hearing her "Hello, is that you, Pluche?" I had the weird impression that Marie was already dead, that I was the victim of a hallucination. I ought on the contrary to be glad that this voice is still the same as ever, that it hasn't been impaired by sickness or sorrow. But not in the least: I visualized Marie's face, how ill she looked, and her voice in contrast rang out like a memory, like the sole surviving relic of one who has vanished without trace. Being in a calmer frame of mind this evening I fully realize that these fantasies don't mean a thing and I shouldn't pay any heed to such irrational states of mind; but some demon or other impels me to put all this down in full. Superstition, I suppose. When I dread something happening I describe it to myself in advance, I make my forebodings as black as I can, I prepare myself for the worst in order to ward off ill luck. An old trick of mankind, already successfully practiced three thousand years ago.

This phone call, in spite of everything, took a load off my mind. At bottom I needed to make this call, and it had seemed to me the most difficult thing to do. Which explains why I spent the morning writing with such fervor. From seven to eleven I covered paper with ink in order to postpone the moment of calling up Marie. Why are we always more fearful of the cure than of what is destroying us? I have noticed this a hundred times over. Happiness demands more energy than unhappiness. Before talking to Marie I was unhappy, I was letting myself sink gently into unhappiness as into a quagmire. I was afraid of hearing her voice, I dreaded what she would say to me. And then her voice was light and gay and we teased each other as if we were both twenty, belying all my sinister forebodings. By the time I hung up my anxiety had evaporated and the world had resumed its normal countenance. It was midday. The sun was shining in through the big window of my studio, which is none too clean. Mme. Chevassu will have to give it a thorough washdown next Tuesday. She's an excellent woman but inclined to take things too easy, on the pretext that I am a bachelor and quite unconcerned about such matters. Sometimes she comes every day and the apartment shines like a new saucepan; sometimes she doesn't turn up for two weeks, as is the case just now, and I live in a world of dust, dirty plates, and my unmade bed. I have never known such a temperamental cleaning woman. For the past ten years I've been putting up with what no one else in the world would put up with. Typical of me. Because Mme. Chevassu's character appeals to me, because I know she is fond of me, because she regards me as the greatest genius in the history of painting, because one day when I was stone-broke she lent me two hundred francs from her own savings, because with me she has a certain shade of familiarity, because sometimes we hurl abuse at each other without losing our tempers, because she embraces me when she comes and when she goes, because she never takes any account of the hours she devotes to looking after me and for which I pay her very haphazardly, thereby gratifying my parsimony by gaining the impression (probably false) that I am getting the best of the bargain, and because of my conception of human relations, which nowadays have become the object of a rigid scale of values, and for twenty other reasons I judge to be equally strong, I forgive her everything. All the same, when she reappears I shan't mince my words. Two weeks' absence is a bit too much!

Mme. Chevassu has one astonishing faculty: she possesses the gift of second sight. For example, she knows who is calling at the mere sound of the telephone bell and tells me who it is before I even pick up the receiver. She announces three days in advance the letters I am going to receive. One afternoon two years ago, while I was quietly painting away, she rushed in after five days' absence, haggard and wild-eyed, crying: "Go round at once to M. Boulard's. There's something wrong there. He needs seeing to." I was up to my eyebrows in my painting; I stared at her aghast. She was so agitated that she started tugging at my arm; I flew into a rage and told her she was crazy, but she literally tore the brushes from my hand and pushed me out of the door. Feeling shaken nonetheless, I ran round to Boulard's place. I had to break down the door: he was lying delirious from peritonitis, all by himself because his wife and children were away on vacation in Brittany. Had I arrived an

hour later he would have croaked. That's Mme. Chevassu for
you! When I mislay something she finds it again in five minutes. It's a splendid sight to see her casting around for my keys
or my pipe, which I always put down in the weirdest places:
a real hunting dog on the track of game. I have long been en-
tranced by this extraordinary faculty. Thinking it over, I believe
I have found the explanation for it. Mme. Chevassu is a primi-
tive person, far closer to the savages of New Caledonia than
to the average Parisian. She has certainly preserved a part of
those mysterious faculties men used to have long ago, in which
instinct took the place of reason and logic. They were in their
way tuned in to nature and could sense from afar, by means
of obscure inner promptings, the pleasures or dangers heading
toward them. "Twentieth-century man" is a concept without
much reality. Most people have anachronistic souls. I know
Frenchmen of the Middle Ages and the eighteenth century
who apparently live without difficulty in the world of the 1960s.
As for Mme. Chevassu, she goes back I don't know how many
thousand years B.C., though this doesn't prevent her from owning
a washing machine and a television set.

The nice thing about being a bachelor is that one leads a life
without any set framework. A wife and children mean that life
has to be organized with plans, obligations, meals at fixed times,
and so on. Impossible to have any sudden whims and gratify
them. Now I am a man of sudden whims. For instance, at midday I had a sudden urge to go and have a chat with old
Raimondet in the Avenue Reille. What was there to stop me?
Ten minutes later I was in the street, trying to decide whether
to walk or take the bus. Walking was not unpleasant. There was
a blue sky and a March dampness in the air; the sun kept coming out and going in again every five minutes. I put my best foot
forward. It takes half an hour to walk from the Rue Boissonnade to the Avenue Reille. I made a detour via the Rue Hallé;
halfway down it the street expands into a sort of crescent I
wanted to see again. A good thing I did so: while I was contemplating this pretty, well-composed scene an idea occurred to

me that provided me with food for thought during the rest of the way, even leading me to stop off in a café to call up Boulard and inform him of my discovery. As it would have taken a long while to explain over the telephone and I still needed time to work it out, we agreed that I should drop into his studio at about four o'clock. In short, I was so taken up with my idea that it was quite a shock to find myself outside old Raimondet's filthy dung-colored shop and very glad to be there. At the time of my first visit I hadn't noticed the signboard, painted in yellowish letters with the intriguing name of "Au Chic d'Alésia." What odd twist of mind had led my junkman to this esoteric formula, evoking God knows what fabulous dressmaker for the warriors of ancient Gaul? I must remind myself to ask him one of these days.

Papa Raimondet stays open all day, instead of closing between noon and 2 P.M. I found him tucked away at the back of his shop in a cavernous gloom; he was seated at the Mac-Mahon table, on which he had spread a newspaper and set out his lunch consisting of garlic sausage, a hot stew steaming in a tin pot, Roquefort cheese, and a bottle of cheap wine. Propped against the bottle was another newspaper, this one for reading while eating—that delight of the single man. I went up to him. He stared at me over his glasses, showing not the slightest surprise at seeing me there, and without even troubling to wish me good morning, said:

"Shall I fetch you a plate?"

However stingy I may be, I was somewhat embarrassed. Landing oneself at mealtimes on anyone, even a tolerant old codger like Raimondet, is pretty rough. I swear before God that in going to the Avenue Reille I had no intention whatsoever of sponging. But how could I refuse an invitation couched with such Spartan simplicity?

"You don't know what you're letting yourself in for," I replied. "I've an appetite like an ogre. I've been thinking hard for the past half hour, while walking, what's more."

"There's enough for two."

"Wait a couple of minutes then. Don't start without me."

I went out and bought two bottles of Fleurie at the Caves de Bourgogne a hundred yards down the road, and some celery salad, *pâté de campagne,* and pickled pig's feet at the Charcuterie du Maréchal Leclerc.

"You'd no need, there was quite enough," said Papa Raimondet, who had waited for me.

To make more room he put his wine bottle on the floor behind him and folded his newspaper. Its title—*Les Nouveaux Temps*—struck me as odd. Out of politeness and though I couldn't conceivably care less, I asked him if there was any news. Whereupon he gave an artful smile, looked at me with that mocking expression adopted by old men when planning to pull your leg, and said:

"The Huns are at Smolensk."

I, like a fool and being totally unsuspicious, carelessly inquired:

"And what are they doing there?"

"Blowing the place sky-high, shelling and shooting. Things are hotting up!"

I must have looked stunned, for my host leaned back in his Voltaire chair and, without actually laughing (which doesn't seem to be his style), emitted a series of gurgles doubtless expressing his highest peak of jubilation. Then he handed me the newspaper. I began to laugh too; it was an old rag from twenty-three years back. Contrariwise the one serving as our tablecloth dated from only yesterday. This contrast went straight to my heart and I said as much to Raimondet while adding, by way of a joke, that reading newspapers out of the past was pushing his passion for old junk a bit far.

"Bah! Old newspapers are far more interesting than today's," he replied. "I've got piles of 'em if you want to look. Take this one: Pétain, Doriot, Déat, Bucard, de Brinon, the exchange of prisoners, Laval, Darlan, the Huns who wanted to gobble us all up and I don't know what. Those chaps were as busy as ants, they had ambition. They were making a new Europe. Whizz, bang, boom! They're all dead and Europe's the same age as when I was born. Old newspapers are full of philosophy. Mark you, at the time they came out they were just as full of rubbish as they are today. But let them lie around for twenty or thirty years and the rubbish turns into philosophy. Besides, there's one thing was better before the war, and that was the murders. In 1935 murderers had to pay for it. They guillotined you as soon as look at you; killing really meant something. Nowadays you can knife six chaps in a row and you merely cop five years with remission. A month back I reread the whole Violette Nozière affair in *l'Intransigeant* and *Excelsior*. As good as a book. Poor girl. What the hell do I want with the newspapers today? Whenever anything really serious happens a neighbor is sure to come and tell me within fifteen minutes. I spend the whole day here, understand; I don't get many people coming in; I'm no longer a young man. With these old newspapers—and I read them from beginning to end, even the small ads—I feel at least thirty or forty years younger and at the same time I can judge events with the outlook I have today. I've lived through what they describe and it's all as if it were a thousand years old. For me it's as good as the movies!"

I like to think that providence has brought Papa Raimondet my way. There can't be many men who spend their days reading prehistoric newspapers. What cast of mind can give rise to such a taste? At heart Raimondet is a fellow rather like me, that is to say someone who dislikes the present, who tends to misanthropy, who lives in the modern world the way a badger lives in a forest. Besides, he rather puts me in mind of a badger, seeking his living wherever it is to be found and then hurrying back to his earth. The world today bores him, our so-called scientific civilization disgusts him, he prefers old tables, rickety chairs, faded engravings, the time-blackened scum which is all he can collect from the past two or three centuries. In reality, people only do what they want to do and if old Raimondet is a junkman it's not by chance. It is the means he has found to manipulate a little of that past he prefers to the present and, all in all, it's in keeping that he should read old newspapers rather than those of our own day.

Fleurie is a rather heavy wine but it has considerable charm and blended perfectly with the stew, which was extremely good. About halfway through our blowout, Raimondet pushed back his cap to scratch his skull (which is bald) and with some embarrassment confided to me:

"I promised you I'd keep my eyes open. I've found something for you. Perhaps you won't like it. But I'd be surprised if you didn't. You'll be a bit taken aback to begin with but you'll like it when you think it over, or else it's me who's crazy. Anyway, it's free, it won't cost you a penny." At this, he raised his voice and shouted "Tarzan!" I heard a scuffling behind a pile of chairs and and small nameless bits of furniture. A dog appeared which up to then had been lying so still that I hadn't even suspected its presence, a charming little mongrel with a thick white coat spotted with yellow, a curly tail, long spaniel's ears, a charming foxy head, and a snout as yellow as its spots.

"I hope you've noticed there hasn't been a squeak out of him while we were eating? This dog's unique. I picked him up yesterday at Saint-Ouen. He's got no master."

Old Raimondet's encounter with the dog Tarzan is as beautiful as a story by Dickens. I only hope I don't spoil it by telling it badly! This good fellow, then, was strolling around Saint-Ouen, a vast beach where thousands of objects that once belonged to the late lamented get washed up, seemingly driven there by Death like a great tide. Everything ends up in this flea market! Another point in which I resemble Raimondet: I love walking about Saint-Ouen, though my purpose in doing so is more disinterested. I like it because these displays of old junk are imbued for me with a sordid and lachrymose poetry in which I take a keen pleasure, whereas he goes there to scrounge such bits of junk as he can sell. He came across the dog a hundred or a hundred and fifty yards from the Jules Vallès market. The poor brute was tethered to a tree by a string fitted with a running noose and had half strangled itself tugging at it. Its tongue was hanging out, the eyes were popping from its head, but it still had enough life left to whimper. It was six-thirty in the morning, a particularly sinister time of day in the month of March and in this place. In the background could be heard the old-clothes men opening up their stalls. Round the dog, not a soul. A desert. A dying animal alone in the middle of a wasteland as foul as the ill-dredged bed of a muddy river. Old Raimondet had never seen anything more sad in his whole life. Without a moment's hesitation he took out his knife and cut the string. The dog was so exhausted that he had to pick it up in his arms. Whimpering and trembling all over the poor thing. tried, in spite of its weakness, to lick its rescuer:

"Now now, it's all over, boy," said Raimondet. "We're going to a café and we're going to tuck into a good dinner and then we're going home to stay with Papa Raimondet, who loves little doggies!" As he stroked it he could feel the beast's ribs protruding like the iron bands around a stoved-in barrel.

While he talked and I listened, my host and I were both gripped with the same rage. Such an atrocity was past belief. Anyone could see that the dog Tarzan is a charming, affectionate, devoted, discreet, intelligent little beast. Into what brutal hands had destiny led him? It's easy enough to reconstruct his tale of woe: his master wanted to be rid of him, probably so as not to have any longer to pay out the few francs his food cost. Tarzan loved this skunk and always came back when he tried to shake him off. The loathsomeness of having tied him up *with a running noose!* Raimondet regards it as premeditated murder. I wholly share his opinion. To kill an animal because it loves you too well . . . Even just writing this brings me out in a sweat of passionate fury. Happily I only have to look up from my paper to see Tarzan's head, his golden eyes staring at me with such intense affection, his ears pricking whenever I make a movement. In fact, it was he old Raimondet had found for me by "keeping his eyes open." The splendid name Tarzan is his invention. He baptized him thus after treating him to a plateful of beef stew at Louisette's, a dive noted for its fried potatoes. I

must confess I was touched at the idea that Raimondet had
made me a party to his good deed and never doubted my reactions. Moreover, if I didn't want Tarzan he was quite ready to
keep him. But Tarzan won my heart from the moment I saw
him and I welcomed him without a second thought. A nice
little dog like this, who is well behaved and even gifted with
exceptional intelligence since he has learned in twenty-four
hours that from now on his name is Tarzan, who is full of affection for those he feels are fond of him, who talks with every
part of his body—tail, ears, eyes, and paws—who has suffered
and needs to forget his sufferings—here is exactly the kind of
companion suited to a man like me, who hasn't even a suspicion
of an obligation in his life. He is going to compel me to think
of little material details such as feeding him, brushing him, taking him for walks; in short, thanks to him I shall have this
daily preoccupation, this pleasant burden which is the fruit of
love and which I must have felt to be somewhat lacking. Tomorrow I shall buy him a basket and take him to the vet,
since he must be alive with fleas. Lastly, there can be nothing
more comic than this name of Tarzan, evoking as it does the
jungle and orangutans, applied to a creature so puny and so
Parisian!

Papa Raimondet extolled the virtues of his protégé for half an
hour. What touched us most was the fact that poor Tarzan had
remained behind the chairs without even stirring throughout half
our meal. Such heroism, when we were gorging ourselves three
feet away, shows what a reign of terror he has been sub-
jected to. But he made up for it: we stuffed him with stew and
pig's feet. Every few moments he would stop eating to say
thank you, either by looking up at us or by placing his paw on
one of our knees. I don't know many human beings capable of
showing their gratitude in such a nice and explicit way. After
a good feed, Tarzan went to sit down beside Raimondet as if to
ask him (shyly) to take him on his knee. "No," said Raimondet,
"this gentleman here is your father." The good little beast, who
obviously understands everything, half turned and came to

stand at attention before me. "Jump up, my lad!" said I, and didn't need to say it twice. To hell with the fleas! Raimondet went to fetch a bottle of pear brandy. I left him at three o'clock accompanied by Tarzan prancing round my legs like a kid being taken to a movie. I had spent a grand afternoon. How right I was to take a fancy to Papa Raimondet.

As I was only five minutes from the Palazzo Mesnardi and it was too early for my date with Boulard, it occurred to me to introduce Tarzan to my niece Lise, who like all children has for years been begging for a dog and obtaining only vague promises. Here's an ingenuous admission: I live so immersed in my work that I am always very surprised when I chance to think of other people; I mean think positively, with the object of giving them some surprise or pleasure and doing something about it. I then tell myself, and this is rather comic, that I can't be so selfish or turned in on myself after all, that I do sometimes have good impulses, that I should certainly have more if my mind were not preoccupied by painting, absorbing all my thoughts and keeping alive in me my obsession about time slipping away. I am as stingy with my time as with my money. This doesn't make for a very nice character but how else can one get along? Mesnard has tried to by squandering both. Result: a life completely messed up, in my opinion. One always gets back to the fact that one can't have everything. I have chosen to have my painting, and so I have not the sweet satisfactions of a life devoted to cherishing my friends.

A fine surprise on arriving at the Castel de la Mesnardière: my sister was out, which means she was feeling better today. Contrariwise my niece was in: school is closed, the teachers are on strike. Children nowadays have all the luck: those blasted teachers would never have gone on strike in my day. Far from it! Firm at their posts, indestructible, with a professional conscience to make one despair.

It's a very curious sensation to be someone's uncle. When I ring at the castle door, my niece welcomes me as if I were unique, with great joy and familiarity certainly, but also with a

touch of solemnity, as if the fact of being a member of her
family endows me with some mysterious virtue. And I, in spite
of myself, fall in with this subtle ceremony. I have a momentary
feeling of being invested with a special dignity; I am not just
anybody, not just any friend of the house but Uncle, a kindly
and benevolent entity who brings warmth, presents, and an
official avuncular affection. Tarzan was greeted with shouts and
cries of joy. Lise flung herself on him like a mother on her little
one. I had to describe in detail where I had found him, how I
had adopted him, what had decided me to take him, and so on.
Tarzan's romantic and unhappy life story held Lise spellbound
like a novel by Jack London and considerably strengthened the
love she had lavished on him from the first moment. A dog is an
animated toy and if, into the bargain, this toy has a history, there
is nothing more splendid in the world. I had to promise to take
my niece one of these days to see Monsieur Raimondet, of
whom she has built herself up a fabulous picture, a blend of
Jean Valjean, St. Vincent de Paul, and General Durakin. Tarzan,
for his part, seemed highly satisfied by his new acquaintance,
whom he treated in the most flattering manner. What vicious
brats must he have had to face in his hell at Saint-Ouen? He
surely never suspected any possible complicity between children
and dogs. As for me, I was deeply moved to see Tarzan and
Lise, these two delightful creatures, making so much of each
other. We spent a most enjoyable three quarters of an hour and
then, as I was preparing to leave, Lise insisted on walking with
me to the end of the street for the pleasure of holding Tarzan's
lead and directing him to suitable lampposts. For a while we
strolled along like this, with Lise importantly clutching my
mongrel's string. I completely forgot to ask if her father was at
home. Before we parted she said to me in that solemn, measured,
rather emphatic tone of voice children sometimes adopt, always surprising to grownups because it is out of proportion, like
their legs that have grown too fast, and reveals a corner of their
souls which, too, has grown faster than the rest:

"What do you think of Mama, Maestro? I'm a little bit anxious about her health. And then, I've noticed for some time how Papa and she hardly talk to each other any more. Do you think they are going to get a divorce? I do."

How stupid the reactions of adults are! I who am so close to childhood, so childish still in many respects, replied like an idiot of forty. I immediately tried to reassure her, made light of it all, babbled about a temporary and trivial disagreement. A divorce, are you crazy, wherever do you get such ideas? Your father and mother adore each other, and so on and so forth. As I churned out all this bilge I could see Lise's face cloud over, reflect disappointment, and freeze stiff, but while I could have kicked myself for my stupidity some demon drove me on, that absurd demon of *duty* whispering that even if it sickened me I must continue to lie, because the truth is the major scandal from which children must be protected at all costs, even when with their keen minds they have guessed at the whole of it, even when they state it themselves without flinching. The worst of it was that I could read my niece's eyes like an open book; I could read in them that contempt and discouragement I know so well from having expressed them so often with my own eyes. With hers, Lise was saying as plainly as could be: "Impossible to talk to grownups. They take nothing seriously because they're scared of reality. My parents are going to separate, Mama is ill, and Pluche doesn't dare to admit it because like all grownups he has a weak and timorous soul. *I* have a soul of iron; I look reality in the face, however terrible it may be." I was so vexed with myself and so wretched that in the end I took her in my arms, kissed her, and said:

"Listen, darling, your mama is going to have an operation, but I swear to you it isn't serious. No more serious than appendicitis. So just you stop worrying. Everyone has operations nowadays. I am absolutely certain that if you stopped ten people in the street and asked them to undress, you'd find that nine of them had scars on their tummies."

"Beginning with me," replied Lise. "I had my appendix out when I was little."

"You see! Right, then. As to your papa and mama not speaking to each other, I've been an ass and humbly crave your pardon. You are quite right: they aren't getting on very well together just now. But they're grownups, and you know how grownups work: they go slowly and they're afraid of words. But you, who aren't a grownup, go very quickly, you see things six months ahead and you call them by their proper names."

The attentive, avid, enthralled, really touching way children look at one when at last one decides to talk to them seriously ought to prevent one from ever talking nonsense to them again. The beautiful little face of Verrocchio's "David" completely relaxed and was smiling up at me although what I was now telling her was less comforting than my earlier fatuous assurances. But it was true, and the truth is beneficial. We know very well, when we are twelve years old, that there is no other staff on which to lean.

"I don't think," I went on, "that there is at present any question of a divorce between your parents. But you must understand that you have something to say about this as well. Do you think this divorce is desirable? I mean, do you think your father and mother would be happier if they were separated? And you, would you be more unhappy if each of them lived their own lives? I know these are difficult questions but we have responsibilities, you and I. If you don't want your parents to divorce, they won't."

"No, I don't want them to," she said with the deliberation of someone who has spent a long time weighing up the pros and cons. "I thought it was nothing to do with me. But if I've got something to do with it, then I say no. I think that a little girl needs both her parents. A divorce is as if half of each of them were to die. If Papa and Mama divorce, Mama will keep me with her. I shall go and see Papa every Thursday from two to six. It won't be any fun at all; I shall prevent him from working and after five minutes we won't know what to say to each other. Mama will be sad at not living any more with Papa, I shall be

sad because Mama is sad, you will be sad too, and Papa won't
be able to work properly. So, no divorce."

"Excellent," I replied. "I'm very glad we've had this talk. It's
been a very useful talk. This is what I propose to do. I shall patch
things up between your father and mother. Give me a few days.
And until then, mum's the word. Everything we've been saying
to each other must be kept buried in the deepest secrecy. You
must swear on your mother's head."

"I swear on my mother's head," Lise solemnly declared. She
even stretched out her arm and spat on the ground. I have complete faith in this oath. Little girls are incorruptible. I have less
faith in myself. How am I going to set about keeping my promise? Ah well, we shall see. I must rely to some extent on circumstances and on adequate inspiration to exploit these circumstances. When I left Lise I was feeling so lighthearted that
I said to her:

"Au revoir, you big ninny. You are my only treasure."

"What about Tarzan?" she retorted with a burst of laughter.
"You have two treasures now, and don't you forget it, Maestro!"

The Impasse de la Gaîté, at the end of which Boulard lives,
doesn't much appeal to me; this raffish and vulgar side of
Montparnasse is too like Pigalle. When he accuses me of not
coming to visit him often enough, I reply that the name of the
place outrages my artistic credo. Gaiety, in fact, is never an impasse; on the contrary, it is the open door to successful artistic
achievement. In art, all things that aren't gay are failures, even
when they're tragedies. This unassailable argument has finally
shut Boulard up; he no longer upbraids me for having a certain
aversion to climbing his six flights of stairs. Another thing I dislike about the house he lives in is that it overlooks the Montparnasse cemetery. He is perfectly happy about this and even
congratulates himself on it because of the silence, the greenery,
the age-old aspect of the place. All of which is true but I don't
like cemeteries, I don't respond to their poetry, if indeed they
have any. One wholly comic quality of Boulard's, which I sometimes tease him about, is the way he finds everything he pos-

sesses or connected with him marvelous, as if the mere fact of
some being or object belonging to him or playing a part in his
life endowed it with a singular beauty and nobility. Thus, the
Montparnasse cemetery, just because it spreads out below his
windows, is a paragon of cemeteries. Worse still, because
Boulard lives alongside a cemetery he has decreed that all
cemeteries are ravishing places and that it's a great privilege to
live near one.

Another characteristic of Boulard's, which I never note without surprise, is his gregariousness. He loves going to weddings,
funerals, private views—things I avoid like the plague; he makes
friends with a mass of people who would bore me to death, he
writes ten letters a day, he maintains close relations with a host
of tradesmen, tramps, municipal street sweepers, hall porters, fellow artists, and art critics, with an intimate knowledge of their
habits, tastes, sorrows, and joys. It took me quite a while to find
out what lay behind all this activity: it's the fact that he loves
to waste his time, he's garrulous, and finally he's lazy. He post-
pones the moment of getting down to work for as long as he
can. Humanity is very entertaining, incomparably more so than
barricading oneself in one's den and smearing paint for hours on
end on granular surfaces while sweating blood and having for a
large part of the time the feeling that it is all too much for one.
And so Boulard prefers men to painting, which is very
understandable and even quite normal but shows a lack of seriousness. One day when I was lecturing him about this and explaining to him that, with his gift, his talent, his understanding of
painting, it was unforgivable to squander it all in this way, he
made the following lofty reply, over which I teased him for the
next four months: "I am not one of those people who feel a need
to justify their existence!" Actually, throughout his life Boulard
has very carefully set up a number of barriers against painting.
It surprises me that he should have waited till he was thirty to
get married, since a wife and children who have to be fed are
at once the most pressing and most honorable excuses for sacrificing serious work, which is difficult, to breadwinning, which is

easy. However great my affection for Mme. Boulard, first name Charlotte, and the Boulard kids, five in all, namely Jacotte, Riquet, Antoinette, Tatave, and Julien, stretching in age from fourteen to three and a half, I spent many years naïvely regretting that my friend should have saddled himself with such a formidable brood, but I now realize that this was in the nature of things. At thirty he had exhausted every possible loophole, he had a little money in hand, a smattering of fame, and he found himself face to face with his easel. An agonizing situation! Charlotte was the nicest girl in Niort; she was anxious to get married; Boulard loved her dearly and saw in her his salvation and happiness, in other words lots of little Boulards and an effective protection against having to settle down and paint in earnest. I was his witness at the wedding, which, with Mesnard's, is indeed the only one I have ever attended, and it was an extremely jolly affair. As a wedding present I did a portrait of the bride and groom in the manner of the *douanier* Rousseau, a charming picture, and I say as much without false modesty; it is amusing the way all good pastiches are and I'm always pleased to see it again every time I visit the Boulards.

One has to face facts, however irritating they may be for a bachelor and a bachelor's philosophy: Boulard, if he has failed in his artistic career, has made a success of his marriage. Charlotte is the happiest of women and the children are remarkable: as nice as their mother, as intelligent as their father, well brought up, alert, amusing, neither shy nor impertinent, exceptionally natural. Boulard rules over his family like a patriarch, instructing, joking, speaking in parables, in short giving proof of a paternal instinct such as one seldom sees. I greatly admire him in this role, in which I myself would put up a lamentable performance. What with all the din, the chirruping, the continuous upheavals, the moral and humorous lectures Boulard launches into at the slightest excuse, I wonder how he still manages to work at all. I have seen him painting with a child on each knee, sucking their thumbs or dabbing their paws on his palette where they made a hideous mess of all his paints.

Charlotte, by some means I can only explain as a miracle, has, after five pregnancies and fifteen years of housekeeping, cooking, and forced economy, remained so fresh and smart as to be the envy of the prettiest girls in Niort.

The result of this life, at once Bohemian and bourgeois, is that Boulard is continually chasing after a hundred-franc note. He fritters away his talent turning out picture books, dashing off insipid frescoes in school visiting rooms and suburban town halls, and selling caricatures to the newspapers under the name of "Couic." What infuriates me is that he does these jobs without taking the slightest trouble, any old how, not giving a damn. This is his one intellectual vice: he despises the work by which he earns his keep, he refers to it contemptuously and, for the past two or three years, with a touch of bitterness. The wonder of it is that he still contrives every now and then to paint a really excellent picture, garrulous like himself but well constructed, witty, even moving, and this makes one regret all those he hasn't had the courage to embark on. Whatever Marie likes to say, he's a good painter who will unfortunately produce very little good work.

Outside Boulard's door there is a doe's foot, a real doe's foot with the hoof and fur which, when one pulls it, rings a little bell somewhere in the back premises. This object, unearthed long ago in the flea market and fixed up by Boulard with the utmost care, has, naturally, a sacred character. It is the finest doe's foot in the world and at the same time an infinitely more convenient implement than an electric bell. Similarly he heats his apartment with a big charcoal stove of the kind one still sees in certain academies where nothing has changed since 1905. If he's to be believed, this stove, though it smokes pretty often and barely manages to warm more than two rooms, is far more efficient and healthy than central heating. Lastly, at Boulard's one can admire various marvels such as a seascape he persists in attributing to Courbet and wouldn't exchange for the "Burial at Ornans," a drawing by Gabriel de St. Aubin which may possibly be genuine, some walnut furniture, and some rather pretty Gothic revival chairs with their seats, alas, caved in. Boulard's powerful imagination makes up for the inadequacies of this furniture and I would swear he sees his chairs in all the new and shining splendor they must have had in 1830.

As I had anticipated, Tarzan aroused the interest of the Boulard family and I was obliged to tell my story a second time, surrounded by a ring of fat red cheeks and snotty little noses. I never weary of marveling at the way children accept the world as it is. These ones, only a second before my arrival, knew absolutely nothing about my dog. A few minutes later he formed part of their world by the same right as their uncles and aunts, the concierge in the Impasse de la Gaîté, myself, the Emperor Charlemagne, and the landscape of the Montparnasse cemetery. From now on, each time I see them they will talk to me about him, I know for sure, and I shall have to give all the latest news about him as if he were my father or son. To my mind this is one of the most charming facets of childhood, when everything represents a new image and adds something to the reality of the world. During all this Boulard had taken Tarzan on his knees and was scratching the top of his head like a true dog lover. He did have one once, actually; he kept it for fifteen or sixteen years, until it died of old age last year and was escorted to the grave amid heart-rending lamentations. He was called Palette; according to Boulard he was the most beautiful animal in the northern hemisphere. For myself, I always felt an invincible revulsion for this hybrid monster with its long greenish coat and bandy legs; it stank like hell, had eyes white with leucoma, and had been so stuffed with food all its life that it could barely drag itself along. My story ended, Boulard went to a cupboard to fetch down some stale ship biscuits, a legacy of the late Palette, and these he solemnly displayed while explaining to me that there was nothing more nourishing for dogs. Tarzan, who is politeness itself, had some difficulty crunching up these titbits, which were as hard as rods of iron, but given time, he managed it. After this I was treated to a complete lecture on how to take care of quadrupeds, how to house-train

them, the occasions when one has to be strict with them, etc.
This gave me a good laugh since Palette, during fifteen years,
pissed on every square foot of the flooring, was never brushed
once, and lived a life of unalloyed happiness. The children
asked my permission to take Tarzan away to play; this I granted
and Boulard and I were left alone.

"Well now, what about your brilliant idea in the Rue Hallé?"
he asked. "Come on, tell me about it."

What with the day's events I had completely forgotten it!
Woe betide the fine ideas one doesn't write down at once on a
piece of paper! A few hours go by and they lose all their
glamour. What had struck me as admirable at midday had gone
quite flat by six o'clock.

"Damn it!" said I, "you know how it is. I was walking along
and with me, when I walk, it's as if I were drinking champagne.
In next to no time I reach a state of intellectual intoxication
which makes me see everything in gaudy colors and ordinary
enough thoughts seem sensational."

"Thoughts are like painting," he replied. "Everything depends
on the lighting. Nothing is original but sometimes you find a
tonal relationship that revives the subject. Tell me anyway. If
it's rot, no matter; and maybe you'll rediscover the tonal
relationships you found this morning."

Poor flimsy idea! Confronted by Boulard, full of health,
strength, patriarchal majesty, zoological knowledge, and good
humor, I suddenly felt in the worst possible mood for it and at
any rate incapable of reconstructing my arguments of the morning. My mind shrank back like a frightened snail into its shell.
My fine discovery of the Rue Hallé seemed to me less and less
original every moment and certainly not worth imparting to
anyone else. In short, a complete internal rout. I am quite used
to this sort of occurrence, which goes, I suppose, with the rest
of my character. It's of the same nature as the wave of discouragement that sometimes sweeps over me and in fact did so
when I woke up this morning; of the same nature, too, as my
bouts of artistic sterility, although of less consequence. It is most

odd, this inability to influence my own mind. At such moments, between one second and the next, without any warning, it transforms itself into a large, dim, and mulish animal. I, normally rather loquacious, not to say animated, am suddenly unable to find any words. I dry up, become flat, arid.

"Oh shit!" I said. "You're getting me down. It was a very fine idea and now it's lost all its colors. Perhaps it will get them back tomorrow. If it does I'll put it in writing for you, I promise. But right now, tell me about yourself."

No one ever puts such a request to Boulard in vain. This was a splendid inspiration on my part. For the next hour and a half he described his life during the past two weeks. Among other things he has been commissioned to paint a fresco for the wedding hall in the town hall of some suburban borough. Forty or fifty square yards to be covered with more or less allegorical figures. Endless discussions with the Muncipal Council, which has its own ideas on the theme and composition, disputes with the Mayor, who wants a certain style of painting, and so on. Boulard is very hot at this sort of narrative, interlarding it with sociological comments, humorous recriminations, details designed to show the enormous stupidity of man in our time, and ironical or burlesque flights of rhetoric. Given the way in which he treats those who employ him, I cannot conceive how he still manages to wangle any commissions. Not only does he stupefy these poor wretches with his theorizing but he also never stops showing up their profound stupidity. Since he's both penetrating and shrewd, he always puts his finger on the spot where it hurts most. He has left behind him an execrable reputation in every town hall, house of culture, people's palace, and banqueting hall around Paris which he has bedaubed with miles of frescoes, thus contributing—without any illusions, incidentally— to the grand scheme of uglifying outer Paris pursued so doggedly for the past hundred years. The description he gave me today of the suburban municipal councilor was a masterpiece. One of these councilors with whom he has to deal, nurtured on the doctrines of socialist realism and a great admirer of Fougeron,

has taken it into his head to get Boulard to feature in his fresco
a group of artillerymen firing a cannon and some farmers har-
vesting their corn. Boulard had to explain to him that these two
activities were hardly ever simultaneous, that they don't exactly
reap corn six miles from Notre Dame, and finally that a cannon
was a rather murderous subject for a wedding hall. I have great
faith in Boulard, who must have expounded all this with a broad
grin and insulting irony. Notwithstanding, the fellow is still un-
convinced. Boulard is at his best in this suburban creep-hole,
expounding the subtle workings of talent to the town clerk, who
listens to him open-mouthed and is still undecided as to whether
he's a humbug or a genius, spurring on one, wrangling with another, despising the lot of them with relish, biting every hand
that feeds him and always with the feeling that he is giving away
too much for the little it will bring him in. He hasn't yet begun
his fresco and, at this rate, won't begin it for a month or so.
Then he will dash it off in two weeks; the whole thing will
be a complete failure save for one excellent passage in the lower
left-hand corner, the hat of some farm hand or a half-full
bottle of red wine. To wind it all up, he declared with the at
once triumphant and long-suffering smile that so perfectly reflects his character:

"One slaves away for three months, one wastes one's youth
and beauty arguing with dreary slobs, one covers fifty square
yards with larger than life-size figures like Michelangelo, and
the municipality, amid weeping and wailing, dishes you out
three thousand francs. Pope Julius II is called Régis Dugrumeau,
he is municipal councilor of Villebouzin en Parisis. Mark my
words, we live in a debased period of art. I, a French artist, a
man of profound and weird genius, well known in my neighborhood as a respectable family man, have as of today's date
one hundred and fifty francs left in the bank. My mother-in-law,
who owns eight farms and, as they say in her circle, 'a nice little
portfolio of shares,' has sent Charlotte a letter in which she
explains how, were she to lend her some money, we would only
spend it. Superb, eh? I don't know how I shall pay the rent in

three weeks' time. And Riquet and Tatave need new pants. In short, anyone in my place would have shot himself twelve times over since this morning. Apart from this, life is fine."

And indeed life was fine. We could hear the children laughing and shrieking with joy in the room next door. Tarzan even barked twice, and they were the happy barks of a dog who has found friends and is enjoying himself. I should add here that Boulard has on occasion asked me for money; this I always lent at once of course, and he has always paid it back within the same week or month with a promptness that could serve as an example to many members of the bourgeoisie. I suggested letting him have some today, but apparently he's expecting some royalties to fall due tomorrow for the illustrations to some humorous book or God knows what. Boulard is very touching when one offers to help him out. One gets the impression that a sudden revolution takes place inside him and for two minutes he ceases to regard men as vicious monkeys or hungry sharks; in a twinkling he revises his whole philosophy and becomes reconciled with the human species—with which, incidentally, he has never completely fallen out.

Pretty Mme. Boulard, who had gone out, returned at this juncture, spruce, perfumed, frankly almost elegant! Seeing me, she flung her arms around my neck and cried:

"Darling, you must stay to dinner! We've got Toulouse sausage. You *are* nice to come and keep Bouboule company. He needs a little distraction, poor pet. He works so hard! He never stops!"

I had forgotten this legend of the martyr to hard work, the man driving himself to death on the job which Boulard, known as Bouboule, has managed by means of his ceaseless and convincing talk to establish in the bosom of his family. I wonder to what extent he is taken in by it himself. However intelligent one may be, one can easily become convinced by one's own humbug and it's true my friend never stops doodling and chasing round the town from morning to night.

One could write an interesting thesis on Charlotte, who was, fifteen years ago, a young middle-class girl, a little out of the

ordinary, no doubt, but extremely correct, very well brought up,
imbued with all the traditions and prejudices of the provinces,
and who has transformed herself into the wife of a Parisian
artist. Such an evolution is something very special, in no way
resembling the transformations we see taking place in the
modern world, where the bourgeoisie of Europe believe they
become emancipated by aping the bourgeoisie of America and
imagine themselves to be quite different people because they
own electric coffee grinders. As for Charlotte, she has truly and
radically changed her personality, her habits, and even her
speech. Take, for instance, that way of calling me "darling." I
shall have to follow this up one of these days and try to disen-
tangle the stages of her metamorphosis.

Hearing their mother's voice, the red cheeks and snotty noses
made their appearance with yells of:

"Pluche is staying to dinner! (*twice*) Super! We're going to
make Tarzan a pie."

Mme. Boulard giggled like a little girl, which is one of her
special hallmarks, I would even say her principal characteristic;
thanks to this she manages often enough to get out of making
conversation. Little Antoinette, who has a big crush on me,
absolutely insisted that I perch her on my left arm while setting
out the plates, a tricky performance. At ten o'clock I tore myself
away, not without regret, from all this friendship, but I was
anxious to get through my thirty pages of journal. Tarzan will
sleep on my bedside rug. Glory, I'm tired! Beddy-byes.

CHAPTER XI

Family Life

> *Even a colour-sense is more*
> *important, in the develop-*
> *ment of the individual, than*
> *a sense of right and wrong.*
>
> OSCAR WILDE

Letter to Boulard

Sunday, March 13th

Dear Old Sod,

First of all, my respects to Madame and best thanks for the sausage. I was truly touched. As usual, with you and yours I spent one of the luminous moments of my life. Here's my idea from the Rue Hallé, which looked a bit brighter again last night; even so, it's not quite as sparkling as yesterday morning.

You know the Rue Hallé. On the right, going up toward the onetime Avenue d'Orléans, there's a crescent, or rather, the street bulges into a semicircle with houses every kind of color—yellow, white, gray. There's also green, red, ocher. In a nutshell, it's a pretty sight. A bit corny, as well, in the Parisian petit-bourgeois style. Anyway, it appeals to me. Yesterday I liked it particularly on account of the light, at once clear and dim, such

as you only get in spring between showers. I'm not saying I won't
do a sketch of it one day.

Looking at the place I had a feeling I've often had when
painting, but never so sharp and sudden; more to the point, I
have never tried to analyze it before. I told myself that, unlike
what people say and what I used to believe myself, the great
painters don't interpret nature, don't transform it according to
their vision or temperament, but on the contrary reproduce it
just as it is. When you wander around Provence and see a typical
bit of the landscape you exclaim: "I say, a Van Gogh!" You're
wrong. It's Van Gogh who was the first to achieve a real likeness
of the Provençal landscape.

Right. What is the function of literature? To show ideas in
their true light, in other words scrub off the prejudices and
banal associations that smother them. The same goes for painting. People don't see objects any more than they do ideas. For
instance, a man looks at a tree. He doesn't see a vertical piece of
wood with leaves but a poetic thingumbob and with it he
associates a mass of ideas that have no business to be there.
Ideas of countryside, ideas of shade, ideas of calm, strength,
gracefulness, etc. Now for me the great landscape painter is the
one who associates no other idea with that of a tree, the one who
doesn't paint the preconceived ideas standing between the tree
and the eye, the one whose vision is so piercing that he immediately grasps the tree in its essential truth. Another example: a
slob stares at Rouen Cathedral. What does he see with his slob's
eye? A hymn to spirituality, the sublime mysticism of the Middle
Ages, and other assorted bollix. But Monet comes along, con-
siders the building with his painter's eye, and sees only splashes
of color. By means of which he paints Rouen Cathedral in all its
truth with the mysticism of the Middle Ages, the spirituality,
and all the trimmings into the bargain.

It follows from this that the great painters and writers
normally can't enjoy success because in neither case do they
show what people are accustomed to see. They show the naked
truth, and this revolts the public. Whether you look or think,

the workings of the mind are the same. People only see nature through more or less thick veils of preconceived ideas which obscure the true shapes for them. It is the eternal history of painting. With the proviso, however, that at certain periods there are less prejudices than at others. In particular in fifteenth-century Italy. Today nobody sees anything because there is no great pictorial stream kept in flow by the studios, masters, apprentices, etc. Each artist works in his own hole, amusing himself by painting his dreams, and these are of no interest.

Such are the ideas one has in the fourteenth arrondissement. Let me know what you think of them. Give Antoinette a special big kiss from me. Hail and farewell.

It is more out of laziness than literary vanity that I have copied out my letter in this journal; I wanted to keep track of my idea in the Rue Hallé without having the trouble of formulating it all over again. I wrote the letter this morning between nine and half past.

For the first time in ages I didn't wake up alone. Tarzan, still as a statue, slept on my bedside rug. I had arranged a sort of nest for him out of an old cushion and blanket. When, at about eight, I half raised one eyelid, I saw two eyes anxiously scrutinizing me. The good Tarzan was sitting up on his backside waiting for me to wake. A ray of sunlight slid through the gap in the curtains and set a gleam on the tip of his snout, leaving the rest of his body in shadow. He really is a charming dog: directly he saw I had stopped sleeping, far from giving vent to some ill-timed outburst he confined himself to ardently wagging his tail, the most discreet and at the same time affectionate way of wishing me good morning. I smiled at him and patted my eider-down with a come-hither hand. He instantly jumped onto my bed, snuggled up against me, and gave me a thousand demonstrations of devotion. Doing good to an animal brings more joy than doing it to a man. Animals have a simplicity in expressing their gratitude we don't often encounter in our own kind. I can rest assured: I shan't obtain from my brother, when I have stripped myself bare for him, one tenth of what Tarzan lavishes on me for far less. Georges will be starchy, awkward, self-important, embarrassed, not knowing which leg to stand on, mortified at having been saved by a nut case like myself; in short, close to feeling resentful. With Tarzan, not a trace of vanity, not the faintest ulterior motive: he is all love. For a good fifteen minutes I couldn't resist being lovey-dovey; as I stroked his ears and his back, as I scratched his head in Boulardesque fashion, I said in cooing, dulcet tones: "Oh, what a lovely dog, Madame. Oh, isn't he *sweet!* What beautiful paws he has and all. And does he love his old Pa? We won't be having our wicker basket today because it's Sunday, but we'll get it tomorrow. Yes, we will! It's a promise. And we'll have a beautiful collar as well, with a metal tag with our name and address on it. Come on, be a good boy and give your old Pa a lovely big kiss. . . ." And so on.

I got up, made coffee for the two of us, then pulled on my mackintosh over my pajamas and we went down together into the Rue Boissonnade, which was wearing its Sunday morning air, meaning that it was empty and one could picture behind its walls the inhabitants having a good lie-in or pottering about their apartments. The sun was shining and there was a deep sweetness in the air. Sunday mornings in Paris are unforgettable. If I hadn't been in my slippers I would have gladly pushed as far as the Dôme or the Coupole to enjoy a coffee and cream with rolls warm and crisp from the oven. Another of Tarzan's qualities: he gets through his duties with a rapidity that calls for the highest praise. Have I by chance stumbled on perfection? I'm beginning to think so. Good old Raimondet! I shall present him with one of my pictures in gratitude for his having procured me such a delightful companion.

I had barely finished copying out my letter to Boulard when a key turned in the lock of the front door and Tarzan began to growl. He has understood that this is his home and that he must pay his whack by acting as watchdog. It was Mme. Chevassu. I might have known. To reappear on a Sunday after a fortnight's absence is just her style. She was particularly Chevassesque this morning, that is to say haggard of eye, matted of hair, lean as a she-wolf. She embraced me on both cheeks and cried:

"This isn't a house here, it's a stable! Lord, what a beastly stuffy smell. So you have a dog now; that's all we needed. Pissing all over the place. As if there weren't enough to do already, I ask you, a *dog!* And how do you think you're going to take him for walks and feed him, poor brute, when you're hardly able to look after yourself? What a laugh!"

"Madame Chevassu," I replied, "you're nothing but an old bitch and you can just bugger off. Every time you open your mouth, out comes a load of bullshit."

Whereupon she burst out laughing. Nothing rejoices her heart more than foul language. For her part, she loves heaping me with violent reproaches. These slanging matches sometimes last for ten minutes. Each of us goes at it with such vigor that it would be impossible for an onlooker to guess we are just fooling. One day last year my brother witnessed one of these turns—an outstandingly successful one, to tell the truth. Mme. Chevassu called me a money grubber, a lousy hack, and a sex maniac; at the peak of her inspiration she even evoked a child I gave her in 1953. I riposted by describing her eczema, harped on her revolting passion for preserving her excrement in jam jars, and, to wind up, blamed it all on her youth, spent in a brothel at Colomb-Béchar. Georges's face was worth painting. Mme. Chevassu, crumpled up with laughter in an armchair, told him between gasps: "Don't take on about it, we're only joking. I love M'sieur Pluche. He's a card, a proper card! Oh my, I'm wetting me drawers!"

Before embarking on the washing-up she announced two imminent telephone calls: "Your girl and your sister." And in fact the phone rang a few minutes later and I heard the busy singsong voice of Lucienne—her telephone voice, the official voice of a respectable woman, quite different from the other, far more winning and natural voice she adopts when we're alone. Was I free today, could we meet? Yes, yes, my love, I'll

come round to your love nest in the Rue de Prony, let's say at
five o'clock. What better Sunday occupation could one have than
going to see one's mistress? The more so since on Sundays M.
Valhubert, a man of tradition and duty, remains in the bosom of
his family. Mme. Chevassu, drawn by curiosity, dishcloth in
hand, contemplated me with a mocking smile.

"You old pig!" she announced. "You don't half lay it on when
you talk to that doll of yours. You should just hear yourself."

There followed an assortment of offensive remarks on the folly
of men of ripe years who chase after chicks, and the even greater
folly of the said chicks in falling for the smooth talk of artists,
for it appears that I am loved. Mme. Chevassu, who has only
caught a glimpse of Lucienne once through the kitchen door, is
categorical about it: I have lighted in this heart a blaze that is
nowhere near dying. The first I've heard of it! If by chance this
crazy female were telling the truth, I should have to think twice
about it. I don't want a "love passion" at any price. God, how
exhausting women are! Here I was, enjoying a delightful affair,
satisfactory from every viewpoint, and now it threatened to end
idiotically in a morass of sentimentality! No, by God! I decided
that for once Mother Chevassu was way off the mark. Why?
Because she's read too much drivel in the newspapers. Through
them she picks up a smattering of civilization and contemporary
ideas. This smattering of civilization is enough to blind her
cave woman's instinct. Over questions of love she no longer sees
straight. She has been corrupted by *True Romance* and *Famous
Love Stories;* she takes us, Lucienne and me, for George Sand
and Chopin. For all that, she gave me a bad fright for a moment.
Thank God the placid behavior of my mistress a few hours later
reassured me. The renewed ringing of the telephone interrupted
this fruitless dialogue. "Hello, is that you, Pluche? Will you
come and lunch with us at the Palazzo? Be here at one." Taking
advantage of the presence of my pythoness I questioned her
about Marie, but instead of providing me with the oracular
pronouncement I was angling for, she plagued me with endless
questions in return. And how is your sister, and what's new

with her, and the little one, *oh là là*, what a dear little soul she is, the sweet pet, and M'sieur Mesnard, is he as distinguished as ever, there's someone at least who's not a layabout like you, the money he must bring in, you ought to follow his example, you're just a vagabond at heart, you'll never grow up, you won't; with your talent you ought to be in the Institute; when are you going to settle down? And so on.

"Be quiet, you horrible old bag!" I cried. "Your beloved Mesnard, who's going to be in the Institute one of these days, is just about to give his wife and daughter the chuck for a young miss of twenty. So lay off all that malarkey."

I'd have done better to keep quiet too. These few words so inflamed Mother Chevassu's curiosity that she stepped up her questions to the point where I was forced into describing my visit to Marie in detail. She savored this like a true connoisseur, occasionally interrupting with groans and exclamations such as: "Well I never!" "*Men!!!*" "I'd never have believed it." "Whoever would have thought?" "M'sieur Mesnard, I can say it now, I've never fancied the look in his eye." Naturally Marie's operation aroused her enthusiasm; I was treated to a complete course on hysterectomy—what my daily help calls "the lot"—with a wealth of detail that turned my stomach and various examples by way of corroboration, including those of Mmes. Bourlotton, Brelet, and Plumeau, local cronies of hers. These three ladies have been through "the lot" and are trotting round today as bright as buttons. Mme. Brelet had a growth the size of a sheep's head, can you imagine? As far as my sister was concerned, I could sleep peacefully, it would all go off all right, they open up your stomach, take everything out, stitch you up again, snicker-snack, and you wouldn't never know nothing had happened! After which, Madame doesn't need to worry: she can go the whole hog without starting a baby. I wonder why I am transcribing all this nonsense with such relish. Probably because I find nothing that comes from Mme. Chevassu without interest. Her language —at once familiar, foul, plebeian, and incoherent—always charms me. Moreover, her jocular way of discussing a matter so serious,

or so apparently serious to me since it concerns my sister, did me
a lot of good. It gave me back a sense of proportion. I couldn't
help concluding that this witch sees no murky aura enveloping
Marie, that her instinct or telepathic powers have discerned
no baneful influence at work since she can laugh about it so
freely. As always when one begins to hope after a period of
anxiety, I launched into a long speech to which Mme. Chevassu
listened with her mind visibly elsewhere. No matter: I was
talking more for my own benefit than hers.

Finding myself sitting once again in the gaudily painted
dining room of the Castel de la Mesnardière, I had that feeling
of slipping back in time combined with the fleeting dizziness
one gets when chance reproduces a situation one has lived
through before. It was ages since I had had my sister, niece,
and brother-in-law all around me. In the old days the four of us
used to have the gayest of meals together, and then these
became increasingly rare. Mesnard and I, being two well-bred
men, now greeted each other with reasonable cordiality, not
unduly feigned on my part, for that matter. I have too many
common memories with him not to feel a sort of involuntary
pleasure on seeing him again. Besides, there occurred a phenomenon I know all too well: whenever several months pass without
my seeing a man for whom I feel only a rather dim affection, he
becomes considerably simplified in my memory; I forget his
particular qualities and shades of character; all I am left with is
the memory of a few clear-cut defects which make up a figure
at once schematic and unprepossessing. The unexpected presence
of the person in question, the old complicities I rediscover, the
qualities that had escaped my memory, the pleasant conversation—all these then give me a happy surprise. Mesnard, I have to
admit, isn't just anybody. To begin with, he has aged very well.
Objectively I find him rather better than myself, despite the air
of youth that I have preserved and he has lost. But in losing it he
has gained a distinction and elegance I rather lack, I think. He's
a handsome fellow with his thick gray hair, his gaunt face and
slim body. I can see why Mlle. Duchateau has fallen for him. I,

on the other hand, have let myself go, because of the boredom of having to look after one's body. But for the fact that I walk a lot— the only exercise I ever take—I would no doubt have a paunch. I never trouble about my appearance, I couldn't care less about it. Mesnard's suits, tailored to perfection, must cost him two thousand francs apiece; he certainly has a good twenty more in his cupboard like the one he was wearing today.

One thing I hadn't forgotten was Mesnard's smile, which I would describe as thin, never quite fulfilling itself, something more like a hint of a smile expressing, for the few seconds it lasts, a blend of irony, wariness, disdain, and a certain expectancy. Expectancy of what? Of what the other person is going to say, of the absurdity of life which never fails to show itself, and so on. Such a smile, a Louis XV smile in style, inspired artists like La Tour, Perronneau, and Lépicié. The mouth that shapes it belongs to a man who is intelligent, none too virtuous, constantly on his guard, always ready to judge the world and to condemn it. Not only a thin but also a hard smile, not hard in its expression but in its outlines, like the smiles of old men. Mesnard when young already had this smile and this mouth, which I used to admire hugely and try to ape, though this was quite absurd given my fat cheeks and innocent air.

What determines Mesnard as a really wealthy man is the fact that his servants work on Sundays. Lunch was served by the manservant named Celestino, a plump lad of twenty-five with a nice face, big peasant's hands, an olive complexion, crinkly hair, a pimply forehead, and the excessive complacency of foreigners who are lavishly well paid. He understands more or less what one says but expresses himself in a gibberish impossible to comprehend. I wouldn't know whether he was Cuban, Mexican, Peruvian, or merely Spanish. What backward country can he come from? It would be hard to wear a white jacket more clumsily. This character, the personification of Mesnard's swank and ostentation, used not exactly to inspire sympathy in me, but I changed my opinion of him today. He's a good guy who must have a warm heart. I became aware of this

from the discreet and attentive way he insisted on Marie's taking more substantial helpings of each dish, even venturing to re-
prove her because she touched nothing on her plate and showing
distress on seeing the futility of his remonstrances. Throughout
the meal this affectionate war between him and my sister never
ceased. What finally reconciled me to him was the genuine and
spontaneous friendship he displayed toward Tarzan, preparing
his dinner for him himself, stroking him while he ate it, crooning
to him in his peculiar jargon. It was plain to see that this boy
has lived among animals, that he loves them and was glad to
come across one in this foreign city to which poverty has driven
him to emigrate.

Another very touching detail during lunch: the tenderness
lavished by Lise on her mother. She was doing her best to curb
all the still childish elements in her nature which might jar on the
poor woman's tired nerves through overebullience. If it hadn't
been instinctive, it would have been the work of a great artist.
This child subdued everything in herself, even her laughter, the
way a musician mutes his tone in a sonata or a painter dims the
colors in a picture to make it softer, more restful, more pale. She
practically never took her eyes off her mother, as if telling herself
that soon she would be seeing her no more and that every
moment spent in gazing at her, in profiting from her presence,
was infinitely precious. One would also guess that she was trying
to present a portrait of herself as the young girl she hasn't yet
become so that Marie, whatever happens, might know this
image. I was deeply moved by this behavior; there was nothing
preconceived about it; it was entirely spontaneous and purely
reflected the anxiety with which the poor child is filled.
Mesnard himself struck me as rather attentive, speaking very
gently to Marie, getting up to put a shawl around her shoulders,
and so on. With him such an attitude doesn't mean a thing; it's
his habitual manner; nevertheless I thought I could discern a
genuine compassion and, if not love, at least affection. A fairly
good impression on the whole. I had tended to imagine Marie
abandoned all alone with her worries in the depths of the

gloomy palazzo and instead of this I found her surrounded with
as much warmth as possible. From the start to the finish of our
lunch she betrayed no sign of fatigue or despondency; on the
contrary she chattered away, told funny stories, smiled, and even
laughed several times, leaving me unable to make out whether
her gaiety was forced or genuine. Had I closed my eyes I would
truly have had the illusion that time hadn't moved on, that we
were not in the present but two or three years back, in a lighthearted period unclouded by any drama. Mesnard was as he
then used to be, in a cheerful mood; with him this doesn't show
itself through excessive demonstrativeness or chatter, but through
a certain way of "sharing in the talk" and every now and then
injecting into it his own grain of salt in the form of some funny
comment or pun, usually so outrageous that one cannot help
laughing. He himself follows it up with a snigger. This mania for
puns, which I have watched grow until it has almost totally
taken over Mesnard's conversation, is to my mind a manifestation of nihilism. It's the doing of a man who, given a serious
mind and a great talent, has made bad use of these and ended
up by despising them. Whence a need to discredit the faculties
with which he has failed to build up anything satisfactory, as
if the ultimate aim of his talent and mind were this absurd
activity. Behind Mesnard's punning I can glimpse the old, sad
philosophy of renunciation and the vanity of all things, so convenient when one has made a mess of one's life. Mesnard is a
mountain who has given birth to a mouse, who in this ludicrous
want of proportion sees the law of the universe and draws from
it the bitter jubilation of the arid skeptic. A mind like his, which
no longer delights in anything but cooking up puns, puts me in
mind of a forty-ton tank being used to hunt rabbits in order to
make war seem ridiculous. Victor Hugo used to say: "Puns are
the droppings of the mind as it flies." I myself would rather say,
before the example of my brother-in-law, that they are the last
outcries of a mind that has had its wings clipped.

After coffee, Marie announced that she was going to lie
down. Lise insisted on accompanying her to her room, promising

that she would be quiet as a mouse, that she would read by the window, so anxious not to leave her alone for one moment that Marie, touched by this love, granted her everything she asked and even gave her permission to take along Tarzan, whose perfect manners she had already begun to appreciate. Fleetingly I thought of the fleas he was carrying, but felt the fleas must be as discreet as he himself since not one of them has jumped onto me in twenty-four hours, when they have had hundreds of opportunities to do so.

So we were left alone, Mesnard and I. I told myself that for once I must be polite and asked him to take me up to his studio to admire his latest works. He appeared grateful for this mark of interest, which he has hardly come to expect from me for several years past. Before the paintings in question, obviously, I wasn't able to say very much. No surprises. It's the same scamped work he was doing last year and the year before that. The silly ass (or shrewd businessman) has even run up a few abstracts because these have been selling passably well for the past five or six years—unless it's to impress Mlle. Duchateau. However hard I flogged my poor brain, I could find nothing to say about the wretched things. To adopt Boulard's expression, it was "painting that isn't worth the trouble." Yet not badly done, by and large. He's a thorough professional. But oh what a bore, this endless procession of daubs. There were hundreds of thousands of francs' worth, and I wouldn't give a cent for the lot.

I should have put down in writing long ago the reasons for this lamentable decline in Mesnard, concomitant with his rise in the social scale. It is as if fate had set him across my path like a drunken helot, so that I might have before my eyes a constant reminder of the pitfalls to be avoided.

To say that Mesnard has been spoiled by money would be an oversimplification and almost nonsensical. Certainly money has played a part in his story, but only a minor one; it only came on the scene following all the rest. At the root of my brother-in-law's damnation as an artist lies one factor at once far more baneful and far more all-embracing than a taste for wealth, namely self-deception. Like most men, Mesnard has mistaken himself for someone else. Worse, he has wanted with all his might to be someone else; to this crazy end he has applied his will, his intellect, his heart. The poor wretch has been had by that old gag of Oscar Wilde's about "making a work of art of one's life," a proposal which has always struck me as the height of lunacy. It's already a labor of Hercules to make a work of art; if on top of this one has to concern oneself with one's life, it is quite beyond human capacity. We live as best we can: it's a matter of no consequence. The vital thing, in every setback, is not to lose sight of one's soul, to remain true to it even if one dislikes it. At bottom, Mesnard has never liked his soul, in which he is to be pitied. I had guessed none of all this, of course, when he married my sister and I gladly gave my blessing to their union.

When I was eighteen to twenty I admired Mesnard for his bad qualities. His would have been a pernicious example for me had I not been protected by a kind of indolence, a kind of stolidity which drove me to despair then but for which I congratulate myself now. At twenty, one is only capable of admiring what resembles something that exists or has existed. Mesnard seemed to me sublime because he responded to the idea I had forged for myself—and that all my friends, himself included, had forged for themselves—of a great artist. He was lighthearted, showy, a prodigious worker, and in love with every woman; he had fits of melancholy à la Musset but also indulged in students' rags. What I marveled at most was the way he threw money about. "One needs lots of money in order to spend it," he used to say, or: "I don't give a damn for money, it's only interesting for what it can buy." This type of maxim, and he had a whole fund of them, made me feel what a poor nature mine was compared to his. I made endless sordid calculations, as much over my art as over life. I let nothing go to waste, neither the smallest dime nor the smallest idea. This propensity made me very unhappy; I would tell myself how I must reform, take an example from Mesnard,

become like him a great liver of life avidly devouring the
world. My reservations, my taste for order and economy, my
cautious nature decidedly didn't go hand in hand with genius.
The blasted question of money, among others, seemed to me
insoluble. My doctrine didn't fit in at all with Mesnard's moral
outlook, which was shared by all discerning and advanced
spirits. I thought in all simplicity that an artist, to do his
work, needed time and tranquillity. So he mustn't fritter away
his life on potboilers. I knew myself: I had barely any needs,
I could hold out for a long time on very little money; but
for this one has to be closefisted. Left to myself I worked
it all out perfectly, I pinched and scraped like Harpagon, I
made ten francs last for four days. When I went out I never
had a dime on me, I used to cadge pipe tobacco from my
friends; in the café I would quite shamelessly let the others
pay for my half pint, I wore my clothes till they were thread-
bare, I never took my shoes to be resoled. A thousand francs
represented forty days of freedom. I thought that freedom,
for an artist, was the greatest blessing, the only blessing on
earth, that no sacrifice was too heavy for it, not even that of
passing for a slob in the eyes of the world. During my bouts
of honest and clear thinking I couldn't see how an artist
could subsist, preserve the integrity of his work, avoid falling
into any compromise on the sacred subject of art, unless he
kept ferocious watch on his accounts and was as mean as a
louse.

This philosophy dimmed whenever I found myself in Mesnard's company. He spent money frenziedly, he was never
in the least concerned to know how he would manage the
next day, he spectacularly mortgaged his life. Sometimes he
would tease me for my stinginess; I was floundering so deeply
in my youth that I didn't know what to reply. This is strange
since generally, when one has a philosophy, one isn't left at a
loss. But as it happens, like all young people who are not wholehearted conformists, I was ashamed of the truth about myself.
When one is twenty the truth is tiresome, I mean the profound

truth, the truth of one's being, which pierces through attitudes like weeds through a well-kept lawn. When one is twenty all truth seems like a nettle or thistle that must be rooted out. At forty-five it is only the thistles and nettles in me that I find of interest, and I could almost root out the smooth turf surrounding them.

Mesnard, in those distant and diverting days of our youth, embodied the most fascinating thing of all: wastefulness. He was the archangel of waste. If I had a philosophy, he had a system, and the most pernicious one for a young artist: doing violence to his nature in every possible way. Nobody would deny, in fact, that he had an artist's nature, similar enough to mine at bottom, but he was ashamed of it. He was nurtured on the idiotic clichés about artists. He had one eye fixed on D'Annunzio. He wanted the same sort of life, full of rumors, adventures, women, ostentation, smart friends, and I don't know what besides. The title of duke, perhaps! He told himself, the poor fool, that externals are not enough, that one must in addition have the soul for this great calling, that when he had fashioned for himself a wholly aristocratic soul the rest would follow. His battles with himself were merciless. I watched them, though of course quite uncomprehending at the time; but looking back later on I was more or less able to reconstruct the whole process and then, one day, I guessed at the secret, as ludicrous as so many secrets are: his desire to have a splendid life story. All this because at the Fine Arts School they had a certain conception of the Philistine and it was essential to be the opposite of this loathsome monster! On what does a man's fate hang, when you come down to it! On a folly of his youth, consisting of setting up one false image against another false image. The Philistine was a mean, miserly, vulgar, hypocritical, self-righteous reactionary. It followed that the artist must be generous, prodigal, discerning, cynical, dissolute, and have revolutionary views. Could one possibly conceive of a more grotesque antithesis? And yet Mesnard has built his whole life on it. The cream of it is that he has never admitted it to anyone.

It all took place in the innermost depths, in the secret recesses of this heart, and it took years for me—for all that I have a fairly sharp eye—to realize it. For a long time I didn't want to believe anything quite so silly, and then I was forced to give in to the evidence. The whole of Mesnard is there in that absurd notion of his youth, brought to fulfillment with inhuman perseverance, actually transformed into ethics, into the man's philosophy. What a strange thing, an individual over whom one can place a grid and use it to explain everything about him! Simplification to such a degree is almost diabolic.

One memory comes back to me this evening, so typical that I am surprised to have lost sight of it for so long. At the time when Mesnard was collecting mistresses, that is between twenty and twenty-five, and only too ready and willing to recount his successes, he often confided to me good-humoredly that with one or other of these lovelies he had given a very poor if not wholly negative performance. Such candor staggered me. I used to think: "How sure he must be of himself to laugh so casually about his flops!" and I would admire him all the more for it. As for me, had such a mishap befallen me I would have been foolishly mortified and most certainly would never have bragged about it. Now at last, twenty years after, I can understand the reason for these deplorable failures, strangely frequent if the truth were known, and realize that his good-natured avowal of them was not so much a proof of cynicism as a mark of anxiety. Mesnard never guessed that this propensity to fiasco was a defense set up by his body against his womanizing—out of vainglory he fought ceaselessly against the natural chastity of artists, called for quite simply by the fact that one must preserve as much strength as possible for one's work. I understood this but would go to the stake on it that he, Mesnard, never did.

Given the Don Juanesque character he took such a delight in playing, how can one explain his marriage at twenty-five to my sister? Nothing easier. One only has to apply the grid in another place. This time we find a fatal principle stemming directly from the Mesnardian philosophy, based on generosity

and prodigality. After having lavished himself on dozens of
women he felt a desire to lavish himself on one alone, to give
her the whole of himself. To be an artist and yet fail so completely to recognize the prime necessities for an artist, namely
egoism and stinginess (stingy with one's self, one's time and
strength, one's emotions, etc.) passes understanding! As an
ordinary man, that is a man not endowed with the creative
instinct, Mesnard with his ideas would certainly have attained
a kind of perfection, there's no denying. He would have possessed the rarest and most charming qualities. But as an artist I
am convinced that he has made of his inner life a hell, an
endless conflict, a struggle of self against self which would have
been tragic had he had a very forceful temperament, and which
has ended by being ridiculous. With him the man has managed
to vanquish the artist, but it was so costly a victory that he
doesn't even benefit from it. Mesnard threw himself into marriage as he did into all his other devious experiments: with
absolute loyalty, without reservations, exalted by the sacrifice
he was making to another being. One has to grant that he has
been an exemplary husband, full of love during the first years,
the soul of tact, altruism personified, taking all the trouble in
the world to see that, thanks to him, Marie should have every
element of happiness at her disposal. Whence, obviously, Marie's
love for him and her present affection, which is very deep. I
suppose that when Mesnard's love for his wife declined nothing
outwardly changed and, down to the fatal encounter with Mlle.
Duchateau, Marie had preserved the illusion that she was loved
perfectly, I mean to say loved with a sort of conjugal perfection.

I remember a conversation I had with her about ten years
after her marriage, around 1955. I was beginning to have a
glimpse of my brother-in-law's true nature and of the underlying reasons for his attitude. I had felt it my duty to impart
these far-reaching discoveries to my sister, for her guidance.
But just then she was making an equally important discovery
on her own account: the discovery of her face, of her body,
which were becoming attractive. I soon saw that she didn't

understand a word of what I was saying, or didn't want to understand because it disturbed too much a certain way of life that was taking shape for her and which she judged to be highly desirable. It was on that day I realized how she and Mesnard formed a couple, with all that this word implies of intimacy, shared philosophy, common ambitions, and mimicry. I inferred from this that Marie, whom I had been counting on to hold Mesnard back from his downward path, was rather going to help him descend it.

Third application of the grid. Mesnard and painting. It is here, naturally, that the deception has assumed its cruelest form. Mesnard's philosophy has fatally led him to sacrifice his art to his life. Generosity and prodigality, excessive delicacy in relations with others, kindnesses, gifts, and ostentation all call for a great deal of money. It is difficult (but not impossible) to be generous when one is poor: one makes up for lack of money by offering one's time. It is *absolutely impossible* to be generous when one is a poor artist, that is to say when one has neither time nor money nor thoughts to spare for others. So I am right in saying that Mesnard sacrificed his art, which might well have been outstanding, to the man he wanted to be. As a painter he had facility, virtuosity, a feeling for what people want, and finally that lesser form of imagination consisting in having endless "ideas for pictures." At the outset of his career, when he was very much under my influence (without my being particularly aware of it, incidentally; this, like all the rest, only came out later) he worked seriously, seeking like me for something of which neither of us had a very clear idea but heading intuitively in the right direction. This lasted until several years after his marriage. Then, when he was about thirty, he underwent a change. This occurred following an exhibition of his pictures in a gallery on the Left Bank: he was well received by the critics, the dealer pushed him; he wanted a certain prize, he maneuvered to win it, he won it, and everything started to go to pieces. Within a year his pictures had trebled in price. With fame he began to have political ideas, which

was particularly comic given his indifference, as monumental
as my own, to such matters. But it is rather an advantage, I
believe, for an artist to appear to belong to the left wing.
Mesnard saw to this. He managed to get himself interviewed
in the progressive weeklies, he offered his opinions about various
events, he signed two or three manifestoes on behalf of some
murderer condemned to death or some smutty film banned
by the censor. I used to wonder what was the point of these
manifestoes, which are always ineffectual: well, they serve to
keep their signatories in the public eye, over and above which
they give them a reputation for being right-minded. In short,
Mesnard was very quickly taken up by the leftist coteries which,
in France, lay down the law to the bourgeoisie, that is to say
the public. Being rich, he now had the means to be left-wing.
Those were the days when anybody and everybody bought
pictures, chiefly the newly rich, who believed that in this way
they could lock away their capital in a safer form than by
investing in stocks and shares. I don't complain about those
days: I benefited from them myself as well. Thanks to this craze
for painting which broke out about 1950 and raged for more
than ten years, I amassed enough money to pay for this apartment in the Rue Boissonnade and my house at Le Cannet, not
to mention my wretched savings, which are shortly going to
return to the pockets of the bourgeoisie. Mesnard took himself
for a magician, and this is the greatest misfortune that can
befall an artist. When he had need of three thousand francs
he could earn them in fifteen minutes by knocking off any old
sketch. Did he want a Mercedes or a Jaguar? He drew one, and
it turned into a real Mercedes or Jaguar. It was intoxicating.
He became intoxicated. Round about 1955 he began to earn
crazy sums by painting in succession whole series of the same
subjects. He spent it all with the wildest extravagance. He
showered his friends with gifts and his wife with jewelry;
he even gave banquets like the doge of Venice. All this money
earned from daubs and squandered on futilities disgusted me
hugely; it was then that I started to cool off toward him. I

don't think at that time I was in any way jealous of him; no envy, no resentment, nothing but sadness at seeing this really genuine talent going to waste on such vulgarities. I drew apart from him. This in spite of myself: we had ceased to be kindred spirits. On his side, Mesnard underwent a change of mood. Still charming, cordial, faultless, but less debonair. He lost a certain freshness of spirit that I had always greatly relished in him. There's an easy explanation: soon he ceased to do anything just *for the pleasure of it*. Always for money. More and more money. This lay at the roots of his depression and the mysterious malady he had around 1960. For almost a year he suffered from violent stomach pains, he could eat hardly anything, he could drink only water. Any group of more than four people paralyzed him, struck him dumb. The doctors stuffed him with drugs which made him no better. I myself knew the only effective medicine perfectly well: this would have been for him to set about painting good pictures again. It is my contention that his illness was purely a moral one: the artist in him was rebelling, fighting his level best against the fatal treatment to which Mesnard was subjecting him. To practice an art is amusing when one gives oneself endless surprises in the course of creation. What surprises? The new, the unexpected, the unknown, anything that isn't obvious. Now in order to make money one must only say what is obvious, what is expected, what is banal and dreary, which serves no purpose at all. Whence the despair of a true artist, whence the despair of Mesnard, whom it made ill for a year without his suspecting the reason for his illness.

How ludicrous! Mesnard, who has built his whole life on hatred for a certain conception of the Philistine, has now become an out-and-out Philistine himself. An artist who makes money to the detriment of his art is a Philistine, a purveyor of painted canvases, a man who makes it his sole aim to amass a fortune in order to spend it. In the old days Mesnard's friends were artists and his dearest friend was myself. Today he sees only picture dealers who butter him up because he makes them richer and millionaires with whom he goes yachting at

Saint-Tropez in the summer. He's quite capable of holding forth
for hours on end about motorcars or real estate. Horrifying.
He is still intelligent, of course, but one can feel an inner
aridity that makes him completely alien to the man he once
used to be. I believe now that the wheel has turned full circle.
The last thread binding Mesnard's life to art was Marie. Not too
stout a thread, but a thread all the same. In spite of her own
changes she preserved a glint of the poetry of our youth, of the
time when Mesnard wanted to bring something new into the
world. With money Marie has become a sort of bourgeoise, but
this is plainly not enough for him. He now wants to break entirely with the past, which, when he chances to glance back at
it, fills him with a vague remorse. He wants to betray through
and through, damn himself completely, enter body and soul
into the suffocating paradise of absolute bourgeoisdom. He wants
a little bourgeois wife all new and pure, who gives off no brightness, not even a memory of brightness, who loves the money,
empty show, fame, self-deception, luxury, intellectual nullity,
sailboats, and all the other claptrap of the bourgeoisie. Mesnard
the onetime painter, that is to say a man of light, is descending
into darkness. He aspires to lose himself in the deepest and
blackest darkness. Even Marie, though so different from what
she used to be, no longer has any part to play in his life. This
evening a divorce seems to me inevitable. Mesnard is no longer
the man for her; she is no longer the woman for him. This
chapter of their lives is closed. And I promised Lise to bring
her parents together! I have been irresponsible—that's the least
anyone could say.

Very few men see themselves in their true light. For most
people this is of no importance; for an artist it is a catastrophe.
For a long time I used to wonder why so many talented artists
I've known have failed to justify their early promise and why,
when you come down to it, given so great a number of gifted
men there is so little talent in the world. It is because talent
isn't everything: one must in addition know oneself, that is to
say accept the heart one has, the sensibility one has, the amount

of breath one has, face squarely up to one's errors, one's short-comings, one's ignorance, one's prejudices, one's follies, in a word one's limitations. Only with this as a starting point can talent open out, produce all its blooms, give everything it has for the greater glory and happiness of its possessor. One must make a clean sweep of everything that is not an essential part of oneself, a true philosophical procedure in the manner of Descartes. Not only did Mesnard fail to carry out this process but also, to the benefit of a by and large pretty wretched human ideal and out of failure to appreciate its true value, he disregarded and flouted the perplexing artist's soul the Creator had bestowed on him. He disliked this soul, just as at first sight we can dislike all profoundly beautiful or serious things, and he never got over this impression.

The parade of Mesnard's canvases in his studio left me thoroughly dejected. This was to be expected. Bad painting is sad: I mean to say, painted sadly. It saddens the heart of whoever looks at it, whereas good painting is joyous and fills the spectator with gaiety. I suppose it's the same with the other arts, literature and music, where seriousness obviously derives not from the subject matter but from the style. Beethoven, Rembrandt, pre-eminently tragic spirits, never make one feel sad. In return, nothing could be more depressing than Mesnard's painting, despite the humor he tries to put into it. Such commonplace texture, such commonplace drawing are quite dismaying. It is only the hand that functions, mechanically reproducing forms discovered once and for all fifteen years ago. Mesnard has a *manner,* a style, so that any picture by him is instantly recognizable, but it all leads nowhere, none of it is of the slightest interest. He has done two thousand paintings which are all exactly the same. The two-thousandth says nothing different from the first. Machine-made goods. How can one comment on manufactured goods to their manufacturer? I confess I haven't the faintest idea. I managed all the same to squeeze a few non-committal sounds from my rebellious throat. Exhausted

by this effort, I let myself collapse into an armchair and said
point-blank, without any preamble:

"You simply can't divorce just now. Marie is ill. Wait for
three months, until she's better. What on earth can three
months more or less matter to you?"

As I had anticipated, he acquiesced immediately and even
with alacrity. Such alacrity must mean he was agreeing to make
a heavy sacrifice, given that he never shows so much warmth
as when he is doing something that costs him dear.

"Naturally I didn't know Marie was ill," he added.

One brief remark and Mesnard falls silent. That is his way.
Not one question about Marie's illness: it wouldn't be good
form. The question is in his eyes. This urbanity, this elliptical
manner drives me wild. Lord, I would almost prefer idiotic
expressions of surprise or emotion. At least they wouldn't strike
me as any more tedious Oh, how hard it is when one knows
someone too well and foresees his responses in advance!

"Why do you always say the obvious?" said I, peevishly. "I
know perfectly well you didn't know. I am telling you that
Marie is ill because if I didn't, you'd never learn it from her
in the present circumstances, and you would be doing something
wrong, something you would certainly find distasteful."

"You're quite right," he replied, going slightly pink.

"Albert," I went on in a gentler and more earnest tone, "for
once you haven't been true to yourself. Before you brought up
the question of a divorce with Marie you forgot to take a look
at her. If you'd done so, you'd have noticed how run-down and
unhappy she looks. But I suppose you are going through one of
those periods when we are so absorbed in what's going on inside us as to become blind to the outside world. Marie has been
facing her illness all alone for weeks now, possibly months: even
I have only known of it for three days. This illness may be
serious. You've had bad luck: unwittingly you've given one more
kick to someone who is already down. Don't misunderstand
what I'm getting at: I'm not telling you all this to make you

feel sorry for her. I'm doing it for your own sake, not Marie's. Besides, she'd be very vexed if she got to know of it."

In spite of his reticence Mesnard couldn't prevent himself from cross-questioning me, even in quite a pressing way. For once I wasn't clumsy.

"My dear man," I declared, "I've already told you too much. My duty toward you lay in telling you that your wife is sick. The least I could do for Marie, who asked me to keep it to myself, is to let it go at that. If you want to find out more, you must apply to her."

I am rather pleased with that maneuver. Mesnard is going to be compelled, on pain of dishonor, to take a step toward Marie, to pay her some attention. I don't know if this will bring them any closer together but at least it will make things more complicated for him.

"I blame myself a lot for having spoken to Marie," he said. "I've been thinking about this divorce for a long time: I say that by way of explanation, not as an excuse. I certainly ought to have realized she wasn't in a condition to cope with such a piece of news. I'm dreadfully sorry. Sometimes one can be cruel through modesty. It seemed to me—wrongly, no doubt—that she was fairly detached from me. I never thought I would be dealing her such a heavy blow."

A normal man would have added a few things in justification, such as: Thanks to me, Marie has lived a life of luxury she would never have otherwise enjoyed; after we're separated I shall continue to maintain her in princely style; I've had enough of you, Pluche, her brother, with your constant faultfinding over the past ten years; I can't put up any longer with this constraint which makes me smother my true feelings and character; I've at last met a woman who . . . and so on. But not Mesnard. He'd rather be chopped into little bits than level a reproach or betray any inner anguish, however slight. Faced with such natures one is overcome by the same sense of discouragement as when faced with people of bad faith. In a desire to show off his generosity of soul Mesnard acknowledges

everything in exactly the same way as others deny everything.
It is impossible to argue with someone like this, but even so it's
not impossible to tell him what is preying on one's mind. Seeing
my brother-in-law's dry, white face, his hard smile, his im-
maculate appearance—this sort of perfect statue of the gentle-
man-artist—I was stung. There was nothing to be got from this
figure of stone apart from civilities or endless acquiescence. I
told myself that I was human, that I had impulses, feelings,
passions, that I didn't give a damn for poses, and that it was
very good of me to enter into this ridiculous game in the
manner of Metternich or Beau Brummell. It was absolutely
vital that I should inject some disturbing realities into this
mean little soul.

"Look," I said, "it's been a long time since we had a real talk.
There was never any need, since we know more or less everything about each other. But today there's a new situation and I
believe I've simply got to get tough with you. You want a divorce. Right. Do you realize what this means? You are sacrificing two people, namely your wife and your daughter, to your
own selfishness. Not your selfishness as an artist—that would be
sacrosanct and I'd be the last to blame you for it—but your selfishness as a man. You've taken up with a girl and you want to
marry this girl *to be happy*. At forty-five, you have a housemaid's
idea that happiness exists somewhere and that one can go in
pursuit of it. You know perfectly well this isn't true, that happiness doesn't exist anywhere except in oneself, and that if you
don't have it in yourself you won't find it in a woman. You aren't
happy, Mesnard. You're even rather unhappy. And it's a completely happy man who's telling you this, one who is also fully
qualified to compare your case with his own. You aren't happy
for one reason only, and it has nothing to do with marriage, or
your wife of whom you're tired, or your daughter from whom
you're going to be separated, or myself who gets you down because I disapprove of your way of life, or your money which
you spend like a lunatic; you're not happy because you paint
lousy pictures. I've never said this right out before, the way

I am doing today, but don't go telling me you weren't aware of my feelings about it. There was a time when you and I were very close friends, we both liked the same things; when you married my sister I was delighted. By your becoming my brother-in-law we grew even closer, if that were possible. Then came the break. One day I no longer felt able to tell you what I thought of your painting, not just because it was bad but because you had made it bad deliberately. For a long time I cherished the illusion that this wouldn't last, that it was all part of a scheme you had to make enough money in one swoop to live at ease for the next ten or twenty years. I hoped for a little cynicism, thanks to which I'd have been able to exonerate you. For ten years I've waited for one cynical remark from you, something like: 'By the way, I've just turned out another bit of rubbish which'll net me ten thousand. Roll on, riches, so that I can get back to things that matter!' I've done everything I could to provide this cynicism. I've given you hundreds of openings. But you've always acted like someone who didn't understand. As I was the only person with whom a bit of cynicism would have done you no harm but on the contrary would have set you up again, I finally concluded from this that you were sunk. Either in the depths of your heart you see your painting for what it is and you are a hypocrite, or else you consider it good and you've become an idiot. Of these two possibilities I don't know which depresses me more. At bottom, Mesnard, I think you have almost ceased to be a hypocrite and the idiot has virtually won the day. Why? On the one hand because you have preserved an artist's pride, which outlives the wreck of a talent, and are convinced that you can't produce anything really bad, that even your worst canvas, no matter how botched, no matter how repulsive, still has its inimitable little gleam of light; on the other because you are successful, because your daubs sell, because the well-to-do middle classes all have a Mesnard in their drawing rooms, because the gossip columnists write about you and you tell yourself that if so many people join in praising your talent they can't be wholly wrong. But they *are* wrong, Mesnard! Have you ever thought who your public is? It's the people who have always been wrong since time began, who buy smart rubbish, who think they have taste because they have money. And now you work only for those fat pigs. You dish up just the sort of crap they want, you are their favorite source of supply. I don't ask how you got to this point since I know. You have committed a sort of crime against yourself. You wanted to be rich, not so as to have no worries and be able to produce good paintings at leisure, but in order to have a lot of suits, cars, houses, servants. Even that would be nothing in itself. But you wanted to be rich because you thought that only wealth would enable your qualities as a man to develop freely, and that is where the real sin lies. One's qualities as a man are nothing, they don't count. The duty of a painter is to paint well, just as the duty of a statesman is to rule well; it's not to be a nice fellow, a good husband, a good father, or a reliable friend. You've sacrificed yourself to public opinion. You've abandoned a great aim for a little one. You were once an artist, that's to say someone above the common run of humanity, someone who has a different morality from ordinary mortals, with inexplicable obligations, inalienable privileges, someone who in any case cannot be compared with even the most discerning or virtuous of men. But you preferred to be a man. And you've succeeded. You are now a man like any other, chasing after happiness and divorcing like a discontented bourgeois."

It was an almighty outburst, but I'd worked myself up into a state. When I embarked on it I was sitting; but before I'd got very far I felt the need to rise and stride about the room. Conversely Mesnard, who was standing, sat down. He didn't interrupt me once. My pacing gradually assumed a concentric motion, to the extent that at one moment I felt rather like a hawk circling around a field mouse. Poor Mesnard! The more I talked, the more he shrank back into his armchair. At the start I had had no intention of being so ruthless, but one remark leads to another, the argument builds up, so to speak, of its own accord, and finally I felt in myself a force it was impossible to quell. I had to see it through to the end, crush the imbecile, pulverize his good conscience, show him the emptiness for which he was preparing to bring calamity down on two beings who are worth far more than he is. Now and then I glanced across at him: I saw the thin white face go to pieces. He was holding his head stiffly, with lowered eyes. I had the impression that each thing I said was demolishing something inside him. This made me feel sorry for him, but not enough to stop. One curious development was rather to the credit of the poor wretch: normally when one tells someone the truth it's as if one were singing: either he doesn't understand a word of it or he loses his temper. With Mesnard I observed the destructive power of the truth for ten minutes on end. It fell on him like bombs on a village: I could, so to speak, watch his little inner defenses collapsing. When I had done, he raised his eyes and looked at me in a way that could have torn my heart, had I had at that moment any heart to tear.

"What have I done to you, Pluche?" he muttered in a low and trembling voice.

It was pitiful and I would doubtless have been moved had I not seen around me, hanging on the studio walls or propped on easels, my brother-in-law's miserable canvases. This display of horrors precluded any softening on my part. Besides, I wasn't expecting such a collapse. I thought Mesnard was more resilient. I can only presume that in ceasing to be a true artist he has lost his strength of spirit. He no longer has the iron heart of the creative man, which enables one to put up with anything. He's a poor *sensitive* devil! A fine result of wealth! In more measured tones I went on:

"You've done nothing to *me*, Mesnard. It's to yourself that you've done such harm. You've sold your soul. I haven't been speaking as a friend, since I haven't been your friend for a number of years, but if you can still be saved it will be due to what I've been telling you Do you think you've the guts to chuck everything, your cars, your comforts, your girl, your reputation? Is my respect worth it? Is your soul worth it? Would you be capable of taking up your painting again where you left it off ten years ago? Are you completely dead as an artist, or are you curable? It's for you to judge. Goodbye."

When one says goodbye one has to leave. Even so I didn't want to go without shaking his hand. He didn't rise from his chair. His face had resumed its impassivity. What will result from this interview? Nothing, probably. Yet it seemed to me that he squeezed my hand harder than usual, like a man who has been profoundly disturbed and knows that what one said wasn't prompted by hate. Apart from this, not a word.

As I went down the stairs I looked into Marie's bedroom to say goodbye and recover my dog. A complete contrast after the storm on the third floor. Here all was peace, serenity, and even a kind of joy. Marie was reading, stretched out on her bed; her daughter sat reading in a chair; Tarzan, lying on the floor with his nose between his paws and one eye on the alert, was watching over his world. The thin but not uncheerful March sun was shining in through the window. And bathing it all that special Sunday silence which is like no ordinary silence in that one can feel, behind it, that nothing in the city is astir.

"I'll leave you two together," said my niece, getting up. "You always have secrets to tell each other. Don't tire Mama, Maestro; she's a bit under the weather. Coming, Tarzan?"

Impossible to show more tact or deftness. This child's an angel. "What a darling!" I exclaimed.

"You can't imagine how sweet she is," said Marie. "So gentle, such good company. A wonderful person to have around. My life won't have been wasted since I've produced a child like her. She's a far better person than I am."

I rounded on her for her modesty, which annoys me, I don't know why—perhaps because there is always something unnatural in every display of modesty—and then added:

"I've been bawling Mesnard out."

"Yes," said Marie. "I suppose it was inevitable. I hope you weren't too hard on him all the same. Albert can be so weak and you can sometimes be a terror. He's not the type to stand up to you."

This kind of judgment, even when delivered by one who knows me as well as Marie does, never fails to stagger me. Me a terror? That's something I can never manage to get into my head. I reassured Marie as best I could while feeling, so it seemed to me, a twinge of resentment on realizing she still loves this mountebank enough to worry in case I shook him up a bit. A small dose of truth can't do much harm, for heaven's sake!

"Oh yes, it can," said Marie. "You don't know what it's like, because you live with the truth like King Mithridates with his poisons. But for most people the truth is cyanide."

As I hate controversies I changed the subject. To keep the conversation going I asked Marie where she went yesterday.

"You'll never guess," she replied, her eyes glittering. "To the lawyer. I made my will. You see, if I've got cancer I shall start going ga-ga quite quickly. I've taken the opportunity while still of sound mind. Besides, it's a great comfort to make one's will. When I was little, I remember, I used to make my will every week. Generally it was to you I bequeathed all my worldly goods, save for once when I was furious with you, I've forgotten why, tore up all my previous wills, and made a new one in favor of Simone Hirsch, who was my best friend at school. Anyway, yesterday after lunch I was feeling very low and everything seemed black as could be. I took a sheet of paper and wrote a letter from beyond the grave: 'Ladies and gentlemen, here is my last will and testament . . .' I covered four pages with it. After which I felt light as a feather, merry as a grig, happy as a lark. I had the feeling of having had a good tidy up and dust round. It was delicious. I couldn't resist the pleasure of taking my literary efforts to the notary. I know it's a bit melodramatic to make a will at my age, as if one took oneself for La Malibrán or the Dame aux Camélias, but after all, one never knows. Besides, I rather like a bit of drama. You yourself pointed out as much to me the other day, in connection with the little suitcase. I've thought some more about that little suitcase and feel pretty ashamed of it. The poor betrayed wife plodding down the street in the dusk, in the rain, all alone, clutching her little suitcase, heading for the cemetery! What could be more grotesque? A fine subject for Delvaux, provided she's stark naked, of course, and viewed from behind."

This business of the will, although told lightheartedly, left me with an unpleasant impression at the time; but on second thought it seems to me fairly true to Marie's character in that she needs every now and then to do something exaggerated or striking, whereby she frees herself from some worry or obsession. There have been dozens of examples of such behavior throughout her life. I believe that yesterday she rid herself of her sinister forebodings by writing her will. At any rate this would explain the rather gay mood I found her in today.

Apparently the will is chiefly concerned with Lise. If one day Marie is no longer there to watch over her, it will be my task to fill this role, and if the father dies too I shall become the child's guardian. Marie doesn't at any price want her to be taken care of by Georges, with whom she would be like someone in exile. She laughed as she evoked my sordid avarice; thanks to it I can be thoroughly relied on to preserve my niece's fortune, which will be appreciable. She hasn't too much faith in Georges, who is a bourgeois and so tends to be dishonest. If only Marie knew the idiot's latest exploit in real estate, she would doubly congratulate herself on her foresight!

"You'll be quite willing, Pluche, won't you, to act as Lise's mother if I die? Perhaps I shouldn't have named you as I have done without even discussing it with you."

"No indeed," I said to myself under my breath, suddenly aware of what the irruption of a child into my life might mean (however tenderly I love her, as indeed I do) and feeling myself break out in a cold sweat. Happily, if there is one thing experience has taught me it is that one has to acquiesce in people's projects when they have to do with a remote and improbable future. It doesn't commit one to anything and avoids futile disputes. Before I could become Lise's guardian not only

would both Marie and Mesnard have to die, but also Mesnard
would have to make the same dispositions as his wife.

"Shut up," I replied. "It's you who'll be burying me. I've
always counted on it. Out of selfishness, of course, so that it'll
be you who has to see to all the funeral arrangements. And
don't worry about Lise. I'll never let her fall into the clutches
of that slob Georges and his slob family. Now I'm going to kiss
you goodbye, as I've a date with a member of the opposite sex."

One of my most deep-rooted obsessions, verging on a fault,
is punctuality. At five o'clock on the dot I was ringing Lucienne's
bell in the Rue de Prony. She burst out laughing as she opened
the door. I have to admit that, what with my filthy mackintosh,
my checked shirt, and Tarzan tethered by a length of string to my
left hand, I presented a pretty uplifting sight. None of this
prevented my lady friend from welcoming me with the sem-
blance of delight she always assumes whenever we meet. I
would say that this delight reflects two thirds sincerity and one
third politeness; I like to think I respond as warmly to the
politeness as to the sincerity. Nothing is rarer than good style in
love. Lucienne, with her perpetual cheerfulness, has it to the
highest degree. This afternoon on her landing, from the tender
and admiring way she considered me, I was struck by one thing
which had never occurred to me before: that I form the romantic
and picturesque side of her life. If she takes me into a new
world, I do the same for her, and even more so. For a second I
saw myself in my getup, with my odd gait, my height, and—no
misplaced humility!—my face, which is not unpleasing. I suddenly understood the attraction a woman like Lucienne might
feel for such a character, at the opposite pole from M. Valhubert and the other *boys* (one of the words in her vocabulary)
she has known.

When I go to visit Lucienne, we always follow a rite which
consists of making the most correct kind of conversation in her
sitting room for half or three quarters of an hour amid the
poufs covered with coarse brocade, hard by Colin rumpling
Babette's skirt in their gilded frame. I sit myself down in a

Louis XV winged armchair, a masterpiece of the Faubourg Saint-Antoine in 1880; the dear child makes it a point of honor to serve me first and foremost with tea and buttered toast, which I munch while recounting my latest adventures. Not for an empire would I renounce this anachronistic ceremony, whereby Lucienne affirms that we are civilized people such as still existed around 1910. She was clad in a ravishingly pretty silk wrap, her little feet in slippers trimmed with swan's-down, her hair loose, in short all set to do her lover honor. A dim glow reigned in the sitting room, caused by the pink shades surmounting porcelain lamps representing shepherds, Chinese, or elephants. Who else can boast today of enjoying such vivid sensations with his mistress? M. Valhubert and I are lucky fellows, there's no denying.

I was still full of my scene with Mesnard, which I recounted in more or less the same terms as heretofore. This story interested Lucienne deeply and she listened to it like someone with a profound experience of life, interrupting from time to time to make me clarify some point, demanding detailed descriptions of Marie and Lise, etc. My tale ended, she put on her serious face and said:

"You've been pretty hard on your brother-in-law. It's to avenge your sister. Mind you, I don't blame you for it, darling, I'd have done just the same. The people one loves are sacred."

At the time this remark seemed to me rather silly and the product of someone too limited to grasp my real motives. I didn't even trouble to take her up on it. But on thinking it over it's not so foolish after all. With her practical mind Lucienne saw at once what I, with my complex mind, had kept concealed from myself. In my violence toward Mesnard, a desire for vengeance certainly played a part. I was angry with him for making Marie suffer; I had to pay back the wound he had inflicted on her. As so often happens, Lucienne in being mistaken, in judging in an oversimple way, turned out to be right. I always marvel at how most people similarly arrive at the truth down the path of error.

I left Lucienne around 10 P.M. I'm hardly spending anything on food just now. This pearl of mistresses provided an extremely worthy, albeit rather light supper: cold lobster, cold chicken, Russian salad, and champagne. Sincerely, if I am frank with myself, have I ever in my life known such a charming woman? No, no, a hundred times no. She's a jewel. But how contrary is the heart of man: I don't value her the least little bit.

One last thing to note before going to bed. When I got home I had an urge to call up Boulard, to tell him about my brother-in-law and the way I laid into him. Lucienne's opinion, although pertinent, was not enough for me.

"Well, old cock," he said, "you didn't wrap any flannel round the poker. In your case it doesn't surprise me. Pluche the good guy, Pluche the debonair has an ugly side to him that few people are aware of. I who know you know equally well that you are spiteful and vindictive. For the past ten years you've been sharpening your teeth against Mesnard, and the said teeth have grown mighty long since he's been lousing up your kid sister. You had to bite him sooner or later. You just leaped at his throat like a wolf and half killed him. Nevertheless I should like to ask one question: would you have been such a bastard if Mesnard weren't such a success?"

Decidedly it has been a day of revelations. According to my sister and my oldest friend I am a holy terror, a wolf who leaps at people's throats. According to this same friend and my mistress I have settled my account with Mesnard when, in all simplicity, I thought it was only on questions of principle that I attacked him seriously. I, who used to despair of myself when I was young for being too transparent, ought to be content. As I grow older I perceive that I know myself less and less, that my character is a deep black pond teeming with fat, unsuspected fish, sharks, deep-sea monsters that surface every now and then. Can I possibly be an enigma? I hope so. It's good for painting.

CHAPTER XII

The Turners in the Tate Gallery

> *No, Dona Maria, I shall*
> *not reproach you, since I*
> *imagine your conscience has*
> *already spoken and that in*
> *the depths of your soul you*
> *repent for having written me*
> *that strange letter.*
>
> **MERIMEE**

Last night I woke at four and couldn't sleep again till six, something that doesn't often happen to me. I'm turning into a thoroughgoing man of letters: to while away the time I entertained myself, while I tossed in the dark on my mattress to the accompaniment of Tarzan's muffled yaps as he dreamed on his old cushion, by telling myself a story, plainly inspired by my set-to with Mesnard. This morning I can remember it pretty well and intend to try and write it down. Perhaps it will be less telling on paper than it was last night in my mind. I suppose it's the same with literature as with painting: I have painted magnificent pictures in bed, halfway between waking and sleeping, compositions as rich, as crazy as the great Delacroix's "Death of Sardanapalus," teeming with reds and golds, naked women, rich materials, horses, objects, ele-

phants, flames, murders, love, clouded skies, Negroes, wild or
ecstatic faces, of which nothing remained in the morning save
a few blurred colors.

A MORAL FABLE

There was once an artist called Jacques, who had talent
but was as poor as could be. There were days when so much
talent and so much poverty were hard to bear. Although he was
happy-go-lucky, Jacques sometimes burst out in recriminations.
"When will this penury ever end?" he would cry. "When will the
world realize that my painting is sublime and buy it, so that
I in turn can buy myself a juicy steak?"

Now it came about that for one whole week Jacques nour-
ished himself solely on coffee and stale bread, what little money
he had having gone to purchase canvas and paints. As he
painted he made up stories to give himself heart for his work.
For example, he dreamed that every morning he found a
gold coin under his pillow so that he was able to live without
care and paint at leisure. "Ha!" said he, "had I a gold coin
each morning, every morning of my life, I'd ask for nothing
more."

"Granted!" said a cavernous voice behind him.

Jacques jumped, and thought he was having hallucinations
due to his empty stomach. Nevertheless he turned and saw a
smiling little man, wearing a bowler hat and carrying a leather
briefcase under his arm. From this traditional disguise he recog-
nized the devil.

"So be it. A gold coin every morning; you will find it under
your pillow, my good sir."

"You're very kind," said Jacques, "but I accept nothing from
the devil."

"Prejudice, absurd prejudice!" retorted the devil. "Give me
your reasons."

"Sir, it's because on seeing you I, who am normally inclined
more or less to atheism, immediately began to believe in God.

Forgive me, but between God and you I prefer God, even if it means dying of hunger in this bitch of an existence. After all, what are sixty or eighty years of privation if Paradise lies at the end? Whereas if I listen to you I shall end up roasting in your furnace for eternity. No thanks! Be serious and, as the Other One says, *get thee behind me!*"

"But we're being perfectly serious. Before you throw me out listen to my proposition. I promise you it's very much in your favor."

"I've heard it all already," replied Jacques. "You want to buy my soul. I've only got one, and I'm hanging onto it. Anyway, I loathe materialism. What will you give me in exchange for my soul? Cars, castles, kitchen boys, yachts, checkbooks. Ugh! I would become one of those sinister millionaires who are eternally bored and have liver complaints. I prefer my soul, thanks to which I paint my pictures and they're good. If I sold you my soul I shouldn't paint any more. Now, I prefer to dash off a watercolor than to have a Rolls. With me you've fallen on barren ground, you see. Anyway, what sort of jerks do you normally deal with? It takes an artist to know the true price of things and not let himself be swindled."

"I could also give you love."

"Love!" cried Jacques. "What would I want with that? I know two dozen models in Montparnasse who are devoted to me and every now and then come to spend a few days with me. Keep your Beatrices and your Juliets: they'd be pregnant in a jiffy and I've enough worries as it is."

"And genius? I can give you genius too, since painting is the only thing you're interested in."

"Ah no," replied Jacques, "that just about takes the cake! You must be at the end of your tether, my poor friend. You're talking rubbish. Genius I already have. What I don't fully have is the certainty of my genius. But just think: it's far better that way. If I knew I was going to paint nothing but masterpieces, that I would never grope, never have to seek out my way in anguish, I'd never paint again. It would cease to amuse

me. Life is a gamble; right to the end one never knows
whether one will win. That's what makes it so stimulating.
Once you start cheating it's goodbye to excitement. And the
excitement is what *I* like. Good night to you."

"Wait," said the devil, "I'll be generous. I grant you this gold
coin every morning under your pillow. I ask nothing in exchange. My conditions are as follows: if for the rest of your
life you content yourself with living on a daily coin of gold,
I will leave you your soul. But once you need more you are
lost. Naturally all my treasures are at your disposal. You'll
only have to snap your fingers."

"A gold coin," said Jacques, "is a napoleon. On the market
that's worth roughly forty francs. Forty francs a day is not
enough to eat and buy canvases. So you're a skinflint into the
bargain! Go on, get out, scram! You're keeping me from my
work. In five, ten years I'll be as rich as Picasso. That's when
I shall need my soul! Artists are farsighted folk, my good man.
Content yourself with the bourgeoisie and politicians."

I had so thoroughly polished and memorized my story last
night that it didn't take me more than half an hour to write
it out. This morning's task went with such a swing that for
a few minutes I wondered whether I wouldn't seriously take
up writing as well as painting. I even went and messed about
with a blank canvas. But nothing's going to come of that
side of things for the time being. I must learn to put up
with this patiently. Sooner or later it will end. At 10 A.M.,
showered, shaved, bright as a new pin, I decided to venture
forth into the world and, for a start, take Tarzan to the vet
for a monster cleanup. Following this, buy him a wicker basket,
which would take its place at the foot of my bed. I must see
to the creature comforts of this good companion, with whom
I count on spending a number of years.

The telephone directory having informed me that a vet
by the name of Barbarin practices in the Boulevard Raspail,
three minutes from my place, I made my way there. It was the

first time I had ever penetrated a vet's waiting room. There were already three people waiting, a crone with a cat in a basket, a woman of around thirty, rather attractive, holding in her arms a white ball of fur of canine aspect, and a moth-eaten man of sixty clutching a dyspeptic Alsatian crippled with infirmity. These three persons were chatting together. When I entered with Tarzan the way they all looked at me made me realize that quite unwittingly I had just become a member of the mafia of animal lovers. I find such experiences enchanting. All at once, following on some instinctively performed action, one penetrates into a secret society. Virtues hide away as much as vices, or rather, one has to join the brotherhood before they reveal themselves. Only embark on a life of sin and you find out that So-and-So, whom you know well and who always seemed an open book, has preceded you long ago down the same path. Similarly, when you set out to befriend people, help the poor, comfort the unhappy, when you embrace the faith, you discover that someone you had assumed for twenty years to be indifferent, self-centered, and frivolous is a lay Franciscan who devotes half of his income to good works. I had a similar impression in M. Barbarin's waiting room, a sinister spot by the way, far from clean, furnished with tubular chairs and adorned with framed photographs of dogs all around the walls. I had hardly taken a seat before the pretty woman smiled at me with an air of complicity, the man offered me his paper, and the crone with the cat addressed me. One thing led to another and the conversation became general; I learned all about the animals there. If their owners could be believed they were exceptional beasts, with an intelligence far superior to that of humans, endowed with an unswerving goodness, fidelity, and trustworthiness. Whereupon I had to tell them about Tarzan. Impossible to dream up a better audience! I was a bard, a troubadour; they shuddered at my tale, they became incensed, they lavished compassion. I enjoyed a rare triumph. The pretty woman, on learning I was an artist, concluded from my beautiful zoophilist's soul that I must possess

considerable talent and asked for my address. Heavens! Was
this a potential mistress or client? She had lovely legs and
sumptuous crocodile-skin slippers. I found both possibilities
equally beguiling. I have rarely seen a face as horrific as that
of the old crone, who must be a positive hyena with her
family and friends but was now like a lamb, a seraph to her
cat, which looked to be in a pretty bad way. The contrast
was stupendous. This witch, reeking of malice, smothered her
little invalid with every attention, tender words, and caresses.
So she had a heart; she was capable of loving and suffering.
Her cat, poor humble little beast, had made this arid soul
blossom like the rose. The same went for the man, visibly
a moron, but this moron has a passion—his decrepit dog—and
here he sat transfigured. What a fascinating place a vet's waiting
room can be!

Barbarin, a fat and jovial fellow, talked to the animals
the way one does to children. His white smock, streaked with
dried blood, was even dirtier than the paint on his walls. A
flaxen-haired nurse, at least seven months pregnant, assisted
him, clad also in a dubious-looking smock.

"Well now," cried Barbarin, grabbing Tarzan by the scruff of
his neck and dumping him on the operating table, "let's see
what's the matter with us. We needn't be frightened, Doctor
Barbarin's going to make us well again in two shakes of our
tail. My, what a beautiful doggie we are!"

In spite of these soothing words, Tarzan was trembling in
every limb and kept casting imploring glances at me. His
panic redoubled when the vet forced open his jaws to study
his tonsils. For all my efforts to explain that my dog was as
fit as a fiddle and all I wanted was to have him washed
and deloused from top to bottom, Barbarin insisted on examining him and, to complete the job, stuffed a suppository of
vitamins up his backside to the accompaniment of the doubtless ritual phrase:

"Allez-oop! Good day, Madame!"

There ensued a voluble dissertation on the need to give

town dogs vitamins in order to supplement the blessings of
nature. Then Tarzan was for a second time swept into the air
by the scruff of his neck and handed over to the pregnant
nurse, Ghislaine by name, so that she could give him the full
beauty treatment, which was terrifying. This consists of shutting
the animal up for twenty minutes in an airtight box with burning
sulphur in it. Only its head is left in the open. Following this
all the fleas are dead and the patient is washed, dried, and
brushed. Cost: twenty francs. Plus consultation fee and the
suppository for which I never asked: fifteen francs. Sum total:
thirty-five francs. Notwithstanding this highway robbery, I
couldn't help feeling drawn toward Barbarin and Ghislaine,
who had a brisk and affectionate way with animals and seemed
genuinely fond of them. Ghislaine dragged Tarzan, digging all his
toes in and whimpering, toward a murky cubicle. I was so
distressed that, rather than return to collect him an hour later,
I stayed on to be present at the operation. At least poor Tarzan would be spared the horrible suspicion that, after having
been taken in and made much of for two whole days, I had abandoned him once again to his fate. While he was cooking in his
sterilizer I talked to him, but fear he was too panic-stricken
to appreciate my pleasantries. I also attended the rest of his
toilet, performed by Ghislaine, who, as she soaped and murmured words of comfort to the dog, told me her life story,
which offered little of interest. The chief fact to emerge from
it was that she is a "Miss" and that "baby's father" is showing
great reluctance to make an honest woman of her. When all
these ordeals were at last at an end and we found ourselves
back on the Boulevard Raspail Tarzan, seeing that I was still
there, that the sun was shining, that freedom existed once
more for dogs of good will, was seized with a frenzied joy translated into capers, leaps three feet in the air to kiss me, wild
barks, and a dozen other symptoms of madness. He was magnificently clean, his coat supple and shining, his muzzle gleaming, and he's already getting plump from the good dinners he
has devoured during the past forty-eight hours. A far cry

from the miserable cur saved from strangulation by Papa Raimondet. This is a different dog, who from now on will know
only health and happiness. After a detour via the Bon Marché
to buy the wicker basket (47 francs) I returned home, where
a surprise was awaiting me. The concierge had a parcel for
me: a red leather collar with gilt studs for posh poodles and a
leash made of a similarly gilt chain. This will suit Tarzan as
well as a mayor's robes would a street sweeper. Never mind:
the intention is touching. The parcel was accompanied by a
note:

> Darling, your dog must be well dressed and do honor to his
> genius of a master. That string was too hideous. Tell him this is a
> present from his Mama and give him a kiss on the snout for me. I
> was very happy to see you last night.
>
> Yours affectionately,
>
> *Lucienne*

It came from a shop in the Rue François Premier. The
dear angel must have ruined herself. I called her up at once
to thank her. Lucienne is decidedly an exceptional woman.
This present, the first she has ever given me, didn't make her
the least bit emotional, as I might well have feared and as
would certainly have happened with an ordinary woman after
such an outstanding event. Affectionate, certainly, glad to have
caused me pleasure, but nothing more. No misplaced sentimentality. If anyone deserves the title of Goddess of Reason
it's Lucienne. Her note is a model of its kind. Save for the
style, it's like the love letters they used to write in the eighteenth
century.

Once back home, I didn't feel like going out again. My desire
to explore the world had subsided. I lunched off a few leftovers: stale bread, sausage, fried eggs, plus an old stump of
Saint-Marcellin cheese. This type of snack gives me as much
pleasure as the richest feast. Finishing off leftovers provides a

rare satisfaction; one gets the illusion of living for free, snatching a meal from Fate, not to mention the happiness induced by the feeling that one has made the very most of one's outlay and let positively nothing go to waste. I feel a similar sort of contentment when, after working for ten or twelve hours non-stop, I suddenly realize I am dead with fatigue, my mind is completely empty, scoured like a saucepan, and it would be impossible for me to lay even one additional stroke of paint on my canvas. Ah, what a sweet passion avarice is and how misunderstood! I wouldn't need much encouragement to claim that nothing great can be accomplished without it. It adduces to my mind incomparable delights of order and precision. The miser only takes from nature what is strictly necessary for his subsistence, meaning that he respects this good, nutritious Nature and shrinks from eating into it, anxious to bequeath it as intact as possible to future generations. Like all benefactors his only reward is mockery, and from those very people for whose sake he has deprived himself. All their admiration goes to the prodigal, the irresponsible, who devour the world as if it belonged to them by right. Thanks to Tarzan, from now on I shall never throw anything away.

Another pleasure of my frugal lunch: while I ate I read Ingres's thoughts, more succulent than any sauce or *foie gras* in the world. These seasoned my leftovers and gave them savor. Could anyone imagine words more sublime than these, copied out here for my future guidance?

> *Form is not in the contour, it lies within the contour. Shadow is not an addition to the contour but makes it. A reflection on the shadows of the contour is unworthy of the majesty of art.*

Munching my stale cheese on my stale bread, washed down with a few drops of red wine, I embarked on an interminable daydream, glowing with a truly filial affection for old Ingres, who could speak of his art in a manner so profound and so rewarding. His paintings and drawings were very vivid to my mind. I could visualize them quite clearly, and found them even more beautiful for knowing what spiritual strength their creator had drawn from the practice of his art. I recalled an anecdote, told to me long ago by poor Derain on one of our rare encounters, and this carried my emotion to a peak. The young Derain went to see Degas, who was then old, blind, and living on the third or fourth floor. Degas, who was about to go out, asked Derain to accompany him. On the stairs his foot missed a step; he tripped and stumbled into the arms of Derain, who caught him and half carried him down to the landing. "This reminds me of something that once happened to me," said Degas. "When I was twenty-five I had occasion to visit Monsieur Ingres. He was also just about to go out. We went down the stairs together. He too missed a step and fell into my arms." In short, I had one of those splendid times that solitude now and then (even quite often) offers one. A good coffee as only I can make it to round it off, and I was feeling, if not cheerful properly speaking, at any rate nice and warm inside and full of all kinds of confused but bright hopes. As you can see, there's nothing like good company. Ingres, Degas, Derain—these are companions after my own heart. Their three ghosts, just then, were more real, more present than many living people I know. They were still close to me when I lighted my pipe and went to subside into my big armchair, so that I could pursue a daydream that was giving me such pleasure. Even Tarzan, discreetly nudging his cold nose against my hand in the guise of a kiss, failed to jerk me out of it.

It took nothing less than the ringing of the telephone bell at about three o'clock to bring me back to the dreary business of living. It was my sister-in-law Véronique, and I could gladly have consigned her to the devil with her rapid social drawl, which in view of the circumstances she felt obliged to make sound silly. Since I am going to refloat Georges and have thus promoted myself to the rank of an official benefactor, she cooed away at me like a sick pigeon. That is the way people like her express their respect or affections. She pressed me so hard to go and lunch with them tomorrow that I finally gave in, though not before I had been driven half mad by the silly cow's clichés. Another case of conjugal mimicry: Véronique has the same arsenal of ready-made phrases as her husband. Come just as you are, it'll only be potluck (which I detest, by the way: I like people to make an effort for me, particularly when they are relieving me of a hundred thousand francs), I know how you artists are, you hate a lot of fuss; Georges has told me all about it, you've been marvelous; we *must* meet more often (thanks for nothing!); there are times in life when we need to stick together; you should hear Georges talking about you, he can't sing your praises enough; he's told me *mahvelous* things about your latest pictures; you *must* let me see them—and so on for ten minutes. Enough to kill one with boredom. One wonders why such creatures are endowed with speech, and what use it is to them. A woman like Véronique has certainly never made one original remark or expressed one interesting thought all her life. Anyway, here I am saddled with this family lunch. What an odd nature I have! Yesterday I was like a tiger with poor Mesnard, and today I'm incapable of telling that fool Véronique: "It's already appalling enough having to fork out, since I must, without being dragged off to lunch with you on top of it; one might as well cut one's throat right away." Strange Pluche! Will tomorrow be the day I get financially skinned? It seems to me a bit abrupt, all the same. If my memory serves me right, my brother mentioned a delay of several weeks before having to pay. I think instead that they want to cosset me, make sure I am still well disposed, suck up to me as if I were a rich uncle, raise me to a high degree of combustion. Lord, they think I'm as stupid as themselves!

This phone call had such an unpleasant effect on me that I have tried to analyze it. It plainly stems from my wretched hundred thousand francs. On the one hand, the idea of parting with the money crucifies me; on the other, something inside impels me to do so. When one is prey to a conflict of this kind, everything that reminds one of it is hateful, especially those who are the cause of it. Whence my start of revulsion on hearing Véronique's voice and, after hanging up, my despair at the thought of having to spend two hours in the company of my executioners tomorrow.

From time to time I surprise myself by doing things that everything in me condemns: reason, self-interest, and even my will. It is as if my salvation depended on it. To be honest, what is driving me to ruin myself for a brother I dislike? All these dirty financial dealings involving the name I bear, that my father and grandfather bore, that I proudly inscribe in the corner of my pictures? No, let's be serious. Such considerations have nothing to do with it. Today everyone is dishonest; successful writers boast of having been thieves and sent to prison; my brother's swindles wouldn't give rise to the slightest prejudice against myself, even if it ever came out that he is my brother, which is most unlikely. It's no good beating about the bush. I know perfectly well that the root of the matter lies elsewhere: in the remote corner of my character where lurks that sense of duty which has so often irked me throughout my life and led me to perform senseless actions. I have been like this from childhood, deliberately adopting the most difficult course of action so that my conscience might be wholly at rest and my soul scrubbed clean. I can see hidden but very strong ties between this propensity and my taste for order and economy. I cannot tolerate disorder in myself; any task left undone and lying about in my mind like a piece of clothing in an untidy room makes me feel miserable. When Georges came to touch me the other day I knew at once that I would cough up. Why? Precisely because I could easily have got out of it and any ordinary person would have done so, because it's the type of heroic deed proffered to me from time to time by Fate, which I have to carry out at all costs for reasons at once compelling and obscure. And so the course of my life is studded with great difficulties that could be avoided; nevertheless I force myself to opt for them out of an excessive desire for inner purity and an almost metaphysical horror of easy solutions. These choices are scarcely pleasant and I don't forbear to curse my lot, yet I always make them, feeling that they fit in with the general purport of my life, in which nothing is easy, nothing is had for nothing but, on the contrary, everything has to be won against heavy odds.

Something it would be amusing to tackle one day would be an analysis of all the latent bourgeois sentiments that still linger on in artists, however great they may be. Indeed, it should never be forgotten that artists, before becoming artists, have been either middle-class children like me or else children of the people, that is to say nurtured on a certain morality, brought up according to certain middle-class or working-class traditions. Whence in every artist (and probably in me) a more or less considerable part of his being still functions according to bourgeois standards. One of my artist friends may be quite uninhibited when it comes to love and yet at the same time a blatant chauvinist and flag-waver, as militaristic as a veteran of the 1914 war; another, an out-and-out anarchist, suffers from sleepless nights when he owes the butcher a hundred francs. These discrepancies strike me very forcibly; I have observed them time and again. And the Birotteau side of artists! How widespread it is! With this difference, that it isn't our own bankruptcies we pay off but those of others. The sense of honesty and honor is far more developed in us than in the bourgeois, because our spirits are very staunch, fortified by the practice of our art at the same time as being very artless. There is nothing staunch or artless about the bourgeois, who easily yields to dishonesty, complaisance, and vice.

These powerful vestiges of bourgeois morality assume a particular prominence in an artist's life and, by their contrast, enhance it all the more. Writing this, I naturally have in mind Flaubert and Degas, stripping themselves bare to pay their families' debts. It seems to me that were such deplorable episodes missing from their life stories, these would be less beautiful, less exemplary. And who knows whether such ordeals weren't profitable to them? Degas, become poor, changed his themes, his models, and his style. In the paintings done in the second half of his life there is a hardness and a pity thanks to which he found his true genius. Without daring to compare myself with these masters, I cannot help drawing a kind of comfort from the fact that I'm a victim of the same misfortune and it gladdens me to think that in this respect I have the same soul as they had. Finally, dare I admit it? I have the ineradicable conviction that nothing but good can ever happen to me. In spite of my hand-to-mouth existence I have always had the feeling of being protected by something. Protected—nothing more than that; not helped nor borne along toward fame; but it is already a great deal, even the main thing, to be protected. Penury at seventy, when one's creative power has declined, what a catastrophe! At forty-five, on the other hand, it may well be a blessing. In ten years' time I ought to know whether I needed to be ruined and whether Providence once again knew better than I did what was necessary for me.

About an hour after my talk with Véronique, Marie rang me in turn. This call nettled me no less than the first one. "Hello, is that you, Pluche?" she said in a voice I found odd, at once gay and on edge. "What did you do to Albert yesterday? He's completely changed." According to her I must have given the poor man a sort of moral shake-up: he must have felt his whole life rock beneath his feet! After my departure he apparently remained more or less prostrate for several hours, giving himself up to a complete examination of his conscience, holding everything up to question, mulling over my reproaches, and trying his best to exculpate himself in his own eyes. Finally he went down to his wife and abruptly announced that he wouldn't be wanting a divorce after all. He asked her to forgive him for having neglected her so long, for his coldness, his drifting away from her; he questioned her at great length as to her health, made her promise to look after herself properly, declared that he was going to take charge

of things and send her to ten doctors if need be. Whereupon
he called in his daughter and kissed her for five minutes on end.
In short, the return of the prodigal husband.

As for me, delighted to learn that against all expectations
my outburst had had some effect, that Mesnard was less wet
than I thought, and that, without expressly meaning to, I had
done my sister a splendid turn, I exclaimed: "Bravo! That's
wonderful! You must be terribly pleased!" But human beings
are hard to satisfy. The trace of anger I had detected in
Marie's voice suddenly rose to the surface and the crazy girl
blasted off at me: I had been too harsh, I had struck too hard.
Mesnard had emerged from my manhandling quite demoralized,
half dead. It was less of a husband I had handed back to
my sister than a ghost, an ectoplasm. You don't speak to a man,
an artist, a sensitive person, the way I did. No offense can
justify such violence. I had broken something in this frail spirit.
Had Marie known it was at the price of a sort of moral murder
that she would get her darling back she'd have opposed it,
she'd rather have sacrificed herself. Naturally she wasn't denying she ought to be grateful to me, but now she was going to
have to put what I had squashed flat back on its feet again,
and that was going to be no easy matter. She had already
made a start, however, welcoming the fickle wretch back
as if nothing had been wrong, explaining to him that his daubs
are not as bad as all that, that brotherly love made me go
too far, that she, Marie, has faith in him, admires him, and so
on and so forth.

Hearing Marie carrying on like an infatuated cow really
turned my stomach. I told her she was a fool, no better than all
the other fools who people the earth and always assume an air
of disgust when one brings them happiness, on the grounds that
one has held it out to them with the left hand instead of the right.
I added that I wouldn't take back one iota of my harangue
to Mesnard (who incidentally has only given her a rather vague
account of it, confining himself to saying that I was merciless)
and that I looked on the said Mesnard as a lousy artist whose

only talent consisted in earning millions and running up an endless chain of daubs. "And at bottom," I concluded, "that suits you down to the ground. Your only fear is that he might stop laying turds and begin to paint good pictures which mightn't sell so well. You're tortured by the idea of no longer having lovely cars, Givenchy dresses, menservants, your Parc Montsouris palace, your gilded life as a dauber's wife. In my own way I love and respect Mesnard more than you do. I may have hurt him but I was trying to save his soul. Whereas you, with your kissing it better, your forgiveness, your encouragement, your adulation, are pushing him down again into the mire."

We squabbled on like this for quite a while. However, Marie has a different temperament from her husband's. After having bawled each other out over the telephone, both of us hurling exaggerations that the other knew the true measure of, she declared superbly:

"If I didn't love Albert, I should still feel toward him like Princess Mathilde, who wouldn't let anyone run Napoleon down in front of her and used to say: 'If it weren't for him, I'd be selling oranges at Ajaccio.' Well, *I'm* telling you the same thing, Pluche. I don't want to hear anything nasty about Albert, even from you."

"If Albert is Napoleon," I retorted, "then I'm Sganarelle. I return your husband to his marriage bed with a ripe kick in the arse and all you can find to say to me is: 'And what if I like being deceived?' "

We both burst out laughing, and this reconciled us. All the same, I shan't act as a retriever again in a hurry!

What a pest women are, and how I congratulate myself on being a bachelor! Nine times out of ten the little darlings debase the man they love. They contrive to place him in such situations that he is forced to deny himself, dishonor himself, capitulate, betray what was pure and strong in him. Marie herself, who is worth more than many others and in certain respects is a truly superior woman, behaves in just the same

way. In the nineteenth century young gentlemen used to ruin
themselves for actresses or tarts; they became debauched and
dishonest, ran up debts as big as themselves, lost their health
in gambling dens and their lives in duels. In the depths of the
provinces their virtuous parents died of grief, cursing the de-
praved creature who had corrupted one of the white hopes of
the legal profession. The fate of an artist who marries a bourgeois
woman seems to me no less deplorable, although with the
opposite results. The tart ruins the bourgeois, and the bourgeois
woman makes the artist rich. Each, in her own way, destroys
her man. Oh Marie, Marie, who would have thought that one
day I would write such things with you in mind!

I ought to rejoice that Mesnard has turned over a new
leaf: it is my doing and implies that he has preserved a
certain moral integrity, a certain rectitude. But I cannot manage
it. I find his reaction surprising and not wholly gratifying.
Ten years of studied imperturbability ending up with this
maudlin scene worthy of Greuze's brush is not the sign of a
very staunch spirit. Was this hard shell of the dandy of the art
world only cardboard then, and did it take only a snap of
the fingers to reduce it to shreds? Had I known, I'd have
snapped my fingers sooner. Mesnard had a good opportunity
yesterday to make use of his impassivity; he should have swallowed what I said to him without a frown and shown us
by his behavior in three or six months' time that he had not
been deaf to my admonitions. I mistrust these feminine natures
which suddenly turn tail, give vent to a lot of emotional
claptrap, and run to weep on their spouses' bosoms. Nothing
is more suspect than these "moral shake-ups." They last for
forty-eight hours, after which the fellow reverts to his former
ways. Besides, what is a moral shake-up? I have never experienced any such thingamajig. At any rate, just supposing
Mesnard has a genuine inclination to make amends, Marie is
there to nurture the seed. I note that no mention was made
of the Duchateau girl. How is he going to settle this detail?
Will he drop her? Will she tiptoe out of his life, furious at

having been left at the altar? To tell the truth, I couldn't care less and have no wish to know. The main thing is that Mesnard's not going to divorce after all, since this divorce was making Marie suffer.

I've left out one rather nice detail. During our brawl on the telephone Marie, in order to soften me up by contrasting Mesnard's generous nature with my barbarousness, announced that he wants to see me again and have a further talk with me. He regrets our estrangement. He feels a kind of gratitude to me. Such a reaction shows what a difference there is between our characters. Now, if someone had talked to me the way I talked to Mesnard, I would have foamed at the mouth, I would have been bitterly resentful, and then, the next day or the day after, without saying a word, without admitting to any of it, I would have turned such criticism to the best account, granted that it was apt. My way may shock, may seem unattractive; even so, I prefer it to my brother-in-law's. It's healthier. So I shall go back in two or three days' time to the Castel. It rather amuses me to see Mesnard in the role of a penitent, with myself acting as his director of conscience. Marie's happiness has to be secured in spite of her silly squawking. To hell with Mesnard and his conscience; in my eyes he is just an instrument, that of the happiness of his wife and daughter, and this comes first and foremost with me.

One person who is going to be pleased and proud of me, and who I hope won't accuse me of having made Daddy cry, is Lise. The more so in that Mesnard, who is a good and solicitous father, loves her dearly and gives her endless proof of it with those presents for which he has such an instinct. Children are scarcely at ease when they know they are the only tie between their father and mother. They have to spend the whole time making up lies to each in turn, not lies of self-interest, what one might call natural lies in order to cover up their lapses, but lies of politeness, complicated lies demanding imagination and spirit, in order to smooth over difficulties as much as possible, spare feelings, create the illusion that they are happy and haven't understood what is going on. Such lies do children the greatest credit; they provide a measure of their delicacy. At least they would do so if parents weren't as a rule so blind and obtuse. From what I know of my niece I feel certain that for the past six months she has been doing her utmost to conceal from the eyes of Mesnard and Marie that frightening perspicacity children have, whereby nothing of what is taking place in the hearts of grownups escapes them.

Strange things, daydreams. When I give myself up to one I know I shan't snap out of it without an effort. This afternoon I was at home and feeling thoroughly relaxed. My daydream did not confine itself to occupying my mind; it circulated through my limbs, it numbed me all over. Lying back almost flat in my armchair, I abandoned myself to this inner loitering which has no end, where one sees the same scenery a hundred times over without tiring of it, where nothing can harm one since everything is muffled by curtains of intellectual fog. In this it resembles certain pictures painted by masters so bowed down with years that they can hardly see any longer. There is no architecture in them, no composition, only a fleeting drafts-manship, a hodgepodge of colors, and yet from time to time, without rhyme or reason, an exquisite and incongruous design emerges from this magma. Such boneless pictures can some-times give the greatest pleasure. For myself, I never weary of them, and one of my happiest memories is that of an after-noon in London long ago, spent wholly in contemplation of the dozens of Turners hanging in the Tate Gallery. Those of his last years are prodigious. One cannot tell where are the sky, the sea, the sun, the ships; everything is fused together, everything intermingles; and yet there is no chaos, rather the contrary: a sort of prophetic vision of nature reconciled with itself, seized at the moment of its final metamorphosis, when its countless elements melt into each other before returning to the bosom of their Creator. Such is the kind of happiness I find in daydreaming. It jumbles all my ideas and feelings together, breaks them down into a host of particles that merge

together in an elemental embrace. Generally I mistrust this
opium and hardly ever smoke it, for one has to paint, in other
words bang away at the world like a deaf man so as to leave
a mark on it, but today I thought I'd risk it. I had no work,
no inspiration to preserve; I'd have been a fool to deprive
myself. I believe daydreaming is contagious: Tarzan, a few
feet away, was dreaming too; I wasn't mistaken; he had the
glazed eye and absent air of those who have descended very
deep inside themselves. Anyway, it is rare for daydreaming not
to bring with it some motif of hope, of diffuse joy, since it
effortlessly and painlessly leads you down into the caverns of
the subconscious where treasures lie hidden. On returning to
the surface one remembers what one glimpsed on the journey,
gleaming in the fitful light—gold and pearls that you may not
touch but that you know are yours.

Being in a spiritual vein this evening I went out at seven
o'clock with the intention of buying myself a couple of slices
of ham and a pound of apples for my supper. I should have
known better! No sooner in the delicatessen than the beast
in me began to paw the ground: I treated myself to the best
things the place had to offer: rabbit *pâté,* celery salad, saveloy,
cold roast veal, red caviar, and pickled gherkins. I added a
bottle of Chiroubles to round it off and a slice of orange tart,
the specialty of the place. Following this a good pipe—always
the best part of the meal—and so, to quote Master Pepys, to
bed.

CHAPTER XIII

Middle-Class Manners

> *"Your poor brother," said
> David to his wife, who was
> just recovering from a con-
> finement, "is in frightful diffi-
> culties. I have sent him three
> bills payable in one, two and
> three months' time. Make a
> note of it."*
>
> BALZAC

Dear Sir and Honored Colleague,

I have read your Sunday epistle with the liveliest interest
and find it remarkable for an idea at once profound and un-
original, and this as we know is the criterion of all great works.
Everything you have to say is true, naturally. Possibly it tends
toward overphilosophizing. When one is a painter it's a bad
thing to go in for philosophy; this gets reflected in one's work
and one is inclined to put too much black in shadows or to
break out into cubes. There was a fellow from Lyons in the
nineteenth century who philosophized like mad—Chenavard I
think it was. Result: his pictures are the bottom. Ditto for André

Lhote, another philosopher of the palette. If you keep on walking down the Rue Hallé, in five years' time you'll be churning out horrors fit to delight the intelligentsia, you'll have exhibitions in New York, they'll be publishing art books in full color on your daubs, and I shall come and spit on your doorstep. This warning had to be given.

Your world-shaking theory about truth in art has inspired me to write a fable in imitation of Hans Andersen, and this I submit for your benevolent approval. The townspeople watch the emperor pass by stark naked and all cry in unison: "What splendid clothes!" The bad artist at the front of the crowd paints these clothes showing every detail; fur collar, red velvet, gold frogging, boots of Russian leather, hat with ostrich feathers incarnadine. Strollers gather round him and admiringly declare: "What a wonderful likeness!" The good artist at the back of the crowd draws in his sketchbook a fat slob in his birthday suit with fat, hairy calves, fat white belly, and fat green buttocks. The people looking over his shoulder declare that he has no talent and his sketch is a load of crap. The Mothers' Union has him flung into jail for lèse-majesté. Meanwhile the bad artist exhibits his stinker at the Salon and is voted a government grant.

What I found interesting in your screed is what you have to say about the mainstream of painting. You're right, it no longer exists. Art ought to be practiced in communal fashion, with chief clerks, underlings, and errand boys who are there to learn the trade. Today people are painters in the same way as they are dentists or watchmakers, all by themselves in their back rooms. A depressing outlook. Masters, I cry in the wilderness, find me masters who will pass on the sacred flame to the generations of daubers to come! Alas! There are no masters! Only slaves (of fashion). Our craft is on the verge of disappearing altogether.

One thing which seems to me typical of the fatuity of contemporary painters, surrealists and postsurrealists in particular, is that these bums, just like the palsied practitioners of 1880, imagine they have revolutionized art simply because they have changed its subject matter. They paint jolly nudes with cows'

heads. But they overwork them just as they did a hundred years
ago at the Salon des Artistes Français, like Carrier-Belleuse or
Roybet. Rather less well, actually. When it comes to style,
Magritte is way below Bouguereau although in the same line
of descent. To think we have had to reach our own memorable
and luminous epoch to fall back into that ancient booby trap
consisting of judging a picture not on its texture, coloring, tonal
values, and technique but on what it represents! Really one
could weep! It all boils down to the old quarrel of academism.
The academic artists of today paint females with cows' heads
academically.

If you want my opinion, painting is done for. It died about
fifty years ago with the last Impressionists. Since then, we've
had nothing but hideous botches, incompetence, driveling, or—
what's worse—virtuosity. Even a talented fellow like Picasso no
longer knows what to do. Besides, he's been ga-ga for the
past twenty years. Painters spend their time inventing theories
or cooking up philosophies. Why? I'll tell you: so as to conceal
their ignorance, to lend an air of grandeur to their facility, their
laziness, their aberrant researches. They have achieved the
staggering result of being a combination of ignorance and virtuosity. The critics and collectors no longer care for truth. They
only admire this virtuosity, which is worthless. Any true and
sincere meaning exasperates them. Anyone who disdains virtuosity, that is to say refuses to speak when he has nothing to say,
strikes them as vulgar.

Of course, there's always Lord Pluche, who works in an aura of
genius and occasionally pulls off a delicate masterpiece. But do
you really think you'll be able to put painting back in the saddle
all on your own? I wonder! It's a sad fate to be a great artist
in a debased age. One is misunderstood and despised during
one's lifetime, without even having the certainty that things
will improve when one is dead. At any rate, you at least manage
to do what you like; you aren't forced to decorate suburban
town halls like less fortunate people burdened with families and
bowed down by the weight of their responsibilities. Even so,

Pluche has soul-searchings, Pluche anxiously contemplates his navel, hoping that another "Raft of the Medusa" or "Massacre at Chios" will sprout from it! By the way, what news of your idiot brother? When do you have to cough up? You must let me meet this estimable sucker one day. I love such types. And this is to my credit, since they hardly ever buy my wares.

Bearing the above in mind, dear sir and honored colleague, I beg to remain:

Léonce-Agénor de la Ville-Boulard, painter in ordinary to the King and to their worships the Municipal Councilors of Corne-au-Cul sur Yvette

I found this letter of Boulard's so good that I pasted it into my journal directly it came. In it he says all sorts of things that have my unconditional support. I like its tone; it reads exactly the way he talks, like an indomitable student discussing basic principles. Here is a letter from a real friend, a man who thinks the same way as oneself about fundamentals. Nothing could be nicer than receiving a good letter like this when one wakes up, a letter to mull over while dipping toast in one's coffee. Most people nowadays, given that they hardly ever write letters any more, being spared by the telephone, have no idea what pleasures they deprive themselves of. Another reason for regretting the life of the eighteenth century, that supreme age of letter writing. It's just my luck: given my loathing of science, I have to be born in the middle of the only civilization based on science that the world has known so far. I missed the bus by about a hundred years. When I think that I could have died in 1895 or 1912, after having been one of the highlights of the admirable nineteenth century like Manet or Degas, it's as much as I can do not to weep from nostalgia.

At a quarter to one I made my way to Georges, who lives in a luxury-type apartment in a Baron Haussmann-style building in the Rue Boissière. Exactly the sort of place where I would pine away, not that it is particularly sinister (on the contrary, the apartment isn't badly situated on the fourth floor and it enjoys the sun for a good part of the day) but the house has a respectable, tight-lipped, falsely smart air which to me stinks, and its surroundings—namely the Avenue Kléber, the Rue de Lubeck, and the Rue Hamelin—ooze the smugness and bad taste of the new-rich middle classes of 1880. It's the ideal setting for Georges. When we used to live in the Boulevard des Batignolles he must have dreamed of setting up his tent one day in this elegant locality, which forms a major upward step in a man's success story. Véronique's expression when she saw that I had a dog with me was a perfect study: vexed at the idea that Tarzan might pee on her carpets and that she would have to feed this useless extra mouth, yet not daring to show it and putting on a brave face against adversity. As I went in I winced. The place had been repainted from top to bottom, with wall-to-wall carpets and even luxury fittings (at least, that contemptible and absurd luxury in which everyone takes such pride these days).

I hadn't been expecting anything like this and my surprise must have registered on my face, for Véronique immediately plunged into an interminable explanation: all this redecoration and improvement had been embarked on three months ago, before that crook Marchepied had made off with the cash, just when Georges had reckoned he was in clover. An ironic fate saw to it that Georges learned of his ruin on the very day the painters were applying the final coat and the carpet layer was hammering in the last nail. "If only we'd known!" wailed the poor woman in a voice at once so desolate and so conventional that I had to bite my tongue not to burst out laughing. One must admit, there is here a highly comic concatenation of circumstances thanks to which, once again, one is brought full face with the fecklessness, improvidence, and incurable lack of responsibility of the bourgeoisie—that levelheaded breed, those models of good sense and prudence. To saddle oneself with all this redecoration, which must cost around thirty thousand francs, relying for the wherewithal on money that hasn't yet come in,

is just the sort of "middle-class madness" that nine times out of
ten leads to disaster.

Funniest of all is the fact that Georges cannot even afford
to quit his apartment and retire with his family into a couple
of attics, as he would have done a century ago, for one thing
because attics don't exist any more, and for another because the
cost of renting three rooms at Vaugirard would come to more
than what he pays in the Rue Boissière, which is an old building
where he has been a tenant for a long time. "And this," concluded Véronique with a wry smile, "is how one can be poor
nowadays with every appearance of being well off!" Following
which she undertook to show me over the apartment from end
to end, even insisting that I inspect the john, freshly papered
with a floral design in the Persian manner. This business of being
shown around the apartment, to which one proceeds before
anything else, is a *must* in such circles. On the rare occasions
when I have taken meals in bourgeois households, I've always
been treated to it. They want to show off their good taste, their
comfort, their imagination regarding questions of furniture and
decoration. Could anything be more grotesque? Who do these
people take themselves for? Do they suppose their rabbit hutch
rivals Versailles? That one is going to be knocked all of a heap?
I suppose they can't get over the fact of having fixed themselves such a charming interior. Nothing gets me down so much
as these posturings. I don't give a damn whether their lavatory
is pink or blue and the curtains are of Genoese velvet. On the
two or three occasions when, out of politeness, I complimented
her on some hideous table or ornament, Véronique, like all her
kind, did not fail to reveal the price she paid for it at the flea
market or some bargain counter. She too was seized five or six
months ago with the mania for prematurely counting her chick-
ens and, just like her fool of a husband, began to chase around
the antique shops, where she picked up a fine assortment of junk
for which she probably wouldn't get a thousand francs the lot
were she to try to sell it again. That at least is my personal reck-
oning, though I charitably refrained from intimating as much to

her, touched as I was by the naïve way she sought to convince me that she had made a series of brilliant bargains. Yet another middle-class mania—describing how one has acquired some treasure for a song. Always this vanity. In the old days it was the smart thing to throw one's money out the window; but nowadays they pride themselves on the bargains they have made, which go to show how immensely knowledgeable they are. What with all this, I was dying of hunger and longing to pass on to more serious matters. I had forgotten the ceremony of the aperitif. Véronique, after showing me all around, led me back to the sitting room, where I found the family group awaiting me: Papa flanked by young Alain and Marie-Christine. Tarzan, startled by this stolid altarpiece with its two side panels, began to bark with rage, which is quite unusual for him and, all in all, was a fairly accurate translation of my state of mind.

The chief adornment of the sitting room is a large painting by Mesnard, a Size 50 canvas superbly framed, a gift of the artist to his brother-in-law and Georges's prize possession. Naturally it is an unmitigated horror dating from 1961 or '62. At the sight of this monstrosity occupying the place of honor I felt a twinge of resentment. I too once gave a picture to these Ostrogoths. Where the devil had they stashed it away? In some attic or down in the cellar. I don't pretend it was a masterpiece, but anyway it was worth ten Mesnards. For these people without taste to prefer a bad painting to a good one just because they are dazzled by the fame of its painter is only to be expected; but they could at least be polite. Or if not polite, then adroit. It would have required a mere minimum of forethought to dig my picture out of its hole, even if only to flatter the self-esteem of their financial savior. And it never even occurred to them. Such stupidity is barely credible. When I think it over, it's even more their stupidity than their turpitude that annoys me. Marie apart, I really can't claim to be cherished by my family! This matter of the picture stuck in my gullet and spoiled my lunch, though this was quite passable; but I took my revenge rather treacherously over coffee, when the three of us—Véron-

ique, Georges, and myself—were left to confer over their misfortune: I strongly advised them to sell the Mesnard, which is
worth a good ten thousand francs. To rub their noses well into
it, I added that this would mean I should only have to lend them
ninety thousand francs instead of a hundred thousand.

"But one can't sell something that's been given to one," muttered Georges weakly. "It wouldn't be correct." (*Correct* is
superb.)

"Oh, come off it!" I jauntily replied. "Necessity knows no law.
If Mesnard knew you needed to flog his picture to get your-
selves out of a jam, he'd urge you to do it like me. And while
we're about it, why don't you also sell that picture of mine I
gave you a few years back? It would bring you in a good
thousand or two. Do that, old man, you have my full permission. I even insist on it. Incidentally, where is my picture? I
don't seem to have seen it. . . ."

Georges's and Véronique's agonized expressions amply re-
warded me. Both of them distinctly blushed. Being the less
sheepish, Véronique was the first to recover her poise.

"But," she exclaimed rather too shrilly, "your painting is quite
lovely, we both simply *adore* it, don't we Georges? You'll never
guess why you haven't seen it. Imagine, it's at the framer's. The
old frame it had wasn't nearly good enough for it, so we decided to give it a new one. It certainly needed it, hee-hee-hee!"

I must have a residue of malice hidden deep in my character,
since my brother and sister-in-law's confusion gave me real joy.
I couldn't resist the pleasure of prolonging it. It isn't every day
one gets the chance to revenge oneself for thirty years' contempt.

"But you're crazy!" I cried, putting on a fine show of in-
dignation. "You're up to the ears in debt and you go and choose
this moment to buy a new frame. You must be raving! Do you
know what a good frame runs to? At least three hundred francs!
The cost of half a hundredweight of fillet steaks. No, but really,
you can't mean it! Georges, you've got me worried! Even worse,
scared. I'm telling you seriously, it's high time you realized the

extent of your disaster and drew the inevitable conclusions. I'm prepared to make a very heavy sacrifice for you but I don't want it to be a useless one."

Get me, teaching the bourgeoisie a lesson, and in their own terms! What a farce! I put on a tremendous act, assuming the tone of old man Duval dressing down his son. The cream of it was that they listened to me with profound respect. Damn it, for once I was speaking the tribal tongue; I was being understood. I could even see a sort of surprise and admiration growing in my audience. Pluche the layabout, Pluche the wastrel, the dauber, the eternal child was showing how he had a head on his shoulders. And I didn't let it go at that. I demanded a complete breakdown of the situation, which I shall now try to describe here in all its details. Besides, it has a certain interest on the sociological plane, offering as it does an insight into the difference in the conception of ruin nowadays as compared with the past.

In the nineteenth century a ruined man was indeed well and truly ruined; he sold everything he had in order to meet his creditors and failing this he was carted off to the debtors' prison. This disastrous conclusion was preceded by a scarifying fandango of promissory notes, protests, and distraints. A bankruptcy tarnished the family name down to the third generation. I don't deny that there still exists a sort of honor in the business world and that certain businessmen may die of chagrin as a result of going bankrupt; nevertheless it has to be admitted that this sense of honor is less punctilious and widespread than it was in 1840, probably for the reason that the material sanctions are less grave. Society has become modified in such a way that total ruin, pitilessly stripping a once wealthy man bare and reducing him to penury, is no longer possible save in a few very rare and unfortunate cases. My brother Georges provides an excellent example of this change in custom. In the first place, as I have said, he isn't moving out of his apartment, which is of vital importance for one's self-respect and reputation. Secondly, he can be sure of never being absolutely penniless. In fact, he has what is known as a good position, being some sort of manager in an industrial firm. Whereas I can recall its name—Porfirex—I am quite incapable of defining its activities.

Georges, having passed through the state civil engineering school, has a diploma in "Arts and Manufactures." Such qualified men are, so it seems, choice morsels for private industries, which snap them up greedily. In this way my brother earns seven thousand five hundred francs a month from Porfirex by pursuing some daily occupation, although I haven't the faintest idea what. When I heard this figure of seven thousand five hundred francs, which had hitherto been kept carefully concealed from me, I felt a faint flicker of hope. It seemed like El Dorado. How could a man earning that much need my miserable savings into the bargain? But alas! He does, there's no getting around it. As I might have known, the hole dug by the vile Marchepied is far deeper than had at first been reckoned. Georges spread out before me a mass of papers of every conceivable hue (predominantly the blue of summonses), from which it emerged that he has to pay over three hundred thousand francs. He has already forked out half this amount, having sold all his investments (for the slyboots had a portfolio) and obtained from Porfirex an advance on salary amounting to eighty thousand francs. The shares, disposed of in a hurry, were naturally sold at their lowest market value. As for Porfirex, he has to repay the loan over the next two years, and this will be done automatically by withholding part of his salary to the tune of three thousand five hundred francs a month. In short, out of his monthly seven thousand five hundred, Georges has only four thousand francs left, with which he has to contrive to keep his home going, pay his taxes, pay a rent that increases every quarter, settle the balance of the decorators' and carpet layer's bills (around fifteen thousand francs) and put aside a further modest sum toward the fifty thousand which still have to be found to cover his debts. When I said that I was unlikely to see my savings again, I was just about right. This genius is in debt for the next ten years at least. The poor wretch will have to go on a starvation diet for a hell of a long time. He has sold his car and dismissed the maid. It was Véronique herself who cooked today's lunch—a futile expense, to my way of thinking, and I now regret even more not having let them off it, in view of the little pleasure it gave me. In future I shall find no difficulty in being much firmer. All in all, the problem amounts to this: maintaining four people on a thousand or fifteen hundred francs a month. It's going to be no picnic.

With Georges and Véronique I tried to plan an austerity campaign for the next three or four years. I think I finally persuaded them to sell the Mesnard. There is also my sister-in-law's jewelry, which should fetch ten thousand francs. And Véronique will have to confine herself to going to the hairdresser only once a month and cut down on the housekeeping. No more beefsteaks and spring vegetables but wholesome stews made from scrag ends. Cut out all wine, port, whisky. How odd the middle classes are! All this advice I gave in my simple-minded way, all these measures I myself would take without hesitation or regret were I in their shoes left them utterly dismayed. No such notions had ever occurred to them. They raised endless objections, each one stupider than the last, the chief of them being that one mustn't go down in the eyes of the world. The ninnies dug their heels in over the whisky in particular. A household without a drop of whisky to offer is condemned to indelible shame. We argued interminably over what should be done with Alain. The boy hates learning, doesn't do a stroke at school, failed his last exams miserably, and has only one desire (I understand him better than any of them), which is to have done once and for all with textbooks. In spite of this his parents would regard it as a crime to cut short his martyrdom and get him some employment. Thirty years on, I find my brother clinging to the same extravagant superstition about diplomas from which my father suffered, like all the rest of his class. Alain has neither plans nor ambition, he no more wants to be a doctor than an engineer or lawyer. This young fathead is still stuck in the fifth grade; his school reports are deplorable. What is the point of

forcing him to take a degree in literature, science, or the law?
It will only drive him crazy and he'll take five years to get
through, if he ever manages to. When I suggested that he might
do his military service early or take some special course that
might enable him to earn six hundred francs a month, it was
like trying to snatch their cub away from a pair of lions. They
could bleed themselves white but Alain would go on fruitlessly
wearing out his pants on the benches of the university for
twenty years if need be, so that he could have "the chance in
life to which he is entitled" (Georges's jargon). My brother
could surely procure some job for his son with Porfirex, where
he could keep an eye on him, help him on, get him promotion,
and finally ensure him a career, but such an idea fills him with
horror. As a result of all this Alain, by the time he's twenty-
five, will be fit for nothing whatsoever. God, how absurd parents
are! Only bachelors, as I've often remarked, really know how to
bring children up properly. In short, we argued for nearly two
hours, with me trying to inject a little common sense and realism
into their romantic brains, while they constantly opposed me with
their illusions, their impracticality, their need to keep face, and
the debris of their "social standing," even going so far as to
accuse me—to crown everything—of being paradoxical! I thought
I knew all there was to know about the bourgeoisie but I must
confess that Georges and Véronique have taught me a little
more. These poor lunatics are at the bottom of the abyss and they
go on play acting, hoping for vague or impossible things to happen instead of sensibly reorganizing what little is left to them
and saving the situation by ruthless economies.

Examples of their fanciful way of thinking: Véronique, who
speaks English like everyone else, that is to say badly, has taken
it into her head to do translations for a publishing house. Which
one? No idea, obviously, but hope springs eternal. They've also
asked a friend of the family, a woman whose husband, either
to keep her occupied or get her off his hands, has bought her
a dress shop, to take Véronique on as an "assistant." Result:
the friend in question has been untraceable for the past eight

days; impossible to get her on the phone. My brother and sister-in-law wore themselves to shadows explaining how there were perfectly sound reasons for this vanishing act and that it in no way meant that this possibility was down the drain. There would be no end to it were I to list here all the idiotic ideas they trotted out, the ludicrous plans they have cooked up, the crazy expectations they are cherishing. "Keep on hoping," "mustn't get downhearted," "look on the bright side," "keep our spirits up"—these phrases recurred time and again in their talk. I found it so nauseating that I deliberately made myself more and more damping. Nothing disgusts me so much as this gratuitous optimism and groundless hope. To me, it's the opposite of courage. I can see nothing in it but an additional torment. Georges and Véronique kept repeating for all they were worth that they "have to face things squarely." But I was the only one to face them in this way, whereas they kept stubbornly looking in another direction.

All of a sudden I was so distressed by their anguish and blindness that, switching as is my wont from extreme parsimony to extreme self-sacrifice, I offered to hand over my money right away. Georges and Véronique were so staggered that for a few minutes they lost their starchiness and thanked me with a sincerity and simplicity far removed from their usual manner. This touched me even more. Typical of me, this sentimentality. At that moment, I swear, I was almost happy over my gesture! My eyes brimmed with tears. I shall never sufficiently mistrust my sensibility: I only need a trace of genuine emotion to be disarmed. How stupid! Georges reaffirmed that we still have five or six weeks' grace and refused to accept anything before it fell due, thanks to which he rose in my esteem. Nine out of ten people would have grabbed the money on the spot, to be sure of getting it.

What a session! I shudder to look back on it. These money problems, these debts closing in like a vice are enough to sour one against life forever. How can anyone put up with so many *material* complications? I cannot help feeling that, were I in

Georges's place, I would be strongly tempted to fling myself in the river, if only to simplify the whole business. True, these people have an experience of money, its drawbacks and advantages, that to me is quite unknown. When it comes to money the bourgeoisie are like bridge players, whom the cards sometimes favor and sometimes don't; even with no court cards in their hand and the rubber three quarters lost, the game continues to absorb them, to be their only passion.

One point bothered me and I finally questioned Georges about it: why, having need of a hefty sum, did he come knocking at my door rather than at Mesnard's, when the latter is far richer than I am and notoriously more generous? Why didn't he ask him for the fifty thousand francs he still needs? The labyrinthine workings of the bourgeois soul are astounding. Apparently the conventions demanded that I should be the first to be approached in view of my status as a brother. In fact, I could quite easily have turned him down. It's almost past belief. But I ferreted out another reason underlying Georges's rambling explanations: the fact that he admires Mesnard inordinately, values his opinion above all others, and would have found it torture to reveal his follies and miseries to this great man. Corollary: as he doesn't admire me or give a fig for my opinion, he doesn't hesitate to skin me alive. Be it noted also that, if one only lends to the rich, conversely one only borrows from the poor.

"But," said I, "I could quite easily have not had a cent. What would you have done in that case? You'd have simply had to go and scrounge off Mesnard."

"I'd have done so with death in my soul," he replied with what I judged to be largely humbug. The monster must have more or less guessed that I had a little nest egg. The bourgeoisie always contrive in some mysterious way to be informed about such things.

I now deplored the divorce between Mesnard and Marie all the more! But for this blasted divorce I'd have run without wasting another moment to the castle to pour out the whole story and procure a substantial contribution from its overlord. Alas! The fact that since yesterday Mesnard has dropped his divorce doesn't mean that I can ask him to share the burden of Georges's debts. On the contrary, he seems to me even more *untouchable*, if I dare venture this pun, than he was last week. I'm going to be squeezed dry, skinned to the bone without even the recourse of moaning about it.

It goes without saying that the atmosphere in the apartment was dismal. Georges and Véronique, like everyone with financial worries, are sleeping badly and this leaves both of them in a chronic bad temper. Despite their efforts to put a brave face on things for my benefit, I felt all the time that each was on the verge of lashing out at the other, the usual effect of adversity on second-rate characters. Véronique probably never stops reproaching her husband for sinking everything they possessed in an idiotic gamble; Georges, for his part, must counter her recriminations with weak little bursts of rage or little fits of weeping in the conjugal bed during sleepless nights. In a word, hell. Alain and Marie-Christine, on the other hand, seemed improved by misfortune. Last year they were happy middle-class children, despising their parents as is customary in such circles while talking exactly the same rubbish. This year they are unhappy middle-class children. They have been kept fully informed of their father's downfall. This catastrophe has made them if not sympathetic at least sufficiently subdued and cowed to appear more attractive. During the meal they joined in the conversation and I found them quite agreeable though ordinary enough children and I couldn't tell on such a brief acquaintance whether they are in fact silly or hypocritical. At all events, and this is something new, they no longer despise their papa when they could for once have good reason for doing so. Marie-Christine can hardly be called pretty. I really fail to understand why they don't enroll Alain as a car salesman: he has all the pleasant nullity required for this calling.

When the time came for me to leave, Georges inquired whether I had any news of "the Mesnards." He hadn't heard

a thing about the divorce: this, it seems, is known only to
Mesnard, Marie, myself, and possibly Mlle. Duchateau. I didn't
see fit to bring him up to date but confined myself to telling
him that Marie was in a poor state of health. This didn't appear
to upset him unduly, despite a few sighs and polite expressions
of sympathy. I added that Lise is more delightful than ever.
This judgment touched Véronique on the raw.

"She's a sweet child," she said in her most shrewish tone,
"but she does a bit too much what she likes. Her parents give
her too free a rein. She's badly spoiled."

Where the hell did she get that from? Lise is admirably
brought up; this at least is one thing Marie and Mesnard have
made a success of. The bourgeoisie really are ghastly. No troubles
are great enough to keep them from indulging in their favorite
vice, namely their love of slander. What has my niece done to
Véronique? Nothing, except to be pretty, intelligent, and good,
all of which is unforgivable. This little swan squashes her pair
of ducklings. Cliché and convention also have a large part to
play in middle-class slander: other people's children are always
spoiled. It is pleasant to observe that the most furious critics are
principally parents cursed with lamentable offspring. Why do
the people for whom one sacrifices oneself have to be so unpleasant, so antipathetic, so alien to my nature? Can there be
nothing rewarding about duty, must it be wholly loathsome?
It's a painful lot, in truth, to have to turn one's pockets inside
out for people one dislikes, who repel one in every respect and
manage to hurt one with everything they say. As I was about to
rise up in wrath against Véronique's ineptitude, Georges said
with a sly smile:

"Oh-oh! We know you have a passion for your niece. We
mustn't say a word against her."

"Precisely," I replied as sternly as I could. "I regard Lise as
an exceptional child, and anyone who wants to remain in my
good books has to think the same way as I do."

Véronique received this full in the face, but being a fool she
prefers her passions to her own self-interest. All I got out of her

by way of an apology was a pinched smile. Georges, who is more simply a coward, felt it necessary to declare with some warmth that Lise is perfect, everyone loves her, he was sorry his own children didn't see more of her, etc. All this was pretty revolting. If I record it, it's so as not to forget it. In fact, these little nastinesses don't linger very long in my memory. A journal like this one is extremely useful; I ought to find it rewarding reading on days when I don't have Mérimée's wise maxim: "Always remember to be suspicious" uppermost in my mind.

When you come down to it, the only member of the Mesnard family for whom Georges and Véronique feel friendship is Mesnard himself, because he is famous and they are overawed by his ritzy style. Lise and Marie cannot appeal to them: they are too natural. Naturalness is not a commodity within just anyone's reach. Fools take it for inadequacy or a pose.

"Alain, Marie-Christine, come and say goodbye to your uncle!" cried Véronique in her most fashionable voice.

I had to kiss eight cheeks as a ransom for my deliverance. I say eight since my brother, although fat and fifty, insisted on licking my face too, which I found grotesque and most unappetizing. I'm in no hurry to set foot in the Rue Boissière again. It's one thing to fork out, but I refuse to be given a boring time on top of it. Where is the charity in these bitter feelings provoked in me by people who owe me so much? I ought to be fond of them, I suppose, by reason of the good I am doing them, but it's something too strong for me and I just can't manage it. The sacrifice of a hundred thousand francs opens up no fountain of milk in my heart; on the contrary, it locks it with a double twist of the key. If there is in literature any reprobate who has beguiled himself by writing on the "beauty of duty" lead him to me! In one sense, duty is worse than necessity; from the latter there is no escape, whereas we know the former could well be dodged at the price of a little selfishness or disgrace. A man who ruins himself for a whore is at least buying pleasure. A man who ruins himself to rescue some relative who has got into difficulties gets nothing out of it but the gloomy satisfaction of doing his duty, and this is scarcely a source of joy. He has no reward, no excitement, nothing but worry. To suffer for one's own follies presupposes that one has enjoyed some benefits from indulging in them or at least from planning them. To suffer from the follies of others is a matter for pure despair. Duty is a calamity without recourse. When a hailstorm destroys one's crops, one doesn't bless the hail. Such is my view of the matter. I abide by it: it's costing me pretty dear.

As I left the bosom of my family I was filled with a depression and rancor I found excessively distasteful because they were base. On finding ourselves back in the street, Tarzan and I both felt the same sense of relief. It had been quite clear to me up there that my poor dog didn't feel at home. He barely touched the food they offered him. Throughout my confabulation with Georges and Véronique he remained sitting in a corner with his ears laid back, rolling his eyes, looking anxious, every now and then throwing questioning glances at me. Anyone would think he had guessed that I wasn't in a festive mood and that he too was anxious to get it over with. I cannot express how much this little beast gladdens my heart. He's so sensitive and smart, one would think he shared my thoughts. He had understood so well my need for comfort after my ordeal that directly we reached the pavement he stood up on his hind legs and placed his front paws on my stomach. Nothing more. But there was all the friendship possible in this gesture. You can rely on me, it implied; there are still some pure souls on earth since I am here.

"Luckily I've got you, my pet," I replied, patting his head. "Come on now. Let's get out of this misbegotten place. Let's get back to our kennel in the Rue Boissonnade."

I had a need to cleanse myself and thought the best way of setting about it would be once again to write up my visit to Georges and Véronique without a moment's delay. I settled down to this at four o'clock. It is now eight and indeed I feel considerably better. What a wonderful thing writing is! What was bottled up inside me before and making me feel sick is now outside me. With my pen, my paper, my paragraphs, my tale dashed off at top speed, every detail filled in, every emotion recorded, I am now purged of all passion. Here is a heavy blow dealt to one of my favorite theories, that all the arts converge on the same goal and produce the same effect on those who practice them. The contentment my painting brings me is very different from what I feel at this moment. How can I explain it? Painting fills me with a universal and all-embracing sense of satisfaction. The happiness I get from it throws a cloak, as it were, over any troubles or depression I may have; it smothers them; it mysteriously quashes them. Whereas writing, or—let's be modest—this mania for scribbling I am caught up in, attacks and destroys them. When I paint I never have the feeling of fighting against something or winning a victory, apart from the old and timeworn victory over matter. When I write I struggle, I rid myself of a curse, I triumph over my mind. The words flow through my head; do the forms only flow through my hand?

Another point. Being a painter, the most developed, the most experienced of my five senses is sight. I am a "visual" man. Yet what I write is strangely devoid of descriptive matter and color. It could hardly resemble less what the critics call "painter's prose," full of adjectives and colors. On the contrary, it is dry and on the intellectual side. I came to realize this three or four days ago, since when I've been seeking an explanation for it. I believe I have now found it. Describing with words, painting with words, doesn't interest me. For this I have my brush. "Visual" people see and sometimes reproduce; they don't describe what they see. I ask something else of writing than I ask of painting, and this it gives to me.

I've noticed how, every time I talk with my brother as for instance today, I am swept violently back into the past. The man's mind, his speech, his manner, his ideas, his prejudices, his conformism, all revive the world of my childhood. I don't feel anything of the kind with Marie, who has been much more closely linked with my life. This can be explained by the fact that Georges is much older than I am and Marie much younger; as a result, through his superiority over me, he always belonged to the camp of the oppressors. It stems also from the fact that Marie and I detached ourselves from our parents' milieu, from the spirit that presided over it and even from its language. Contrariwise Georges, although he has since risen in the social scale, has never outgrown it. In whatever he says I find all the things that used to be said at home in the old days. He talks and thinks like my father and is even growing to resemble him physically. I have changed my moral outlook, if ever I can be said to have shared that of my parents. I have changed my world; or rather, my mind and my sensibilities have led me to a world at the opposite pole from the one into which I was born—a world where things do not have the same values, where honor, for instance, delicacy, rudeness, and elegance are vested in entirely different objects.

Unlike most people, I haven't retained very happy memories of my childhood. This is one of the reasons why I find encounters with my brother so distasteful. Everything his presence stirs up in my memory is painful. Marie herself hardly played any part in my life at that time. When she was born, I was six and already had a wide experience of society. A gap of six years between two children doesn't begin to be bridged until the end of adolescence. When I was ten, Marie was only four. Her devotion to me took the form of a blind loyalty and that remarkable strength of character little girls display when they side with a brother they admire—all very touching, and I was deeply conscious of it, but how could one confide in a little girl of four? My thoughts were too subtle and I was myself too involved in groping my way through my emotions. In short, I was all alone against society, my one and only ally being a child even weaker than I. The first time Marie gave evidence of real, adult understanding and stood up for me was at the age of twelve, when I was eighteen and won my first victory over my family.

My first victory, I say. This was when I enrolled at the

Ecole des Beaux-Arts in 1938. My parents thought and reasoned like characters in a Labiche farce, only they were less comic. Just imagine, I had been forced to fight like a lion in order to get into this school at once thick with dust and devoid of tradition, retrograde yet welcoming any phony innovations, where no serious teaching was any longer to be found—a place, to put it bluntly, in a state of complete decadence. My battle lasted a year. My father was horrified by the Beaux-Arts. For him it was hell and he had a son who wished to go to hell, who would exhibit himself naked, painted blue and crowned with feathers, at the Beaux-Arts Ball, who would slop around the cafés of Montparnasse and, at best, only learn a starveling's profession. Red-eyed my mother would argue with me; my brother, pride of the family with his technical diploma in "Arts and Manufactures," pretended to see my point of view while insidiously extolling the advantages of a *real* profession. Of all these people, not one of them had any inkling of what sort of person I was. Georges was particularly odious with his protective and ironic manner and his cherished conviction that I was a young lunatic who would soon be brought to see reason. This dashing engineer, himself so sensible, following in Father's bourgeois footsteps, dying to be even more bourgeois still while taking credit upon himself for making fun of his ways, amenable, conformist, dreaming of a stolid career cozily embedded in the established order, made me even fiercer in my determination. The idea that he and my parents were convinced I was the same as they were, that I was just going through a rebellious phase like so many other young morons, that "it would all pass over," made me boil with rage. I took it as an insult. Only Marie followed me down my secret paths. She fanatically admired my early masterpieces, she was sure I had genius. Knowing our mutual devotion, they tried to mobilize her against me too, but she always intrepidly resisted all pressure. Better still, she used to report back to me their various efforts to subvert her and encourage me to resist. Impossible to forget an alliance like that. I haven't.

The cream of it all was that, having finally won the right to enter the sanctuary in the Rue Bonaparte, six months had barely elapsed before I was burning to leave it. The teaching they dished out in that place in 1938 was quite senseless. I had for masters nitwits wholly devoid of talent, though this wouldn't have mattered so much if they hadn't been entirely lacking in any craftsmanship as well. At eighteen, having learned what little I knew all on my own, I still knew more than they did. And to think that they held exhibitions, were acclaimed, became members of the Institut de France, and held sway over the salons and artistic life! The pictures my masters painted were out-and-out trash; they revolted me and I never concealed my opinion of them. This earned me the reputation of being an obnoxious, unruly, pretentious lout, and it followed me around for ten years. After one or two semesters I had set the whole bunch of nonentities of both older and younger French schools against me. What a letdown! I who had had to quarrel with my family before I could get into the Beaux-Arts and *learn the profession* found there nothing but ignorant hacks who almost led one to regret Bonnat and J. P. Laurens. As for my companions, they placed all their hopes in one day being able to churn out imitations of Othon Friesz or Gromaire. I used to talk to them about the artists I admired, who at that time were Dunoyer de Segonzac, Matisse, Derain, Bonnard. They hardly even knew their names. I wasn't at the Beaux-Arts, I was at the Sorbonne. Such was my start in life.

I was all the more unhappy in that I had thoughtlessly made a sort of agreement with my parents. I had explained to them that the Beaux-Arts would at least provide me with the means of earning a living until fame descended on me: I could teach drawing in the state schools and colleges. I could hardly see myself instructing a class of young drips from the rising generation how to make charcoal drawings of plaster casts; but this prospect had reassured them and they had at long last consented that I should be a painter. By the end of a few months I was convinced that I would never get anywhere. I was too serious-minded for the tricksters at the Beaux-Arts, detested by almost all the teachers and little relished by their pupils, save for Mesnard and Boulard, whom I got to know at that time and who were worth incomparably more than all the rest put together. Nothing I did pleased anyone. Sometimes I was regarded as a fanatic of the avant-garde, sometimes as a hundred years behind the times; they could never decide which. Only a war could extricate me from this hornets' nest. It broke out on September 3, 1939. I joined up. My flabbergasted parents dared not oppose this decision, which had every appearance of patriotism and suited me admirably.

No sooner had I joined up, of course, than the army stunned me with boredom and I regretted my impulsive gesture. Nor had I paused to consider that I was going to have to fight. I'm not a coward but I was appalled by the possibility of being idiotically killed by a burst of machine-gun fire, of losing my sight or my right hand. What had I, an artist, to do with this war with which I wasn't remotely concerned? I realized my utter stupidity and understood how, in the manner of all fools, I had extricated myself from one false position only by flinging myself into a worse one. At nineteen one has very healthy ideas about life: I could see no common yardstick between the loss of my right arm and the defeat of my country. To achieve the work I had been created for, to build this up slowly, at my leisure, making it ever more extensive, ever more profound, ever more dazzling, seemed to me infinitely more important than hacking Germans to pieces or even defending the soil of my forefathers. How long would this damned war last? One year, two, or four years like the last one? I was going to waste my time on a lot of nonsense that would never be of the slightest use to me: foot drill, arms drill, training, route marches, etc. No chance of any peace and quiet for a single moment of the day what with fatigues, capricious sergeants, and my rowdy comrades; and later on the fighting and the

trenches, just as with Father, who had bored me with his
heroic memories all through my childhood. To die at nineteen
without having had time to embark on my life's work seemed
to me a perfectly hideous fate; I was completely bowled over
by it for three weeks. What an unimaginable loss mankind
was going to suffer! I can envisage easily enough how a writer
can go to war for the reason that he wants to defend his
language, which is his true native land, by force of arms. But
a painter? A painter's fatherland is anywhere with men who
have eyes to see and love beauty. I was willing enough to
die of hunger for my art, I was fully prepared to do so;
but I refused to die for a load of tripe. I mean by a load of
tripe the ambitions of Master Hitler and the invasion of France.
I wasn't particularly French at that time. To tell the truth, I
was nothing at all; I was a citizen of the worldwide Republic
of Painting. My heroes weren't called Du Guesclin, Turenne,
or Napoleon, but Leonardo, Rembrandt, Dürer, Poussin, Char-
din, Delacroix, Manet, Degas, Van Gogh. Splendid heroes,
whose exploits had merely consisted of bringing mankind fresh
reasons for finding the world beautiful! I was fiercely on the
side of the creators against that of the destroyers. Among the
latter I ranked any imbecile capable of demolishing Strasbourg
Cathedral with shellfire. In a word, I was the opposite of a
soldier. I would never have had the courage to order fine
houses in the old part of some town to be destroyed and reduced to rubble for strategic advantages. Destroying a work of
art seemed to me a sin more unforgivable than killing men. Men
can be turned out in any quantity required, whereas Ingres's
"Portrait of M. Bertin" is unique. If it goes up in flames,
no one will ever be able to re-create it. It was for this
reason chiefly that I never wanted to become an officer, so as
to avoid the heartbreak of ordering the annihilation of some
marvel, and why, despite the drawbacks inherent in being a
private, I preferred to remain one. I might add that this
status, where one is lost in the crowd with no responsibility
of any kind, no obligation other than serving, pleased me far

more than being a leader of men, for which I didn't feel the least bit inclined.

My despair came to an end after three weeks for the very same reasons that had induced it. This was the result of an emotional process very revealing of my character, and I find it odd that I shouldn't have noted it before. I was terrified at the idea of being killed, losing a limb, or being made blind. Suddenly these wild fancies swung in the other direction and a blissful superstition took hold of me. I was convinced overnight that my future work, on account of which I was so afraid of dying, would on the contrary protect me like a sheltering wing. It was inconceivable that a man like me, chosen to add something unique to the world, should come to any harm. Providence, having assigned me a mission on this earth, would see to it. And so I had nothing to fear. The war could last as long as it liked; it was written in the stars that I should return intact to hearth and home. All the major departures in my life have had similar origins; I mean that when pondering what line of conduct to adopt I have never based my decision on logical arguments or reasoning but on irrational impulses that anyone else would find childish; it is for this very reason that they win me over. Strangest of all is the fact that, after having been invaded by superstition in this way, my mood completely changed. I became gay as a lark, bellicose, eager to get to the front, burning to face the foe so as to put my new-found theory to the test. I was not mistaken. In May 1940, during the German offensive, I won the Croix de Guerre and Military Medal without in the least deserving them, without even an instant's fear or for that matter ceasing to consider war for what it is, namely the utmost folly. Providence again watched over me on this occasion by never putting me in the position of having to kill a man; though it would doubtless have come easily to me in the heat of the moment it would cause me much grief now. Apparently my way of advancing between the bullets and grenades impressed my captain. With all this, I must confess that what little war

I waged did not displease me. Besides, I had the luck to wage
it at twenty, an age when it's still amusing. This cut me off
once and for all from my youth and set me free. I went off
to war a child; I returned from it eleven months later a man.

My brother, a sublieutenant in the reserve of the Engineer
Corps, not only failed to cover himself with glory like young
Pluche but also allowed himself to be captured and carted off
to Germany, where he squatted as a prisoner for five years.
This deplorable event carried the scorn Marie and I felt for
him to a high peak. It is pleasant in this connection to
establish yet again that in the strictly futile and bourgeois
occupation that war is, it was the artist who behaved like a
brave man and the bourgeois who behaved like a poltroon.
Georges never stopped bleating about the motherland; for me,
such a notion was almost unthinkable (and still is, what's more).
I couldn't understand how, ardent patriot as he was, he didn't
try to escape. One has to suppose that such a thought never
crossed his mind. According to the ecstatic tales he told us
on his return, he felt perfectly at home in his oflag in company
with all the other sheep he was penned up with, feeling sorry
for himself, receiving parcels, and acting in bedroom farces
dressed as a woman. I believe he found a kind of glory in
his tribulations and enjoyed the role of victim. In which he is
more a man of his time than I am. I loathe victims and see
nothing else wherever I look. Another spicy detail: in 1945
Georges, like all his ilk, swamped us with his stories of life in
captivity: these, fifteen years later, seemed to me as ridiculous
and boring as my father's war stories and, although different
in spirit, were tainted with the same stupidity. I saw here the
two faces of the bourgeoisie, each as hateful as the other. My
father the bourgeois victor, my brother the bourgeois defeated,
the former as insupportable in his triumph as the latter in his
abjection. I even remember having had an odd impression at
the time that the roles could easily have been reversed, my
brother a *poilu* and my father a prisoner. It was the same
being in two different persons.

My cross and medal proved very useful to me after I was
demobilized in August 1940. They kept my parents' mouths
shut. Impossible to force a hero to study law. Besides, I was no
longer disposed to submit to them. One of the benefactions
war bestowed on me was that in eleven months it aged my
character by ten years. I mean by this that during those
eleven months I had discovered a portion of the world infinitely more vast than the one I had known during the previous
nineteen years, and as a result I was able to be detached over
the little family outbursts of rage. My reasoning in August
1940 ran as follows: "Either I go home to Papa and Mama,
who will give me a room, feed me, and sooner or later
drive me crazy with their middle-class ideas on the need
to have a profession, or I set myself up in some garret in
Montparnasse without asking anyone for anything." Young as
I was I had understood that since liberty was the greatest of
blessings it was natural for it to be the most expensive. I had
also realized that life is a perpetual paraphrase of the legend
of Hercules placed between vice and virtue. To choose my
parents would obviously be to choose vice. Even so it took
me a good month to make up my mind: I was scared of
penury. During this month I gave myself a vacation. I put
off the decision from one day to the next, so delighted was
I to have come back whole from the war, to be young and
in good health, to have nothing else to do in life but win
fame. I ate like a horse and slept like a log. Then one morning
without particularly thinking about it I took the plunge, in
other words rented a small room without water or heating in
the Rue Vavin. My father, still dazzled by my ribbons, gave
me five thousand francs and let me take my bed with me. That
is all I ever had from him. Apart from my upkeep from my birth
to the day I enlisted in the army and these five thousand
francs, I can't have cost him very dear. Show me many other
sons who go off at twenty to make their own way for themselves and never ask for another penny! Although I pay little
heed to such things, I believe my father, on the other hand,

spent a great deal on Georges, who was his favorite, subsidizing him for a long time, treating him to the premium to an apartment, and showering him with presents when he married. At a rough guess I would say that Georges cost him eight or ten times more than I did, though this never prevented him from holding my brother up as an example to me all my life—this good son who gave him cause for nothing but satisfaction.

The best part of it all is that the poor fool—I'm referring now to my father—through his futility and lack of foresight found himself more or less without a cent in 1950, a time when he was first attacked by the illness he died of two years later. He was then sixty-seven and, my mother having died in 1948, was vegetating rather sadly in our old house in the Batignolles. Who paid for it all—daily help, nurse, doctor, medicines? Who kept the poor wretch alive? Who undertook the chore of going round for a chat every other day? Pluche, damn it! This sort of occurrence has periodically repeated itself in different guises ever since my birth: high-minded persons, after having taken a thorough dislike to me, plagued my life, pestered and criticized me with their superior wisdom, have fallen on evil times and then, abandoned by their own kind, turned to me for help. And I, who am goodhearted and a man of duty, go to inconceivable lengths for imbeciles from whom I have reaped nothing but rebuffs. Will this be counted in favor of my salvation? I am not even so sure of that, since I cannot manage to be taken in by my devotion, nor can I regard it without irony.

Georges's behavior during the illness and death of my father was really rather splendid. In two years he paid him four visits and didn't contribute so much as a hundred francs to the old man's upkeep. Alas, he was bowed down with obligations, poor fellow: a wife who was "entitled to a certain level of comfort," a child, a position to maintain, hospitality to be returned, a still unsettled career, etc. Anyway, I was there, wasn't I? My paintings were selling nicely just then, or at least people were beginning to show an interest in them.

Every time I manage to put something by, think I am getting out of the wood, begin to feel I can breathe, wham! a brick for which I am not responsible lands smartly on my head. I may say that, up to 1950, I had my full share of lean kine. Just when the horizon was beginning to brighten, when I had moved out of the Rue Vavin to treat myself to a decent studio in the Rue Notre-Dame des Champs and finally saw ten years of toil beginning to bear fruit, duty obliged me to three quarters ruin myself for a man who scarcely cared at all for me and toward whom I felt only dim affection. Marie helped me as best she could in all this, but Mesnard hadn't yet taken wing and she was none too well off. At least she came every day to the Boulevard des Batignolles, brought flowers, prattled away, tidied the place up, lavished the only gift she possessed: her presence. One must grant to Georges that, when our father died, he shed abundant tears and declared *urbi et orbi* that he was grief-stricken. His attitude was highly admired by friends and acquaintances, who found Marie and me ungrateful by comparison. And this is the type for whom I am going to sacrifice my hundred thousand francs of savings.

When I stopped writing I looked at the clock. It was eleven. All at once I realized I was hungry as a wolf. I nipped round to the Coupole, where Tarzan and I copiously celebrated our independence, our happiness, our friendship, our contempt for fools, he with a majestic platter of stew and I with oysters, *tête de veau sauce gribiche,* and a bottle of Pouilly. Nothing like a good supper to put one's ideas into perspective. It is now half past midnight. It's odd, this itch of mine to write: impossible to let the paper alone. Before going to bed I have still felt impelled to scribble these few lines. Who on earth would be interested to know that I've been eating oysters and calf's head at the Coupole? Me. I like this detail. On a fine evening in the month of March the celebrated Pluche, a great but unrecognized artist, treated himself to oysters and calf's head, which made him forget his troubles and helped him to reoccupy his soul—a feckless, amusing, selfish, in other words happy soul. After which the celebrated Pluche returned to his household gods smoking his pipe and chatting to his dog. The celebrated Pluche is now going to snuggle down in his feather bed, telling himself he has lived another day of his life, that he has lived a great many already and no doubt will live a great many more, that he has need of almost nobody and nothing and that it is quite a good thing, on the whole, to live in intellectual and emotional autarchy. Artists surely have tendencies to hermaphroditism.

CHAPTER XIV

Serendipity in the Suburbs

> *To begin with, transfer the money voted for the Fine Arts to state orphanages instead of cluttering up public places and provincial museums with works commissioned from artists.*
>
> DEGAS

As I took my shower this morning I had an idea which set me up for the next twenty minutes: this was that all impotence, incompetence, or technical inadequacy has a comforting side to it—it represents a return to youth, when everything is difficult, when one doesn't yet know oneself and is feeling one's way in the dark. Skill, sureness of touch, strength, staying power are the privileges of age. From time to time these are withdrawn from me and I find myself back amid all the uncertainties of my eighteen years. It is odd that I should feel cheered by such a notion, since I felt very uncomfortable in my skin when I was young. I feel far happier in it now that I have brought to light and accounted for everything within me, now that I know myself inside out and have experienced the act of creation countless hundreds of times. But anything connected with one's youth possesses a strange power. I get a kick from this youth that only wells up at awkward moments.

It was half past eight. There came a ring at the door; I ran to open it still dripping from my ablutions. It was Boulard, with little Antoinette trotting behind him. The place immediately filled with noise. Boulard loves descending on people unannounced in this way, which is at once touching and exasperating. Touching because he imagines his friends are as delighted to see him as he is to visit them. Exasperating because such inconsiderate behavior implies that one is, like him, available at any hour of the day and has nothing else to do but gossip with one's friends. This man, in other respects so shrewd and wise, has preserved this trait from our youth, when we were fresh and eager, still marveling at being friends with no secrets or private activities to hide from each other. So I was both pleased and annoyed by his intrusion. He was grinning from ear to ear, happy to be alive, happy to be here, regarding his mere presence, along with his daughter's, as an unhoped-for gift he was bestowing on me.

"Yes, it is Agamemnon, your king, come to awake you," he declared on entering. "Hither has he fared with Iphigenia, for favorable winds are blowing in the direction of East Suburbia and he has in mind a marvelous plan for spending the day with you in that progressive municipality where he is engaged on a sublime masterpiece. So go and don your artist's gear. It will be entertaining, rustic, radical-socialist, and humanitarian, you'll see. We'll have a good laugh and chew the rag; you can even lend me a hand, since today's the day I begin my fresco. I'll draw the harvesters and you the gunners, since that's what the pompous asses want. You're going to have a whale of a time, my lad. You can do me a 75-mm. cannon down to the last detail, yum-yum! At lunchtime we'll have a monster blowout at a bistro I've located nearby where they think the world of me. And then I'll introduce you to the municipal councilors, who are well worth looking over. Can you be ready in ten minutes?"

Out of a spirit of contradiction and because I was in a sour mood, I began by refusing on the feeblest of grounds. But Boulard is not so easily deterred and stuck firmly to his plan, having moreover every intention of making me carry out a good chunk of his work. Antoinette threw her weight in too, repeating with that kind of lisp whose charm she is already well aware of: "Do come wiv us, Pluffe. We're going to fpend a lovely day making Daddy'v frefco. I infift you come." Faced with the joint efforts of these two friends my cantankerousness evaporated within a few minutes, the more so since I was only resisting out of bad temper. In actual fact, Boulard and Antoinette (known as Tonton) were highly welcome with their proposal. I had a long, empty day ahead of me and here they were, offering me a way to fill it blithely; I'd have had to be a real sourpuss to turn up my nose.

"I see our friend is having one of his bad days," declared Boulard. "Our friend's genius is constipated and that makes him prickly. Come on now, man! Instead of sitting here watching your arteries harden, I am offering you a day out with one of the wittiest men in Europe. You'll work, and that won't do you any harm, even if it's only a bit of trash like painting a 75-mm. cannon for the town hall of Noisy-l'Humide."

"Heev quite right," Antoinette chipped in; "it won't do you any harm, Pluffe. Tonton wantf you to come."

Boulard owns a car which can barely stand comparison with anything save a worn-out rubbish bin. It has the same dirty color with its scratched and battered gray bodywork, and even the same sickly-sweet smell when one gets into it. It's an old two-horsepower Citroën that he bought secondhand seven or eight years ago, and in mileage it must have traveled at least five times around the world. This miserable knocked-up, shuddering hunk of metal still manages to go, which never fails to astound me every time I see it. Downhill, Boulard achieves peaks of forty miles an hour. Were he to be believed, this vehicle is the most accomplished one ever to emerge from the Citroën works; it boasts an indefatigable engine, undreamed-

of comfort, it holds the road exceptionally well, and is even an
object of beauty reminiscent of Philip II's state coach in the
Lisbon Museum. Its owner wouldn't exchange it for a Rolls
(which eats too much gas). When I had settled into my seat
Antoinette, who likes talking about herself in the third person,
said in the most feminine tone of voice:

"Tonton iv going to fit on Pluffe's kneev becov there ivn't
any room behind."

Indeed, Boulard's jalopy was stacked with painting equipment. I've never seen it when it wasn't stuffed with canvases,
brushes, easels, and paintboxes. All this as dirty and dusty
as the car itself and seemingly ossified. One would think Boulard
had stocked up his vehicle once and for all time, so as to
be ready for some eventuality that hardly ever arises. I had
been foolish to hang back: once in the car I felt perfectly
happy. By redistributing the canvases and other paraphernalia
we contrived to organize room on the back seat for Tarzan,
who immediately wriggled and squirmed in order to get his
nose through the window and enjoy the pleasure of being
buffeted by the wind. A thin March sun was shining; the
sky was by and large blue. Another charming Paris morning.
Really it's too bad that it has been painted so often and by
so many, so that one can no longer reproduce these bright
mornings without copying twenty other artists!

Nothing is so touching as the solemnity with which children
perform actions they set store by. For Antionette it was a great
privilege to be sitting through the whole journey on the
knees of Pluche, who is a friend of Papa, who is one of
the major institutions of this world and often talked about at
home. So she held herself as erect as a queen, deeply conscious of the honor being bestowed on her, confident that
she was filling the idlers who watched us ride by with envy and
admiration.

It's a good thing the car doesn't go very fast, since Boulard is
a terrifying driver. For one thing, he never stops talking; this
wouldn't matter if only he didn't keep wildly gesticulating,

letting go of the wheel to jab his finger into my chest, looking
around at his passenger regardless of what lies ahead of him,
totally absorbed in what he is saying. I always wonder why he
doesn't have more accidents. Today I saved him from four, one
of which would doubtless have been fatal, by urgently drawing
his attention to the traffic lights, the pavement, pedestrians, and
other cars. Drives with Boulard are like his conversation: they go
on a long time, with a mass of digressions, halts, and detours. I
have nothing against this; far from it! On such questions I am the
same: I nearly always prefer the digressions to the central topic,
maintaining that it is in the former one finds most pleasure and
instruction. This morning, for instance, after going down the
Boulevard de Port-Royal, we turned off along the Avenue des
Gobelins, where Boulard wanted to show me the front of a
movie house carved and decorated by Rodin, which is indeed a
most handsome, extraordinarily incongruous piece of work. It
takes the form of a loggia; there are columns, a balustrade,
masks of comedy and tragedy, and two tall, sinuous figures
surmounted by palmettes. We spent fifteen minutes in ecstasy.
This work of art set amid virtual tenements, what a symbol of
our condition, we artists of the twentieth century! The loggia is
hemmed in between two ramshackle buildings whose ignoble
walls rear up on either side. There old Rodin's lascivious allego-
ries dwell, like divinities in exile among the savages, just as we
are in exile ourselves in this world, which for the past fifty years
has been making giant strides toward total ugliness. Poor old
Rodin! He also came too late. This French Michelangelo not
only lacked a Pope Julius II but also a good epoch. One gets the
feeling that the Third Republic diminished and whittled away
his genius, that had he been born four hundred years earlier, in
Italy, with the means of those days, he would have produced an
oeuvre thirty times more vast.

Clambering back into the car I imparted these views to
Boulard, who immediately launched into an immense dissertation
on the drawbacks of the modern world, a topic which as a rule
inspires him and I rather enjoy. There is something magical

about Boulard's company, due to the way his mind ceaselessly
throws out weird flashes of insight, ideas possibly not original
but seemingly so on account of the angle from which he ap-
proaches them. The magic lies, for me, in the fact that whereas
the prospect of seeing him often tires or depresses me before-
hand, because I know him too well and he talks too much, after
the first five minutes I find no one in the world so entertaining.

"D'you know what the curse of artists is?" he said, jabbing his
finger in the air. "I'll tell you. It's democracy. The older I grow,
the more of a monarchist I become. Do you know the story of
the statues in Albi Cathedral? They were condemned to be torn
down in 1790 by the committee of the Tarn Department, as
being 'monuments to superstition.' Superb, eh? Those pure gems
of the sixteenth century! It was only thanks to the efforts of a
local art-loving engineer that they were saved. I'm not making
this up; there's a plaque on their base to say so. We've got to re-
sign ourselves, old thing: we can't expect anything from the
people and we've turned up at the worst possible time. Artists
can only flourish during periods when the people have no say
whatsoever. Nowadays their voices are all we hear, or those who
speak for them and lay it on thick. The people used to be like
dogs: they had everything but the power of speech. Now they've
been given it. What a shower of bull. The people have no need of
beauty; they want ideas. The smallest extra home comfort suits
them far better than the victory of Austerlitz or the galleries of
the Louvre. Taking things to their logical conclusion, democracy
will suppress all beauty and national glory in favor of comfort.
That is its mission and it will carry it out, I guarantee you. In a
hundred years' time there'll be no more war and no more art. All
over and done with. When a revolution breaks out the first thing
the plebs always does is to knock down the statues and set fire
to the palaces. The historians, who never see further than the
ends of their own noses, believe they do this out of rage or
resentment. They're wrong; they do it out of instinct. The plebs
knows beauty is its worst enemy. It symbolizes the idleness and
happy lives of its oppressors. Look at the decline of art in

France and the rest of the world since 1789. And this is only the beginning. The plebs are obviously right, from their point of view. They will always prefer a washing machine on the installment plan to a picture, and it's only natural. The washing machine brings them greater comfort.

"Basically, all this is the fault of science. Science is the enemy of the mind. I've been aware of this for a long time, but never quite dared to admit it. However cunning, however unimpressionable, philosophical, and the rest of it one may be, one always ends up becoming contaminated by the idiocies all around one. What with reading so many panegyrics to science in the press and hearing them on the radio, I finally got intimidated. After all, I used to tell myself, science is pretty awful but it can't be as bad as all that; besides, there are more happy people today than there were under Louis XV. I'm telling you all this to show you how a completely independent-minded man like myself still has his moments of stupidity. Because these arguments, my boy, are a load of crap. Science is bad through and through. I am one hundred per cent in favor of obscurantism and I'd chop old Galileo's head off without a moment's hesitation. The old codgers of the fifteenth century who had the men of science burned at the stake weren't as silly as people like to make out. On the contrary I think they were very sensible and farsighted. They knew that so long as man held science at bay the earth would be inhabitable and that directly they stopped crushing this hateful breed of scientists in the egg it would be all washed up. And they were perfectly right. After Hiroshima don't let anyone start beating me over the head with the Inquisition's burnings at the stake. If it comes to choosing between the Ignorantine monks and the atheist scientists I don't hesitate. As for all the people who are happier today than they were under Louis XV, that may be true but it's irrelevant. For one thing, I'd have been far happier myself under Louis XV.

"For centuries humanity has resisted the temptations of comfort. D'you really suppose that people who were capable of reading Plato two thousand five hundred years ago wouldn't equally have been able to invent electricity and even airplanes if they'd applied themselves a bit to the problem? But they simply didn't care. They knew not only that it was of no interest but also that it was harmful, since the ultimate goal of science is comfort, and comfort is the antithesis of intelligence. It's the body versus the mind. And they had chosen the mind. Whether you take an individual or a nation, it's the same thing: impossible to do gymnastics and write sonnets at the same time. It has got to be one or the other. Up to the nineteenth century mankind wrote sonnets. Since the nineteenth century it has been doing gymnastics. As far as getting strong and developing its muscles goes, it hasn't done so badly. But the brain has shrunk appallingly. And the heart. And the passions. Not to mention the artistic sense. So, in the circumstances, you can't blame me if I say the plebs can go and stuff themselves. They're a formidable herd of pigs being fattened. The pigs will get fatter and fatter, pinker and pinker, happier and happier; they'll fornicate more and more in their ultramodern sties furnished with every conceivable electrical household gadget. Each pig will have his car, his TV, his refrigerator, his dishwashing machine, and even color reproductions of masterpieces of the Impressionist school to create the illusion that he has a soul. Thanks to democracy and science the day will come when there will be no more pain in the world and the devil will have won the game. There's no doubt about it, a world without pain is an idea of the devil's. Whereas suffering, cruelty, unhappiness, and the consequent blossoming of the heart are from God.

"And that, my old sod, is why, alone of all my kind, I am savagely reactionary. I call for the complete destruction of everything invented since 1789. I'm telling you this in confidence, of course, and under the seal of secrecy, so you can judge how childish I can be, since there's no way of putting things into reverse and the world is done for. It's a great pity. My system was the only one capable of saving it. For an artist, to support the left, to work for revolution against the aristocracy merely amounts to sawing off the branch one's sitting on. The nature of the artist is essentially aristocratic and artists can exist only in an unjust, cruel, and intelligent world. The just, merciful, and idiotic world science is evolving for us means our annihilation. Nowadays all artists are left-wing, or pretend to be, because this is rewarding. They have one eye fixed on the future, like mere television dealers or petit bourgeois dazzled by trips to the moon. What slobs! Besides, it's completely misunderstanding the mission of the artist, who is not a man of the future but a man of all time. I've always thought, for instance, that if Van Eyck or Watteau came along today and produced Van Eycks or Watteaus identical with the ones we know, nobody would understand them and they would be regarded as scandalous innovations."

At the time, as always happens when Boulard starts to hold forth, I shared his views and confined myself to agreeing more or less vigorously with the better passages of his disquisition. This man is altogether persuasive and paralyzing. One can sense in him such a copious fund of arguments and words and he is so inexhaustible that one hasn't the strength to argue. Thinking it over, however, that is to say right now, I can see what it was that prevented me from giving him my wholehearted support while he rattled on: his excessive pessimism. Every prediction of whatever kind, whether pessimistic or optimistic, is false. The more well-founded it appears, the more deeply rooted in logic, the greater the risk it runs of being given the lie. The world never evolves in the way we anticipate. If experience teaches us anything, it is that nothing is truly black or white. That is why Boulard annoys me with his wholly black future. It's either doctrinairism or bad temper. So it isn't serious. Not to mention the fact that people prophesy in their own image, which is of necessity never that of the world. There is an underlying bitterness in Boulard, who hasn't become a Rubens or a Veronese and never will, and who has nurtured secret but burning regrets about it. Since he hasn't been Rubens when he so richly deserved to, he doesn't want new Rubenses to be born at any price. For the peace of his soul the matrix has to be lost forever. Thank God, it's not possible that men should cease to commit abominable crimes, kill each other, oppress each other, torture each other, and all the rest of it. In consequence there will always be artists to hymn the ruins amid the ruins, and life is beautiful!

"Papa, I'm hungry," said Antoinette, suddenly abandoning the graceful and languid pose she had been holding for the past half hour and which was sending my arm to sleep. "Give me a focolate bifcuit, pleave."

"Just help yourself, Tonton," replied Boulard, switching quite naturally from apocalyptic to paternal tones. "They're in the back, in the paper bag. These kids are perfect gluttons. Eating, always eating, that's all they ever talk about. Just look at those plump thighs and chubby paws! And those cheeks! They reek of health while Papa wears himself to a shred slopping paint in the suburbs. Take it from me, one really has to love children to become a family man!"

Five minutes of acrobatics. Antoinette clambering over me to get to the back seat. Rustlings of paper, conversation with Tarzan. A second bout of clambering in the opposite direction. Antoinette returns to perch with my arm around her and proceeds to consume her chocolate biscuit, which makes her round cheeks all smeary and scatters a mass of crumbs over my lap. To add to the discomfort I pull my pipe out of my pocket, fill it and light up. "Here we are!" cries Boulard. The car stops. Men, dog, and child climb out and shake themselves.

The air in the suburbs is keener than in Paris. The sun had a look of wanting to grow stronger and two thirds of the sky was blue. I have rarely seen a landscape as ugly as the one in which we found ourselves. Not that I dislike gimcrack houses and sinister suburban streets as a matter of course. If they make a good composition I enjoy them as much as the Trianon or the Château de Chambord. But in this place where Boulard had brought me, everything was hideous and discordant. It wouldn't even have inspired Utrillo, who wasn't exactly choosy. When one reflects that this place was an honest village not a hundred years ago and sees the heap of squalor it has now become, one finds oneself out-Boularding Boulard as regards his theories! Modern cafés, hideous shop signs, buildings of cement and plaster, movie house in ferroconcrete, despairing ironwork of the balconies, lampposts as depressing as telegraph poles. I wonder what kind of people can live there. Speaking for myself, I couldn't stick it for a week; I'd either run away or commit suicide. There's not a trace of humanity. Everything has been mass-produced by machines and is of a perfect, impeccable ugliness. The town hall, the scene of Boulard's exploits, is a specimen of that monumental and indigent architecture that flourished around 1936 and, although built thirty years ago, has an unfinished air while at the same time looking as if it might fall down at any moment. What is it made of? It is the color of wine dregs, with streaks of damp and cracks in its walls, finished with roughcast that is flaking, and rusty iron shutters. Even the sunlight, when it happens to stray over it, fails to cheer it up. What a weird notion on the part of the town councilors to commission a fresco for this hangar fit only for demolition! Can it really mean that they find it beautiful, worthy of further embellishment? The souls of such people are as incomprehensible to me as those of Kanakas.

In spite of everything I have to admit that once inside the wedding hall I had a pleasant surprise. It's a large room, well lit and clean, with a fine stretch of wall to be decorated behind the mayor's platform. The benches are upholstered in red plush, following tradition, and there are two Louis Philippe-style armchairs for the bridal pair. Boulard already had everything prepared. The municipality had advanced money for the purchase of paints; they had even erected a scaffolding for the artist, who could trot from one end of the wall to the other as he chose. This vast surface gave me a faint twinge of jealousy. Here was something one could have a lot of fun with, devising a whole pictorial world. What a tragedy that these idiotic town councilors should have fixed on the crazy theme of peasants and artillery-men! One could have done some biblical, mythological, or alle-

gorical scene worthy of Tintoretto. Oh well, never mind! One
could still have fun doing gunners and harvesters. Boulard had
prepared a rough sketch: the harvesters were on the left with
their wives and babies, trusses of hay, sheaves of corn, agricultural implements, bottles of wine, straw hats. They stood
beaming foolishly in conventional poses. The military on the
right were fiddling with the breech of their 75-mm. cannon. One
of them was hurling a grenade; another was charging with fixed
bayonet at some invisible enemy. I burst out laughing at this
absurd composition, and so did Boulard. He had run it up with
his eyes shut, so to speak, without giving a damn for how it
would look when blown up to forty or fifty square yards. When
I rebuked him for his insolent lack of professional conscience,
he retorted:

"Look, mate, don't go telling me it's a lousy job, I know that
just as well as you do. But it's quite good enough for these
cretinous town councilors. I would even add that the more
shoddy, corny, conventional, and silly it is, the more they'll like it.
For the few pennies they're paying me, you don't suppose I'm
going to ruin my constitution, do you? My good man, were I to
produce for them a sublime fresco on the lines of Carpaccio or
even Puvis de Chavannes, they'd utter shrieks of horror and
make me start all over again. You don't know these birds like I
do. They want crap, so I'm giving them crap. That too is
professional conscience of a sort. In my way I am a martyr to
commercial probity. 'The customer's always right'—that's my device. I may do violence to my genius but the customer is served
according to his tastes. What's more, I've a family to feed."

I made no reply, knowing too well this type of profession
of faith Boulard has dished up to me time and again during
the past ten or fifteen years. For my part, I have expounded
to him my way of looking at this kind of thing a thousand times
over, namely that one must always do one's best, even if it only
earns one peanuts; that this is the only way to safeguard one's
soul and one's talent; that one should never despise one's work,
however humble it may be, since such contempt ends by per-

vading one's whole life and soon there is nothing left that one finds worthy of application; that this misplaced pride only harms its owner; and so on. But he is deaf to these arguments, with which I belabor him with the brutality of a guardian angel. Or at least he doesn't take any heed of them, however dolefully he listens to me at the time. As a result, like Mesnard, he hardly ever paints purely for pleasure. Such are the baleful effects of laziness. Indeed, laziness is at the bottom of it all, and Boulard prefers turning out horrible daubs which demand no mental effort and bore him to good things that he would enjoy doing.

One comic detail. He had rigged out his gunners in a sort of dung-colored uniform bearing no relation to anything ever seen in any army. I pointed this out to him, adding that it would have been more picturesque, in my opinion, to dress his military as German or French troops of the 1914 war.

"You don't know suburban town councilors," he cried. "These brutes not only are pacifists but they're anxious to cause no offense. French soldiers! Are you crazy? French soldiers don't fight and they kill nothing but time. As for the German brand, they never existed. The town councilors don't want to do anything that might impede the union of the peoples of Europe. German troops firing a cannon on the wall of their wedding hall might risk causing a breakdown in the Common Market negotiations. Their very words, old man. I also suggested Russian and American soldiers. Same veto. They have to have soldiers from nowhere firing on farm laborers from nowhere. That's the conception the suburban elect enjoy of reality, war, life in general, and the demands of artistic composition in particular."

Boulard knew what he was doing when he lured me into his town hall: in face of this vast expanse of wall I was seized with a thirst to paint such as I hadn't felt for two whole months. From the half-quizzical, half-respectful way he was looking at me I realized I had been maneuvered and that he had only dragged me there so that I could get his work started for him, but I was so heartened by this unexpected inspiration that I pretended not to notice.

"How shall we share the work out?" he asked hypocritically. "Will you take the gunners or the yokels? Which do you fancy most?"

"I fancy all of it," I replied. "I'll take the lot. I'll rough out the whole caboodle. We've five hours ahead of us. That'll just do me."

"That's dandy," he declared, sprawling back in one of the bridal thrones. "Go to it. Enjoy yourself. I'll let you know when it's time for lunch. Meanwhile don't hesitate to sing out if you need me. Only too honored to give the master any help I can."

Imagine, the goon had brought a book with him, he was so sure his ruse would work! Barely had I clambered up onto the scaffolding than he shamelessly pulled it out of his pocket and buried his nose in it. This organized laziness struck me as so remarkable that I couldn't help laughing.

"Well hell," cried Boulard, "you've been doing damn-all for weeks, I offer you the wall of the Sistine Chapel on a plate, I discreetly fade away, and now you take it out on me! I find such ingratitude disgusting!"

Decidedly I shall never learn how the creative instinct functions. The profoundest of ideas leave me flat after ten minutes whereas an absurd subject hatched out in the pea brain of a town councilor electrifies me. The old machinery miraculously set itself going again in my head, which was suddenly all whirring and filled with that anticipated delight that never lets one down. In actual fact, no one has ever discovered anything better for inspiration than a commission. Here was a commission to be executed; little did it matter that it had been given to Boulard and not to me, since I was taking it under my own wing. With a commission there's no beating about the bush, no soul-searching; it's simply a question of work, of pouring all one's talent into a subject in which it is entirely absorbed. What a marvelous invention a commission is! It does away with the first and most precipitous obstacle: the idea to be translated into paint. It enables one to smuggle through all the treasures one has stored up inside one.

I have been referring all the time to a fresco. This proved to

be an incorrect term Boulard had been deliberately using in
order to whet my appetite, since it is a type of work unfamiliar
to me and he thought I would be all the more eager to try it out.
Fresco work calls for very rapid execution, since the paint diluted
in limewater dries almost as soon as applied and one cannot
therefore retouch anything. As a result, one has not only to be
extremely adroit and sure of oneself, but also to have meticulously
prepared what one is going to do. I was rather surprised that
Boulard, who loves ambling along, daydreaming, having second
thoughts, breaking off to chat with callers, should have accepted
this constraint. Actually it turned out to be an honest-to-God oil
painting. Everything had been made ready. The wall had been
covered with a stretch of canvas of a rather coarse grain, as was
best suited to such a wide expanse. I think it was above all the
special and peculiar smell of the canvas that set my mouth
watering. I sniffed it up the way a hungry man inhales the
aroma of a roast leg of lamb. There was a good supply of
charcoal pencils. By the end of an hour I had roughed out the
design, well balanced and even rather impressive. I was
drenched with sweat, not from climbing up and down the
scaffolding but from drawing—the usual effect work has on me.
In any case, such perspiration is not unpleasant; it stems from
an intoxicating inner fire and offers a fine example of the action
of the spirit on the body. My shirt gets so soaked with sweat
that, if it ever occurred to me to weigh myself after a few hours'
hard painting, I'm sure I would discover I had lost a good two
pounds. It's not surprising that I feel so well during creative
periods: this liquid pouring out of me purges me of all evil
humors.

Having made a good job of the drawing, I started painting
in a few of the figures, taking the size of the canvas into
account, that is to say using broad brush strokes and stressing
the contours with bands of black or green. I gave the soldiers
calmly ferocious faces rather like those one sees in Mantegna's
compositions. My fancy led me to paint one of these fellows

with bare feet. I then moved over for a spell on the agricultural side.

"Put me in wiv the peavantf, Pluffe," Antoinette demanded as she skipped along behind me, fascinated by it all. "I'll keep ftill av long av you like."

Tarzan, no less fascinated than Antoinette, was sitting gazing at me with extreme devotion, quite thrown off balance to see me so active, wagging his tail every time my eyes chanced to fall on him. I put him in alongside the child. They made a charming group which I placed at the foot of the canvas, on the left. Antoinette gave me a delightful half hour. She's a real Rubens baby and I did her as such, with hardly any pressure of the brush. A real treat! As for Tarzan, I have the feeling no dog in the whole history of painting is as alive as the portrait I did of him. I managed to convey not only his good little animal's soul but also the glossiness of his coat. At noon the sound of voices brought me down to earth: Boulard was talking to a skinny, dark, bony-looking man with thinning hair and a sallow complexion—a sort of lemur of suburban committeedom. As I was beginning to feel tired I descended from my perch and went up to them.

"Monsieur Duproux is the mayor's deputy," explained Boulard. "Monsieur Duproux," he added in the naïve and earnest tone he adopts when he's about to pull someone's leg, "let me introduce Monsieur Joseph Bridau, my assistant. He's a good lad who's never had a proper chance in life. In spite of his many gifts he hasn't got on the way he deserved to. I employ him from time to time, to help him earn a little money. He needs every penny, I might add. He has a half-wit brother for whom he's wholly responsible and two young children. Their mother ran away with a Senegalese last year. Ah, Monsieur Duproux, nobody knows what terrible lives artists have to lead! Come and say how d'you do to Monsieur Duproux, my boy. Monsieur Duproux, although a Social Democrat, is quite a connoisseur. He's an expert on contemporary trends in painting and it's chiefly thanks to him that you have the honor to be working in this town hall."

Duproux looked me up and down with that lofty disdain all true democrats display toward the poor. He held out a flabby but surprisingly horny hand, which I shook.

"Pleased to meet you, sir," I murmured humbly.

"What do you think of the sketch this young fellow's laid out under my guidance, Monsieur Duproux?" said Boulard.

"Ah well," replied Duproux, "we must wait and see. Just so. I withhold judgment. These are only the first stages. I shall wait until you put your own personal hallmark on it, *maître*."

"He doesn't do too bad a job for a beginner," said Boulard. "Obviously you won't find here the superior stamp of originality you are entitled to expect, but I can assure you it's an excellent piece of work. Tomorrow the groundwork will have been thoroughly prepared and I shall get down to things myself. Then you'll see."

"Just so," repeated Duproux, pretending to ignore me.

"It is reward enough in itself," said I, "being assistant to the great Boulard. Did you know, monsieur, that he won the bronze medal at the Montauban Biennale in 1949 for a 'Shepherd Bringing Home His Flock at Dusk'? A masterwork. And the diploma of French quality at the Carcassonne Fair in 1954, for his 'Lunch-Break at the Berliet Factory'? That picture was a landmark in modern art. He's been recommended for the ribbon of a Chevalier of Arts and Letters."

"Fancy that!" said Duproux. "But you've been keeping this hidden from me, *cher maître*."

"What can you expect, monsieur? Our good Boulard is a modest man. With him, work comes first and foremost. He's not interested in honors. But he'll end up a member of the Academy. Why, only this morning I had all the trouble in the world to stop him from snatching the brushes out of my hands. He was burning to paint, he was champing at the bit. But I was adamant. Blocking out a canvas, putting each mass in its proper place, isn't worthy of a Boulard; that's students' work."

We carried on like this for a good fifteen minutes. Nothing could have been more comic than this Duproux, who didn't lower his gaze three times on a mere insect like me. When we parted he offered me two fingers while looking the other way. In contrast, completely abject before Boulard, who had now become an important personage thanks to my spoofing.

We went for lunch to the bistro where they think the world of Boulard. A nice little place, indeed, where everything is modern, in other words bare, shabby, and depressing and where, in broad daylight, writhing strips of pale blue neon lighting burn in the ceiling, giving the customers' faces a spectral hue. We were installed in the back room, decorated in rustic style with checkered curtains and tablecloths. The proprietress insisted on serving us herself. One has to face it, Boulard's an amazing man. He's known this woman only two weeks but one would swear he's been on intimate terms with her for twenty years. He asked her for news of her daughter, who is about to have a baby, her garage-hand son-in-law, her husband who suffers from gallstones, her old mother, and I don't know what else besides. All this with an air of profound interest and knowing hints. She, for her part, displayed toward him the tactful familiarity of one deeply conscious of the honor such friendship conferred; she was showing herself in her best light and offering all that was best in herself to this man who, from his very first words to her, appealed unerringly to all that was best in her. This gift Boulard has of drawing people to him, raising them high above themselves, making them—merely through the consideration he shows them—more intelligent, more noble than they normally are, is something I never tire of marveling at and goes to prove he is the exact opposite of a misanthropist. He loves human beings, this is a fact, and they love him in return; he makes them better than they are through his sympathy, and they are grateful for the high opinion he has of them. Whenever I see him in this guise, laying himself out to please all and sundry, finding time to scratch Tarzan's head, explaining in detail the ingredients to be put into his dinner, teaching Antoinette amusing little object lessons with a mocking tenderness that is a masterpiece of paternal art, skillfully analyzing to me the way Delacroix and Bonington painted historical scenes, I cease to be surprised at his laziness. Obviously life and what he gets out of it interest him far more than the antlike toil the evolution of a painting involves. He has too generous a nature for this vocation, which calls for selfishness and parsimony. In his way Boulard is a prodigal like Mesnard, although of a far superior species to the latter since he, at least, hasn't put his talent to the service of his worldly desires.

Hand in hand with the touching side to all this, here's the comic one: from the mere fact that Boulard got to know her two weeks before I did Mme. Lenègre—for that is the name of the proprietress—has acquired the sacred character of everything belonging to him. Not that he exaggeratedly sang her praises or gave me an overblown description of her, but one could feel he regards her as a paragon among bistro owners, a sort of showpiece in an ethnographical museum. The same approach to Citizeness Lenègre with regard to me: as introduced by Boulard, I wasn't just another customer but a man way out of the normal run, endowed with mysterious and marvelous abilities. For all that I am familiar with the quirk in Boulard's character which leads him to magnify everything connected with him, I sometimes let myself get carried away by it. I was flattered by Mme. Lenègre's respect; I basked happily in this glory reflected from Boulard. How absurd! Naturally, Mme. Lenègre went into ecstasies over Antoinette, whose visit her father had announced the week before as a historic event in the district. Antoinette sat receiving the homage of her vassals like a young princess. Even Tarzan profited from the general enchantment: a dog patronized by M. Boulard just had to be an exceptional animal. All this devotion took material shape in the form of a rabbit stew specially prepared by Mme. Lenègre herself for the great man. Just the sort of food suited to our expedition, the nip in the air, the voracity of artists and their simple souls. M. Lenègre, who is taking things easy on account of his gallstones, nevertheless ap-

peared during the dessert to offer us a glass of Calvados. Through
the half-open door I caught two or three glimpses of the serving
girl poking her nose inquisitively at the illustrious guests. It was
I who gave the signal to leave, being eager to get back to the
town hall.

My itch to paint never deserted me all day. I worked like an
angel till dusk had completely fallen and I could no longer see
anything even six inches off. When the lights were switched on
and I could contemplate my work as a whole, I was pretty
satisfied with it. Everything was in its proper place, half the
canvas was colored in, it was full of movement, vigorous, and
even rather diverting. What a wonderful time one has with
great surfaces like this! Considering my harvesters and gunners,
I could almost have taken myself for Delacroix painting "Helio-
dorus Driven from the Temple." This work done for another's
benefit gladdened me as much as if I had done it for my own
renown and for posterity. The thought that it wouldn't bring me
in a penny caused me no regrets. I had forgotten that there is
nothing finer in the world than the practice of painting! Tonight I am in the same state of happy fatigue as I feel during
periods of great productivity. At such times nothing is overwhelming enough to scare me or get me down. It is the happiness
of an apple tree that has borne a good crop of apples.

"Well," I asked Boulard, "are you pleased with it?"

"Ummmmm," he replied. "It's too good. I shall have to tone it
down. You must realize, my employers aren't called François I
or Lorenzo de' Medici. Anything slightly energetic or even
smacking of truth strikes them as a personal affront. You must
forgive me, but I'm anxious to keep my rich patrons. So no
imagination. Dullness is the order of the day. All the same I'll
see how much of it I can salvage."

I'd have appreciated a little more warmth in the compliment,
but one mustn't ask of people what they are unable to give.
Boulard only pays compliments through third parties. He only
speaks well of me behind my back, to people who sometimes
pass it on to me; never to my face. This restraint annoys me since

I like being praised and, frankly, the higher the praise the more I like it. Since painting is the hardest thing in the world, one's need is for praise rather than criticism if one is to persevere. The more so since I myself know perfectly well what is good and what is bad in my pictures. There is a schoolmasterish, proofreader side to Boulard against which I constantly rebel while appreciating it at the same time. I only note this so as not to forget it, since today he went as far as he was capable in overt praise.

Night had fallen by the time we got back to Paris. I am particularly fond of these late drives back into Paris, on account of the yellow light of the lampposts, which gives the darkness a chestnut hue verging on ocher. I never weary of this color; it gives me as much pleasure as the noonday blue on the Montagne Sainte-Victoire. Another pleasure of returning to Paris: from one mile to the next one can see the city closing in. First there is the pure, bare countryside; then come the scattered and as it were elastic buildings of the outer periphery; next the frail suburbs with their little gardens and patches of wasteland, giving way in turn to the *faubourgs* and lastly the city itself, hard as rock. I always get the same satisfaction from plunging into this gigantic conglomeration where six million troglodytes dwell, from tracing backward in this way the various stages of petrifaction begun a thousand years ago. Here is a weird poetry such as was never known by the people of the eighteenth century, so happy according to Boulard. In those days the city was no doubt more beautiful but small, patched with greenery, far more tender and soft than today. Cattle grazed at the barrier of the Etoile, goats wandered down the Rue Saint-Honoré, and there must have been chicken runs in the Faubourg Saint-Antoine. At the heart of Paris one could still reach out and touch the countryside, whereas today one has to travel a long way to find it. Whence a specifically modern charm to which I am very responsive.

Boulard didn't want us to part company but it was well past seven o'clock by the time we reached Denfert-Rochereau. I felt a need to be alone and have a few hours to write up my

account of the day. So I was adamant, in spite of the pleadings
of Antoinette, in whose heart I am beginning to be supplanted
by Tarzan. Rather than go and carouse in the Impasse de la
Gaîté, I preferred to grab a snack at the Dôme and proceed
straight home.

I was expecting the desolate sight of my unmade bed, dust
and disorder. A happy surprise: Mme. Chevassu had been;
everything was cleaned and swept, and she had even put out
fresh sheets and towels. Being in an ebullient mood she had
left me a note, which I've pasted in below, as it provides a specimen of her style:

> Dear Sir, the place was a horrible pigsty as usual, I gave it a good
> scrubbing, how you can make such a mess of it I don't know sir.
> Wherever you've run off to today, you never do a stroke of work,
> it's a shame with your gifts. Another hussy or God knows what
> making you waste more of yore time. You owe me 137.80 F.
> There's milk in the freezer and I've left bread. Nobody rang
> while I was here. Your girl spits in your eye and if you want my
> advice I think she's right because yore an old goat and a layabout.
> I hope she deceives you good and proper!! Kind regards. Mme.
> Chevassu.

I'm really an excellent audience. As I read this epistle I
couldn't help laughing out loud. I can picture the old bag sitting
at my desk, sucking her pencil, searching for the *mot juste* like a
lady novelist. Maybe I'm giving myself illusions, but in her letter
I detect much friendship and I'd even venture to say a true
kindred spirit. Coming on top of the good work I've done today,
this tutelary harridan's letter rounded off my happiness. I haven't
had such a day since heaven knows when. Truly, happiness costs
nothing!

People who maintain that one's moral state is subject to one's
physical condition are either blind or abject materialists. I've
never observed anything of the kind in myself; always the
opposite. This evening, after doing a good day's work and with

my spirit at peace, I feel twenty years old. No tingling of any kind, not the faintest twinge of pain through the whole extent of my body. Better still: I've had a cold for the past two days, I was sneezing, my throat was sore, I thought I should be coughing and sniffling all next week. But the cold came out with my sweat in that wedding hall. Come to think of it, I've never had an illness which a few hours' work hasn't cured. Accordingly, what need have I of doctors? I haven't seen one more than three times in twenty years. Painting is my panacea. When I stop painting I shall die—I'm as certain of this as that two and two make four. Then all the ailments kept at bay so long by painting will pounce on me.

CHAPTER XV

Conversation with a Man of Our Time

> The ancients, Sir, are the an-
> cients, and we are men of
> to-day.
>
> **MOLIERE**

One should never be surprised at anything and as a rule very
little surprises me; all the same, to see Mesnard turning up at
my place at lunchtime laden with victuals and bottles of wine
like a country cousin took the wind out of my sails. How long
can it have been since he set foot in the Rue Boissonnade? Five,
six, eight years? And here he was suddenly ringing at my door
without a word of warning, equipped with parcels and a sunny
smile, just like in the days of our youth. Since I'm vindictive by
nature, nurse grudges, and find it hard to let bygones be bygones, the lack of resentment shown by certain people is, to me,
a source of eternal astonishment. I envy this ability they have of
wiping out the past because they have decided to do so, of
acting as if nothing had happened, and I find it very difficult
to fall in with them. In the opinion of Boulard, Lucienne, and
Marie—and they should know—I treated Mesnard to some home
truths of the most wounding nature. Result: four days later he
comes to call on his executioner bearing gifts. This was no
Frenchman, this was no contemporary of mine, this was not my

brother-in-law, but a Saracen warrior from the fourteenth century requesting or proposing an amnesty; this was a knight advisedly purging his simple soul of its burden.

Directly he came in his smile, which betrayed signs of real friendship and even a trace of humility, disarmed me. I opened my arms to him as if it were the Mesnard I once knew who stood before me, not without a shock of surprise at such an uncharacteristic gesture on my part.

"I was hoping you'd be in," he declared without preamble. "Would it be a nuisance if we had lunch together? I've brought the wherewithal."

Wherewithal was the word. His parcels contained enough to feed a full board of company directors and items of the choicest kind: caviar, *foie gras,* lobster with mayonnaise, Parma ham, Russian salad, a cake, and, to wind up, a quantity of those tropical fruits called litchis that smell like grapes. The feast was rounded off with two bottles of Krug champagne. In all this I could recognize Mesnard's munificence, which led him to spend three hundred francs at the lowest estimate and to choose what he knew was most likely to please me. And after all my grousing over his fastidiousness and ritzy ways! One has to admit that this is sometimes all to the good. The most touching thing about it was that he hadn't laid himself out like this in order to coax me round or bribe me, but simply to give me pleasure, taking delight in the pleasure I would feel.

Another cause for astonishment: his lighthearted manner, the ease with which he brushed aside the past ten years. Throughout our lunch he was just as he had been at thirty, when we used to see each other every day and shared the same opinions about everything. I find such characters quite incomprehensible. How can one snuff out the past in this way, behave as if nothing had ever been? It's simply denying the world and living in a dream. For me, being the opposite of a dreamer, what has once been can never be forgotten. While Mesnard chatted in his dry, witty way, I couldn't help thinking of everything that had set us apart. This is one of the drawbacks of being by inclination a *realist.* I can never dismiss any event from my life: it is ever present in my mind in all its details and episodes. Whereas he, being wholly taken up with courtesies, felt no preoccupations of this kind. There is in extreme urbanity a sort of pragmatism that must be very convenient. The perfectly well-bred man never takes past history into account: he sees only the present situation, he takes it as it is and faces it with his impeccable poise. I shall probably never be capable of such wisdom. Besides, I suspect that it is I who am in the right. My concern is not to abolish an evil by pretending not to see it, but to see everything, feel everything, welcome in me a wide variety of passions so that I can paint them.

I was the only one to do honor to Mesnard's sumptuous repast. The poor man has a delicate stomach, he never does more than nibble at things and drinks nothing but water. I got the impression that my appetite gratified him. He kept piling fresh helpings onto my plate, marveling at my voracity and the gusto with which I knocked back the Krug. It's no good mincing matters: this lunch was quite delightful and put me in a thoroughly good humor. I was even oddly moved by this reunion. Deep inside me I felt a strange sort of joy. Could it perhaps be that, all unknown to me, my heart was suffering for Mesnard's absence from my life? The friendships of one's youth, compounded of so many discoveries made together, so much shared anger and joy, such a deep union of characters, leave a deep nostalgia in one's heart. Let us be completely frank: I was glad to discover that my friend of 1945 was not dead as I believed, and that on certain points we still understand each other implicitly. He has retained a certain spark from the old days. The same spell was working on him, I believe; perhaps an even stronger spell since, having taken the decision, through what was after all a courageous step, to break the ice that had formed between us during the past ten years, he was more inclined to welcome it than I was.

For a whole hour we merely talked about this and that, making no reference to our feelings or our personal affairs.

It is amusing to note the slant whereby our conversation assumed a more intimate tone and how we finally touched on our
main preoccupation. It began through painting. I was taking
every possible care, determined to stick to harmless generaliza-
tions and avoid saying anything personal and therefore wounding. Mesnard, when he first came in, had glanced up at his
picture, for which I once nearly ruined myself buying an old
ebony frame with a green velvet slip. Not a word of comment.
Silence on my side too, of course. At the end of our meal, as I
was filling my pipe, he got up and planted himself in front of
his painting. I wondered what he was thinking, whether he was
feeling any regrets or whether he was repudiating the charming
thing. No reaction. Following this he went to rummage among
my canvases piled up around the walls, studying some of them
for a long time, occasionally delivering bits of criticism, all of it
justified, incidentally, and proving that he had lost none of his
discernment. Having inspected everything thoroughly, he assumed a serious expression, lowered his eyes, and said in his
cold voice:

"You are a great man, Pluche. These paintings are excellent.
They show such mastery that one isn't even aware of it."

I was simultaneously delighted and abashed. This man was
returning good for ill. I would have given anything to be able to
return the compliment.

"Come off it!" I said with false modesty. "One just does what
one can. The chief thing is to like doing it. There isn't one of
these canvases I didn't enjoy working on at some time or another.
Besides, if it comes to mastery, you have just as much as I have.
Why don't you want to enjoy your work as well? That's what it
all boils down to."

"You think that's what it all boils down to?" he said. "I
wonder. I'm not so sure. Or else, perhaps we don't have the
same conception of enjoyment. . . ."

At this he gave me one of those urbane smiles he lavishes on
all and sundry, half forced, half confiding, but meaning very
little, and we got down to the crux of the matter. Like the

majority of contemporary artists, Mesnard is basically a victim of
our age and he makes up for a lack of aesthetics by philosophy.
For a good hour, allowing for my interruptions, I had to listen
to this philosophy, which contained, of course, a certain measure
of truth and a fairly pertinent analysis of the present day but
led to unacceptable conclusions. So far as I could gather, his
purpose in coming here was less to have a serious discussion—
that is, on points of detail—than to justify himself in a more
subtle fashion over my accusations last Sunday by proving to
me that there is a metaphysical background to his bad painting.
It's odd, this passion people have had for the past thirty or forty
years for believing that philosophy excuses everything and that
it's enough to be lucid to ensure one's salvation. A lot of good
Mesnard's lucidity does him! It's a fair bet that Clouet, Holbein,
Fragonard, and Cézanne were infinitely less lucid than he and
talked less well, but they possessed that absolute intelligence
that has no need of speeches, that profound intuition that comes
from a genuine experience of creation. By painting to their very
best, they learned from it more about life and humanity than if
they had philosophized till the cows came home. Actually I've
finally come to believe like Boulard that philosophy is the last
resource of the lazy and the ignorant.

"For me, you see," Mesnard went on in a warmer tone than
usual, "enjoyment lies to a great extent in life. And this is
something it took me rather a long time to understand. Not till
I was thirty or thirty-five, I'd say. Up to then your outlook,
your morality hung over me and prevented me from seeing a
number of things. To begin with, that I was living in the
twentieth century, which is not the same as the nineteenth,
unlike what I believed for a long time. Basically it was you,
Pluche, who kept me in the nineteenth century until I was
thirty, if not older. Why? Because you are man of that century.
You lash out like Flaubert, you are a contemporary of Delacroix, at a pinch of Manet. Mind you, I'm not saying you do
painting a hundred years out of date but that you are driven by
the spirit that prevailed in those days over the French school:

creative optimism. Today there is no more French school, that is the great novelty, and there's hardly any painting left anywhere.

"In the past it was simple: there was good painting and bad, and they divided the field between them like Cain and Abel. The bad painters did pictures that were accurate likenesses, anecdotal, traditional, and dreary. The more literal and trivial the likeness, the more childish the anecdote, the more the Boeotians liked it. The bad painters were Abels, for whom everything went right; they became rich, they became members of the Academy, they were respected members of the state. The good painters were Cains, who scared people and earned their curses. And then the world grew older. Abel, the happy Abel who had such an easy conscience, who was so right-minded, who prospered in such a satisfactory way, gradually became a figure of opprobrium. People began to find considerable style and merit in Cain. The brilliant career of Abel Detaille, as compared with the tragic one of Cain Van Gogh, suddenly appeared hideously vulgar. In short, every painter today wants to be a Cain. There's not a single Abel left in modern painting, which doesn't mean the level of talent has increased but that everyone makes believe he's setting the house on fire.

"This leads to various consequences. In the first place, everything's in a muddle: one doesn't know any longer what is good and what is bad painting since both of them look the same; secondly, pictorial skill is wholly draining away since nowadays it's more important to appear a genius than actually to be one, in other words to have a whole bagful of tricks without any craftsmanship; thirdly, Cain is a solitary type clinging fiercely to his cave and having no contact with the rest of men: and so there are no longer any artistic movements, no longer any groups of artists reproducing a common world and a universal sensibility, but only individual initiators with no link between them, no solidarity, each of them expressing only the more or less well-marketed sensibility of a poseur. The art market has been swamped by thousands of painters all trying to persuade the buying public that they possess an unsullied talent in its

inimitable pristine state, because they have entirely rid themselves of the disciplines of painting without incidentally having
taken the trouble to master them. The collector has no judgment either and will buy anything so as to be sure he's not
making a mistake. In the old days his device used to be: 'I
choose this one because it is beautiful.' Nowadays it's: 'You never
can tell!'

"Ever since last Sunday I've been thinking about this problem
and it has enabled me to see clearly an idea that first occurred to me around 1950; I have never squarely faced up to
it before, although it more or less determined the course of
my life. This is that the arts are not a mass of little springs,
each flowing for itself alone and knowing nothing but itself;
they are mighty rivers. I can see no river in the world today
in which one can throw oneself, to be carried with a minimum
of assurance into future ages. One man on his own hasn't a
strong enough pair of legs to swim to the distant banks of posterity. In the great epochs everyone is saved. The least gifted
still has the style of his time, and this gives his work a sparkle,
however small. In the base epochs everyone is engulfed, including the man of genius, who is the biggest dupe of all. Anyway, Pluche, how often have I heard you inveighing against
the second half of the twentieth century, declaring that in it
art has descended to the most abject level! How is it that,
smart as you are, you haven't carried the argument through,
in other words concluded that it is useless to try to bring beauty
into an age which not only doesn't know what it is but worse,
through its inability to recognize it, is beginning to replace it
by the products of industry and science? Beauty as mankind has
conceived it since the days of antiquity no longer exists. For
proof, look at the lengths to which people go to preserve or
acquire what is left of the past—a unique phenomenon in history. It's because they know or guess they will never see the
like again. Art is dead. The museums are like the reservations for
red Indians in America. When I chance to visit the Louvre—
which I don't very often—and see the people painted by Rem-

brandt, Hals, even by Monet or Bazille, I have the feeling I'm looking at a vanished species.

"Last Sunday you accused me of not being a cynic. And yet I am, though in a different way from the one you'd like. For you, cynicism is a proof of moral healthiness. For me it is more a sort of sickness I've caught from watching the development of painting over the past thirty years. Painting is heading toward nothingness; it has almost got there. One has to face facts: the world has no more need of painting, no more need of art. The future belongs to electricians. My cynicism consists of this, that I have weighed up the modern world for what it is worth, adapted myself to it, and take from it the best it can provide: possessions, luxuries, comfort, a certain form of happiness deprived from material wealth. It's pretty grim, I grant you, it's worth nothing compared to the intellectual ferment of the eighteenth century or the creative naïveté of the nineteenth, but what is the alternative? One has to keep up with the times, as they say. My times are moving in a direction I haven't chosen and would certainly never have chosen: I am going along with them. My times are heading for damnation: I am damning myself too. Quite a relative sort of damnation, as it happens, and pretty painless. I am an artist in a century that has a horror of art; I am fighting the century with its own weapons and, though I say it myself, I have come out the winner. I have reached the certainty that nothing, but literally nothing, will remain of our time. It will sink without trace, like the seventh century A.D., for instance. So what is the point of sitting all alone in my corner producing brilliant paintings? No one would understand them today and they would vanish in the general shipwreck tomorrow. The only possible philosophy is to enjoy this civilization, unremittingly hostile to us as it is, take what we can of its good things and dispense them among those we love. I think finally that, for a human being, the means to live in the fullest sense, to make the best of oneself, vary with each age. Under Clovis the world belonged to the Frankish warriors, brandishing battle-axes with their hair coiled in topknots; in the Middle

Ages it belonged to the master builders of the cathedrals; during the Italian quattrocento it belonged to the painters and sculptors; in the days of Louis XV it belonged to the philosophers; and so on. And who does it belong to now? To the rich, since money has become the measure of everything. I mean it quite sincerely, Pluche, when I say that it seems to me I have found myself more completely by conforming to the spirit of this century the way I've done—or the way it's come about, if you prefer—than by resisting it. I am rich."

All through this rigmarole I had to keep holding myself down on my chair. As I listened to it my face must have been a comic sight: the face of the devout confronted by the devil! In fact, there is something devilish in the way truth and error were mingled in what Mesnard said. Such a mixture is characteristic of Evil, which uses truth to drive us down the path of error and contaminates our minds with honeyed words. Another link with the devil; the desperate materialism, not to say nihilism, into which Mesnard has subsided. I don't think I have omitted anything from his system; I have merely translated and condensed it, since he doesn't express himself so concisely. I've cut out all the meanderings, allusions, reservations, digressions, and implications that pepper his style, but which I cannot manage to convey in mine. In particular, he never actually said the words: "I am rich." These have been added by me, but they don't strike me as unfair. Everything he had to say was building up to this statement; it was dancing in his mind and came out, so to speak, directly through my pen. It is interesting to note how, on certain points, his ideas resemble Boulard's. I already found it striking this afternoon; I find it even more so tonight. One thing is certain—my brother-in-law and my friend have shared a common experience. They have more or less progressed at the same pace and in directions which I, in my simple-minded way, would never have suspected. What an example for me, these two artists, one of them my dearest friend, as the other was once, and both of them formerly or still so close to me! Of the three of us I am the only one not to have caught the disease of the age, or—let's not mince matters—not to have been corrupted. Why should this be? To what mysterious element in my artistic purpose is it due? Compared with them, I feel that I go through the world almost without seeing it. Like them, I know a mass of contemporary daubers, I have looked at hundreds of contemporary daubs, yet for all the effect they have on me it is as if the last works in the history of painting to have left any impression on my retina were those of Cézanne or just possibly Bonnard.

What problems, I ask you, does painting pose today that it hasn't posed since time began? Either they have been solved and it isn't worth going over them again, or else they have not and it's best to stay clear of them since they never will be. I am always astounded when I hear an artist propounding theories, holding forth about the conditions of art, its possibilities, its fetters, its contingencies. Like the man in the street I ask myself: "Where on earth does he get it all from?" Not only do I feel a sense of astonishment that anyone could so waste his time on empty subtleties (that I would never bother my head with) but also I am filled with suspicion. Do I tend to oversimplify? Possibly, but I can't help thinking that a successful piece of work contains its whole justification, its whole philosophy, its whole explanation in itself and that only unsuccessful works lead to fast talk in an attempt to compensate thereby for their inadequacy.

What has happened to the majority of artists today has happened to Mesnard and Boulard: they have lacked the necessary strength of spirit to build up a worth-while body of work in an age that, more than any other, has a pitiless hatred of art in spite of the grotesque cult it pretends to make of it. They have been made dizzy by the accelerated evolution of styles during the past sixty years. Progress and art are galloping in opposite directions. Within sixty years the airplane has developed from a bird cage floundering along barely twenty feet above the ground to a magical strip of metal crossing the Atlantic in three hours. During these sixty years painting has joined in the same race; unwittingly, artists have not wanted to lag behind the engineers, and this is an unparalleled piece of stupidity. They have seen a world that was changing every week, with new or different products every year; they have told themselves that they must proceed with the same speed and variety. The only thing these madcaps have forgotten is the one essential; that progress does not exist in questions of art or thought and that if it has taken sixty years to create modern aviation, it takes a whole civilization to create or re-create painting. In sixty years one just has time to destroy it. Or to break its flow, since to destroy entirely needs more than fools or ignoramuses; it needs well-organized barbarism. Now in most respects we are still at the stage of Napoleon III as regards our sensibility and ways of behavior.

These last two days, yesterday and today, have most definitely been decisive in my life. I don't believe I have ever seen so clearly what an artist should or should not be. Right now it even gives me a feeling of fear when I look back. In Mesnard and Boulard I see two doubles of myself, two negatives; I see what I might have become had I not been endowed by heaven with this strange virtue of imperviousness, this inner stolidity, these blinkers vast as battlements; if, to put it in a nutshell, I were not a blockhead. And God how it bores me, this philosophy they pound me with! It's all very well for Boulard to make fun of the "philosophers of the palette," as he calls them, but he philosophizes just as merrily himself. What really lies at the back of this philosophy, at the back of these two little dramas? Laziness, of course, the alibis for which are varied ad infinitum. One always gets back to this. In art more than anywhere else, laziness is the mother of all the vices. Each idles away his time as he thinks best. Mesnard's alibi is Cain and Abel, Boulard's is his family. On the whole I prefer Boulard; his laziness is at least healthy, since it consists of not working at all, whereas Mesnard's consists of working badly.

"Listen, Albert," I said, "there are a lot of things I could say in reply and you must know quite well I don't agree with you. In the first place, what exactly is this theory according to which one can fulfill oneself and live to the full only by conforming to the general imbecility? That doesn't wash with me at all. For forty-five years I have practiced exactly the contrary every day. I am in a state of total war with the century. I do the opposite of what it does in every respect, I think the opposite of what everyone thinks; as a result of this I am very happy and have fulfilled myself to the extreme tips of my toes and my feelings. Happiness can never be gained by bowing to circumstances but only by following the dictates of the heart one has, which is difficult to locate and hard to fathom. The search for this heart demands humility, firmness, perseverance, and a certain deafness toward the tumult of the outside world. In short, I believe we each possess a built-in fate and are happy only when we are following it. I have sometimes wondered, my inner self being what it is, whether I would have been a different man had I had a lot of money or lived at the time of Gustavus Vasa, or (better still) in the event that God didn't exist and the worst of horrors were of no importance. Each time I have reached the conclusion that these contingencies wouldn't change a thing, that at any time and in any circumstances I would still be Pluche, an artist, endowed with his own particular character, aspirations, spirit of contradiction, and scruples.

"Your analogy of Cain and Abel is not a bad one but it doesn't prove very much, except that the dreary good pupils have realized that to become successful they must disguise themselves as dunces. There has always been bad painting. The kind we see today doesn't resemble the bad painting of the past, I grant you, but it's bad painting just the same. It will never help Abel to make horrible faces like Cain and rig himself out in a wolfskin; he will still never manage to hit the right spot with his club, even admitting his arms are strong enough to raise it. Besides, this Cain of yours lacks the principal characteristic of Cain: he's not unhappy; on the contrary, he's doing extremely well for himself, exactly like Abel. Bad painting, like the devil, has an ambiguous face but the true believer

is never taken in by it. The only difference between the bad
painters of today and those of the past is that today they
are ignorant into the bargain and their ignorance discourages
the good ones. How can people let themselves be so easily taken
in by the devil when his tricks are so wretched?

"As to your vision about the future of painting, it may be
correct but this shouldn't stop one from doing one's best. Do
you know the story of St. Louis Gonzaga playing tennis? Somebody came and asked him: 'What would you do if it was revealed to you that the world would come to an end in fifteen
minutes' time?' St. Louis Gonzaga scratched his head, thought
for a couple of seconds, and replied: 'I should go on playing
tennis.' The same goes for painting. 'All will be lost,' you tell
me, 'not one painting from the twentieth century will survive.'
'What the hell,' I reply, 'I shall go on with the one I've got in
hand and, what's more, I shall paint it with the greatest possible care, I shall try to make it the finest thing I've ever done.'
You see, Albert, your trouble is precisely that of being a man
of the twentieth century, in other words someone who lets himself be intimidated. Believe me, it's true: it's a man of the
nineteenth century who's telling you. What does it mean, being
a man of the twentieth century? It means that you cook up a
nihilist philosophy because you dislike the world around you,
instead of saying to hell with the world and transforming it by
thinking of other things."

One never knows where one is with people like Mesnard. I
mean, one stumbles on their true selves in places where one
had imagined nothing but their vanity was left. I thought I
might have caused him further offense by talking in this way.
But not at all. All he did was sigh and say with an amused
smile:

"Pluche, you're a bonehead, you don't understand a thing,
you talk like a sergeant major, and the worst of it is that you're
right. I shan't ask you how it is you manage to have so few
problems, since you would reply that for one thing you loathe
the word 'problems' and for another that there is only one

problem for artists, and this is to have talent. You see, I know
you pretty well although we haven't seen much of each other
these last years."

"Albert," I replied, "let's drop all this. I'm treating you like
a pompous father: I want you to be happy the same way as I
am. It's idiotic. Only one thing matters, and that is that we
have spent the afternoon together. I am very happy to have you
here. Does Marie know of your expedition to the distant land of
the Rue Boissonnade?"

It's wonderful how the right words can sometimes come to
the aid of one's wishes! They descend out of the blue just when
one is least expecting it. For the past half hour I had been
racking my brains to find a means of bringing Marie into the
conversation, and now it arrived almost of its own accord, almost without my being aware of it! At the mention of his
wife's name Mesnard once again lowered his eyes, which must
be his way of shutting down his face when some emotion threat-
ens to betray itself. Assuming a flat tone of voice that I even
judged to be "cautious," he replied that he had said nothing,
that he had come here off his own bat, following on a lot of
serious thought. I didn't ask what his thoughts had been, since
I instantly guessed them: to take the first step, to come and see
me after the way I slanged him last Sunday was an act of
heroism. This heroism tempted him, forced itself on him as being
the most difficult, most noble, most magnanimous and thus the
only possible attitude. A lesser man would have remained fretting
or fuming in his corner. But not Mesnard: he wanted to prove to
himself that the harsh things I had said, even if they had hurt
him, had not impaired his generous spirit. He wanted to show me
how he was rising above my violence, was acknowledging only
that part of my admonitions which was true, and was tacitly
thanking me for it.

The annoying thing about men like Mesnard in relation to
men like me is that the men like me end up by being contaminated by their delicacy. Having raised the subject of Marie,
all sorts of questions were burning the tip of my tongue but

through a sudden and, for me, most unwonted attack of shyness I didn't dare put them to him. For instance, I should have liked to ask him if he had really abandoned his ideas of a divorce. I just couldn't. It would have seemed to me the height of bad taste. In the same way, impossible to get out a single word about Mlle. Duchateau, a character who intrigues me inordinately. In view of the crisis of heroism Mesnard is going through, he may well drop her. I should have every reason for wishing this and yet, I don't know why, something tells me it would be a pity. Poor Mesnard and poor Duchateau! I don't much fancy myself at breaking up romances and making people unhappy.

"Supposing you had pelted me with rotten eggs," said Mesnard in answer to my question, "and had thrown me out: it would only have upset Marie still more. Whereas tonight I shall tell her all about our lunch together and it will be the finest surprise imaginable. Don't you agree?"

I assured him that I would never throw out any man who turned up at my door with caviar, *foie gras,* and champagne. Having known me for so long he must have realized this, the old fox!

"Marie will be all the more pleased," I added, "since she thinks I've behaved like a louse toward you. Incidentally, she told me as much to my face. Last Monday she and I had a row over the phone such as we haven't had since we were young."

I think this revelation gave Mesnard a certain amount of pleasure. If anything can restore a tottering marriage, it's the description to one of the two parties of an act of loyalty performed by the other. There is no husband who isn't agreeably tickled to learn that his wife has sided violently with him against the world, especially if he knows in his heart of hearts that he is in the wrong and that she is defending him out of love and blind solidarity. I told Mesnard that I had got the best possible impression from this virulence of Marie's. Any woman who can draw on so much energy to plead in favor of the man she loves cannot possibly be smitten with a serious illness.

"I hope you are right," he replied rather sadly, implying: "If the result of the tests is bad, I shall find it hard to forgive myself for treating her so coldly these past months." Poor Mesnard! I was touched by this silent but most explicit remorse.

I don't quite know how he veered from his wife to his daughter; at any rate I got the impression that this switch to a fresh topic was more than just a simple association of ideas and had a definite purpose on his part. In his reticent way, with short, caustic remarks between silent pauses, he gave me a glimpse of an emotion I always find embarrassing when it is revealed in my presence: paternal love. And yet there is nothing silly about it and love in general, whatever its object, never causes any unpleasant reaction in me. Why am I always put out by demonstrations of paternal love? Probably because it is the blindest of all, the one that feeds most avidly on illusions and false appearances. Whence the extreme forms it assumes. Behind the father's lack of critical spirit and caution I can see all the disappointments or unwelcome surprises lying ahead, and the succession of griefs so deeply felt and so seldom tempered by philosophy or fatalism. This deception irritates me all the more in that it isn't brought about by the children but entirely built up by the parents. Anyway, I have a horror of people who cherish illusions, and parents fall more than anyone else into this category.

That Mesnard loves his daughter there can be no doubt; I would even say he adores her. Beneath his understatements and mocking tone one doesn't have to be very bright to discern his affection for her, and this is considerable. One feels his attention is centered on her almost the whole time, that he is always observing her, although from a distance and pretending to look the other way. Besides, I've noticed that whenever he is talking about her, quoting something she has said or describing something she has done, the smile never leaves his mouth. There is no mistaking that smile: despite its mocking twist it is a true expression of joy and love. Like all parents, of course, he cherishes a totally false image of his child, whom he regards in a highly conventional, traditional way as far more childish and innocent than she is, while at the same time taking pride in her intelligence. It's as if, as soon as someone has produced a child, he ceases by the same token to have any understanding of a child's nature. Indeed, I believe parents respond above all to what is incomplete in children. As they are fully absorbed in shaping their minds and hearts, they see nothing but scaffolding, lumps of clay, a shapeless mass in which they like to recognize (wrongly) a rough outline of their own characteristics, whereas children are, on the contrary, very complete and finished in their ways. They are not embryos of men but beings of a different species. In his daughter Mesnard can only see those points where she is beginning to resemble him (whence his light irony; in gently mocking her he mocks himself) and those where she differs from him, which fascinate him. He has no eyes for what is properly speaking childish in Lise, that is to say of a special nature as foreign to the adult state as the Prussian character is to the Chinese. I didn't venture to explain all this to him as I am noting it down here, since these are arguments parents are deaf to, as I have observed time and again, and even find rather distressing.

Toward five o'clock Mesnard looked at his watch. He rose with the air of a man preparing to leave but still with something to say and not quite knowing how to put it. His expression became more furtive than usual and he even bluntly turned his head away.

"While on the subject of Lise," he began in an inconsequent, almost careless tone that made me prick my ears as being the herald of grave tidings, "if anything should happen to me, say I'm in a car smash or a chimney pot falls on my head or I get galloping consumption, would you be willing to take care of her? Become her guardian, for instance? If I knew she were safe in the hands of you and her mother, I'd have no further worries."

At the time I was struck above all by the coincidence and could think only of the similar decision taken by my sister three days before. But now that I am describing them in writing, things are assuming a strange force and significance. I suddenly have a suspicion that perhaps I have put an entirely wrong interpretation on Mesnard's visit. Coming from me, this wouldn't surprise me particularly, since I am pretty slow on the uptake and as a rule rather prone to see the light only after the event. Thinking it over, this visit during which Mesnard began by expounding what he believes to be his truth, and ended by placing in my safe custody what he holds dearest in the world, takes on the appearance of a last will and testament, which I don't like at all. This father and mother who, with three days between them, have entrusted their child to me, plainly without any question of collusion—what is behind it all? What obscure foreboding has each of them had? I know one shouldn't attach too much importance to these so-called "portents"; nevertheless it's a fact that sometimes they do not appear to us without purpose and we are appalled when, after the castastrophe, we recall them to mind. To give them immediate and serious attention is one way of exorcising them. That at least is my doctrine and I find it often works. Nothing should be overlooked when it is a question of warding off tragedy. I could almost make horns behind my back, like Italian peasant women.

What can have been going on in Mesnard's head to lead him to ask me to be Lise's guardian in case anything goes wrong? Two possible explanations. The first is that his wife's illness, of which he has only just learned, has put him in a morbid frame of mind. It suddenly brought home to him the fact that human beings are frail; during the twenty years he has been married he has always regarded his wife as being as indestructible as himself. And now illness has got its grip on her; this has led him to realize his own frailty and fear for the future of his child. I am only noting this theory down so as not to forget it, since I don't believe it. It's too simple, too plausible. I incline more toward the second explanation, which I find a poisonous one, and it must be the correct one just because I dread it. And

I know why I dread it: because with all the violent things I said last Sunday I set going a mechanism whose workings are beginning to come clear to me. Indeed, the fact that Mesnard, after our ten years of estrangement, after our scene last Sunday, should have taken this unprecedented step means that he has been completely knocked sideways by what I said to him, that he has accepted this in good faith, that in spite of his turbid philosophy he is convinced at heart that it is I who am in the right. The moral collapse Marie spoke of was no joke: it was an even greater one than I had imagined. Mesnard has reached the point of thinking that his life, since it makes no more sense on the artistic plane, has by the same token lost its value, doesn't deserve to be prolonged, and that its end is near. This is perhaps what the poor wretch has grasped on account of me. Through my voice, my appearance, my words, my brutal manner which he had forgotten, I violently swept him back ten years to a time when he still believed that, for an artist, art is the only reason for living and that if he betrays it he is ripe for the coffin. Please God I am mistaken, for I find such an idea most painful. It makes me feel like a doctor who has administered a horse pill to a patient with a severely weakened constitution and killed him. I blame myself for not having suspected that Mesnard had preserved a certain purity of spirit and that, by talking the way I did to a man of honor, I was driving him to despair. But Marie understood it, and this explains her fury on the telephone. I blame myself for not having foreseen that he would come to visit me and would solemnly entrust me with the upbringing of his daughter, thus paying me homage while at the same time teaching me an almighty lesson in generosity. In short, I have misjudged him. I have believed him to be a completely lost soul when he has merely been weak. God, if only he should now have the courage to paint two or three good pictures! But courage is not enough. Mesnard no longer knows what patience is, his mind no longer has that iron resistance so indispensable for carrying a work through to the end, digging down to the deepest part of oneself; ten years of bad habits have spoiled his hand. How will he extricate himself from the fix I have put him in? I think of what Delacroix said: "To finish demands a heart of steel." Poor Mesnard has become incapable of finishing anything and he lost his heart of steel ages ago, if he ever so much as had one.

Oh well! I mustn't overdramatize. I'm carrying on like a lunatic rushing from one extreme to the other. After a surfeit of bloody-mindedness, I'm falling over myself with pity. Besides, one should never *put oneself in other people's skins;* their skins were not made to fit us. If I myself were in Mesnard's skin right now, I should probably already be dead. But he isn't dead; in fact, for ten years now he has survived the slow scuttling of his genius without any difficulty. This could go on for another thirty years. There's a fair chance I shall have a good laugh when I reread this journal one day.

As he left me, he shook my hand with a smile (yet another) that rather pained me—the smile as if of a man in exile. Perhaps I am romancing when I write this, but that's exactly the impression it gave me. To me it seemed this smile was saying: "You're a lucky one, you are, to be so content with life, to paint the way you want, to have a gigantic appetite, to be free of any worries or complications, to have only difficult aims. . . ." I was so shaken by this mark of his bewilderment that I did something incredible: I kissed him on both cheeks, an unprovoked assault that left him completely nonplussed, and heard myself say: "Come back whenever you like; I shall always be glad to see you!" Happily, this kind of invitation never leads to anything with people as discreet as my brother-in-law.

What a bundle of contradictions I am. The glimpse I have just had into Mesnard's case has quite upset me; I feel honored by his request and at the same time terrified of the responsibility it may involve. I would do anything for my niece but the prospect that one day she might be an orphan, that I might have to share my life with her, concern myself with her education, her language, her soul makes my blood run cold. Must I, who have so carefully dismissed all complications from my life, banished from it all material constraints, rigorously made it a masterpiece of seediness in order to be constantly in good shape for my work—must I now see this admirable structure knocked sideways? My future doesn't look too rosy tonight.

What wouldn't I give to be caught up right now in a period of frantic creativity! I should be painting all day; my work would enwrap me like a cocoon, I wouldn't see anybody, the world could come apart and join together again without my even noticing. Instead, I am bogged down in the sticky warm placenta of life, I have emotions, I want this, I don't want that, I influence the march of events. Ugh! I who hate living have landed myself a proper plateful of it! What in God's name led me to try and find a solution for Mesnard and his problems! For it's all your doing, Pluche, with your excessive nature, talking to a fashionable painter as if he were Michelangelo.

Ah well, *insh allah!* We live and learn. Meanwhile Tarzan is snuffling. That means he wants to go out and wee-wee. It's eleven o'clock. The night is as black as prune juice. Let us away to sprinkle and spray the pavement of the Boulevard Edgar Quinet. Tomorrow I shall go and see Papa Raimondet, who is a philosopher and may perhaps swing me up to those heights where they soar at the Chic d'Alésia; following which I shall arrange to dine with Lucienne, who is as soothing as the chain of the Alps.

CHAPTER XVI

Sixteenth (and Last) Day of Sterility

> *It is necessary to navigate.*
> *It is not necessary to live.*
>
> **POMPEY**

To each man his dove. Mine alighted on my finger this morning.
It was still dark. I half opened one eye to consult my clock:
5:23. I then opened the other eye and decided two things: first,
that I no longer felt sleepy; second, that I wanted to get out
of bed. At the same time an immense joy spread through every
part of my body. Beginning in the feet, it sprang into the knees,
exploded in the elbows, and planted an enormous grin on my
face. For the first time in two months (or three or four, I can't
now remember, it could be eternity!) I was filled with curiosity.
I wanted to see the world, so teeming, so full of diversity, so
rich in happy surprises. Or rather, I wanted to know what I
was going to extract from myself to present as a gift to the
world. When I think that only yesterday morning, like all those
previous mornings, I was clinging to slumber like a limpet,
forcing myself to go back to sleep, cowering in my bed like a
rabbit in its hole, I can't get over it! Yesterday I was a fetus, I
was an embryo. I was scared of everything; my bed was my
mother's womb. I had only one desire: to remain in this snug

warmth. The thought that whether I liked it or not I would at any moment have to face a world offering nothing but hostility and woe made me desperate. The idea of me, a weak, defenseless, idiot, naked, helpless creature confronting this monster appalled me! I simply wasn't up to it. Poor little old Pluche, curled up in his blanket, piteously repeating: "The dawn is a fearsome thing!"

But no, the dawn is not a fearsome thing! It is exquisite, it is divine. Each dawn is as beautiful as the first day of creation. The world is all new. The earth is still soft and moist from the Flood. One can do whatever one likes with it. It is Man's trusty beast of burden. It is there, we only have to stoop down to take it, give it the shape of which our spirits dream, mold it in our own guise. Nothing is impossible. This morning I had the sudden certainty that my Flood was over. Painting was singing inside me; I was bursting with ideas and plans; I was young and intrepid. I couldn't wait a second longer to get my feet on the floor. Whereas it rained bucketfuls all yesterday, by a coincidence that came as no surprise at all it was superb weather the whole of today, real summer weather far ahead of its time and even out of place in March. I shall have to look in the paper tomorrow: I'm sure it hasn't been so fine and hot at this time of year since 1875. Not a single cloud dared to venture into the sky, which until evening remained of a blue worthy of the earthly paradise.

Another intuition came to me as I got up and added further to my happiness, since I welcomed it without any shadow of doubt; this was that everything which has been getting me down during the past two weeks was going to end today, and end well. The soiled feeling that had brought me so low had gone. There was no more tension around me. Tragedy had gone up in smoke. It wasn't the first time I had observed something of this kind. One can be lying ill at death's door and then, one fine day, mysteriously wake up cured. One's illness has decamped in the night. The patient is like the garrison of a besieged town at its last gasp and on the brink of surrender, when all at once, unable to believe its eyes, it perceives that under cover of darkness the enemy has crept away in its stockinged feet. The same goes for personal troubles. Mine have fled during the night. That's the way it had to be, I thought, since I'm about to start painting again, since I have at least forty canvases to cover with paint and need absolute freedom of mind and spirit.

At 5:23 then, I sent the blankets flying, leaped from my couch, went for a triumphant piss, and then dashed into the kitchen singing at the top of my voice. Tarzan, overjoyed to see me so merry, threw himself into the spirit of the thing by dancing a fine saraband around the apartment and leaping all over me. This is the right way of awakening! There will be plenty more like it stretching into the future, for the next six months or maybe a year. I haven't yet started to paint again but I can barely conceive how I could ever have been sterile, me, Pluche, with so many things to say by means of brushes and tubes of color. Me sterile, me idle, me drifting like a corpse down a river is something strictly speaking inconceivable! Who has really written this journal I now leaf through in disbelief, finding the observations I read in it unintelligible? Could it have been me? Me the creator, the toiler, the Gargantua of contemporary painting, with enough in my head and fingers to cover a hundred square yards of canvas a month? And what about this idea of writing my "diary of sterility"? Had I no spirit then? My natural state is one of unbroken creativity, and this in turn engenders order, peace, gaiety, and perspicacity. I was fast asleep. I had my eyes shut. Title of this journal: *Pluche Asleep.* Today I have recovered my normal sight, seeing everything without looking at anything; I am once again at the center of the world, I embrace it in its totality and in all its details. It is as transparent, as easy to fathom as yesterday it was opaque and hostile. Oh, how fascinating it is to be oneself! Jonah stepping out of the whale.

The smell of coffee and toast spreading through the apartment at half past five in the morning is intoxicating. It galvanizes me, the way the smell of gunpowder galvanized the horses of Géricault's dragoons. It is the smell of hard work and contentment. Without bragging, I brewed myself this morning the finest coffee of my life, and this I may say includes a good number of pretty fine ones. Tarzan and I gorged ourselves like a couple of pigs, though this didn't prevent us from enjoying one of those splendid early morning talks between bachelors.

"Tarzan, my treasure, comfort of my middle age, at least you are going to discover what it is to be happy," said I. "You're going to sniff up the goodly smell of fresh oil paint, as appetizing as anything that ever came out of a kitchen. You're going to learn to know the real Pluche, Pluche the Great, who bears no resemblance to the slug who adopted you. Pluche the Great is a good and awe-inspiring man; he scares everybody except dogs. He sings from morning to night and when he's not singing he whistles. He is covered all over with colors like a redskin chief. He has a ready wit and the temper of an angel, he is full of fun and always good for a laugh. Up to now you have been sharing the existence of an ordinary man, bowed down by his fellows. From today onward you are *the Dog Tarzan*, a distinguished figure who will be mentioned in books because he was the companion of a fellow of the same caliber as Delacroix or Courbet. Did you know it is impossible to get a fellow of this sort down? There's a good reason: he is protected by a thick layer of paint which he renews every morning. An idyllic life lies ahead of us. Fifteen hours of work a day. We're going to wallow in an orgy of paint. We're going to put Titian, Rubens, and all the rest of them to rout."

Nothing in common between the foregoing and a monologue. Tarzan interrupted me twenty times with expressions of assent and encouragement. He sat gazing at me, waggling his ears and his tail, barking, placing his paw on my knee, and reaching up to sweep his tongue over my cheek. In short, he gave every sign of unqualified enthusiasm and support. I could swear by the Almighty that no detail of what I said escaped him, that he understood everything and rejoiced in his heart over my resurrection. It's incredible how expressive a dog's face can be. One can read ten times more emotions and thoughts in it than in a man's.

"You had better know what happened to me," I went on; "or precisely, I have to describe it to you so as to get a clear idea of it myself. I ran away. Every now and then I take to my heels and beat it. I keep running for two, three, four months. I become a wandering Jew. I run for miles. Miles away from painting, from my destiny, miles away from myself. I run like a madman. I tell myself I'm running so fast that nothing will ever be able to catch up with me. Just when I imagine I have at last reached an inaccessible spot, a sudden twist brings me face to face with myself. In actual fact I have never budged an inch, I have been running on the same spot. And this is just as well, since if I had really run away, if I had ditched everybody including myself, if I had truly thrown over my destiny to take on another one, I would have lost my soul. What is curious to observe is that about halfway through my flight, let's say after two months' sprinting, I begin to have a vague suspicion that running away is no help but will inevitably bring me back to my point of departure. This is at once despairing and comforting. I said things take a sudden twist. That's not the right word, there's no sudden twist. From day to day I see the end of my journey drawing nearer. Long before I have reached it I can discern its shape. To begin with, this intrigues me. I am thrilled to think that at last I am going to know a new landscape. But gradually the landscape changes and assumes an air of familiarity. The closer I draw to it, the more it resembles the place I started from. At bottom the only benefit one gets from flight is what one meets on the way, while it lasts. Sometimes it's a woman. Sometimes a dog."

At the word "dog" Tarzan, who was sitting beside me, beat a tattoo on the floor with his tail. I got up and went to sit at my writing table, so that I could carry out a difficult task: making out Georges's check. I had dillydallied long enough. The hallmark of a man running away is to indefinitely postpone

unpleasant chores, and this poisons his life since by so doing he
piles up all his troubles ahead of him instead of putting them
behind him. The man who doesn't run away, on the other hand,
hastens to liquidate all his worries because he is brave, and
bravery is frugal. I threw myself on my checkbook and accomplished my ruin in nine seconds flat. This gave me the
keenest pleasure: it was done now, never again in my life
would I think of these hundred thousand francs! So long as I
hadn't given them away they made me feel quite ill; they were
catarrh, migraine, rheumatism, colic. With one stroke of the
pen I had driven these ailments out of me. I no longer have a
cent but once again feel fit and ready for anything. Now it's
Georges's turn to suffer. It's for him now to do what he can with
this money, for him to writhe and burn over it. It isn't a check
I've sent him, it's a curse and I'm damned glad to have palmed
it off on him. Whereupon, pursuing the same impulse, I tore the
check up and made out another one for ninety thousand francs
only. With this unlooked-for ten thousand, this windfall, this gold
mine, I decided to go out directly the shops opened and buy
myself a mass of tubes, canvases, and brushes. I would treat
myself to a fabulous stock of equipment such as I had never
possessed before. Had it been my own money I would never
have dared; but since it was now Georges's I had no such
scruples!

What proves that I have finally emerged from my limbo is
that while I took my shower a thousand ideas were exploding
in my head. When I am enjoying an outburst of creativity the
morning shower has the same effect on me as water does on a
garden. Hopping about under the spray I thought of thirty
pictures which left cruel gaps in my *oeuvre* and urgently demanded to be done before I died. At the prospect that I might
easily die tomorrow, stupidly run down by a three-wheeled van,
I was seized with panic. When I begin to be afraid of death it
means I am pregnant with a large number of pictures. I don't
tremble for myself, I tremble for my work, which must be

brought to its conclusion, and for this purpose I am only the very precious instrument.

From this my thoughts, my dear little thoughts freshened by hot water, led me to Mesnard. I don't know if his visit yesterday did him any good. At any rate, it did a lot to me. It quite revived me. The spectacle of this poor slob wasting his life, piling up daubs, winning success after success, so unhappy, so helpless, so corrupted by his gimcrack philosophy, showed me by comparison what a splendid fellow I am—a fact I now and then forget. Those crappy paintings of his, inspected at his place last Sunday, paraded before my eyes. I felt a crazy longing to show the world what I am capable of. One of the great driving forces of creativity is the comparison of oneself with other artists, the desire to do better than they, better than any living artist whoever he may be, and the knowledge that one can. One longs to impose one's own style as being the only good and fruitful one. The act of creation takes place *against* something. Certainly the apple tree needs to produce its apples, but it also needs the world to see it covered with apples, to admire its apples, bigger, redder, and more tasty than all the apples on earth. As the water cascaded over me I was profoundly convinced that I was not the contemporary of Mesnard, Buffet, Magritte, Max Ernst, Fautrier, Balthus, or Dali himself; I loathed them, I was going to pulverize these midgets, since I belonged to the family of Poussin, Goya, Degas, and Bonnard; I, alone in our own day, formed part of the timeless mafia of ogres, and this was just fine! I was seized with a spirit of emulation, I told myself Tintoretto hadn't said *everything*, nor had Michelangelo, nor had Rembrandt, nor Ingres, nor Manet; that any amount of avenues in painting remained to be explored, down which they had barely ventured, down which they had merely taken a few timid steps; that I was the only one with the ability to take up painting where they had left off and to carry it as far forward again as they had carried it themselves. Yesterday there was nothing left to say; painting was empty and dead; there was nothing worth beginning on, since one would only produce a faint murmur. This morning everything was still to be said. Yesterday I could have died without regrets and even with some satisfaction. This morning I longed to live to be ninety-nine like Titian.

At eight o'clock Tarzan and I, all shining in the sun, innocent as the first man and first dog, found ourselves in the Rue Boissonnade, which is pretty innocent too, at that time of day. Moreover, today innocence pervaded everything: the Boulevard Montparnasse, the Boulevard Raspail, and even the Vavin cross-roads, that famous place of perdition. We had a brisk walk as far as the Quai Voltaire, where my dealer in artist's materials has his shop. There I spent a whole hour, turning the place upside down until I had completely exhausted my ten thousand francs. I am sure a trapper in Arkansas in 1880, fitting himself out in some emporium for a lengthy expedition, never felt greater satisfaction in purchasing boots, carbines, cartridges, fur jackets, smoked beef, pemmican, and woollen shirts than I did in stocking up with a profusion of Chinese white, French vermilion, and all the wonders they sell in shops for artists. The trapper's delight stems from the fact that he is a man of experience who knows what he needs, picks the best at the best value, buying with discrimination and looking ahead to the use he will make of his purchases. Nothing will be wasted, everything will be put to the fullest use. This goes for me too. I felt the same delight this morning, more completely than I had ever known it before, since I had a fabulous sum to spend. Here I am now, set up for a whole year. Such wealth goes to my head. I regard it almost *religiously!* To think that I had to be brought to ruin before I could have, for once in my life, the means to treat myself to an amount of equipment on a level with my ambitions! I was wrong to complain about duty! Since my parcel weighed nearly two hundredweight and measured at a rough guess about fifteen cubic feet, the dealer agreed to have it delivered to me.

Leaving the shop, Tarzan and I felt energetic enough to cover another twenty miles; for all this, I made my way home at a fairly brisk pace, anticipating that Marie would call me up

during the morning, since it was today she was due to learn the
result of the biopsy. I hadn't been back five minutes before the
doorbell rang. I went to open the door; it was Marie and Lise
bursting joyously in, triumphant and bubbling over. Marie
planted half a dozen smacking kisses on my cheek. Lise and
Tarzan similarly indulged in mutual congratulations. In between Marie's bubbles and gasps (out of breath from having
climbed my four flights of stairs at a run) I gathered that she
had come straight from the laboratory, that the biopsy was
negative, that she couldn't wait a second to come and tell me,
that Mesnard himself didn't yet know, that she could only stay
for a moment, and so on. Although this news didn't surprise me
in the least, given that it had so to speak been revealed to me
already by the thirst to paint that once again seized me this
morning, I felt blessedly relieved all the same. Revelations are
all very well, but one can never be quite sure if one is right
about them. Marie plunged into a mass of projects: they're going
to operate on her next week; following this a period of con-
valescence on a Greek island with Albert. One reassuring detail,
proving that she is already cured before her operation: the spirit
of domination has reinstated itself in her heart. I realized this
from the way she airily declared that Mesnard would be able
to work very well in Greece, that she was going to take charge
again of this fascinating man, give him back the orderliness and
solitude indispensable for an artist if he is to be happy both in his
home and in his creative life. For a moment I felt a flash of pity
for the poor devil, who appeared to me like a slave subsiding once
more under his master's thumb! Like me, Marie is emerging from
the Flood. Her life is like a huge cupboard she hasn't looked into
for months and in need of spring-cleaning from top to bottom.
She is going to throw herself wholeheartedly into this tidying-up
process. We were still standing in the hall and, taking advantage
of the fact that Lise had slipped into my studio to look at my
pictures, Marie rapidly whispered:

"I was quite ludicrous the other day on the phone. Please
forgive me. Albert has told me how sweet you were to him

yesterday. He's had a bad shake-up. Our trip to Greece will do him even more good than me. He'll find landscapes and a light there that will intrigue him a lot. Promise me one thing, Pluche: if you don't like the pictures he brings back, don't tell him so."

"If I understand rightly," I laughingly told her, "you'll see to it that they are pretty, in other words frightful. All right. It's a promise, I won't say a word. Besides, I have more or less decided not to discuss painting any more with Mesnard. I don't see why I should stop you from having Rolls-Royces."

"Pluche," she said, "you've told me time and time again that one should only give people the sort of advice they can follow. When you try to force Albert to paint the way you do, you're being quite unreasonable. Why do you have this passionate urge to save the world? The world doesn't want to be saved."

"You're right," I replied, still laughing, "but one can't change one's nature. I can't stop myself trying to save people. Probably so that I can have the pleasure of being nasty to them first."

"Maestro," Lise called from the room next door, "come here a moment, I've a secret to tell you."

Lise is already quite a woman. Her visit to my studio was only a maneuver to lure me in there and get me alone.

"You're a wizard," she murmured in my ear. "And your pictures are very good, you know. I've been looking at several while I was waiting for you. They are almost as good as Papa's."

Marie, from the hall, shouted to us to be quick. She wanted to get back at top speed to the Castel to announce the good news to Papa, who wasn't as yet in the know. This didn't prevent me from detaining my sister and my niece on the doorstep to tell them my own good news. When I'm about to plunge into work again it's a kind of uncontrollable urge I have to proclaim it to the world and even to say I have already begun when the canvases are still virgin white. What can be the reason behind this passion, which tends more to exasperate people than give them any pleasure? I think it's of the same nature as the accounts young men give of their amorous exploits, dazzled as they are by their capacities. At forty-five I am the same with regard to painting: always dazzled by my fecundity, always eager for the world to recognize and admire it. And then, this shameless contentment contrasts nicely with the morose faces of my colleagues who "have problems" or who are eternally "seeking something" they will never find.

"Oh Pluche, I'm so glad," cried Marie. "You're working, how marvelous! Make me one more promise: not to come and see me when I'm at the clinic. You'd find it an awful bore and clinics are the last place to inspire anyone."

Things fall back into place just as easily as they get out of hand. A very strong reason for not being pessimistic. Marie isn't going to die. Providence has protected me once again. It has warded off this cup of woe. Decidedly I have a gift for keeping tragedy at arm's length. I say a gift advisedly, and feel I owe this gift to heaven, since it goes mysteriously hand in hand with my gift as a painter.

At heart, in spite of several moments of anguish last week, I never really believed Marie would die. Such a death would have been out of my line, it wouldn't have fitted in with my destiny. It would, as Stendhal said, have been a pistol shot in the middle of a concert. My life is a private concert of chamber music which certainly veers between major and minor but until the end of my days my special guardian spirits will scrape at their fiddles in complete tranquillity, uninterrupted by fusillades or the thud of bombs. The fact has to be faced: I have no biography. If any books are written about me when I'm dead, on the lines of *Pluche, the Man and His Work*, they won't find much to say about the man. All the better. Having no biography strikes me as the height of stylishness. My story consists of my pictures. They contain all of me. There will also be this journal, these sixteen days of my life at the age of forty-five, which provide a very false image of me since, during these sixteen days, the only work I managed to do was to paint a stuffed squirrel in half an hour and sketch out Boulard's absurd composition. The real Pluche is probably not to be found in any of these whining pages. The real Pluche is a painting machine and, incidentally, the merriest man I know.

At least my journal has one virtue: the story set out in it has a happy end. Marie, for whom I feared, for whom I trembled, is going to live. She won't change, she will remain the same kind, greedy, frivolous, intelligent, pretty person she is. Simply, she is going to live. Mesnard will live on too, in order to paint bad pictures. He is not the sort of man to die of grief. I wasn't half romancing yesterday! Money keeps people alive. They will remain true to themselves, and alive. My story ends well: nobody dies. Every ending in which nobody dies is beautiful, even if life does nothing more than keep limping along just the same as before, since to live is the most beautiful thing of all. God must have said that before me.

This day will have been a very full one, as if the world, before I go underground, has enjoyed giving me one last fireworks display. From morning till evening I have had the impression of being a traveler on the point of departure, with people coming to shake my hand on the platform. Ten minutes after Marie and Lise left, Mme. Chevassu turned up with a string bag full of provender dangling against her legs like some monstrous third breast.

"Up already?" she yapped, embracing me. "What's up with you? Fell out of bed, did you? I've brought you cutlets for lunch, spinach and Camembert. For once you're going to eat at home instead of ruining your stomach in restaurants where they only serve leftovers. And this little beast," she added, giving Tarzan a whack on the spine which made him jump, "who'd look after him, I ask you, if I wasn't here? I've been and fetched some heart from the butcher especially for him, poor little thing."

Mme. Chevassu being a good audience, I couldn't forbear to announce to her that I was about to embark on a period of frantic creativity, but today she was in a mocking mood; instead of the admiring cries I was counting on, she confined herself to coldly declaring: "There's no one to beat you when it comes to fine talk, but as far as work goes, I'll believe it when I see it."

Whereupon the telephone rang. It was Ravuski. This to begin with gave me no pleasure and even caused me some apprehension. The people who pay you seldom call you up to say nice things. For once I was wrong. Ravuski has had a brain wave, the dear man, after a considerable amount of thought. He is going to stage a major exhibition of my paintings. An astonished world is going to rediscover me, the way it rediscovered Balthus last year. This bracketing together with the doleful troubadour of anemic little girls made me scowl into the receiver. I acquiesced fairly coldly. Ravuski was so cock-a-hoop just because an idea had strayed into his featherbrain that he wanted to mount the exhibition without delay. In fact, it will be held next month. This unseemly haste appalls me. After trying in vain to curb him, I told him he could hold his exhibition without me, seeing that I'm up to my ears in work and that I don't intend to waste my time on his social shenanigans. This call lasted half an hour. It left me at once delighted and as ill-tempered as a wild bull. Happy events always occur at the wrong moment. I've asked Ravuski twenty times to mount an exhibition during the periods when I couldn't get down to anything. And he has to decide to hold one now, just when painting is oozing out of my every pore and I shan't have a minute to spare. And he expects me to jump with joy into the bargain. At the end of our discussion I suddenly found the explanation for his sudden eagerness to glorify me: three or four people have talked to him about me during the past fortnight and one of my pictures has apparently fetched an unusually high price at an auction. This is a case for quoting Degas: "I win the Derby and all they give me is my ration of oats." How stupid people are! Even picture dealers. That's the way he ought to have begun. But this idiot told himself that he shouldn't show too keen an interest, unless he wanted to make me think he was organizing his exhibition for love. I'm far happier that he is pursuing his own interest. That at least shows he is serious. The bourgeoisie will obviously never understand the workings of an artist's mind.

As I hung up, I wondered why I wasn't more astonished. After all, in this step of Ravuski's there is something wholly unexpected and staggering. I merely welcomed it as my due and rather turned up my nose at it, what's more. Tonight I can see why I took it so calmly: because I more or less had the feeling that Providence, having snatched a hundred thousand francs from me, had to give them back to me in some fashion or other. According to Ravuski, a dreamer like all businessmen, the exhibition should bring in *hundreds of thousands* of francs. If it brings in merely *one* I shall consider myself very lucky. I should add that this gentleman, who could fill his gallery to overflowing with what he has already bought from me, suggested that I should add ten more canvases belonging to myself, on which he will take only twenty per cent commission if they are sold.

Mme. Chevassu hadn't revealed to me that she had bought food for two people and not just one, having taken it into her head to share my lunch with me. I was advised of this around twelve-thirty.

"Try not to eat like a pig for once," said my daily help. "I've put out a clean tablecloth."

I forget the countless inanities we swapped during this meal, in which each of us played his usual comedy role, I as the elderly art student and she as the old campaigner. I can only remember that for a minute or two over the dessert she adopted a superb pose: with her head leaning on her fist, her sharp elbow propped on the table, her hair tousled like a maenad's, her long, thin nose casting a shadow on her cheekbone, lolling between a glass of red wine and the dirty plates, she looked exactly like a picture by Degas. A perfection of composition and coloring. I was on the verge of getting out my sketchbook. But I restrained myself. I had made up my mind not to touch either pencil or brush the whole day. I am saving up my urge to paint for tomorrow, intact like a sweet held in one's cheek. This last wait to which I am subjecting myself is too delectable to be broken into.

The chief pleasure of lunching with Mme. Chevassu is that

she clears the table, does the washing up, and puts everything away. At two o'clock, when she left, the apartment was impeccably clean and tidy. I contemplated it the way Napoleon may have contemplated his strategic positions before battle, thinking voluptuously of the glory hole it will become tomorrow when I have unpacked all my supplies and settled down to work. I've had enough of living in such orderly surroundings for the past four months. The time has come for work to mess it all up, the time has come to end this immobility of an Egyptian tomb that descends on places where nothing gets created.

My last idle afternoon was whiled away between friendship and love. Friendship rang the bell at three o'clock, love at five. As proof that the erstwhile man is dead in me, love gave me less pleasure than friendship. At three o'clock, then, dringg! Tarzan barked and pricked his ears in excitement. I went to open the door: it was Raimondet puffing and panting, propelling before him a tall nineteenth-century mahogany easel with a crank-handle and shaft to adjust its height.

"Do you like it?" he asked in his abrupt way, without even saying good afternoon. "If you do, it's yours."

Dear Raimondet had extracted this marvel out of a job lot of old junk he had just come by. Thinking only of the joy he would bring me, he had closed down the Chic d'Alésia, chartered a taxi and brought it to me straightaway. In all my life I have never been given such a sumptuous and at the same time useful present. For it was a present in due and proper form. Raimondet would not even permit me to pay the taxi fare. I have always dreamed of owning an easel like this one, practical, ingenious, sturdy, and above all handsome! I had equally made up my mind to do without one in view of the astronomical price this type of object fetches in the flea market or the antique shops—and here a poor old codger I didn't even know a month ago had brought one round to my place on the very day inspiration began to flow in me again. Isn't this a small miracle of friendship? I settled Raimondet in my armchair, poured him out a glass of brandy, and tried to express my gratitude, which, in any case, could be read all over my face. Tarzan, for his part, cut a series of capers that must have shown this good man he wasn't dealing with a pair of ingrates. He appeared to be touched by our welcome, so far as one could judge from so undemonstrative a character. We sat chatting for more than an hour, smoking our pipes and swigging brandy. There must be some sort of link between him and me; only last night I was thinking how nice it would be to see him, and today here he was.

I couldn't refrain from confiding to him how much my fingers were itching to paint. I even described to him, going into details of style and outlining the subject matter, several pictures I was proposing to start on, although only a moment before I hadn't had the slightest notion of them. With me, inventing paintings off the cuff in this way is the sure sign of a great stirring in the depths. It means that my caldron of colors, forms, sensations, philosophy, and metaphysics is full and running over and that I must set about skimming it off. Naturally I shall never paint any of the pictures I described to Raimondet, but I needed to describe them in order to be rid of them. It is as if the really new and difficult works ahead of me lie smothered beneath many others, more accessible and hence misleading, in which I should get myself fruitlessly bogged down unless I can contrive to discard them. In brief, it is more convenient and time-saving to describe ten bad pictures than to paint them. The really funny thing is that, being full of conviction and verve, these idle word pictures of mine make a great impression on people, who keep on referring to them for years after.

Raimondet, with his subtle and certainly profound mind, was quick to understand that I wasn't the same man as at our last meeting, that he should let me talk on without interruption, and that at this moment I was more in a frame to impart messages to the world than to receive them. Besides, judging by the way I was wound up, he would have found it hard to get a word in. Seeing him so attentive, I launched into an endless and complacent chronicle of my working day: up at 5 A.M., coffee, getting progressively immersed in the act of creation, the state of intense intellectual awareness induced by the search for a likeness in art, the feeling one has of constantly running one's finger along the knife-thin edge of truth, and so on and so forth. As I evoked all this, so obvious and even trivial for me, I thought Raimondet must be having some difficulty in following me, but the pleasure it was giving me was only the greater for this. There is no better listener than the man who only half understands, dares not raise objections, listens to what you say as to a new and difficult kind of music. With him one feels the same freedom and almost the same joy as in front of a canvas.

"Well, so we're not going to see very much of you from now on," said Raimondet, rather intimidated. "Would it put you out too much if I paid you a short visit now and then?"

This bashful declaration of affection touched me. I assured him that he would always be welcome, but only after six in the evening, the time when I generally stop working. Not wishing to lag behind him in generosity, I gave him the squirrel I painted eight days ago, which he vigorously refused, arguing that there was no common yardstick between the ancient object he had brought me and a "work by a master." In the end my firmness got the better of his resistance; but I wonder now, tonight, if I was right to insist, if I wasn't slightly tactless toward this man who is so tactful himself. He was glad to have made me a gift. And I slightly tarnished his pleasure by making him a gift in return, by reducing to a simple exchange of courtesies what had been a spontaneous act of friendship. He barely said thank you. I put this down to his usual gruff manner; but now I'm inclined to think he was embarrassed and disappointed and I blame myself for it. True tact would have consisted in my taking the squirrel to him at the Chic d'Alésia in a few days' time. (Damn, I again forgot to ask him the reason for his shop sign.) I hope the demonstrations of warmth displayed by Tarzan and me on his departure did something to wipe out this bad impression.

The second surprise of the afternoon was a ring at the door from Lucienne, who—a unique circumstance—came to see me without prior warning. She happened to be in the neighborhood, apparently; she had come up on the off-chance, having a couple of hours to spare. I had been meaning to see her as well today— as recorded in this journal under yesterday's date—and I had forgotten her just as I had Raimondet. What a weird coincidence, these two people coming to me as if I had actually summoned them! Could Mme. Chevassu be right? Could Lucienne, able to hear the scratching of my pen on my paper from the depths of the Rue de Prony, be more in love with me than I thought? She was very affectionate and looking particularly pretty in her mid-season orange coat. But my mind couldn't have been less inclined to dalliance. I had no need of affection this afternoon. I was an unfeeling male, wholly concentrated on action, already absorbed by it. I did my best to be nice to her, but my thoughts kept flying off in other directions from one moment to the next. Stupendous color relationships kept flitting through my brain as I talked. Lucienne is much too worldly-wise to ask direct questions: but through her eyes, her mouth, her eyebrows I could see how this new man, preoccupied by some-thing utterly remote from herself, disconcerted and saddened her. I finally told her of the work I was about to plunge into, and this fired my enthusiasm. The contrast, with me so absent-minded a moment before and now suddenly so full of warmth, was striking.

"Can we still go on seeing each other as much as we have done during the past few months?" she asked in a small voice.

"Out of the question!" I replied, with more alacrity than I would have wished. I regretted this at once, but it was just too bad, I'd said it! Besides, I have noticed how the words I speak unthinkingly like this nearly always express my true feelings. Consequently it's wrong to repent of them. I like Lucienne but I like my painting even more. If I hurt her, it is because some-thing inside me judged it necessary to inflict this wound. While I was contemplating the pretty, grave, and disconsolate face of my mistress a dirty voice I know all too well was crying in my head: "I hope to God she's not going to turn into a clinging vine and poison my life while I'm trying to work!"

I who regard myself as a decent sort of chap am astonished to discover how hard I can sometimes be. This hardness gives me no pleasure—on the contrary, I loathe it, I am miserably aware of how vulnerable the beings are on whom I vent it, but there's no way of holding myself back. Someone inside me, someone stronger than myself, impels me to lash out and bruise. It is like a sort of ordeal to be gone through, in order to reach some distant goal that I cannot see though it is plainly vital that I should aim at it. Poor Lucienne, who came to see me today only to be slapped down! She didn't stay long and I did nothing to detain her. The deliveryman from the art shop drove her away barely half an hour after her arrival. The vast package of canvases, paints, brushes, and stretchers I immediately rushed to unpack was the final blow for her. There was an agonizing moment when she saw her rival face to face. She saw the one and only object on which my desires were fixed, and this was not herself. Discreetly she withdrew. This didn't prevent her from bidding me the tenderest of farewells and begging me to telephone her soon. Maybe I will, maybe I won't. We shall see.

My journal is ended. My story is done. Tomorrow painting will set up a void around me. Life will beat it far into the distance. No more of this humanity, no more of this suffering meat! I shall pass into the pure and delectable world of oil paint. Tomorrow my studio will smell good like a carpenter's shop, where the craftsmen's sweat blends with the scent of wood shavings. It will be filled with exquisite and nauseating odors—of cheap tobacco, linseed oil, turpentine, new canvases, drawing paper, and drying paints. Painting is like a cooking pot simmering on to infinity, distilling a warm, sickly, and appetizing aroma. The paints exude a smell of savory stew which permeates the air, impregnates the walls and one's clothes, joining forces with the pipe tobacco, embracing the musty redolence of pig's brawn, red wine, and Camembert cheese—foods proper to the creative man, who leaves them lying about on the table all day along with the dirty plates. Painters reek like lions, and their studios have a violent stench like the cages at the Vincennes Zoo.